GEORG[ES SIMENON]

MAIGRET AND THE HEADLESS CORPSE

Translated from the French by Eileen Ellenbogen

A Harvest Book
A Helen and Kurt Wolff Book
Harcourt Brace & Company
San Diego   New York   London

Requests for permission to make copies
of any part of the work should be mailed to:
Permissions Department, Harcourt Brace & Company,
6277 Sea Harbor Drive, Orlando, Florida 32887-6777.

First published in France in 1955 under the title
Maigret et le corps sans tête

Maigret is a registered trademark of the
Estate of Georges Simenon.

Library of Congress Cataloging-in-Publication Data
Simenon, Georges, 1903–1989
Maigret and the headless corpse.
Translation of: Maigret et le corps sans tête
"A Helen and Kurt Wolff book."
I. Title
PZ2637.I53M25813 1985   843'.912   84-25228
ISBN 0-15-655144-6 (pbk.)

Printed in the United States of America
FHIGE

Contents

Maigret and the Headless Corpse

Chapter 1

The Fouled
Propeller

In the faint, gray light of early dawn, the barge lay like a shadow on the water. Through the hatchway appeared the head of a man, then shoulders, then the great gangling body of Jules, the elder of the two Naud brothers. Running his hands through his tow-colored hair, as yet uncombed, he surveyed the lock, the Quai de Jemmapes to his left, and the Quai de Valmy to his right. In the crisp morning air he rolled a cigarette, and while he was still smoking it a light came on in the little bar on the corner of the Rue des Récollets.

The proprietor, Popaul, came out onto the pavement to take down his shutters. His hair, too, was uncombed, and his shirt open at the neck. In the half-light, the yellow façade of the bar looked more than usually garish.

Rolling his cigarette, Naud came down the gangplank and across the quay. His brother, Robert, almost as tall and lanky as himself, emerging from below deck in his turn, could see, through the lighted window, Jules leaning on the bar counter and the proprietor pouring a tot of brandy into his coffee.

It was as though Robert were waiting his turn. Exactly as his brother had done, he rolled a cigarette. As the elder brother left the bar, the younger came down the gangplank, so that they met halfway, in the street.

"I'll be starting the engine," said Jules.

Often, in the course of a day, they would not exchange more than a dozen laconic sentences, all relating to their work. They had married twin sisters, and the two families lived on the barge, which was named *The Two Brothers*.

Robert took his elder brother's place at the bar, which smelled of coffee laced with spirits.

"Fine day," said Popaul, who was a tubby little man.

Naud, without a word, glanced out of the window at the sky, which by now was tinged with pink. The slates and tiles of the rooftops and one or two paving stones below were still, after a cold night, coated with a translucent film of rime, which was just beginning to melt here and there. Nothing seemed quite real, except the smoking chimney-pots.

The diesel engine spluttered. The exhaust at the rear of the barge spurted black fumes. Naud laid his money on the counter, raised the tips of his fingers to his cap, and returned across the quay. The lockkeeper, in uniform, was at his post, preparing to open the gates. Some way off, on the Quai de Valmy, there were footsteps, but, as yet, not another soul in sight. Children's voices could be heard below deck on the barge, where the women were making coffee.

Jules reappeared on deck, and leaned over the stern, frowning. His brother could guess what the trouble was. They had taken on a load of gravel at Beauval from

Wharf No. 48 on the Ourcq Canal. As usual, they were several tons overweight, and the previous night, as they were drawing away from the dock at La Villette, headed for the Saint-Martin Canal, they had churned up a good deal of mud.

As a rule, in March, there was no shortage of water. This year, however, there had been no rain for two months, and the Canal Authority was hoarding its reserves.

The sluice-gates opened. Jules took the wheel. His brother went ashore to cast off the moorings. The propeller began to turn, and, as they had both feared, thick mud, churned up by the blades, was soon bubbling to the surface. Leaning with all his weight on the boat-hook, Robert tried to head the barge toward the lock. It was as though the propeller were spinning in a vacuum. The lockkeeper, used to this sort of thing, waited patiently, clapping his hands together to keep warm.

The engine shuddered with a grinding sound. Robert looked at his brother, who switched off.

Neither of them could make out what had gone wrong. The propeller, protected by the rudder, could not have scraped the bottom. Something must have got caught in it, a loose cable, maybe, such as is frequently left lying about in canals. If that was the trouble, they were going to have a job disentangling it.

Robert went behind the boat, leaned over, and felt about in the muddy water with his hook, trying to reach the propeller. Jules, meanwhile, fetched a smaller boat-hook. His wife, Laurence, poked her head through the hatchway.

"What's up?"

"Dunno."

Silently, the two men felt about with their boat-hooks, trying to reach the fouled propeller. After a few minutes of this, Dambois the lockkeeper, known to everyone as Charles, came down to the quay to watch. He asked no questions, but just stood by, silently puffing at his pipe, the stem of which was held together with string.

From time to time, people hurried past, office workers on their way to the Place de la République, nurses in uniform making for the Hospital of Saint-Louis.

"Got it?"

"I think so."

"What is it? Rope?"

"I couldn't say."

Jules Naud had certainly hooked something. He managed, after a time, to free the propeller. Bubbles rose to the surface.

Gently, hand over hand, he drew up the boat-hook and, with it, a strange-looking parcel, done up with string, and a few remnants of sodden newspaper.

It was a human arm, complete from shoulder to fingertips, which, through long immersion, was drained white, and limp as a dead fish.

At Police Headquarters, 3rd Division, situated at the far end of the Quai de Jemmapes, Sergeant Depoil was just going off night duty when he saw the lanky figure of the elder Naud standing in the doorway.

"I'm from the barge *The Two Brothers,* up near the lock at the Récollets. We were just pulling out when the propeller jammed. We've fished up a man's arm."

Depoil had served fifteen years in the 10th *Arrondissement*. His first reaction, like that of all the other police officers to be subsequently involved in the case, was incredulity.

"A *man's* arm?" he repeated.

"Yes, a man's. Dark hair on the back of the hand, and . . ."

There was nothing remarkable in the recovery, from the Saint-Martin Canal, of a corpse which had fouled someone's propeller. It had happened before, more than once. But as a rule it was a whole corpse, sometimes that of a man, some old tramp, most likely, who had taken a drop too much and stumbled into the water, or a young thug knifed by someone from a rival gang.

Dismembered bodies were not all that uncommon either. Two or three a year were about average, but invariably, in the Sergeant's long experience, they were women. One knew what to expect right from the start. Nine out of ten would be cheap prostitutes, the kind one sees loitering in lonely places at night.

One could safely conclude, in every case, that the killer was a psychopath.

There was not much one could teach the local police about their neighbors. At the Station, they kept up-to-date records of the activities of every crook, every shady character in the district. Few crimes were committed—from shoplifting to armed robbery—that were not followed in a matter of days by the arrest of the perpetrator. Psychopathic killers, however, were rarely caught.

"Have you brought it with you?" asked Depoil.

"The arm?"

"Where is it?"

"At the quay. Can we go now? There's this load we've got to deliver, Quai de l'Arsenal. They'll be waiting for it."

The Sergeant lit a cigarette and went to the telephone to notify the Salvage Branch. Next, he rang his Divisional Superintendent, Mangrin, at his home.

"Sorry to get you out of bed, sir. A couple of bargees have just fished a human arm out of the canal. No! A man's . . . That's how it struck me too . . . What's that, sir? . . . Yes, he's still here . . . I'll ask him."

Holding the receiver, he turned to Naud:

"Would you say it had been in the water long?"

Jules Naud scratched his head.

"It depends what you mean by long."

"Is it in a very bad state?"

"Hard to tell. Two or three days, I'd say."

The Sergeant repeated into the instrument:

"Two or three days."

Doodling on his notepad, he listened while the Superintendent gave his instructions.

"Can we go?" repeated Naud, when he had hung up.

"Not yet. As the Superintendent quite rightly says, we don't know what else you may have picked up, and if you moved the barge, we might lose it."

"All the same, I can't stop there for ever. There are four others already, lined up to go through the lock. And they're beginning to get impatient."

The Sergeant had dialed another number, and was waiting for a reply.

"Hello! Victor? I hope I haven't waked you. Oh! You're having breakfast, are you? Good. I've got a job for you."

Victor Cadet lived in the Rue du Chemin-Vert, not far from the Police Station, and it was unusual for a month to go by without some call upon his services from that quarter. He had probably retrieved, from the Seine and the canals of Paris, a larger and more peculiar assortment of objects, corpses included, than any other man.

"I'll be with you as soon as I've got hold of my mate."

It was seven o'clock in the morning. In the Boulevard Richard-Lenoir, Madame Maigret, already dressed, as fresh as paint and smelling faintly of soap, was busy in the kitchen getting breakfast. Her husband was still asleep. At the Quai des Orfèvres, Lucas and Janvier had been on duty since six o'clock. It was Lucas who got the news first.

"There's a queer thing!" he muttered, turning to Janvier, "They've fished an arm out of the Saint-Martin Canal, and it's not a woman's."

"A man's?"

"What else?"

"It could have been a child's."

There had, in fact, been one such case, the only one, three years before.

"What about letting the boss know?"

Lucas looked at the time, hesitated, then shook his head.

"No hurry. He may as well have his coffee in peace."

By ten minutes to eight, a sizable crowd had gathered on the quay where *The Two Brothers* was moored. Anyone trying to get too close to the thing lying on the ground covered with sacking was ordered back by the policeman on guard. Victor Cadet's boat, which had been lying downstream, passed through the lock and came alongside the quay.

Cadet was a giant of a man. Looking at him, one wondered whether his diving suit had had to be made to measure. His mate, in contrast, was undersized and old. He chewed tobacco even on the job, and stained the water with long brown streamers of spittle.

It was he who secured the ladder, primed the pump, and, when everything was ready, screwed on Victor's huge spherical diving helmet.

On deck, near the stern of *The Two Brothers,* could be seen two women and five children, all with hair so fair as to be almost white. One of the women was pregnant, and the other had a baby in her arms.

The buildings of the Quai de Valmy were bathed in sunshine, golden, heart-warming sunshine, which made it hard to credit the sinister reputation of the place. True, there was not much new paint to be seen. The white and yellow façades were streaked and faded. Yet, on this day in March, they looked as fresh as a scene by Utrillo.

There were four barges lined up behind *The Two Brothers,* with washing strung out to dry, and restless children who would not be hushed. A smell of tar mingled with the less agreeable smell of the canal.

At a quarter past eight, Maigret finished his second cup of coffee, wiped his mouth, and was just about to light up his morning pipe when the telephone rang. It was Lucas.

"Did you say a *man's* arm?"

He, too, found it hard to believe.

"Have they found anything else?"

"We've got the diver, Victor, down there now. We'll have to let the barges through fairly soon. There's a bottleneck building up at the lock already."

"Who's on duty there?"

"Judel."

Inspector Judel, a young policeman of the 10th *Arrondissement*, was conscientious if somewhat dull. He could safely be left in charge at this early stage.

"Will you be going yourself, sir?"

"It's not much out of my way."

"Do you want one of us to meet you there?"

"Who have you got?"

"Janvier, Lemaire . . . Hang on a minute, sir. Lapointe's just come in."

Maigret hesitated. He was enjoying the sunshine. It was warm enough to have the windows open. Was this just a straightforward, routine case? If so, Judel was quite competent to handle it on his own. But at this stage, how could one be sure? If the arm had been a woman's, Maigret would have taken a bet that there was nothing to it.

But since it was a man's arm, anything was possible. And if it should turn out to be a tricky case, and he, the Chief Superintendent, should decide to take over, the day-to-day Headquarters routine would to some extent be affected by his choice of assistant, because, whoever it was, Maigret would want him to see the case through to the end.

"Send Lapointe."

It was quite a while since he had worked in close collaboration with Lapointe. His youth, his eagerness, his artless confusion when he felt he had committed a *faux pas,* amused Maigret.

"Had I better let the Chief know?"

"Yes. I'm sure to be late for the staff meeting."

It was March 23. The day before yesterday had been

the first day of spring, and spring was in the air already—which was more than could be said in most years—so much so, in fact, that Maigret very nearly set off without his coat.

In the Boulevard Richard-Lenoir he hailed a taxi. There was no direct bus, and this was not the sort of day for shutting oneself up in the Métro. As he had anticipated, he arrived at the Récollets lock before Lapointe, to find Inspector Judel gazing down into the black waters of the canal.

"Have they found anything else?"

"Not yet, sir. Victor is still working under the barge. There may be something more there."

Ten minutes later, Lapointe drove up in a small black police car, and it was not long before a string of glittering bubbles heralded Victor's return to the surface. His mate hurried forward to unscrew the metal diving helmet. The diver lit a cigarette, looked around, saw Maigret, and greeted him with a friendly wave of the hand.

"Found anything?"

"There's nothing more there."

"Can we let the barge go?"

"It won't turn anything up except mud, that's for sure."

Robert Naud, who had been listening with interest, walked across to his brother.

"Start the engine!"

Maigret turned to Judel.

"Have you got a statement from them?"

"Yes, they've both signed it. Anyway, they'll be at the Quai de l'Arsenal, unloading, for the best part of a week."

The Quai de l'Arsenal was only a couple of miles downstream, between the Bastille and the Seine.

The overloaded barge was very low in the water, and it

was a slow business getting it away. At last, however, it scraped along the bottom into the lock, and the gates closed behind it.

The crowd of spectators dispersed, leaving only a few idle bystanders who had nothing better to do, and would very likely hang around all day.

Victor was still wearing his diving suit.

"If there's anything else to find," he explained, "it'll be upstream. An arm's light enough to shift with the current, but the rest, legs, torso, head, would sink."

There was not a ripple to be seen on the canal, and floating refuse lay, seemingly motionless, on the surface.

"Of course, there's nothing like the current you get in a river. But each time the level is raised or lowered in the lock, there's movement, though you'd barely notice it, all along the reach."

"In other words, the search ought to extend right up to the next lock?"

"He who pays the piper . . ." said Victor, inhaling and blowing smoke through his nostrils. "It's up to you."

"Will it be a long job?"

"That depends on where we find the rest of the body —assuming, of course, it's in the canal at all."

Why would anyone, getting rid of a body, dump part of it in the canal, and the rest somewhere else—say on some patch of waste ground?

"Carry on."

Cadet signaled to his mate to move the boat a little way upstream, and indicated that he was ready to be screwed into his diving helmet.

Maigret moved away, followed by Judel and Lapointe.

They formed a solitary little group on the quay, observed by the spectators with the instinctive respect accorded to authority.

"You'll have to search all rubbish dumps and waste ground, of course."

"That's what I thought," said Judel. "I was only waiting for you to give the word."

"How many men can you spare?"

"Two right away. Three by this afternoon."

"Find out if there have been any gang fights or brawls locally in the past few days, and keep your ears open for anyone who may have heard anything—screams, say, or someone shouting for help."

"Very good, sir."

Maigret left the local man on guard over the human arm, which lay covered with sacking on the flagstones of the quay.

"Coming, Lapointe?"

He made for the bar on the corner, with its bright yellow paint, and pushed open the glass door, noting the name, Chez Popaul, inscribed on it. Several local workmen in overalls were having snacks at the counter.

The proprietor hurried forward.

"What can I get you?"

"Do you have a telephone?"

Before the words were out of his mouth, he saw it. It was on the wall next to the bar counter, not enclosed in a booth.

"Come on, Lapointe."

He had no intention of making a phone call where it could be overheard.

"Won't you have something to drink?"

"We'll be back," promised the Chief Superintendent, not wishing to give offense.

Along the quay there were blocks of apartments and concrete office buildings, interspersed with one-story shacks.

"There's bound to be a bistro with a proper telephone booth somewhere around here."

Walking along, they could see, across the canal, the faded flag and blue lamp of the Police Station and, behind it, the dark, massive Hospital of Saint-Louis.

They had gone about three hundred yards when they came to a dingy-looking bar. The Chief Superintendent pushed open the door. Two steps led down into a room with a tiled floor, dark red tiles of the kind commonly seen in Marseilles.

The room was empty except for a large ginger cat lying beside the stove. It got up, stretched lazily, and went out through an open door at the back.

"Anyone there?" called Maigret.

The staccato tick-tick of a cuckoo clock could be heard. The room smelled of spirits and white wine, especially spirits, and there was a faint whiff of coffee.

Someone was moving about in a back room. A woman's voice called out rather wearily, "Coming!"

The ceiling was low and blackened with smoke, and the walls were grimy. Indeed, the whole place was murky, except for faint patches of sunlight here and there. It was like a church lit only by stained-glass windows. A scribbled notice on the wall read: *Snacks served at all hours*, and another: *Patrons are welcome to bring their own food*.

There were, for the time being, no patrons to take advantage of these amenities. It was plain to Maigret and La-

pointe that they were the first that day. There was a telephone booth in a corner, but Maigret was waiting for the
woman to appear.

When at last she did appear, she shuffled in, sticking
pins in her dark, almost black hair. She was thin, sullen-
faced, neither young nor old, perhaps in her early or middle
forties. Her felt slippers made no sound on the tiles.

"What do you want?"

Maigret and Lapointe exchanged glances.

"Have you a good white wine?"

She shrugged.

"Two white wines. And a *jeton* for the phone."

He went into the telephone booth, shutting the door behind him, and rang the Public Prosecutor's office to make
his report. The Deputy to whom he spoke was as surprised
as everyone else to hear that the arm fished out of the canal
was a man's.

"The diver is working upstream now. He says if there's
anything more to find, that's where it will be. The next step,
as far as I'm concerned, is to have Doctor Paul examine
the arm as soon as possible."

"I'll get in touch with him at once and call you back, if
that suits you."

Maigret, having read out the number on the dial, went
over to the bar. Two glasses of wine stood ready poured on
the counter.

"Your very good health," he said, raising his glass to the
woman.

For all the interest she showed, he might not have
spoken. She just stared vacantly, waiting for them to go,

so that she might finish making herself presentable, or whatever it was she had been doing when they arrived.

She must have been attractive, once. She had, like everyone else, undoubtedly once been young. Now, everything about her, her eyes, her mouth, her whole body, was listless, faded. Was she a sick woman, anticipating a dreaded attack? Sometimes sick people who knew that, at a particular hour of the day, the pain would recur, wore that same look of apathy mixed with apprehension, like drug addicts in need of a shot.

"They're calling me back," murmured Maigret, sounding apologetic.

It was, of course, like any other bar or café, a public place, impersonal in a sense, yet both men had the feeling of being intruders who had blundered in where they had no right to be.

"Your wine is very good."

It really was good. Most Paris bistros advertise a *petit vin du pays*, but this, as a rule, turns out to be a wholesale product, straight from Bercy. This wine was different. It had a distinctive regional flavor, though the Superintendent could not quite place it.

"Sancerre?" he ventured.

"No. It comes from a little village near Poitiers."

That accounted for the slight flinty tang.

"Is that where you come from?"

She did not answer. She just stood there, motionless, silent, impassive. Maigret was impressed. The cat, which had come into the room with her, was rubbing its back against her bare legs.

"What about your husband?"

"He's gone there to get more."

More wine, she meant. Making conversation with her was far from easy. The Superintendent had just signaled to her to refill the glasses when, much to his relief, the telephone rang.

"Yes, it's me. Did you get hold of Paul? When will he be free? An hour from now? Right, I'll be there."

The Deputy talked. Maigret listened in silence, with an expression of deepening disapproval, as it sank in that the Examining Magistrate in charge of the case was to be Judge Coméliau. He was the most pettifogging, niggling man on the Bench, and Maigret's very own private and personal enemy.

"He says, will you please see to it that he's kept in the picture."

"I know."

Maigret knew all too well what he was in for: five or six phone calls a day from Coméliau, not to mention a briefing session every morning in the magistrate's office.

"Ah, well," he sighed, "we'll do our best."

"Don't blame me, Superintendent. There just wasn't anyone else available."

The sunlight had penetrated a little farther into the room, and just reached Maigret's glass.

"Let's go," he said, feeling in his pocket for change. "How much?"

And, outside in the street:

"Have you got the car?"

"Yes, I left it over by the lock."

The wine had put color in Lapointe's cheeks, and his

eyes were bright. From where they were, they could see a little group of onlookers watching the diver's progress from the edge of the quay. As Maigret and the Inspector came up to them, Victor's mate pointed to a bundle in the bottom of the boat. It was larger than the first.

"A leg and foot," he called out, and spat into the water. This time, the wrapping was in quite good condition. Maigret saw no necessity to take a closer look.

"Shall we need a hearse?" he asked Lapointe.

"There's plenty of room in the trunk, of course."

The prospect did not commend itself to either of them, but they did have an appointment at the Forensic Laboratory, a large, bright, modern building overlooking the Seine, not far from the junction of the river and the canal. It would not do to keep the pathologist waiting.

"What should I do?" Lapointe asked.

Maigret could not bring himself to say. Repressing his revulsion, Lapointe carried the two bundles, one after the other, to the car, and laid them in the trunk.

"Do they smell?" asked the Superintendent, when Lapointe rejoined him at the water's edge.

Lapointe, who was holding his hands out in front of him, nodded, wrinkling his nose.

Doctor Paul, in white overall and rubber gloves, smoked incessantly. He subscribed to the theory that there was no disinfectant like tobacco, and often, during a single autopsy, would smoke as many as two packs of Bleues Gauloises.

He worked briskly and cheerfully, bent over the marble slab, chatting between puffs.

"Naturally, I can't say anything definite at this stage. For one thing, there's not a great deal to learn from a leg and an arm on their own. The sooner you find the rest of the body, the better. Meanwhile, I'll do as many tests as I can."

"What age would you say?"

"As far as I can tell at a glance, a man somewhere between fifty and sixty—nearer fifty than sixty. Take a look at this hand."

"What about it?"

"It's a broad, strong hand, and it's done rough work in its time."

"A laborer?"

"No. A farm worker, more likely. Still, it's a fair bet that that hand hasn't gripped a heavy implement for years. This was not a fastidious man. You can tell by the nails, especially the toenails."

"A tramp?"

"I don't think so, but, as I say, I can't be sure till I have more to go on."

"Has he been dead long?"

"Again, I can only hazard a guess—don't take my word for it. I may have changed my mind by tonight or tomorrow. But, for the time being, I'm fairly confident that he died not more than three days ago, at the very outside."

"Not last night?"

"No, the night before that, possibly."

Maigret and Lapointe were smoking too, and, as far as they could, they kept their eyes averted from the marble slab. As for Doctor Paul, he seemed to be enjoying his work, handling his instruments like a juggler.

He was changing into his outdoor clothes when Maigret was called to the telephone. It was Judel from the Quai de Valmy.

"They've found the torso!" he announced, sounding quite excited about it.

"No head?"

"Not yet. According to Victor, it won't be so easy. Because of its weight, it will probably be sunk in the mud. He's found an empty wallet and a woman's handbag, though."

"Near the torso?"

"No, quite a long way off. There probably isn't any connection. As he says, every time he goes down, he finds enough junk to open a stall in the Flea Market. Just before he found the torso, he came up with a child's cot and a couple of slop pails."

Paul, holding his hands out in front of him, was waiting before taking off his gloves.

"Any news?" he asked.

Maigret nodded. Then to Judel:

"Can you get it to me at the Forensic Lab?"

"I'm sure we can manage it."

"Right. I'll be here, but be quick about it, because Doctor Paul . . ."

They waited outside the building, enjoying the fresh air, and watching the flow of traffic on the Pont d'Austerlitz. Across the Seine, several barges and a small sailing boat were unloading at the quayside opposite a warehouse. Paris, in the morning sun, was throbbing with youth and gaiety. It was the first real spring day. Life was full of promise.

"No tattoo marks or scars, I suppose?"

"None on the arm or leg, at any rate. From the condition of the skin, I'd say he was not an outdoor type."

"Hairy, though."

"Yes. I have a fair idea of what he must have looked like. Dark, broad-shouldered, but below medium height, with well-developed muscles, and coarse dark hair on the arms, hands, legs, and chest. A real son of the soil, sturdy, independent, stubborn. The countryside of France is full of men like him. It'll be interesting to see his head."

"If we ever find it!"

A quarter of an hour later, two uniformed policemen arrived with the torso. Doctor Paul, all but rubbing his hands, got to work at the marble slab like a craftsman at his bench.

"As I thought," he grumbled. "This isn't a skilled job. What I mean to say is: this man wasn't dismembered by a butcher or a Jack-the-Ripper, still less by a surgeon! The joints were severed by an ordinary hack-saw. The rest of the job, I'd say, was done with a large carving knife. All restaurants have them, and most private kitchens. It must have been a longish job. It couldn't have been done all at once."

He paused.

"Take a look at this chest. What do you see, and I don't mean hair?"

Maigret and Lapointe glanced at the torso, and looked away quickly.

"No visible scars?"

"I don't see any. I'm certain of one thing. Drowning wasn't the cause of death."

It was almost comical. How on earth would a man found in pieces in a canal contrive to drown?

"I'll examine the organs next, and especially—in so far as it's practicable—the contents of the stomach. Will you be staying?"

Maigret shook his head. He had seen quite enough. He could hardly wait to get to a bar and have a drink, not wine this time, but a drop of the hard stuff, to get rid of the foul taste in his mouth, which seemed to him like the taste of death.

"Just a minute, Maigret. What was I saying? D'you see this white line here, and these small white spots on the abdomen?"

The Superintendent nodded, but did not look.

"That's an old operation scar. Quite a few years old. Appendectomy."

"And the spots?"

"Now there's an odd thing. I couldn't swear to it, but I'm almost sure they're grapeshot or buckshot wounds, which confirms my feeling that the man must have lived in the country at some time or other. A small farmer or game-keeper, maybe. Who knows? A long time ago, twenty years or more, someone must have emptied a shotgun into him. There are seven, no, eight of these scars in a curve, like a rainbow. Only once before in the whole of my life have I ever seen anything like them, and they weren't so evenly spaced. I'll have to photograph them for the record."

"Will you give me a ring?"

"Where will you be? At the Quai des Orfèvres?"

"Yes. In my office, and I'll probably lunch in the Place Dauphine."

"As soon as I have anything to report, I'll let you know."

Maigret led the way out into the sunshine and mopped his forehead. Lapointe felt impelled to spit several times into the gutter. He, too, it seemed, had a bitter taste in his mouth.

"As soon as we get back to Headquarters, I'll have the trunk fumigated," he said.

On their way to the car park, they went into a bistro for a glass of marc brandy. It was so potent that Lapointe retched, held his hand to his mouth, and, for a moment, with eyes watering, wondered anxiously whether he was going to be sick.

When he felt better, he muttered:

"Sorry about that."

As they went out, the proprietor of the bar remarked to one of the customers:

"That's another of them come from identifying a corpse. It always makes them that way."

Situated as he was, directly opposite the mortuary, he was used to it.

Chapter 2

Red
Sealing Wax

When Maigret came into the great central lobby of the Quai des Orfèvres he was, for a second or two, dazzled, because even this lobby, surely the grayest and dingiest place on earth, was sunlit today, or at least gilded with luminous dust.

On the benches between the office doors, there were people waiting, some handcuffed. As Maigret went past, to report to the Chief of Police on the Quai de Valmy case, a man stood up and touched his hat in greeting.

With the familiarity born of daily meetings over many years, Maigret called out:

"Well, Vicomte, what have you got to say for yourself? You can't complain this time that it's just another case of someone chopping up a whore."

The man known to everyone as the Vicomte did not seem to object to his nickname, although he must have been aware of the innuendo. He was, in a discreet way, a homosexual. For the past fifteen years he had "covered" the Quai des Orfèvres for a Paris newspaper, a press agency, and some twenty provincial dailies.

In appearance, he was the last of the Boulevard dandies, dressed with Edwardian elegance, wearing a monocle on a black ribbon around his neck. Indeed, it could well have been the monocle (which he hardly ever used) that had earned him his nickname.

"Have they found the head?"

"Not to my knowledge."

"I've just spoken to Judel on the phone. He says, no. If you get any fresh news, Superintendent, don't forget me."

He returned to his bench, and Maigret went into the Chief's office.

The window was open, and from there, too, one could see river craft plying up and down the Seine. The two men engaged in pleasant conversation for ten minutes or so.

The first thing Maigret saw when he went through the door of his own office was a note on his blotting pad. He knew at once what it was—a message from Judge Coméliau, of course, asking him to phone him as soon as he got in.

"Chief Superintendent Maigret here, Judge."

"Ah! Good morning, Maigret. Are you just back from the canal?"

"From the Forensic Lab."

"Is Doctor Paul still there?"

"He's working on the internal organs now."

"I take it the corpse hasn't been identified yet?"

"With no head, there's not much hope of that. Not unless we have a stroke of luck . . ."

"That's the very thing I wanted to discuss with you. In a straightforward case, where the identity of the victim is known, one can tell more or less where one is going. Do you follow me? Now, in this case, we haven't the faintest idea who may be involved. Within the next hour, or the next day or two, we may be in for a nasty shock. We must be prepared for the worst, the very worst, and therefore would do well to proceed with extreme caution."

Coméliau enunciated every syllable, and liked the sound of his own voice. Everything he said or did was of "extreme" importance.

Most examining magistrates were content to leave matters in the hands of the police until they had completed their inquiries. Not so Coméliau. He always insisted on directing operations from the outset, owing, no doubt, to his exaggerated dread of "complications." His brother-in-law was an ambitious politician, one of a handful of Deputies with a finger in every departmental pie. Coméliau was fond of saying:

"You must understand that, owing to his position, I am more vulnerable than my brother-magistrates."

Maigret got rid of him eventually by promising to inform him immediately of any new development, however trivial, even if it meant disturbing him at his home in the evening. He looked through his mail, and then went to the Inspectors' Duty Room, to give them their orders for the day.

"Today is Tuesday, isn't it?"

"That's right, sir."

If Doctor Paul had estimated correctly that the body had been in the Saint-Martin Canal about forty-eight hours, then the crime must have been committed on Sunday, almost certainly during the evening or night, since it was hardly likely that anyone intent on getting rid of a number of bulky and sinister packages would be so foolhardy as to attempt it in broad daylight with the Police Station not five hundred yards away.

"Is that you, Madame Maigret?" he said playfully to his wife, when he had got her on the line. "I shan't be home for lunch. What were we having?"

Haricot mutton. He had no regrets. Too stodgy for a day like this.

He rang Judel.

"What news?"

"Victor is having a snack in the boat. The whole body has been recovered, except the head. He wants to know if he's to go on looking."

"Of course."

"I've got my men on the job, but they haven't come up with anything much so far. There was a bit of trouble in a bar on the Rue des Récollets on Sunday night. Not Chez Popaul. Farther up toward the Faubourg Saint-Martin. A concierge has reported the disappearance of her husband, but he's been missing for over a month, and the description doesn't fit."

"I'll probably be along sometime this afternoon."

On his way to lunch at the Brasserie Dauphine, he looked in at the Inspectors' Duty Room.

"Ready, Lapointe?"

He really did not need his young assistant just to share the table at which he always sat in the little restaurant in the Place Dauphine. This thought struck him as they walked along in companionable silence. He smiled to himself, remembering a question that had once been put to him on this subject. His friend, Doctor Pardon of Rue Popincourt, with whom he and his wife dined regularly once a month, had turned to him one evening and asked very earnestly:

"Can you explain to me, Maigret, why it is that plainclothes policemen, like plumbers, always go about in pairs?"

He had never thought about it, though on reflection he had to admit that it was a fact. He himself, when he was out on a case, almost always took an inspector with him.

He had scratched his head.

"I imagine it goes back to the days when Paris was a lawless city, and it wasn't safe to go into some districts alone, especially at night."

It was not safe even today to make an arrest singlehanded, or venture into the underworld on one's own. But the more Maigret had thought about it, the less this explanation had satisfied him.

"And another thing. Take a suspect who has reluctantly made some damaging admission, either in his own home or at Headquarters. If there had been only one police officer present at the time, it would be that much easier to deny everything later. And a jury will always attach more weight to evidence when there is a witness to corroborate it."

All very true, but still not the whole truth.

"Then there's the practical angle. Say someone is being shadowed. Well, you can't watch him like a hawk and make a telephone call at the same time. And then again, more often than not, your quarry will go into a building with several exits."

Pardon had smiled then as Maigret was smiling now.

"I'm always suspicious," he said, "of tortuous answers to simple questions."

To which Maigret had retorted:

"Well, then, speaking for myself, I usually take an inspector along for company. I'm afraid I'd be bored stiff on my own."

He did not repeat this conversation to Lapointe. One should never poke fun at the illusions of youth, and the sacred fire still burned in Lapointe. It was pleasant and peaceful in the little restaurant, with other police officers dropping in for a drink at the bar, and four or five lunching in the dining room.

"Will the head be found in the canal, do you think?"

Maigret, rather to his own surprise, shook his head. To be honest, he had not given the matter much thought. His response had been instinctive. He could not have said why, he just had a feeling that the diver, Victor, would find nothing more in the mud of the Saint-Martin Canal.

"Where can it be?"

He had no idea. In a suitcase at a baggage checkroom, maybe. At the Gare de l'Est, a few hundred yards from the canal, or the Gare du Nord, not much farther away. Or it might have been sent by road to some address or other in the provinces, in one of the fleet of heavy, long-distance trucks that the Superintendent had seen lined up in a side street off the Quai de Valmy. These particular trucks were red and green, and Maigret had often seen them about the streets, heading for the highways. Until today, he had had no idea where their depot was. It was right there in the Rue Terrage, next to the canal. At one time during the morning, he had noticed twenty or more of them strung out along the

road, all inscribed: "Zenith Transport. Roulers and Langlois."

When Maigret directed his attention to details of this
kind, it usually meant that he was thinking of nothing in
particular. The case was interesting enough, but not absorb-
ing. What interested him more, at the moment, was the
canal itself and its surroundings. At one time, right at the
beginning of his career, he had been familiar with every
street in this district, and could have identified many a
night prowler who slunk past in the shadow of the buildings.

They were still sitting over their coffee when Maigret
was called to the telephone. It was Judel.

"I was in two minds about calling you, sir. I wouldn't
exactly call it a lead, but one of my men, Blancpain, thinks
he may be on to something. I posted him near where the
diver is working, and about an hour ago his attention was
attracted by an errand boy on a delivery bicycle. He had a
feeling he'd seen him before, earlier, more than once, at
regular intervals of about half an hour, in fact. People have
been coming to the quay all day to watch the diver. Most of
them stay for a bit and then wander away, but this character, according to Blancpain, kept to himself, and seemed
to be drawn there by something more than curiosity. Errand
boys, as a rule, work to a pretty tight schedule on their
rounds, and don't have all that much time to waste."

"Has Blancpain spoken to him?"

"He was intending to, but as soon as he made a move toward him—very casually, so as not to scare him off—the
boy hopped onto his bicycle and pedaled away at top
speed toward the Rue des Récollets. Blancpain did chase

after him, but couldn't make much headway in a crowded street on foot—he had no transport—and finally lost him in the traffic of the Faubourg Saint-Martin."

There was a brief silence. It was all very vague, of course. It might mean nothing. On the other hand, it could be a breakthrough.

"Was Blancpain able to describe him?"

"Yes. A fellow of between eighteen and twenty—probably a country boy—very healthy complexion—fair—longish hair—wearing a leather jacket and a turtle-neck sweater. Blancpain couldn't read the name of the firm on his bicycle, but he was able to see that one word ended in 'ail.' We're checking on all the local shopkeepers who employ an errand boy."

"What news from Victor?"

"He says that as long as he's getting paid for it, he doesn't care whether he's under water or on dry land, but he's sure it's a waste of time."

"What about the rubbish dumps and waste ground?"

"Nothing so far."

"I should be getting the pathologist's report shortly. I'm hoping that will tell us something about the dead man."

At half past two, when Maigret was back in his office, Paul rang to report his findings, which would later be confirmed in writing.

"Do you want it at dictation speed, Maigret?"

Maigret drew a writing pad toward him.

"I've had to rely on guesswork to some extent, but I think you'll find I'm not far out. First of all, here's a description of your man as far as one can be certain in the absence of the head. Not very tall, about five foot eight. Short, thick neck and, I feel sure, round face and heavy jowl. Dark hair, possibly graying a little at the temples. Weight: a hundred and sixty-seven pounds. I would describe him as thickset, stocky rather than tubby, muscular rather than fat, though he did put on a bit of weight toward the end. The condition of the liver suggests a steady drinker, but I wouldn't say he was an alcoholic. More probably the sort who likes a glass of something, white wine mostly, every hour or even every half-hour. I did, in fact, find traces of white wine in the stomach."

"Any food?"

"Yes. It was lucky for us that his last meal—lunch or dinner, whichever it was—was indigestible. It consisted mainly of roast pork and haricot beans."

"How long before he died?"

"Two to two and a half hours, I'd say. I've sent scrapings from under his toenails and fingernails to the laboratory. Moers will be getting in touch with you direct about them."

"What about the scars?"

"I can confirm what I told you this morning. The appendectomy was performed five or six years ago, by a good surgeon, judging from the quality of the work. The buckshot scars are at least twenty years old, and if you ask me, I'd say nearer forty."

"Age?"

"Fifty to fifty-five."

"Then he would have got the buckshot wound as a child?"

"In my opinion, yes. General health satisfactory, apart from the inflammation of the liver that I've already mentioned. Heart and lungs in good condition. There's a very old tuberculosis scar on the left lung, but it doesn't mean much. It's quite common for babies and young children to contract a mild form of TB which no one even notices. Well, that's about it, Maigret. If you want any more information, bring me the head, and I'll do my best to oblige."

"We haven't found it yet."

"In that case, you never will."

There, Maigret agreed with him. There are some beliefs in the Quai des Orfèvres which have been held for so long that they have come to be taken for granted. The belief, for instance, that, as a general rule, only the corpses of cheap prostitutes are found dismembered. And the belief that, although the torso is usually found, the head is not.

No one questions these beliefs, they are just accepted by everyone.

Maigret stumped off to the Inspectors' Duty Room.

"If I'm wanted, I'll be upstairs in the lab."

He climbed slowly to the top floor of the Palais de Justice, where he found Moers poring over his test tubes.

"Is that my corpse you're working on?" he asked.

"I'm analyzing the specimens Paul sent up to us."

"Found anything?"

The laboratory was immense, and full of pathologists absorbed in their work. Standing in one corner was the dummy used in the reconstruction of crimes, for instance, in a case of stabbing, to determine the relative positions of victim and assailant.

"It's my impression," murmured Moers, who always spoke in a whisper, as though he were in church, "that your man seldom went out of doors."

"What makes you think that?"

"I've been examining the particles of matter taken from under his toenails. That's how I can tell you that the last pair of socks he wore were navy-blue wool. I also found traces of the kind of felt used for making carpet slippers, from which I conclude that the man practically lived in his slippers."

"If you're right, Paul should be able to confirm it, because if one lives in slippers over a long period, one ends up with deformed feet, or so my wife always tells me, and . . ." He broke off in mid-sentence to telephone Doctor Paul at the Forensic Laboratory. Finding that he had already left, he rang his home.

"Maigret here. Just one question, Doctor. It's Moers's idea really. Did you get the impression that our man wore carpet slippers most of the time?"

"Good for Moers! I almost said as much to you earlier, but it was just an impression, and I didn't want to set you on a false trail. It came into my mind, while I was examining the feet, that the man might have worked in a café or a bar. Barmen, like waiters and policemen—especially policemen on traffic duty—tend to get fallen arches, not because they do much walking, but because they stand for long hours."

"You mentioned that the fingernails were not well kept."

"That's true. It's not very likely that a hotel waiter would have black fingernails."

"Nor a waiter in a large brasserie or a respectable café."

"Has Moers found anything else?"

"Not so far. Many thanks, Doctor."

Maigret stayed in the laboratory for almost an hour,

roaming about, and leaning over the benches to watch the technicians at their work.

"Would it interest you to know that there were also traces of soil mixed with potassium nitrate under the nails?"

Moers knew as well as Maigret where such a mixture was most often to be found: in a cellar, especially a damp cellar.

"Was there much of it?"

"That's what struck me. This was ingrained, occupational dirt."

"In other words, a man who regularly worked in a cellar?"

"That would be my guess."

"What about the hands?"

"There are traces of the same mixture under the finger-nails, and other things too, including minute splinters of red sealing wax."

"The kind used for sealing wine bottles?"

"Yes."

Maigret was almost disappointed. It was beginning to look too easy.

"In other words, a bistro!" he muttered grumpily.

Just then, in fact, it seemed to him more than likely that the case would be over that same evening. He saw, in his mind's eye, the thin, dark woman who had served him with a drink that morning. She had made a deep impression on him, and she had been in his mind more than once that day, not necessarily because he had associated her with the dismembered man, but because he had recognized her as someone out of the ordinary.

There was no lack of colorful characters in a district such as the Quai de Valmy. But he had seldom come across anyone as negative as this woman. It was hard to put it into words. As a rule, when two people look at one another, an interchange of some sort, however slight, takes place. A relationship is established, if only a hostile one.

Not so with this woman. Her face, when she had seen them standing at the bar, had betrayed no trace of surprise or fear, no trace of anything, indeed, but a profound and seemingly habitual lassitude.

Or was it indifference?

Two or three times, between sips of wine, Maigret had looked her straight in the eye, but there had been no response, not so much as the flicker of an eyelash.

Yet it was not the insensibility of a moron. Nor was she drunk or drugged, at least not at that moment. He had made up his mind there and then that he would pay her another visit, if only to discover what kind of people her customers were.

"Are you on to something, sir?"

"Maybe."

"You don't sound exactly overjoyed."

Maigret did not care to pursue the subject. At four o'clock he went in search of Lapointe, who was catching up on his paper-work.

"Would you mind driving me over there?"

"To the canal?"

"Yes."

"I hope they'll have had time to fumigate the car."

There were brightly colored hats in the streets already, with red this year as the dominant color, brilliant poppy-red. The awnings, plain orange or candy-striped, were down over the street cafés. There were people at almost every table, and there seemed to be a new air of cheerful briskness about the passers-by.

At the Quai de Valmy, a small crowd was gathered near where Victor was still searching the bed of the canal. Among them was Judel. Maigret and Lapointe got out of the car and went over to him.

"Nothing more?"

"No."

"No clothing?"

"We've been working on the string. If you think it would help, I'll send it up to the lab. As far as we can tell, it's just the ordinary coarse string most shopkeepers use. Quite a lot was needed for all those parcels. I've got someone making inquiries in the local hardware shops, so far without results. Then there's what's left of the newspapers that were used for wrapping. I've had them dried out, and they're mostly last week's."

"What's the most recent date?"

"Saturday morning."

"Do you know that bistro in the street just beyond the Rue Terrage, the one next door to the surgical instruments place?"

"Chez Calas?"

"I didn't notice the name; it's a murky little place below street level, with a big charcoal stove in the middle, and a zinc bar counter painted black, stretching almost from end to end."

"That's it. Omer Calas's place."

When it came to local landmarks, the district police had the edge on the Quai des Orfèvres.

"What sort of place is it?" asked Maigret, watching the

air bubbles which marked Victor's comings and goings under water.

"Quiet. They've never given us any trouble, as far as I know."

"Would you say Omer Calas was a townsman or a countryman?"

"A countryman, I should think. I could look up his registration. It's always happening. A man comes to Paris as a personal servant or chauffeur, and ends up married to the cook and running a bistro in double harness."

"Have they been there long?"

"Longer than I have. As far back as I can remember, it's always been much the same. It's almost opposite the Police Station, and I occasionally drop in for a drink. They have a good white wine."

"Who looks after the bar? The proprietor?"

"Most of the time—except for an hour or two every afternoon, when he's at a brasserie in the Rue La Fayette playing billiards. He's keen on billiards."

"When he's away, does the woman look after the bar?"

"Yes, they have no staff. I seem to remember they did have a little waitress at one time, but I've no idea what became of her."

"What sort of people go there?"

"It's hard to say," said Judel, scratching the back of his head.

"All the bistros hereabouts cater to more or less the same class of customer, and yet no two are alike. Take Chez Popaul, opposite the lock. It's busy from morning to night. There it's neat spirits and rowdy talk, and there's always a blue haze of tobacco smoke about the place. Any time after eight at night you're sure to find three or four women in there, waiting for their regular fellows."

"And Omer's place?"

"Well, for one thing it's a bit off the beaten track, and for another, it's dark and rather gloomy. You must have noticed the atmosphere yourself. They get dockers from thereabouts dropping in for a drink in the morning, and a few take their sandwiches along at lunchtime, and order a glass of white wine. There's not much doing in the afternoon, and I daresay that's why Omer goes off for his game of billiards after lunch. As I said, there are no regulars at that time, just the occasional passer-by. Trade picks up again at the end of the day.

"I've been in myself once or twice of an evening. It's always the same. A hand of cards at one of the tables, and a couple of people, no more, drinking at the bar. It's one of those joints where, if one doesn't happen to be a regular, one is made to feel out of place."

"Is the woman Omer's wife?"

"I've never thought to ask. I can easily find out, though. We can go over to the station now, if you'd like, and look them up in the records."

"I'll leave that to you. You can let me know later. Omer Calas is away from home, it seems."

"Oh? Is that what she told you?"

"Yes."

By now, the Naud brothers' barge had docked at the Quai de l'Arsenal, and the cargo of gravel was being unloaded by crane.

"I should be grateful if you would compile a list of all the bistros in the district, drawing my attention to any whose proprietor or barman has been absent since Sunday."

"Do you think . . . ?"

"It's Moers's idea. He may be right. I'm going along there."

"To Calas's?"

"Yes. Coming, Lapointe?"

"Shall we be needing Victor tomorrow?"

"We can't chuck the taxpayer's money out of the window. I have a feeling that, if there had been anything more to find, he'd have found it today."

"That's what he thinks, too."

"Tell him he can give up as soon as he feels like it, and not to forget to let me have his report by tomorrow."

Maigret paused on his way, to take another look at the trucks in the Rue Terrage, and read the inscription, "Roulers and Langlois," over the great archway of the depot.

"I wonder how many there are," he murmured, thinking aloud.

"What?" Lapointe asked.

"Trucks."

"I've never driven into the country without finding myself crawling along behind one. It's damned near impossible to pass them."

The chimneypots, which had been rose-pink that morning, were now a deepening red in the setting sun, and there were pale green streaks here and there in the sky, green streaks almost the same color as the green sea at dusk.

"Do you really believe, sir, that a woman could have done it?"

He thought again of the thin, dark woman who had poured their drinks that morning.

"It's possible . . . I don't know."

Perhaps Lapointe felt, as he did, that it was all too easy.

Confront the men of the Quai des Orfèvres with a thoroughly tangled and apparently insoluble problem, and you will have every one of them, Maigret most of all, fretting and grumbling over it. But give them something that, at first sight, seems difficult, and later turns out to be straightforward and commonplace, and those same men, Maigret included, will not be able to contain their disappointment.

They were at the door of the bistro. On account of its low ceiling, it was darker than most, and there was already a light switched on over the counter.

The same woman, carelessly dressed as she had been in the morning, was serving two men, office workers by the look of them. She must have recognized Maigret and his colleague, but she showed no sign of it.

"What will you have?" was all she said, without so much as a smile.

"White wine."

There were three or four bottles with drawn corks in a bucket behind the counter. Presumably it was necessary to go down to the cellar from time to time to get more. The floor behind the bar was not tiled, and there was a trap door, about three foot square, leading, no doubt, to the cellar below. Maigret and Lapointe had not taken their drinks to a table. From the conversation of the two men standing beside them at the bar, they gathered that they were not, in fact, office workers, but male nurses on night shift at the Hospital of Saint-Louis on the other side of the canal. From something one of them said to the woman, it was evident that they were regulars.

"When do you expect Omer back?"

"You know he never tells me anything."

She replied un-self-consciously, and with the same indifference as she had shown when Maigret had spoken to her earlier in the day. The ginger cat was still stretched out beside the stove, with every appearance of having been there all day.

"I hear they're still searching for the head!" said the man who had asked about her husband. As he spoke, he glanced at Maigret and his companion. Had he seen them on the quay earlier in the day? Or was it just that he could tell by the look of them that they were policemen?

"It hasn't been found, has it?" he went on, addressing himself direct to Maigret.

"Not yet."

"Do you think it will be found?"

The other man subjected Maigret to a long stare, and then said:

"You're Chief Superintendent Maigret, aren't you?"

"Yes."

"I thought so. I've often seen your picture in the papers."

The woman still did not bat an eyelid. For all one could tell, she had not even heard.

"It's weird, carving up a man like that! Coming, Julien? How much, Madame Calas?"

With a slight nod to Maigret and Lapointe, they went out.

"Do you get many of the hospital staff in here?"

"A few."

She did not waste words.

"Has your husband been away since Sunday?"

She looked at him blankly and asked, as though it were a matter of indifference to her:

"Why Sunday?"

"I don't know. I thought I heard . . ."

"He left on Friday afternoon."

"Weɪe there many people in the bar then?"

She seemed to be trying to remember. At times, she looked so withdrawn—or bored, was it?—that she might have been a sleepwalker.

"There are never many people in the afternoon."

"Was there anyone at all? Try and think."

"There may have been. I don't remember. I didn't notice."

"Did he have any luggage?"

"Of course."

"Much?"

"A suitcase."

"What was he wearing?"

"A gray suit. I think. Yes."

"Do you know where he is now?"

"No."

"Didn't he say where he was going?"

"I know he must have taken the train to Poitiers. From there, he'll have gone on by bus to Saint-Aubin or some other village in the district."

"Does he stay at the local inn?"

"As a rule."

"Doesn't he ever stay with friends or relatives? Or on one of the estates where he gets his wine?"

"I've never asked him."

"You mean to say that if you needed to get in touch with him urgently, to pass on some important message, for instance, or because you were ill, you wouldn't know where to find him?"

This too appeared to be a matter of indifference to her.

"Sooner or later he'd be bound to come back," she said in her flat, monotonous voice. "The same again?"

Both glasses were empty. She refilled them.

Chapter 3

The Errand
Boy

It was, all in all, one of Maigret's most frustrating interrogations. Not that one could call it an interrogation in the accepted sense, with life going on as usual around them. The Chief Superintendent and Lapointe stood at the bar for a long time, sipping their drinks like ordinary customers. And that was what they really were. True, one of the male nurses had recognized Maigret earlier, and had addressed him by name, but the Superintendent, when speaking to Madame Calas, made no reference to his official standing. He would ask a question. She would reply, briefly. Then there would be a long silence, during which she completely ignored him.

At one point, she went out of the room through a door at the back, which she did not bother to shut behind her. The door presumably led into the kitchen. She was gone some time. They could hear her putting something on the stove. While she was away, a little old man came in and, obviously knowing his way about, made straight for a corner table, and took a box of dominoes from the shelf underneath. He tipped the dominoes onto the table and jumbled them up, as though intending to play all by himself. The clink of the pieces brought the woman back from the kitchen. Without a word, she went to the bar and poured a pink apéritif, which she slapped down on the table in front of him.

The man waited. A few minutes later, another little old man came in and sat down opposite him. The two were so much alike that they could have been brothers.

"Am I late?"

"No. I was early."

Madame Calas poured an apéritif of a different sort, and carried it over to the table. On the way, she pressed a switch, and a light came on at the far end of the room. All without a word spoken, as in a mime.

"Doesn't she give you the creeps?" Lapointe whispered to Maigret. That was not the effect she had on the Superintendent. He was intensely interested in her, more so than in anyone he had met for a very long time.

Had he not in his youth dreamed of an ideal vocation for himself, a vocation which did not exist in real life? He had never told anyone, had never even given it a name, but he knew now what it was he had wanted to be: a guide to the lost.

In fact, curiously enough, in the course of his work as a policeman, he had often been able to help people back onto the right road, from which they had misguidedly strayed. More curiously still, recent years had seen the birth of a new vocation, similar in many respects to the vocation of his dreams: that of the psychoanalyst, whose function it is to bring a man face to face with his true self.

To be sure, he had discovered one of her secrets, though

secret was perhaps hardly the word for something that all her regular customers must be aware of. Twice more she had retreated to the back room and, the second time, he had clearly heard the squeaking of a cork in a bottle.

She drank. He was quite sure of one thing. She never got drunk, never lost her self-control. Like all true alcoholics, whom doctors are powerless to help, she knew her own capacity. She drank only as much as was needed to maintain her in the state of anesthesia which had so puzzled him at their first meeting.

"How old are you?" he asked her, when she was back at her post behind the counter.

"Forty-one."

There was no hesitation. She said it without a trace of either coquetry or bitterness. She knew she looked older. No doubt she had stopped caring years ago about other people and what they thought of her. She looked worn out, with dark shadows under the eyes, a tremor at the corner of the mouth, and, already, slack folds under the chin. She must have lost a great deal of weight, judging by her dress, which was far too big, and hung straight down from her shoulders.

"Were you born in Paris?"

"No."

She must know, he felt sure, what lay behind his questions. Yet she did not shrink from them. She was giving nothing away, but at least he got a straight answer to a straight question.

The two old men, behind Maigret, were playing dominoes, as no doubt they did every evening at this time.

What puzzled Maigret was that she did her drinking out of sight. What was the point, seeing that she did not care what people thought of her, of slinking off into the back room to have her swig of wine or spirits, or whatever it was, straight out of the bottle? Could it be that she still retained this one vestige of self-respect? He doubted it. It is only when they are under supervision that hardened alcoholics resort to subterfuge.

Was that the answer? There was the husband, Omer Calas. He might well object to his wife's drinking, in front of the customers at least.

"Does your husband go regularly to Poitiers for his wine?"

"Every year."

"Once a year?"

"Sometimes twice. It depends."

"On what?"

"On our trade."

"Does he always go on a Friday?"

"I can't remember."

"Did he say he was going on a business trip?"

"To whom?"

"To you."

"He never tells me anything."

"Would he have mentioned it to any of the customers, or a friend?"

"I've no idea."

"Were those two here last Friday?"

"Not when Omer left. They never come in before five."

Maigret turned to Lapointe.

"Ring the Gare Montparnasse, will you, and find out the times of the afternoon trains to Poitiers. Have a word with the stationmaster."

Maigret spoke in an undertone. Had she been watching him, Madame Calas would have been able to lip-read the message, but she did not trouble to do so.

"Ask him to make inquiries among the station staff, especially in the ticket office. Have him get the husband's description."

The telephone booth, unlike most, was not at the far end of the room, but near the entrance. Lapointe asked for a *jeton*, and moved toward the glass door. Night was closing in, and there was a bluish mist outside. Maigret, who had his back to the door, heard quickening footsteps, and turned to catch a glimpse of a young face which, in the half-light, looked blurred and very pale. Then he saw the dark outline of a man running in the direction of La Villette, followed by Lapointe, who had wrenched open the door to dash out and give chase. He had not had time to shut the door behind him. Maigret went outside, and stood on the pavement. He could now barely see the two running figures, but even after they had disappeared from view he could still hear their rapid footsteps on the cobbles.

Lapointe must have seen a face he recognized through the glass door. Maigret had not seen very much, but he could guess what must have happened. The fugitive fitted the description of the errand boy who, earlier in the day, had watched the diver at work in the canal, and fled when approached by a policeman.

"Do you know him?" he asked Madame Calas.

"Who?"

It was no use pressing the point. Anyway, she might well have been looking the other way when it all happened.

"Is it always as quiet as this in here?"

"It depends."

"On what?"

"On the time of day. And some days are busier than others."

As though to prove it, a siren sounded, releasing the workers at a nearby factory, and a few minutes later there was a noise in the street like a column on the march. The door opened and shut and opened and shut again, a dozen times at least. People sat down at the tables, and others, like Maigret, stood at the bar.

Most of them seemed to be regulars, as the woman did not ask what they wanted, but silently poured their usual drinks.

"I see Omer's not home."

"No."

She did not go on to say: "He's out of town," or "He left for Poitiers on Friday."

She merely answered the question, and left it at that. What was her background? He could not even hazard a guess. Life had tarnished her, and eroded some part of her real self. Through drink, she had withdrawn into a private world of her own, and her links with reality were tenuous.

"Have you lived here long?"

"In Paris?"

"No. In this café."

"Twenty-four years."

"Was your husband here before you?"

"No."

He did some rapid mental arithmetic.

"So you were seventeen when you first met him?"

"I knew him before that."

"How old is he now?"

"Forty-seven."

This did not altogether tally with Doctor Paul's estimate of the man's age, but it was not far out. Not that Maigret was convinced he was on the right track. His questions were prompted more by personal curiosity than anything else. For it would surely be a miracle if, without the smallest effort on his part, he were to establish the identity of the headless corpse on the very first day of the inquiry.

There was a hum of voices in the bar, and a floating veil of tobacco smoke had formed overhead. People were coming and going. The two players, absorbed in their game of dominoes, seemed unaware that they were not the only people on earth.

"Do you have a photograph of your husband?"

"No."

"Not even a snapshot?"

"No."

"Have you got any of yourself?"

"No. Only the one on my identity card."

Not one person in a thousand, Maigret knew from experience, can claim not to possess a single personal photograph.

"Do you live upstairs?"

She nodded. He had seen from the outside that the building was a single-story structure. The space below street level comprised the café and kitchen. The floor above, he assumed, must consist of two or three rooms, more likely two, plus a lavatory or storeroom.

"How do you get up there?"

"The staircase is in the kitchen."

Shortly after this exchange, she went into the kitchen, and this time he heard her stirring something in a saucepan. The door burst open noisily, and Maigret saw Lapointe, flushed, bright-eyed and panting, pushing a young man ahead of him.

The little fellow, as Lapointe was always referred to at the Quai des Orfèvres, not because he was undersized but because he was the youngest and most junior of the Inspectors, had never looked so pleased with himself in his life.

"I didn't catch him until we were right at the end of the street!" he said, grinning broadly and reaching out for his glass, which was still on the counter. "Once or twice I thought he'd given me the slip. It's just as well I was the five-hundred-meter champion at school!"

The young man, too, was panting, and Maigret could feel his hot breath.

"I haven't done anything," he protested, appealing to Maigret.

"In that case, you have nothing to fear."

Maigret looked at Lapointe.

"Have you seen his identity card?"

"Just to be on the safe side, I kept it. It's in my pocket. He works as an errand boy for the Maison Pincemail. And he's the one who was snooping on the wharf this morning, and made a quick getaway when he saw he'd been noticed."

"What did you do that for?" Maigret asked the young man.

He scowled, as boys do when they want to show what tough guys they are.

"Well?"

"I've nothing to say."

"Didn't you get anything out of him on the way?" he asked Lapointe.

"We were both so winded we could hardly speak. His name is Antoine Cristin. He's eighteen, and he lives with his mother in rooms in the Faubourg Saint-Martin."

One or two people had turned around to look at them, but not with any great interest. In this district, a policeman bursting into a bar was quite a common sight.

"What were you up to out there?"

"Nothing."

"He had his nose pressed against the glass," Lapointe explained. "The minute I saw him, I remembered what Judel had said, and I nipped out to get him."

"If you had done nothing wrong, why try to get away?"

He hesitated, took a quick look around to satisfy himself that there were at least a couple of people within earshot, then said, with a theatrical curl of the lip: "Because I don't like cops."

"But you don't mind spying on them through glass doors?"

"There's no law against it."

"How did you know we were in here?"

"I didn't."

"What did you come for, then?"

He flushed, and bit his fleshy lower lip.

"Come on, let's have it."

"I was just passing."

"Do you know Omer?"

"I don't know anyone."

"Not even Madame?"

She was back in her place behind the bar, watching them. But there was no trace of fear or even anxiety in her face. Had she anything to hide? If so, her nerve was beyond anything Maigret had ever encountered in a criminal or accessory to a crime.

"Do you know her?"

"By sight."

"Don't you ever come in here for a drink?"

"Maybe."

"Where's your bicycle?"

"At the shop. I'm off at five."

Maigret made a sign to Lapointe, one of the few secret signs used by plain-clothes detectives. Lapointe nodded. He went into the telephone booth and rang, not the Gare Montparnasse, but the Police Station just across the road, and eventually he got hold of Judel.

"We've got the kid here, at Calas's place. In a minute or two, the boss will let him go, but he wants someone standing by in case he makes a run for it. Any news?"

"Nothing worth mentioning. Four or five reports of scuffles in bars on Sunday night; someone who thinks he heard a body being dropped in the water; a prostitute who claims she had her handbag snatched by an Arab . . ."

"So long."

Maigret, very bland, turned to the young man.

"What will you have, Antoine? Wine? Beer?"

"Nothing."

"Don't you drink?"

"Not with cops, I don't. You'll have to let me go, you know."

"You're very sure of yourself."

"I know my rights."

He was a broad-shouldered, sturdy country lad, with a wholesome complexion. Paris had not yet robbed him of his robust health. Maigret could not count the number of times he had seen kids just like him end up having black-jacked some poor old soul in a tobacconist's or dry-goods shop, to rob the till of a couple of hundred francs.

"Have you any brothers or sisters?"

"I'm an only child."

"Where's your father?"

"He's dead."

"Does your mother go out to work?"

"She's a cleaning woman."

Maigret turned to Lapointe:

"Give him back his identity card. All in order, is it? The correct address, and so on?"

"Yes."

The boy looked uncertain, suspecting a trap.

"Can I go?"

"Whenever you like."

He went without a word of thanks or even a nod, but on his way out he winked furtively at the woman, a signal which did not escape Maigret.

"You'd better call the station now."

He ordered two more glasses of white wine. There were fewer people in the café now. Only three customers, other than Lapointe and himself, and the two old men playing dominoes.

"You don't know him, do you?"

"Who?"

"The young man who was here just now."

Unhesitatingly, she said:

"Yes."

It was as simple as that. Maigret was disconcerted.

"Does he come here often?"

"Quite often."

"For a drink?"

"He drinks very little."

"Beer?"

"And occasionally wine."

"Does he usually come in after work?"

"No."

"During the day?"

She nodded. Her unshakable composure was beginning to exasperate the Superintendent.

"When he happens to be passing."

"You mean when he's around this way on his bicycle? In other words, when he's out delivering?"

"Yes."

"And what time of day would that be?"

"Between half past three and four."

"Does he have a regular round?"

"I think so."

"Does he stand at the bar?"

"Sometimes he sits at a table."

"Which one?"

"This one over here, next to the till."

"Is he a particular friend of yours?"

"Yes."

"Why wouldn't he admit it?"

"He was showing off, I expect."

"Does he make a habit of it?"

"He does his best."

"Do you know his mother?"

"No."

"Are you from the same village?"

"No."

"He just walked in one day, and you made a friend of him. Is that it?"

"Yes."

"Half past three in the afternoon. That's when your husband is out playing billiards in a brasserie, isn't it?"

"Most days, yes."

"Is it just a coincidence, do you think, that Antoine should choose that particular time to visit you?"

"I've never thought about it."

Maigret hesitated before asking his next question. The very idea shocked him, but he had a feeling that there were even more shocking revelations to come.

"Does he make love to you?"

"It depends what you mean."

"Is he in love with you?"

"I dare say he likes me."

"Do you give him presents?"

"I slip him a note from the till, occasionally."

"Does your husband know?"

"No."

"Doesn't he notice that sort of thing?"

"He has, from time to time."

"Was he angry?"

"Yes."

"Isn't he suspicious of Antoine?"

"I don't think so."

Entering this dark room, two steps down from the street, they had stepped into another world, a world in which all the familiar values were distorted, in which even familiar words had a different meaning. Lapointe was still in the telephone booth, talking to the stationmaster.

"Will you forgive me, Madame Calas, if I ask you a more intimate question?"

"If you want to, you will, whatever I say."

"Is Antoine your lover?"

She did not flinch or even look away from Maigret.

"It has happened from time to time," she admitted.

"You mean to say you have had intercourse with him?"

"You'd have found out sooner or later, anyway. I'm sure he'll tell you himself before long."

"Has it happened often?"

"Quite often."

"Where?"

It was a question of some importance. Madame Calas, in the absence of her husband, had to be available to serve anyone who might happen to come in. Maigret glanced up at the ceiling. But could she be sure of hearing the door open, up there in the bedroom?

In the same straightforward manner in which she had answered all his questions, she nodded toward the open kitchen door at the back of the room.

"In there?"

"Yes."

"Were you ever interrupted?"

"Not by Omer."

"By whom?"

"One day, a customer wearing rubber-soled shoes came into the kitchen, because there was no one in the bar."

"What did he do?"

"He laughed."

"Didn't he tell Omer?"

"No."

"Did he ever come back?"

It was intuition that prompted Maigret to ask. So far he had judged Madame Calas correctly. Even his wildest shots had hit the target.

"Did he come back often?" he pressed her.

"Two or three times."

"While Antoine was here?"

"No."

It would not have been difficult to tell whether or not the young man was in the café. Any time earlier than five o'clock, he would have had to leave his delivery bicycle at the door.

"Were you alone?"

"Yes."

"And he made you go into the kitchen with him?"

For a second, there was a flicker of expression in her eyes. Mockery? Perhaps he had imagined it. All the same, he believed he could read an unspoken message there:

"Why ask, when you know the answer?"

She understood him as well as he understood her. They were a match for one another. To be more precise, life had taught them both the same lesson.

It all happened so quickly that Maigret wondered afterwards whether he had imagined the whole thing.

"Are there many others?" he asked, lowering his voice. His tone was almost confidential now.

"A few."

Then, standing very still, not bending forward toward her, he put one last question:

"Why?"

To that question, there was no answer but a slight shrug. She was not one to strike romantic attitudes or dramatize her situation.

He had asked her why. If he did not know, it was not for her to tell him.

The fact was that he did know. He had only wanted confirmation. He had got it. There was no need for her to say anything.

He now knew to what depths she had sunk. What he still did not know was what had driven her there. Would she be equally ready to tell him the truth about her past?

That would have to wait. Lapointe had joined him at the bar. He gulped down some wine and then said:

"There's a weekday train to Poitiers that leaves at four forty-eight. The stationmaster says that neither of the ticket-office clerks remembers anyone answering the description. He's going to make further inquiries, and call us at Headquarters. On the other hand, he thinks we'd do better to ring Poitiers. It's a slow train, and it goes on south from Poitiers, so there would have been fewer people stopping there than had boarded the train at Montparnasse."

"Put Lucas on to that. Tell him to ring Saint-Aubin and

the nearest villages. Where there isn't a police station, let him try the local inn."

Lapointe asked Madame Calas for some *jetons*, and she handed them over listlessly. She asked no questions. Being interrogated about her husband's movements might have been an everyday occurrence. Yet she knew what had been found in the Saint-Martin Canal, and could not have been unaware of the search that had been going on all day almost under her windows.

"Did you see Antoine last Friday?"

"He never comes on Friday."

"Why not?"

"He has a different round that day."

"And after five o'clock?"

"My husband is usually back by then."

"So he wasn't here at any time during the afternoon or evening?"

"That's right."

"You've been married to Omer Calas for twenty-four years?"

"I've been living with him for twenty-four years."

"You're not married?"

"Yes. We were married at the Town Hall in the 10th *Arrondissement*, but not until sixteen or seventeen years ago. I can't remember exactly."

"No children?"

"One daughter."

"Does she live with you?"

"No."

"In Paris?"

"Yes."

"How old is she?"

"She's just twenty-four. I had her when I was seventeen."

"Is Omer the father?"

"Yes."

"No doubt about it?"

"None whatever."

"Is she married?"

"No."

"Does she live alone?"

"She's got rooms in the Ile Saint-Louis."

"Has she a job?"

"She's assistant to one of the surgeons at the Hôtel-Dieu, Professor Lavaud."

For the first time, she had told him more than was strictly necessary. Could it be that, in spite of everything, she still retained some vestige of natural feeling, and was proud of her daughter?

"Did you see her last Friday?"

"No."

"Does she ever come to see you?"

"Occasionally."

"When was the last time?"

"Three or four weeks ago."

"Was your husband here?"

"I think so."

"Does your daughter get on well with him?"

"She has as little to do with us as possible."

"Because she's ashamed of you?"

"Possibly."

"How old was she when she left home?"

There was a little color in her cheeks now, and a touch of defiance in her voice.

"Fifteen."

"Without warning?"

She nodded.

"Was there a man?"

She shrugged.

"I don't know. It makes no difference."

The room was empty now, except for the two old men. One was putting the dominoes back in their box, and the other was banging a coin on the table. Madame Calas got the message, and went over to refill their glasses.

"Isn't that Maigret?" one of them asked in an undertone.

"Yes."

"What does he want?"

"He didn't say."

Nor had she asked him. She went into the kitchen for a moment, came back to the bar, and said in a low voice:

"My meal is ready. Will you be long?"

"Where do you have your meals?"

"Over there." She pointed to a table at the far end of the room.

"I won't keep you much longer. Did your husband have an attack of appendicitis several years back?"

"Five or six years ago. He had an operation."

"Who did it?"

"Let me think. A Doctor Gran . . . Granvalet. That's it! He lived in the Boulevard Voltaire."

"Where is he now?"

"He died, or so we were told by another of his patients."

Had Granvalet been alive, he could have told them whether Omer Calas had a rainbow-shaped scar on his abdomen. Tomorrow, they would have to track down the assistants and nurses who had taken part in the operation. Unless, of course, they found Omer safe and well in some village inn near Poitiers.

"Was your husband ever, years ago, involved in a shotgun accident?"

"Not since I've known him."

"Did he ever join a shooting party?"

"He may have, when he lived in the country."

"Have you ever noticed a scar, rather faint, on his stomach, in the shape of a rainbow?"

She frowned, apparently trying to remember, and then shook her head.

"Are you sure?"

"I haven't seen him undressed for a very long time."

"Did you love him?"

"I don't know."

"How long did you remain faithful to him?"

"For years."

She said this with peculiar emphasis.

"Were you very young when you first knew each other?"

"We come from the same village."

"What village?"

"It's really a hamlet, about midway between Montargis and Gien. It's called Boissancourt."

"Do you go back there often?"

"Never."

"You've never been back?"

"No."

"Not since you and Omer came together?"

"I left when I was seventeen."

"Were you pregnant?"

"Six months."

"Was it generally known?"

"Yes."

"Did your parents know?"

In the same matter-of-fact tone, about which there was a kind of nightmare quality, she said dryly:

"Yes."

"You never saw them again?"

"No."

Lapointe, having finished passing on Maigret's instructions to Lucas, came out of the telephone booth, mopping his brow.

"What do I owe you?" asked Maigret.

For the first time, she had a question to ask.

"Are you going?"

And, taking his tone from her, he replied,

"Yes."

Chapter 4

The Boy on the Roof

Maigret hesitated a long time before taking his pipe out of his pocket, which was most unlike him; and when he did, he assumed an absent-minded air, as though he had just got it out to keep his hands occupied while he was talking.

The staff meeting in the Chief's office had been short. When it was over, Maigret and the Chief stood for a few minutes talking by the open window, and then Maigret made straight for the little communicating door which led to the Department of Public Prosecutions. The benches all along the corridor in the Examining Magistrates' Wing were crowded, two police vans having driven into the courtyard a short while before. Maigret recognized most of the prisoners waiting handcuffed, between two guards, and one or two, apparently bearing him no ill-will, nodded a greeting as he went past.

By the time he had got back to his office the previous evening, there were several messages on his pad requesting him to phone Judge Coméliau. The Judge was thin and nervy, with a little brown mustache that looked dyed, and the bearing of a cavalry officer. His very first words to Maigret were:

"I want to know exactly how things stand."

Obediently Maigret told him, beginning with Victor's search of the Saint-Martin Canal, and his failure to find the head. Even at this early stage, he was interrupted.

"The diver will be continuing the search today, I presume?"

"I didn't consider it necessary."

"It seems to me that, having discovered the rest of the body in the canal, it's logical to assume that the head can't be far away."

This was what made him so difficult to work with. He was not the only meddling magistrate, but he was certainly the most pig-headed. He wasn't a fool, by any means. It was said by lawyers who had known him in his student days that he had been one of the most brilliant men of his class.

One could only suppose that he had never learned to apply his intelligence to the hard facts of life. He was very much a man of the Establishment, guided by inflexible principles and hallowed taboos, which determined his attitude in all things. Patiently, the Chief Superintendent explained:

"In the first place, Judge, Victor is as much at home in the canal as you are in your office and I am in mine. He has gone over the bottom inch by inch, at least a couple of hundred times. He's a conscientious fellow. If he says the head isn't there . . ."

"My plumber is a conscientious fellow, too, and he knows his job, but that doesn't prevent him from assuring me, every time I send for him, that there can't possibly be any defect in my water system."

"It rarely happens, in the case of a dismembered corpse, that the head is found near the body."

Coméliau was making a visible effort, with his bright little eyes fixed on Maigret, who went on:

"It's understandable. It's no easy matter to identify a torso or a limb, especially when it's been some time in the water, but a head is easily recognizable. And because it's less cumbersome than a body, it's worth taking the trouble to dispose of it further afield."

"Yes, I'll grant you that."

Maigret, as discreetly as he could, had got out his tobacco pouch and was holding it in his left hand, hoping that something might distract the magistrate's attention, so that he could fill his pipe.

He turned to the subject of Madame Calas, and described the bar in the Quai de Valmy.

"What led you to her?"

"Pure chance, I must admit. I had a phone call to make, and there was no telephone booth in the first bar I went into, only a wall instrument, making private conversation impossible."

"Go on."

Maigret told him of Calas's alleged departure by train for Poitiers, and of the relationship between the proprietress of the bar and Antoine Cristin, the errand boy. And he did not forget to mention the crescent-shaped scar.

"Do you mean to tell me that you believed this woman when she said she didn't know whether or not her husband had such a scar?"

This infuriated the Judge, because he could not understand it.

"To be perfectly frank, Maigret, I can't understand why you didn't have the woman and the boy brought in for questioning in the routine way. It's the usual practice, and generally produces results. I take it her story is a pack of lies?"

"Not necessarily."

"But claiming she didn't know where her husband was or when he would return . . . Well, really! . . ."

Coméliau was born in a house on the Left Bank, with a view over the Luxembourg. He was still living in it. How could such a man be expected to have the smallest insight into the minds of people like Omer Calas and his wife?

At last! The flicker of a match, and Maigret's pipe was alight. Now for the disapproving stare. Coméliau had a perfect horror of smoking, and this was his way of showing it when anyone had the impudence to light up in his presence. Maigret, however, was determined to outface him.

"You may be right," he conceded. "She could have been lying to me. On the other hand, she could have been telling the truth. All we have is a dismembered corpse without a head. All we know for certain is that the dead man was aged between forty-five and fifty-five. So far, he has not been identified. Do you imagine that Calas is the only man to have disappeared in the past few days, or gone off without saying where? Madame Calas is a secret drinker, and her lover, the errand boy, is scared of the police. Does that give me the right to have her brought to Headquarters as a suspect? What kind of fools will we look if, in the next day or so, a head is found, and it turns out not to be the head of Omer Calas at all?"

"Are you having the house watched?"

"Judel of the 10th *Arrondissement* has a man posted on the quay, and I went back myself after dinner last night to take a look around."

"Did you get any results?"

"Nothing much. I stopped one or two prostitutes in the street, and asked them a few questions. It's one of those districts where the atmosphere is quite different at night from what it is by day, and I was hoping that if there was anything suspicious going on around the café on Sunday night, one of these women would have seen or heard it."

"Did you discover anything?"

"Not much. I did get what may be a lead from one of them, but I haven't had time to follow it up.

"According to her, the woman Calas has another lover, a middle-aged man with red hair, who either lives or works in the district. My informant, it must be admitted, is eaten up with spite, because, as she put it, 'that woman takes the bread out of our mouths.' If she were a pro, she said, they wouldn't mind so much. But she does it for nothing. All the men, it seems, know where to go. They only have to wait till the husband's back is turned. No one is refused, I'm told, though, of course, I haven't put it to the test."

In the face of such depravity, Coméliau could only heave a distressful sigh.

"You must proceed as you think fit, Maigret. I don't see any problem myself. There's no need to handle people of that sort with kid gloves."

"I shall be seeing her again shortly. And I intend to see the daughter as well. As to identification, I hope we shall be able to clear that up through the nurses who were present at the operation on Calas five years ago."

In that connection, one curious fact had emerged. The previous evening, while Maigret was wandering about the streets, he had suddenly remembered another question he wanted to put to Madame Calas, and had gone back to the bistro. Madame Calas was sitting half asleep on a chair and four men were playing cards at a table. Maigret had asked her the name of the hospital where her husband had been operated on.

He had formed an impression of Calas as a fairly tough character, not at all the sort to pamper himself, fret about his health, or fear for his life. Yet when it came to undergoing a simple operation, without complications, virtually without risk, he had not chosen to go into hospital but, at considerable expense, to a private clinic at Villejuif. And not just any private clinic, but a religious establishment, staffed by nuns.

Maigret looked at his watch. Lapointe must be there by now. He would soon be telephoning to report.

"Be firm, Maigret!" urged Coméliau, as the Superintendent was leaving.

It was not lack of firmness that was holding him back. It was not pity either. Coméliau would never understand. The world into which Maigret had suddenly been plunged was so different from the familiar world of daily life that he could only feel his way, tentatively, step by step. Was there any connection between the occupants of the little café in the Quai de Valmy and the corpse thrown into the Saint-Martin Canal? Possibly. But it was equally possible that it was mere coincidence.

He returned to his office, feeling restless and disgruntled, as he nearly always did at this stage of any inquiry.

Last night, he had been collecting and storing information without stopping to consider where it was all leading. Now, he was faced with a jumble of facts which needed sorting out and piecing together.

Madame Calas was no longer simply a colorful character, such as he occasionally encountered in his work. She was his problem, his responsibility.

Coméliau saw her as a sexually promiscuous, drink-sodden degenerate. That was not how Maigret saw her. Just what she was, he could not say yet, and until he knew for sure, until he felt the truth in his bones, as it were, he would be oppressed by this indefinable uneasiness.

Lucas was in his office. He had just put the mail on his desk.

"Any new developments?"

"Have you been in the building all the time, sir?"

"With Coméliau."

"If I'd known, I'd have had your calls transferred. Yes, there has been a new development. Judel is in a terrible stew."

It was Madame Calas who came at once into Maigret's mind, and he wondered what could have happened to her. But it had nothing to do with her.

"It's about the young man, Antoine. I think that was the name."

"Yes, Antoine. What's happened? Has he vanished again?"

"That's it. It seems you left instructions last night that he was to be kept under observation. The young man went straight to his lodgings, at the far end of the Faubourg Saint-Martin, almost at the junction with the Rue Louis-Blanc. The man detailed to follow him had a word with the concierge. The boy lives with his mother, who is a cleaning woman, on the seventh floor of the building. They have two attic rooms. There's no elevator. I got all this from Judel, of course. Apparently, the building is one of those ghastly great tenements, housing fifty or sixty families, with swarms of kids spilling out onto the stairs."

"Go on."

"That's about all. According to the concierge, the boy's mother is an estimable woman with plenty of guts. Her husband died in a sanatorium. She has had TB herself. She claims to be cured, but the concierge doubts it. Well, when he had heard all this, Judel's man rang the Station for further instructions. Judel, not wanting to take any chances, told him to stay where he was and watch the building. He stood guard outside until about midnight. All the tenants were in by then. He went in after the last of them, and spent the night on the stairs.

"This morning, just before eight, a thin woman went past the lodge, and the concierge called out to him that this was Antoine's mother. He saw no necessity to stop or follow her. It was not until half an hour later that, having nothing better to do, he thought of going up to the seventh floor, to have a look around.

"It did strike him as odd then that the boy hadn't yet left for work. He listened at the keyhole, but couldn't hear a sound. He knocked, and got no answer. In the end, after examining the lock and seeing that it was anything but secure, he decided to use his skeleton keys.

"The first room he came to was the kitchen. There was a bed in it, the mother's bed. In the other room there was a bed too, unmade. But there was no one there, and the sky-light was open.

"Judel is furious with himself for not having foreseen this, and given instructions accordingly. It's obvious that the kid got out through the skylight during the night, and crawled along the rooftops looking for another open sky-light. He probably got out through a building in the Rue Louis-Blanc."

"They've checked that he's not hiding in the tenement, I take it?"

"They're still questioning the tenants."

Maigret could imagine Judge Coméliau's sarcastic smile when he was told about this.

"Nothing from Lapointe?"

"Not yet."

"Has anyone turned up at the mortuary to identify the corpse?"

"Only the regulars."

There were about a dozen of these, elderly women for the most part, who, every time a body was found, rushed to the mortuary to identify it.

"Didn't Doctor Paul ring?"

"I've just put his report on your desk."

"If you speak to Lapointe, tell him to come back here and wait for me. I won't be far away."

He walked toward the Ile Saint-Louis. He skirted Notre-Dame, crossed a little iron footbridge, and soon found him-self in the narrow, crowded Rue Saint-Louis-en-l'Ile. The housewives were all out doing their shopping at this time of day, and he had difficulty in pushing past them as they crowded around the little market stalls. Maigret found the grocer's shop above which, according to Madame Calas, her daughter Lucette had a room. He went down the little alleyway at the side of the shop and came to a cobbled courtyard shaded by a lime tree, like the forecourt of a village school or country vicarage.

"Looking for someone?" shrilled a woman's voice from a window on the ground floor.

"Mademoiselle Calas."

"Third floor, left-hand side, but she's not at home."

"Do you know when she'll be back?"

"She very seldom comes home for lunch. She's not usually back before half past six in the evening. If it's urgent, you can get her at the hospital."

The Hôtel-Dieu, where Lucette Calas worked, was not far away. All the same, it was no easy matter to find Professor Lavaud. This was the busiest time of the day. The corridors were crowded with hurrying men and women in white coats, nurses pushing trolleys, patients taking their first uncertain steps. There were doors opening onto other corridors leading heaven knows where.

"Please can you tell me where I can find Mademoiselle Calas?"

They hardly noticed him.

"Don't know. Is she a patient?"

Or they pointed to a corridor.

"Down there."

He was told to go first in one direction and then in another, until at last he reached a corridor where stillness and silence reigned. It was like coming into port after a voyage. Except for a girl seated at a table, it was deserted.

"Mademoiselle Calas?"

"Is it personal business? How did you manage to get this far?"

He must have penetrated one of those sanctums not accessible to ordinary mortals. He gave his name, and even went so far as to produce his credentials, so little did he feel he had any standing here.

"I'll go and see if she can spare you a minute or two, but I'm afraid she may be in the operating theater."

He was kept waiting a good ten minutes, and he dared not light his pipe. When the girl came back she was accompanied by a nurse, rather tall, with an air of self-possession and serenity.

"Are you the gentleman who wished to see me?"

"Chief Superintendent Maigret from Police Headquarters."

The contrast with the bar in the Quai de Valmy seemed all the greater on account of the cleanliness and brightness of the hospital, the white uniform and starched cap of the nurse.

Lucette Calas seemed more astonished than distressed. Obviously, she had not the least idea what he had come about.

"Are you sure I'm the person you want to see?"

"You are the daughter of Monsieur and Madame Calas, of the Quai de Valmy, aren't you?"

It was gone in a flash, but Maigret was sure he had seen a spark of resentment in her eyes.

"Yes, but I . . ."

"There are just one or two questions I'd like to ask you."

"I can't spare much time. The Professor will be starting his round of the wards shortly, and . . ."

"It will only take a few minutes."

She shrugged looked around, and pointed to an open door.

"We'd better go in there."

There were two chairs, an adjustable couch for examining patients, and a few surgical instruments that Maigret could not identify.

"Is it long since you last saw your parents?"

She started at the word "parents," and Maigret thought he knew why.

"I see as little of them as possible."

"Why is that?"

"Have you seen them?"

"I've seen your mother."

She was silent. What more explanation was needed?

"Have you anything against them?"

"What should I have, except that they brought me into the world?"

"You weren't there last Sunday?"

"I was out of town. It was my day off. I spent it in the country with friends."

"So you can't say where your father is?"

"You really should tell me what this is all about. You turn up here and start asking questions about two people who admittedly are, in the strictly legal sense, my parents, but from whom I have been totally estranged for years. Why? Has something happened to him?"

She lit a cigarette, saying:

"Smoking is allowed in here. At this time of day, at any rate."

But he did not take advantage of this opportunity to light his pipe.

"Would it surprise you to hear that something naa happened to one or the other of them?"

She looked him straight in the eye, and said flatly:

"No."

"What would you expect to hear?"

"That Calas's brutality to my mother had gone too far for once."

She did not refer to him as "my father," but as "Calas."

"Does he often resort to physical violence?"

"I don't know about now. It used to be an almost daily occurrence."

"Didn't your mother object?"

"She put up with it. She may even have liked it."

"Have you anv other possibilities in mind?"

"Maybe she put poison in his soup."

"Why? Does she hate him?"

"All I know is that she's lived with him for twenty-four years, and has never made any attempt to get away from him."

"Is she unhappy, do you think?"

"Look, Superintendent, I do my best not to think about her at all As a child I had only one ambition—escape. And as soon as I could stand on my own feet, I got out."

"I know. You were just fifteen."

"Who told you?"

"Your mother "

"Then he hasn't killed her."

She looked thoughtful, then, raising her eyes to his, said: "Is it him?"

"What do you mean?"

"Has she poisoned him?"

"I shouldn't think so. We don't even know for sure whether anything has happened to him. Your mother says he left for Poitiers on Friday afternoon. He goes there regularly, it seems, to get his supplies of white wine from the vineyards around there."

"That's right. He did even when I lived with them."

"A body has been recovered from the Saint-Martin Canal. It may be his."

"Has no one identified it?"

"Not so far. The difficulty is that the head has not been found."

Was it perhaps because she worked in a hospital that she did not even blench?

"How do you think it happened?" she asked.

"I don't know. I'm feeling my way. There seem to be several men in your mother's life, if you'll forgive my mentioning it."

"You surely don't imagine it's news to me!"

"Do you know whether your father, in childhood or adolescence, was wounded in the stomach by a shotgun?"

She looked surprised.

"I never heard him mention it."

"You never saw the scars, of course?"

"Well, if it was a stomach wound . . ." she protested, with the beginning of a smile.

"When were you last at the Quai de Valmy?"

"Let me think. It must be a month or more."

"Was it just a casual visit, keeping in touch with home, as it were?"

"Not exactly."

"Was Calas there?"

"I make it my business only to go there when he's out."

"In the afternoon, was it?"

"Yes, he's always out then, playing billiards somewhere near the Gare de l'Est."

"Was there a man with your mother?"

"Not on that occasion."

"Did you have any special reason for going to see her?"

"No."

"What did you talk about?"

"I can't remember. One thing and another."

"Was Calas mentioned?"

"I doubt it."

"You wouldn't by any chance have gone to ask your mother for money?"

"You're on the wrong track there, Superintendent. Rightly or wrongly, I have too much pride for that. There have been times when I've gone short of money, and, for that matter, food, but I've never gone to them begging for help. All the more reason not to do so now, when I'm earning a good living."

"Can't you recall anything that was said on that last occasion at the Quai de Valmy?"

"Nothing special."

"Among the men you saw in the bar from time to time, do you remember a fresh-complexioned youth who rides a delivery bicycle?"

She shook her head.

"Or a middle-aged man with red hair?"

This did strike a chord.

"With smallpox scars?" she asked.

"I don't know."

"If so, it's Monsieur Dieudonné."

"Who is Monsieur Dieudonné?"

"I know very little about him. A friend of my mother s
He's been going to the café for years."

"In the afternoon?"

She knew what he meant.

"Whenever I've seen him, it's been in the afternoon. But
you may be wrong about him. I can't say for sure.
He struck me as a quiet sort of man, the kind one thinks of
as sitting by the fire after dinner in his slippers. Come to
think of it, he always seems to be sitting by the stove, facing
my mother. They behave like people who have known each
other for a very long time. They take one another for
granted, if you see what I mean. They could be mistaken
for an old married couple."

"Do you happen to know his address?"

"He's got a muffled kind of voice. I'd know it again if I
heard it. I've known him get up and say: 'Time to get back
to work.' I imagine his place of work must be somewhere
near there, but I don't even know what he does. He doesn't
dress like a manual worker. He might be a bookkeeper, or
something of the sort."

A bell sounded in the corridor. The girl sprang to her
feet.

"It's for me," she said. "I'll have to go, I'm afraid."

"I may have to take up a little more of your time. If so, I'll call on you in the Rue Saint-Louis-en-l'Ile."

"I'm never there except in the evening. Please don't make it too late. I go to bed early."

He watched her go down the corridor. She was shaking her head slightly, puzzled by what she had just heard.

"Excuse me, Mademoiselle. How do I get out of here?"

He looked so lost that the girl at the desk smiled, got up, and led him along the corridor to a staircase.

"You'll manage all right from here. Down the stairs, then left, and left again."

"Thank you."

He did not have the temerity to ask her what she thought of Lucette Calas. He scarcely knew what he thought of her himself.

He stopped at a bar opposite the Palais de Justice for a glass of white wine. When, a few minutes later, he got back to his office, he found Lapointe waiting for him.

"Well, how did you make out with the nuns?"

"They couldn't have been nicer. I expected it to be rather an embarrassing experience, but they made me feel quite at home . . ."

"What about the scars?"

Lapointe was less enthusiastic on this subject.

"In the first place, the doctor who did the operation died three years ago, as Madame Calas told us. The sister in charge of records showed me the file. There's no mention of any scar, which isn't surprising. On the other hand, I did discover one thing: Calas had a stomach ulcer."

"Did they operate?"

"No. Apparently they always do extensive tests before an operation, and record their findings."

"There's no reference to any distinguishing marks?"

"None at all. The sister very kindly went and spoke to the nuns who were present at the operation. None of them remembered Calas very clearly. One thought she remembered his asking for time to say his prayers before they gave him the anesthetic."

"Was he a Catholic?"

"No, he was scared. That's the kind of thing nuns don't forget. They wouldn't have noticed the scars."

They were back where they started, with a headless corpse that could not be identified with any certainty.

"What do we do next?" murmured Lapointe.

With Maigret in his present disgruntled mood, he judged it wiser to keep his voice down.

Perhaps Judge Coméliau was right after all. If the man found in the Saint-Martin Canal was Omer Calas, then it might indeed be true that there was no way of getting the evidence they needed except by subjecting his wife to cross-examination. A heart-to-heart talk with Antoine, the fellow with the bicycle, if only they could lay their hands on him, would also be helpful.

"Come on."

"Shall I get the car?"

"Yes."

"Where are we going?"

"To the canal."

On his way out, he gave instructions to the Inspectors concerned to order a search in the 10th *Arrondissement* for a red-haired man with a pock-marked face, Christian name: Dieudonné.

The car nosed its way between buses and trucks. When they came to the Boulevard Richard-Lenoir, and were almost at Maigret's own front door, he suddenly growled:

"Take me to the Gare de l'Est."

Lapointe looked at him in bewilderment.

"There may be nothing to it, but I'd like to check all the same. We were told that Calas had a suitcase with him, when he left on Friday afternoon. Suppose he came back on Saturday. If he's the man, then whoever killed and dismembered him must have got rid of the suitcase somehow. I'm quite sure it isn't still in the house at the Quai de Valmy, and I bet you we won't find the clothes he's supposed to have been wearing there, either."

Lapointe nodded agreement.

"No suitcase has been recovered from the canal, nor any clothes, in spite of the fact that the dead man was stripped before being carved up."

"And the head hasn't been found!" exclaimed Lapointe, taking it a stage further.

There was nothing original about Maigret's reasoning. It was just a matter of experience. Six murderers out of ten, if they have anything incriminating to get rid of, deposit it in the luggage checkroom of a railway station.

And it was no distance from the Quai de Valmy to the Gare de l'Est.

Lapointe eventually found somewhere to park the car, and he followed Maigret to the luggage checkroom.

"Were you on duty last Sunday afternoon?" he asked the clerk.

"Only up to six o'clock."

"Did you take in a lot of luggage?"

"Not more than usual."

"Have any suitcases deposited on Sunday not been claimed yet?"

The clerk walked along the shelves, where suitcases and parcels of all shapes and sizes were stacked.

"Two," he said.

"Both left by the same person?"

"No. The ticket numbers aren't consecutive. The canvas carryall, anyway, was left by a woman, a fat woman. I remember her because of the smell of cheese."

"Are there cheeses in it?"

"No, the smell has gone. Maybe it was the woman herself."

"What about the other one?"

"It's a brown suitcase."

He pointed to a cheap, battered case.

"Is it labeled?"

"No."

"Can you describe the person who handed it in?"

"I could be wrong, but I'd swear it was a country fellow."

"Why a country fellow?"

"That's how he struck me."

"Because of his complexion?"

"Could be."

"What was he wearing?"

"A leather jacket, if I remember rightly, and a peaked cap."

Maigret and Lapointe exchanged glances. Antoine Cristin was in both their minds.

"What time would it have been?"

"Round about five. Yes. A little after five, because the express from Strasbourg had just come in."

"If anyone comes to claim the case, will you please ring the Police Station at the Quai de Jemmapes immediately."

"What if the fellow takes fright and runs?"

"We'll be here, anyway, within minutes."

There was only one way of getting the suitcase identified. Madame Calas would have to be brought to see it.

She looked up mechanically when the two men came in, and went to the bar to serve them.

"We won't have anything just now," said Maigret. "Something has been found which you may be able to identify. The Inspector will take you to see it. It's not far from here."

"Had I better close the bar?"

"There's no need. It will only take a few minutes. I'll stay here."

She did not put on a hat. She merely changed out of her slippers into shoes.

"Will you tend to the customers?"

"I doubt if it will be necessary."

Maigret lingered for a moment on the pavement, watching Lapointe drive off with Madame Calas beside him. His face broke into a mischievous smile. He had never before been left all by himself in a bistro, just as if he owned it. He was so tickled by the notion that he went inside and slipped behind the bar.

Chapter 5

The Bottle of
Ink

The patches of sunlight were exactly where they had been the morning before. One, on the rounded end of the zinc counter, was shaped like an animal, another fell like a spotlight on a print of a woman in a red dress, holding a glass of foaming beer.

The little café, as Maigret had felt the previous day, like so many of the cafés and bars in Paris, had something of the atmosphere of a country inn, deserted most of the week, suddenly coming to life on market day.

Although he was tempted to help himself to a drink, he could not permit himself to give way to such a childish whim. Sternly, with his hands in his pockets and his pipe clenched between his teeth, he went over to the door at the back.

He had not yet seen what lay behind that door, through which Madame Calas was always disappearing. Not surprisingly, he found a kitchen, rather untidy, but less dirty than he would have expected. Immediately to the left of the door was a dresser, painted brown, on which stood an open bottle of brandy. So, wine was not her tipple, but brandy, which—since there was no glass to be seen—she presumably swigged straight out of the bottle.

A window looked onto the courtyard, and there was a glass door, which was not locked. He pushed it open. Stacked in a corner were barrels, discarded straw wrappers, and broken buckets. There were rust-rings everywhere. Paris seemed far away, so much so that it would not have surprised him to find a mass of bird droppings, and hens scratching about.

Beyond the courtyard was a cul-de-sac, bounded on both sides by a blank wall, and presumably leading off a side road.

Mechanically, he looked up at the first-floor windows of the bistro. They were very dirty, and hung with faded curtains. Was there a flicker of movement up there, or had he imagined it? It was not the cat, which he had left stretched out by the stove.

He went back into the kitchen, taking his time, and then up the spiral staircase which led to the floor above. The treads creaked. There was a faint musty smell, which reminded him of little village inns at which he had stayed.

There were two doors on the landing. He opened the first, and was in what must have been the Calases' bedroom. The windows looked out onto the Quai de Valmy. The double bed, of walnut, had not been made that morning, but the sheets were reasonably clean. The furniture was what one would expect in this sort of household, old, heavy stuff, handed down from father to son, and glowing with the patina of age.

A man's clothes were hanging in the wardrobe. Between the windows stood an armchair covered with red plush and, beside it, an old-fashioned radio set. The only other furniture was a round table in the middle of the room, covered with a cloth of indeterminate color, and a couple of mahogany chairs.

No sooner had he come into the room than he felt that something was not quite as it should be. What was it? He looked searchingly about him. Once again, his glance rested on the table covered with a cloth. On it was a bottle of ink, apparently unopened, a cheap pen, and one of those blotters advertising an apéritif that are often put on café tables for the convenience of customers. He opened the blotter, not expecting to find anything of interest, and indeed he found nothing but three blank sheets of paper. Just then, he thought he heard a board creak. He listened. The sound had not come from the lavatory, which led off the bedroom. Returning to the landing, he opened the door to the other room, which was as large as the first. It was used as a storeroom, and was piled high with battered and broken furniture, old magazines, glasses and other bric-à-brac.

"Is there anyone there?" he called loudly, almost certain that he was not alone in the room.

For a moment, he stood absolutely still, and then, without making a sound, shot out his arm and jerked open a cupboard.

"No tricks this time!" he said.

It did not greatly surprise him to discover that it was Antoine cowering there in the cupboard, like a trapped animal.

"I thought it wouldn't be long before I found you. Come on out of there!"

"Are you arresting me?"

The young man, terrified, was staring at the handcuffs which the Superintendent had taken out of his pocket.

"I haven't made up my mind yet what I'm going to do with you, but I'm not having any more of your Indian rope tricks. Hold out your hands."

"You've got no right. I haven't done anything."

"Hold out your hands!"

He could see that the boy was only waiting for a chance to make a dash for it. He moved toward him and, leaning forward with all his weight, pinned him against the wall. When the boy had tired of kicking him in the shins, Maigret managed to fasten on the handcuffs.

"Now then, come along with me!"

"What has my mother been saying?"

"I don't know what she's going to say about all this, but, as far as we're concerned, we want to know the answers to a few questions."

"I'm saying nothing."

"You come along with me, just the same."

He motioned him forward. They went through the kitchen and into the bar. Antoine looked around, startled by the emptiness and the silence.

"Where is she?"

"The proprietress? Don't worry, she'll be back."

"Have you arrested her?"

"Sit down over there, and don't move!"

"I'm not taking orders from you!"

He had seen so many of them at that age, all more or less in the same plight, that he had come to expect the defiant posturing and back talk.

It would please Judge Coméliau, at any rate, that Antoine had been caught, though he himself did not believe that they would learn much from him.

The street door was pushed open, and a middle-aged man came in. He looked around in surprise, seeing Maigret very much in command in the middle of the room, and no Madame Calas.

"Is Madame not here?"

"She won't be long."

Had the man seen the handcuffs and, realizing that Maigret was a police officer, decided that discretion was the better part of valor? At any rate, he touched his cap, muttered something like "I'll come back later," and beat a hasty retreat.

He could not have got as far as the end of the street when the black car drew up at the door. Lapointe got out first, opened the door for Madame Calas, and then took a brown suitcase from the trunk.

She saw Antoine at first glance, frowned, and looked anxiously at Maigret.

"Didn't you know he was hiding upstairs?"

"Don't answer!" urged the young man. "He has no right to arrest me—I've done nothing. I challenge him to prove anything against me."

Briskly, Maigret turned to Lapointe.

"Is the suitcase his?"

"She didn't seem too sure at first, then she said it was, then that she couldn't swear to it without seeing what was in it."

"Did you open it?"

"I wanted you to be present. I signed for it, but the clerk was most insistent that he must have an official requisition as soon as possible."

"Get Coméliau to sign it. Is the clerk still there?"

"I imagine so. I couldn't persuade him to leave his post."

"Call him. Ask him to try and get someone to take over from him for a quarter of an hour. That shouldn't be too difficult. Tell him to hop into a taxi and come here."

"I understand," said Lapointe, looking at Antoine. Would the baggage clerk recognize him? If so, it would make everything a lot easier.

"Phone Moers as well. I want him here too, with a search warrant. And tell him to bring the photographers."

"Right you are, sir."

Madame Calas, who was standing in the middle of the room as though she were a stranger to the place, asked, as Antoine had done before her:

"Are you going to arrest me?"

"Why should I?" countered Maigret. She looked at him in bewilderment.

"Am I free to come and go?"

"In the house, yes."

He knew what she wanted, and, sure enough, she went into the kitchen and disappeared, making straight for the brandy bottle, no doubt. To lend color to her presence there, she rattled the crockery, and changed out of her shoes—which must have been pinching her, since she so seldom wore them—into slippers.

When she returned to her place behind the counter, she was herself again.

"Can I get you anything?"

"Yes, a glass of white wine—and one for the Inspector. Perhaps Antoine would like a beer?"

His manner was unhurried, hesitant even, as though he had not quite made up his mind what to do next. He took a leisurely sip of wine, and then went over to the door and locked it.

"Have you the key of the suitcase?"

"No."

"Do you know where it is?"

In "his" pocket, she supposed.

In Calas's pocket, since, according to her, he had his suitcase with him when he left the house.

"Have you a pair of pliers or a wrench of some sort?"

She took her time getting the pliers. Maigret lifted the suitcase onto a table. He waited for Lapointe to come out of the phone booth before forcing the flimsy lock.

"I've ordered a white wine for you."

"Thank you, sir."

The metal buckled and eventually broke. Maigret lifted the lid. Madame Calas had not moved from behind the counter. She was watching them, but did not seem greatly concerned.

In the suitcase were a gray suit of quite good quality, a pair of shoes, almost new, shirts, socks, razor, comb, toothbrush, and a cake of soap still in its wrapping.

"Are these your husband's things?"

"I suppose so."

"Aren't you sure?"

"He has a suit like that."

"And it's not in the wardrobe?"

"I haven't looked."

She was no help, but, at the same time, she did not hinder them. As before, her answers to questions were curt and guarded, though, unlike Antoine, she was not on the defensive.

While Antoine was scared stiff, the woman gave the impression of having nothing to fear. The comings and goings of the police seemed to be a matter of indifference to her. They could carry on, as far as she was concerned, whatever they might discover.

"Anything strike you as odd?" Maigret said to Lapointe, while they were rummaging in the suitcase.

"You mean everything shoved in higgledy-piggledy like that?"

"Well, that's how most men would pack a suitcase. But there's something else. Calas, or so we're told, was setting out on a journey. He took a spare suit, and a change of shoes and underclothes. It's reasonable to assume that he packed the case upstairs in his bedroom."

Two men in housepainters' overalls rattled at the door, peered in through the glass, mouthed inaudible words, and went away.

"If that is so, can you think of any reason why he should have taken his dirty washing with him?"

One of the two shirts had, in fact, been worn, as well as a pair of trousers and a pair of socks.

"Do you mean you think someone else may have put the stuff in the suitcase?"

"He could have done it himself. The likelihood is that he did. But not at the start of his journey. He was packing to come home."

"I see what you mean."

"Did you hear what I said, Madame Calas?"

She nodded.

"Do you still maintain that your husband left on Friday afternoon, taking the suitcase with him?"

"I can only repeat what I have already told you."

"You're sure you don't mean Thursday, Friday being when he came back?"

She shook her head.

"Whatever I say, you'll believe what you want to believe."

A taxi drew up at the door. Maigret went to open it. As the station clerk got out, he said:

"It can wait. I won't keep you a minute."

The Superintendent ushered him into the café. The man looked about him, taking his time over it, getting his bearings, wondering what it was all about.

His glance rested on Antoine, who was still sitting on a bench in the corner. Then he turned to Maigret, opened his mouth, and gave Antoine another searching look.

All this time, which seemed longer than it was, Antoine was scowling defiance at him.

"I really do believe," began the man, scratching his head. He was conscientious, and there was some doubt in his mind.

"Well then! From what I can see of him, I'd say he was the one."

"You're lying," shouted the young man furiously.

"Maybe I ought to see what he looks like standing up."

"Stand up."

"No."

"Stand up!"

Maigret heard Madame Calas's voice behind him.

"Get up, Antoine."

The clerk looked at him thoughtfully.

"I'm almost sure," he murmured. "Does he wear a leather jacket?"

"Go and have a look upstairs in the back room," said Maigret to Lapointe.

They waited in silence. The station employee glanced toward the bar. Maigret could take a hint.

"A glass of white wine?" he asked.

"I wouldn't say no."

Lapointe returned with the jacket that Antoine had worn the previous day.

"Put it on."

The young man looked to the woman for guidance, re-signed himself grudgingly, and held out his wrists for the handcuffs to be removed.

"Can't you see, he's just trying to suck up to the cops? They're all the same. Mention the word 'police,' and they shake in their shoes. Well, what about it? Do you still say you've seen me before?"

"I think so, yes."

"You're lying."

The clerk addressed himself to Maigret. He spoke calmly, though it was possible to detect an undercurrent of feeling in his voice.

"This is a serious business, I imagine. I shouldn't like to get an innocent person into trouble. This boy looks like the one who deposited the suitcase at the station on Sunday. Naturally, not knowing that anyone was going to ask me about him, I didn't take much notice of him. Perhaps if I saw him in the same place, under the same conditions, lighting and so on . . ."

"I'll have him brought to you at the station sometime today or tomorrow," said Maigret. "Thank you. Your very good health!"

He saw him to the door, and locked it after him. There was, in the Chief Superintendent's attitude to the case, a kind of diffidence that puzzled Lapointe. He could not have said when he had begun to notice it. Perhaps the previous day, right at the start of the inquiry, when they had come together to the Quai de Valmy, and pushed open the door of the Calas bistro.

Maigret was pursuing his investigations in the normal way, doing all that was required of him, but surely with a lack of conviction that was the last thing any of his subordinates would have expected of him? It was difficult to define. Half-heartedness? Reluctance? Disinclination? The facts of the case interested him very little. He seemed to be wrapped up in his thoughts, which he was keeping very much to himself.

It was particularly noticeable here in the café, especially when he was talking to Madame Calas, or furtively watching her.

It was as though the victim were of no account, and the dismembered corpse meant nothing to him. He had virtually ignored Antoine, and it was only with an effort that he was able to attend to the routine aspects of his work.

"Phone Coméliau. I'd rather you did it. Just give him a summary of events. You'd better ask him to sign a warrant for the arrest of the kid. He'll do it in any case."

"What about her?" asked the Inspector, pointing to the woman.

"I'd rather not."

"What if he insists?"

"He'll have to have his own way. He's the boss."

He had not bothered to lower his voice, in spite of the presence of the other two, whom he knew to be listening.

"You'd better have a bite to eat," he advised Madame Calas. "It may not be long before you have to go."

"For long?"

"For as long as the Judge thinks fit to hold you for questioning."

"Will they keep me in prison?"

"At the Central Police Station to begin with, I expect."

"What about me?" Antoine asked.

"You too. But not in the same cell!" Maigret added.

"Are you hungry?" Madame Calas asked the boy.

"No."

She went into the kitchen just the same, but it was to have a swig of brandy. When she came back, she asked:

"Who will look after the place when I'm gone?"

"No one. Don't worry. It will be kept under supervision."

He was still watching her with that same thoughtful expression. He could not help himself. It seemed to him that he had never encountered anyone so baffling.

He had experience of artful women, some of whom had stood up to him for a long time. In every case, however, he had felt from the first that he would have the last word. It was just a matter of time, patience, and determination.

With Madame Calas, it was different. She did not fit into any category. If he were to be told that she had murdered her husband in cold blood, and had carved him up single-handed on the kitchen table, he would not have found it impossible to believe. But he would not have found it impossible to believe, either, that she simply did not know what had become of her husband.

There she was in front of him, a living creature of flesh and blood, thin and faded in her dark dress, which hung from her shoulders like a shabby window-curtain. She was real enough, with the fire of her inner life smoldering in her somber eyes, and yet there was about her something insubstantial, elusive.

Was she aware of the impression she created? One would say so, judging from the cool, perhaps even ironic manner in which she, in her turn, appraised the Chief Superintendent.

This was the reason for Lapointe's uneasiness a little while back. The normal process of conducting a police inquiry with a view to apprehending a criminal was being overshadowed by the private duel between Maigret and this woman.

Nothing which did not directly concern her was of much interest to the Chief Superintendent. Lapointe was to have further proof of this when, a minute or two later, he came out of the telephone booth.

"What did he say?" asked Maigret, referring to Coméliau.

"He'll sign the warrant and send it across to your office."

"Does he want to see him?"

"He presumed you'd want to interrogate him first."

"What about her?"

"He's signing two warrants. It's up to you what you do with the second one, but if you ask me . . ."

"I see."

Coméliau was expecting Maigret to go back to his office, and have Antoine and Madame Calas brought to him there separately, so that he could grill them for hours, until they gave themselves away.

The head of the dead man had still not been found. There was no concrete proof that the man whose remains had been fished out of the Saint-Martin Canal was Calas. All the same, they did now have strong circumstantial evidence, namely the suitcase, and it was by no means unusual to obtain a full confession, after a few hours of interrogation, in cases where the cards were more heavily stacked against the police.

Judge Coméliau was not the only one to see the matter in this light. Lapointe was of the same opinion, and he could scarcely hide his astonishment when Maigret instructed him: "Take him to Headquarters. Shut yourself up with him in my office, and get what you can out of him. Don't forget to order some food for him, and something to drink."

"Will you be staying here?"

"I'm waiting for Moers and the photographers."

Looking unmistakably put out, Lapointe motioned to the young man to stand up. As a parting shot, Antoine called to Maigret from the door:

"I warn you, you'll pay for this!"

At the Quai des Orfèvres, at about this time, the Vicomte, having poked his nose into most of the offices in the Palais de Justice, as he did every morning, had started on the Examining Magistrates.

"Any news, Monsieur Coméliau? Have they still not found the head?"

"Not yet. But I can tell you more or less officially that the identity of the victim is known."

"Who is it?"

Coméliau graciously consented to give ten minutes of his time to answering questions. He was not altogether displeased that, for once, it was he and not Maigret whom the press was honoring with its attentions.

"Is the Chief Superintendent still there?"

"I presume so."

Thus it came about that news of the inquiries in progress at the Calas bistro and the arrest of a young man, referred to only by his initials, appeared in the afternoon editions of the newspapers, two hours after the Vicomte's interview with Coméliau, and the five o'clock news on the radio included an announcement to the same effect.

Left on his own with Madame Calas, Maigret ordered a glass of wine at the bar, carried it across to a table, and sat down. As for her, she had not moved. She had remained at her post behind the bar where, as proprietress, she had every right to be.

The factory sirens sounded the midday break. In less than ten minutes, at least thirty people were crowded around the locked door. Some, seeing Madame Calas through the glass, indicated by gestures that they wanted to speak to her.

Suddenly, Maigret broke the silence.

"I've seen your daughter," he said.

She looked at him, but said nothing.

"She confirmed that she last came to see you about a month ago. I couldn't help wondering what you found to talk about."

It was not a question, and she did not choose to make any comment.

"She struck me as a sensible young woman, who has done well for herself. I don't know why, but I had the feeling that she was in love with her boss, and might be his mistress."

Still she did not flinch. Was it of any interest to her? Did she feel any affection for her daughter, even the smallest remnant?

"It can't have been easy at the beginning. It's tough going for a girl of fifteen, trying to make her own way, alone, in a city like Paris."

She was still looking at him, but her eyes seemed to see through and beyond him. Wearily, she asked:

"What is it you want?"

What, indeed, did he want? Was Coméliau right after all? Ought he not to be engaged at this very moment in making Antoine talk? As for her, perhaps a few days in a police cell were just what was needed to bring about a change of heart.

"I'm wondering what made you marry Calas in the first place, and, even more, what induced you to stay with him all those years."

She did not smile, but the corners of her mouth twitched, in contempt, perhaps, or pity.

"It was done deliberately, wasn't it?" went on Maigret, not quite sure himself what he meant.

He had to get to the bottom of it. There were times, and this was one of them, when it seemed to him that he was within a hair's breadth not merely of solving the mystery but of sweeping aside the invisible barrier that stood between them. It was just a question of finding the words which would evoke the simple, human response.

"Was *the other one* here on Sunday afternoon?"

This, at least, did get results. She started. After a pause, she was reluctantly compelled to ask:

"What other one?"

"Your lover. Your real lover."

She would have liked to keep up the pretense of indifference, asking no questions, but in the end she yielded:

"Who?"

"A red-haired, middle-aged man, with smallpox scars, whose Christian name is Dieudonné."

It was as though a shutter had come down between them. Her face became completely expressionless. What was more, a car had drawn up at the door. Moers, and three men with cameras, had arrived.

Once again, Maigret went to the door and unlocked it.

Admittedly, he had not triumphed. All the same, he did not consider that their tête-à-tête had been altogether a waste of time.

"Where do you want us to search, sir?"

"Everywhere. The kitchen first, then the two rooms and the lavatory upstairs. There's the courtyard as well, and, of course, the cellar. This trap door here presumably leads to it."

"Do you believe the man was killed and dismembered here?"

"It's possible."

"What about this suitcase?"

"Go over it thoroughly. The contents too, of course."

"It will take us the whole afternoon. Will you be staying?"

"I don't think so, but I'll look in again later."

He went into the telephone booth and rang Judel at the Police Station opposite, to give him instructions about having the place watched.

When he had finished, he said to Madame Calas:

"You'd better come with me."

"Shall I take a change of clothing, and things for washing?"

"It would be advisable."

She stopped on her way through the kitchen for a stiff drink. Soon she could be heard moving about in the bedroom above.

"Is it safe to leave her on her own, sir?"

Maigret shrugged. If a crime had been committed here, steps must have been taken long before this to remove all traces of it, and dispose of anything incriminating.

All the same, it did surprise him that she should take so long getting ready. She could still be heard moving about, turning taps on and off, opening and shutting drawers.

She paused again in the kitchen, realizing no doubt that this was the last drink she would get for a long time.

When at last she reappeared, the men gaped at her in amazement, which in Maigret's case was mixed with a touch of admiration.

In the space of twenty minutes or less, she had completely transformed herself. She was now wearing a most becoming black coat. Under her carefully brushed hair and charming hat, her face seemed to have come to life. Her step was lighter, her carriage more upright. There was self-respect, even a hint of pride, in her bearing.

Was she aware of the sensation she was creating? Was there, perhaps, a touch of coquetry in her make-up? She did not smile, or show any sign of being amused at their astonishment. She looked inside her bag to make sure she had everything, and then, drawing on her gloves, said, almost in a whisper:

"I'm ready."

She was wearing face powder and lipstick. The scent of eau de Cologne, mingled with the fumes of brandy on her breath, seemed somehow inappropriate.

"Aren't you taking a suitcase?"

She said no, almost defiantly. Would it not be an admission of guilt to take a change of clothing? At the very least, it would be an acknowledgment that there might be some justification for keeping her in custody.

"See you later!" Maigret called out to Moers and his assistants.

"Will you be taking the car?"

"No. I'll get a taxi."

It was a strange experience, walking by her side, in step with her, there in the sunlit street.

"The Rue des Récollets would be the best place to find a taxi, I imagine?"

"I expect so."

"I should like to ask you a question."

"You surprise me!"

"When did you last take the trouble to dress as you are dressed now?"

She looked thoughtful, obviously trying to remember.

"Four years ago or more," she said at last. "Why do you ask?"

"No particular reason."

What was the point of explaining, when she knew as well as he did? He managed to stop a taxi just as it was driving past. He opened the door for her, and got in beside her.

Chapter 6

The String

The truth was that he had not yet made up his mind what to do with her. If anyone but Judge Coméliau had been in charge of the case, things would have been different. He would have been prepared to take a risk. With Coméliau, it was dangerous. Not only was he finicky, a stickler for the rules, scared of public opinion and parliamentary criticism, but he had always mistrusted Maigret's methods, which he considered unorthodox. It had come to a head-on collision between them more than once in the past.

Maigret was well aware that the Judge had his eye on him, and would not hesitate to hold him responsible if he were to step out of line or if anything, however trivial, should go wrong.

He would have much preferred to leave Madame Calas at the Quai de Valmy until he had a clearer insight into her character, and some clue as to her connection, if any, with the case. He would have posted a man, two men, to watch the bistro. But then Judel had posted a constable outside the tenement in the Faubourg Saint-Martin, and what good had that done? The boy Antoine had got away just the same. And Antoine was just an overgrown kid, with no more sense than a thirteen-year-old. Madame Calas was a different proposition. The newspapers in the kiosks already carried the story of the little café and its possible connection with the crime. At all events, Maigret had seen the name Calas in banner headlines on the front pages. Suppose, for instance, that tomorrow morning the head-lines read: "Madame Calas disappears." He could just imagine his reception on arrival at the Judge's office.

While pretending to look straight before him, he was watching her out of the corner of his eye. She did not seem to notice. She was sitting up very straight, and there was an air of dignity about her. As they drove through the streets, she looked out of the window with interest and curiosity.

Just now she had admitted that she had not worn her street clothes for at least four years. She had not told him what the occasion was on which she had last worn her black dress. Perhaps it was even longer since she had been in the center of town, and seen the crowds thronging the Boulevards.

Since, on account of Coméliau, he was not free to do as he liked, he had had to adopt a different procedure.

As they were approaching the Quai des Orfèvres, he spoke for the first time.

"Are you sure you have nothing to tell me?"

She seemed a little taken aback.

"What about?"

"About your husband."

She gave a slight shrug, and said confidently:

"I didn't kill Calas."

She called him by his surname, as country women and
shopkeepers' wives often call their husbands. But in her
case it seemed to Maigret to strike a false note.

"Shall I drive up to the entrance?" the taxi driver turned
around to ask.

"If you will."

The Vicomte was there, at the foot of the great staircase,
in company with two other journalists and a number of
photographers. They had got wind of what had happened,
and it was useless to try to conceal the prisoner.

"One moment, Superintendent."

Did she imagine that Maigret had tipped them off? She
held herself erect, as they took photographs, even following her up the stairs. Presumably Antoine, too, had under-
gone this ordeal.

They were upstairs in his own domain, and still Maigret
had not made up his mind. In the end, he made for the
Inspectors' Duty Room. Lucas was not there. He called to
Janvier.

"Take her into an empty room for a few minutes and
stay with her, will you?"

She could not help hearing. The Superintendent felt
oppressed by the mute reproach of her look. Was it reproach, though? Was it not rather disillusionment?

He walked away without another word, and went to his
own office, where he found his desk occupied by Lapointe,
in shirt sleeves. Facing the window, Antoine was sitting
bolt upright in a chair, very flushed, as though he were
feeling the heat.

Between them was the tray sent up from the Brasserie

Dauphine. There were traces of beer in the two glasses, and a couple of half-eaten sandwiches on plates.

As Maigret's glance traveled from the tray to Antoine, he could see that the boy was vexed with himself for having succumbed. No doubt it had been his intention to "punish" them by going on hunger strike. They were familiar with self-dramatization in all its forms at the Quai des Orfèvres, and Maigret could not help smiling.

"How is it going?" he asked Lapointe.

Lapointe indicated, by a lift of the eyebrows, that he was getting nowhere.

"Carry on, boys."

Maigret went across to Coméliau's office. The magistrate was on his way out to lunch.

"Well, have you arrested the pair of them?"

"The young man is in my office. Lapointe is dealing with him."

"Has he said anything?"

"Even if he knows anything, he won't talk, unless we can prove something against him, and rub his nose in it."

"Is he a bright fellow?"

"That's exactly what he isn't. One can usually make an intelligent person see sense in the end, or at least persuade him to retract self-contradictory statements. An idiot will just go on denying everything, even in the teeth of the evidence."

"What about the woman?"

"I've left Janvier with her."

"Will you be dealing with her yourself?"

"Not for the moment. I haven't got enough to go on."

"When do you expect to be ready?"

"Tonight, maybe. If not, tomorrow or the next day."

"And in the meantime?"

Maigret's manner was so bland and amiable that Coméliau wondered what he was up to.

"I came to ask your advice."

"You can't keep her here indefinitely."

"That's what I think. A woman especially."

"Wouldn't the best thing be to have her locked up?"

"That's up to you."

"But you would prefer to let her go?"

"I'm not sure."

Frowning, Coméliau considered the problem. He was furious. Finally, as though he were throwing down a challenge, he barked:

"Send her to me."

Why was the Chief Superintendent smiling as he disappeared down the corridor? Was it at the thought of a tête-à-tête between Madame Calas and the exasperated Judge?

He did not see her again that afternoon. He merely went into the Inspectors' Duty Room, and said to Torrence:

"Judge Coméliau wants to see Madame Calas. Let Janvier know, will you?"

The Vicomte intercepted him on the stairs. Maigret shook him off firmly, saying:

"Coméliau's the man you want to see. He'll be making a statement to the press, if not immediately then very shortly, you can take my word for it."

He stumped off to the Brasserie Dauphine, stopping at

a bar for an apéritif. It was late. Almost everyone had had lunch. He went to the telephone.

"Is that you?" he said to his wife.

"Aren't you coming home?"

"No."

"Well, I hope you'll take time off for lunch."

"I'm at the Brasserie Dauphine. I'm just about to have something."

"Will you be home for dinner?"

"I may be."

The brasserie had its own distinctive blend of smells, among which two were dominant: the smell of Pernod around the bar, and that of coq-au-vin, which came in gusts from the kitchen.

Most of the tables in the dining room were unoccupied, though there were one or two of his colleagues lingering over coffee and Calvados. He hesitated, then went across to the bar and ordered a sandwich. The sun was still shining brilliantly, and the sky was clear, except for a few white clouds scudding across it. A sudden breeze had blown up, scattering the dust in the streets, and molding the women's dresses against their bodies.

The proprietor, behind the bar, knew Maigret well enough to realize that this was not the time to start a conversation. Maigret was eating absent-mindedly, staring into the street with the mesmerized look of a passenger on board ship watching the monotonous and hypnotic motion of the sea.

"The same again?"

He said yes, probably not knowing what he had been eating, ate his second sandwich, and drank the coffee which was put in front of him before he had even ordered it.

A few minutes later he was in a taxi, heading for the Quai de Valmy. He stopped it at the corner of the Rue des Récollets, opposite the lock, where three barges were lined up, waiting to go through. In spite of the filthy water whose surface was broken from time to time by unsavory-looking bubbles, there were a few anglers, tinkering with their floats as usual.

As he walked past Chez Popaul, with its yellow façade, the proprietor recognized him, and Maigret could see him, through the window, pointing him out to the people at the bar. All along the road, huge long-distance trucks were parked, bearing the name "Roulers and Langlois."

On his way, Maigret passed two or three little shops, of the sort to be found in all densely populated, residential districts of Paris. In front of one a trestle, piled high with fruit and vegetables, took up half the pavement. A few doors farther on, there was a butcher's shop which seemed to be empty, then, almost next door to Chez Calas, a grocer's shop, so dark that it was impossible to see into it.

Madame Calas must have had to go out sometimes, if only to do her marketing. These presumably were the shops she went to, wearing her slippers no doubt, and wrapped in the coarse, black, woolen shawl that he had noticed lying about in the café.

Judel must have interviewed the shopkeepers. The local police, being known to them, inspired more confidence than the men from the Quai des Orfèvres.

The door of the bistro was locked. He peered through the glass, but could see no one in the bar. Through the open kitchen door, however, he could see the flickering shadow of someone moving about out of sight. He rapped his knuckles on the glass, but had to knock several times more before Moers appeared and, seeing him there, ran to unlock the door.

"I'm sorry. We were making quite a lot of noise. Have you been waiting long?"

"It doesn't matter."

It was he who remembered to lock the door again.

"Have you had many interruptions?"

"Most people try the door and then go away, but some are more persistent. They bang on the door, and go through a whole pantomime to be let in."

Maigret looked around the room, then went behind the bar to see if he could find a blotting pad, like the one advertising an apéritif that he had seen on the table in the bedroom. There were usually several of these blotters dotted about in cafés, and it struck him as odd that here there was not even one, though the place was well supplied with other amenities, including three games of dominoes, four or five bridge cloths, and half-a-dozen packs of cards.

"You carry on," he said to Moers. "I'll be back shortly."

He threaded his way through the cameras set up in the kitchen, and went upstairs, returning with the bottle of ink and the blotting pad.

He sat down at a table in the café, and wrote in block capitals:

"CLOSED UNTIL FURTHER NOTICE."

He paused after the first word, thinking perhaps of Coméliau closeted at this very minute with Madame Calas.

"Are there any thumbtacks anywhere?"

Moers answered from the kitchen:

"On the left-hand side of the shelf under the counter."

He found them, and went out to pin his notice above the door. Coming back, he felt something brush against his leg, something alive, and looked down to see the ginger cat gazing up at him and mewing.

That was something he had overlooked. If the place was going to be left unoccupied for any length of time, something would have to be done about the cat.

He went into the kitchen, and found some milk in an earthenware jug, and a cracked soup plate.

"Who can I get to look after the cat?"

"Wouldn't a neighbor take it? I noticed a butcher's shop on my way here."

"I'll see about it later. Anything interesting, so far?"

They were going through the place with a fine-tooth comb, sifting through the contents of every drawer, searching every corner. First Moers, examining things under a magnifying glass or, when necessary, his portable microscope, then the photographers, recording everything on film.

"We began with the courtyard, because, with all the junk there is out there, it seemed the most likely place to choose if one had something to hide."

"I take it the trash baskets have been emptied since Sunday?"

"On Monday morning. All the same, we examined them thoroughly, especially for traces of blood."

"Nothing?"

"Nothing," repeated Moers, after a moment's hesitation.

Which meant that he thought he might be on to something, but was not sure.

"What is it?"

"I don't know, sir. It's just an impression that all four of us had. We were discussing it when you arrived."

"Go on."

"Well, there's something peculiar about the setup, at least as far as the courtyard and the kitchen are concerned. This isn't the sort of place you'd expect to find spotlessly clean. You only have to open a few drawers to see that everything is stuffed in anyhow, and most of the things are thick with dust."

Maigret looked about him. He saw what Moers meant, and his eyes brightened with interest.

"Go on."

"There was a three days' pile of dirty dishes on the draining board, and several saucepans. There's been no washing up done since Sunday. An indication of slovenly habits, you might think. Unless it's just that the woman lets things slide when her husband's away."

Moers was right. She wouldn't bother to keep the place tidy, or even particularly clean.

"In other words, one would expect to find dirt everywhere, dirt accumulated over a period of a week or ten days. In fact, in some drawers and inaccessible corners, we did find dirt that had been there even longer. In general, however, there was evidence that the place had been recently and extensively scrubbed, and Sambois found a couple of bottles of bleach in the courtyard, one of them empty and, judging from the condition of the label, recently bought."

"When would you say this spring cleaning had been done?"

"Three or four days ago. I can't be more definite until I've made one or two tests in the lab, but I should know for certain by the time I come to write my report."

"Any fingerprints?"

"They bear out our theory. Calas's prints are all over the drawers and cupboard, only on the inside, though."

"Are you sure?"

"Well, at any rate, they are the same as those of the body in the canal."

Here, at last, was proof that the dismembered corpse was that of the proprietor of the bistro in the Quai de Valmy.

"What about upstairs?"

"Nothing on the surface, only inside the wardrobe door and so on. Dubois and I have only been up there to look around. We'll make a thorough job of it later. What struck us was that there wasn't a speck of dust on any of the furniture, and that the floor had been thoroughly scrubbed. As for the bed, the sheets were changed recently, probably three or four days ago."

"Were there dirty sheets in a laundry basket, or anywhere else?"

"I thought of that. No."

"Was the washing done at home?"

"I couldn't see any evidence of it. No washing machine or tub."

"So they must have used a laundry?"

"I'm almost sure of it. So unless the truck called yesterday or the day before . . ."

"I'd better try and find out the name of the laundry. The neighbors will probably know."

But before the words were out of Maigret's mouth, Moers had gone over to the dresser and opened one of the drawers.

"Here you are."

He handed Maigret a bundle of bills, some of which bore the heading: "Récollets Laundry." The most recent was ten days old.

Maigret went into the telephone booth, dialed the number of the laundry, and asked whether any washing had been collected from the bistro that week.

"We don't call at the Quai de Valmy until Thursday morning," he was told.

So the last collection of laundry had been on the previous Thursday.

No wonder it had struck Moers as odd. Two people do not live in a house for almost a week without soiling some household linen. Where was it, then, and in particular where were the dirty sheets? The ones on the bed had certainly not been there since Thursday.

He was looking thoughtful when he went back to join the others.

"What was it you were saying about the prints?"

"So far, in the kitchen, we have found prints belonging to three people, excluding yourself and Lapointe, whose prints I know by heart. The prints most in evidence are a woman's. I presume they're Madame Calas's."

"That can easily be checked."

"Then there are the prints of a man, a young man I

should guess. There aren't many of them, and they are the most recent."

Antoine, presumably, for whom Madame Calas must have got a meal in the kitchen when he turned up in the middle of the night.

"Finally, there are two prints, half obliterated. Another man's."

"Any more of Calas's prints inside the drawers?"

"Yes."

"In other words, it looks as though very recently, on Sunday possibly, someone cleaned the place from top to bottom, but didn't bother with turning out drawers and cupboards?"

They were all thinking of the dismembered corpse, which had been recovered piecemeal from the canal.

The operation could not have been undertaken in the street or on open ground. It must have taken time, and each part had been carefully wrapped in newspaper, and tied with string.

What would any room look like, after being used for such a purpose?

Maigret's remorse at having delivered Madame Calas into the merciless clutches of Judge Coméliau was beginning to subside.

"Have you been down to the cellar?"

"We've been everywhere, just to get our bearings. At a glance, everything looked quite normal down there, but there again, we'll be going over it thoroughly later."

He left them to get on with their work, and spent some time in the café roaming about, with the ginger cat following him like a shadow. The bottles on the shelf reflected the sun, and there were warm pools of light on the corner of the bar counter. He remembered the great stove in the middle of the room, and wondered whether it had gone out. He looked inside, and saw that there were still a few glowing embers. Mechanically, he stoked it up.

Next, he went behind the counter, studied the bottles, hesitated, and then poured himself a glass of Calvados. The drawer of the till was open. It was empty except for a couple of notes and some small change. The list of drinks and prices was posted near the window to his right.

He consulted it, took some loose change out of his pocket, and dropped the money for the Calvados into the till. Just then he caught sight of a figure beyond the glass door, and gave a guilty start. It was Inspector Judel peering in.

Maigret went to unlock the door.

"I thought you'd probably be here, sir. I rang Headquarters, but they didn't seem to know where you'd gone."

Judel looked around, and seemed surprised at the absence of Madame Calas.

"Is it true, then, that you have arrested her?"

"She's with Judge Coméliau."

Judel caught sight of the technicians at work in the kitchen, and jerked his chin in their direction.

"Have they found anything?"

"It's too early to say."

And it would take too long to explain. Maigret could not face it.

"I'm glad I found you here, because I didn't want to take action without your authority. I think we've found the man with red hair."

"Where?"

"If my information is correct, practically next door. Unless, that is, he's on night shift this week. He's a warehouse man with Zenith Transport, the firm . . ."

"Rue des Récollets. I know. Roulers and Langlois."

"I thought you would wish to interview him yourself."

Moers called from the kitchen:

"Can you spare a minute, sir?"

Maigret went over to the door at the back of the café. Madame Calas's black shawl was spread out on the kitchen table, and Moers, having already examined it through his magnifying glass, was focusing his microscope.

"Take a look at this."

"What is it I'm supposed to see?"

"You see the black wool fibers, and those brownish threads like twigs, intertwined with them? Well in fact, those are strands of hemp. It will have to be confirmed by analysis, of course, but I'm quite sure in my own mind. They're almost invisible to the naked eye, and they must have rubbed off onto the shawl from a ball of string."

"The same string that . . . ?"

Maigret was thinking of the string used to tie up the remains of the dismembered man.

"I could almost swear to it. I don't imagine Madame Calas very often had occasion to tie up a parcel. There are several kinds of string in one of the drawers, thin white string, red string, and twine, but not a scrap of string anything like this."

"I'm much obliged to you. I take it you'll still be here when I get back?"

"What are you going to do about the cat?"

"I'll take it with me."

Maigret picked up the cat, which did not seem to mind, and carried it outside. He considered entrusting it to the grocer, but decided that it would probably be better off with the butcher.

"Isn't that Madame Calas's cat?" asked the woman behind the counter, when he went in with it.

"Yes. I wonder if you'd mind looking after it for a few days?"

"So long as it doesn't fight with my own cats."

"Is Madame Calas a customer of yours?"

"She comes in every morning. Is it really her husband who . . . ?" When it came to putting such a grisly question into words, she balked, and could only look toward the canal.

"It looks like it."

"What's to become of her?"

And before Maigret could fob her off with an evasive answer, she went on:

"Not everyone would agree with me, I know, and there are plenty of grounds for fault-finding, but I think she's a poor, unhappy creature, and, whatever she's done, she was driven to it."

A few minutes later, Maigret and Judel were in the Rue des Récollets, waiting for a break in the stream of trucks leaving the depot, to cross over safely to the forecourt of Roulers and Langlois. They went to the glass box on the right, on which the word "Office" was inscribed in block letters. All around the forecourt were raised platforms, like those in a railway freight yard, piled high with boxes, sacks, and crates, which were being loaded onto the trucks.

People were charging about, heavy packages were being roughly manhandled. The noise was deafening.

Maigret had his hand on the doorknob when he heard Judel's voice behind him:

"Sir!"

The Superintendent turned around to see a red-haired man standing on one of the platforms, with a narrow log-book in one hand and a pencil in the other. He was staring intently at them. He was broad-shouldered, of medium height, and wearing a gray overall. He was fair-skinned with a high color, and his face, pitted with smallpox scars, had the texture of orange rind. Porters loaded with freight were filing past him, each in turn calling out a name and number, followed by the name of a town or village, but he did not seem to hear them. His blue eyes were fixed upon Maigret.

"See that he doesn't give us the slip," said Maigret to Judel.

He went into the office, where the girl at the inquiry desk asked him what she could do for him.

"I'd like to speak to someone in authority."

There was no need for her to reply. A man with close-cropped, gray hair came forward to find out what he wanted.

"Are you the manager?"

"Joseph Langlois. Haven't I seen you somewhere before?"

No doubt he had seen Maigret's photograph in the papers. The Chief Superintendent introduced himself, and Langlois waited in uneasy silence for him to explain his business.

"Who is that red-haired fellow over there?"

"What do you want him for?"

"I don't know yet. Who is he?"

"Dieudonné Pape. He's been with us for over twenty-five years. It would surprise me very much if you'd got anything against him."

"Is he married?"

"He's been a widower for years. In fact, I believe his wife died only two or three years after their marriage."

"Does he live alone?"

"I suppose so. His private life is no concern of mine."

"Have you got his address?"

"He lives in the Rue des Ecluses-Saint-Martin, very near here. Do you remember the number, Mademoiselle Berthe?"

"Fifty-six."

"Is he here all day, every day?"

"He puts in his eight hours, like everyone else, but not always in the daytime. We run a twenty-four-hour service here, and there are trucks loading and unloading all through the night. This means working on a three-shift system, and the rota is changed every week."

"What shift was he on last week?"

Langlois turned to the girl whom he had addressed as Mademoiselle Berthe.

"Look it up, will you?"

She consulted a ledger.

"The early shift."

The boss interpreted:

"That means, he came on at six in the morning and was relieved at two in the afternoon."

"Is the depot open on Sundays as well?"

"Only with a skeleton staff. Two or three men."

"Was he on duty last Sunday?"

The girl once more consulted her ledger.

"No."

"What time does he come off duty today?"

"He's on the second shift, so he'll be off at ten tonight."

"Could you arrange to have him relieved?"

"Can't you tell me what all this is about?"

"I'm afraid that's impossible."

"Is it serious?"

"It may be very serious."

"What is he supposed to have done?"

"I can't answer that."

"Whatever you may think, I can tell you here and now that you're barking up the wrong tree. If all my staff were like him, I shouldn't have anything to worry about."

He was far from happy. Without telling Maigret where he was going or inviting him to follow, he strode out of the glass-walled office and, skirting the trucks in the forecourt, went over to Dieudonné Pape.

The man stood motionless and expressionless, listening to what his boss had to say, but his eyes never left the glass box opposite. Langlois went to the storage shed, and seemed to be calling to someone inside, and indeed, within seconds, a little old man appeared, wearing an overall like Pape, with a pencil behind his ear. They exchanged a few words, and then the newcomer took the narrow log-book from the red-haired man, who followed the boss around the edge of the forecourt.

Maigret had not moved. The two men came in, and Langlois loudly announced:

"This is a Chief Superintendent from Police Headquarters. He wants a word with you. He thinks you may be able to help him."

"I have one or two questions to ask you, Monsieur Pape. If you'll be good enough to come with me."

Dieudonné Pape pointed to his overall.

"Do you mind if I change?"

"I'll come with you."

Langlois did not see the Superintendent out. Maigret followed the warehouse man into a sort of corridor that served as a cloakroom. Pape asked no questions. He was in his fifties, and seemed a quiet, reliable sort of man. He put on his hat and coat, and, flanked on the right by Judel and on the left by Maigret, walked to the street.

He seemed surprised that there was no car waiting for them outside, as though he had expected to be taken straight to the Quai des Orfèvres. When, on the corner opposite the yellow façade of Chez Popaul, they turned not right toward the town center, but left, he seemed about to speak, but then apparently thought better of it, and said nothing.

Judel realized that Maigret was making for the Calas bistro. The door was still locked. Maigret rapped on the glass. Moers came to let them in.

"In here, Pape."

Maigret turned the key.

"You know this place pretty well, don't you?"

The man looked bewildered. If he had been expecting

a visit from the police, he had certainly not expected this.

"You may take off your coat. We've kept the fire going. Take a seat, in your usual place if you like. I suppose you have your own favorite chair?"

"I don't understand."

"You're a regular visitor here, aren't you?"

"I'm a customer, yes."

Seeing Moers and his men in the kitchen with their cameras, he peered, trying to make out what was going on. He must have been wondering what had happened to Madame Calas.

"A very good customer?"

"A good customer."

"Were you here on Sunday?"

He had an honest face, with a look in his blue eyes that was both gentle and timid. Maigret was reminded of the way some animals look when a human being speaks sharply to them.

"Sit down."

He did so, cowering, because he had been ordered to do so.

"I was asking you about Sunday."

He hesitated before answering: "I wasn't here."

"Were you at home all day?"

"I went to see my sister."

"Does she live in Paris?"

"Nogent-sur-Marne."

"Does she have a telephone?"

"Nogent three-one-seven. She's married to a builder."

"Did you see anyone besides your sister?"

"Her husband and children. Then, at about five, the neighbors came in for a game of cards, as usual."

Maigret made a sign to Judel, who nodded and went to the telephone.

"What time was it when you left Nogent?"

"I caught the eight o'clock bus."

"You didn't call in here before going home?"

"No."

"When did you last see Madame Calas?"

"On Saturday."

"What shift were you on last week?"

"The early shift."

"So it was after two when you got here?"

"Yes."

"Was Calas at home?"

Again, he hesitated.

"Not when I came in."

"But he was, later?"

"I don't remember."

"Did you stay long in the café?"

"Quite a time."

"How long would that be?"

"Two hours, at least. I can't say exactly."

"What did you do?"

"I had a glass of wine, and we talked for a bit."

"You and the other customers?"

"No, I talked mostly to Aline."

He flushed as he spoke her name, and hurriedly explained:

"I look upon her as a friend. I've known her for a long time."

"How long?"

"More than ten years."

"So you've been coming here every day for ten years?"

"Almost every day."

"Preferably, when her husband was out?"

This time he did not reply. He hung his head, troubled.

"Are you her lover?"

"Who told you that?"

"Never mind. Are you?"

Instead of replying, he asked anxiously:

"What have you done with her?"

And Maigret told him outright:

"She's with the Examining Magistrate at the moment."

"Why?"

"To answer a few questions about her husband's dis-appearance. Don't you read the papers?"

As Dieudonné Pape sat motionless, lost in thought, Maigret called out:

"Moers! Take his prints, will you?"

The man submitted quietly, appearing more anxious than frightened, and his fingertips, pressed down on the paper, were steady.

"See if they match."

"Which ones?"

"The two in the kitchen. The ones you said were partly rubbed out."

As Moers went out, Dieudonné Pape, gently reproach-ful, said:

"If all you wanted to know was whether I had been in the kitchen, you only had to ask me. I often go in there."

"Were you there last Saturday?"

"I made myself a cup of coffee."

"What do you know about the disappearance of Omer Calas?"

He was still looking very thoughtful, as though he were hesitating on the brink of some momentous decision.

"Didn't you know he'd been murdered, and his dismembered corpse thrown into the canal?"

It was strangely moving. Neither Judel nor Maigret had been prepared for it. Slowly, the man turned toward the Superintendent, and gave him a long, searching look. At last he said, gently reproachful still:

"I have nothing to say."

Maigret, looking as serious as the man he was questioning, pressed him:

"Did you kill Calas?"

And Dieudonné Pape, shaking his head, repeated:

"I have nothing to say."

Chapter 7

The Cat

Maigret was finishing his meal when he became aware of the way his wife was looking at him, with a smile that was maternal and yet, at the same time, a little teasing. At first, pretending not to notice, he bent over his plate, and ate a few more spoonfuls of his custard. But he could not help looking up in the end:

"Have I got a smut on the end of my nose?" he asked grumpily.

"No."

"Then why are you laughing at me?"

"I'm not laughing. I'm smiling."

"You're making fun of me. What's so comical about me?"

"There's nothing comical about you, Jules."

She seldom called him "Jules"; only when she was feeling protective toward him.

"What is it, then?"

"Do you realize that during the entire dinner you haven't said a single word?"

No, he had not realized it.

"Have you any idea what you've been eating?"

Assuming a fierce expression, he said:

"Sheep's kidneys."

"And before that?"

"Soup."

"What kind of soup?"

"I don't know. Vegetable soup, I suppose."

"Is it because of that woman you've got yourself into such a state?"

Most of the time, and this was a case in point, Madame Maigret knew no more about her husband's work than she read in the newspapers.

"What is it? Don't you believe she killed him?"

He shrugged, as though he were carrying a burden and wished he could shake it off.

"I just don't know."

"Or that Dieudonné Pape did it with her as his accomplice?"

He was tempted to reply that it was of no consequence. Indeed, as he saw it, this was not the point. What mattered to him was understanding what lay behind the crime. As it was, not only was this not yet clear to him, but the more he knew of the people involved, the more he felt himself to be floundering.

He had come home to dinner instead of staying in his office to work on the case, for the very reason that he needed to get away from it, to return to the jog-trot of everyday life, from which he had hoped to go back with sharpened perceptions to the protagonists in the Quai de Valmy drama. Instead, as his wife had teasingly pointed out, he had sat through dinner without opening his mouth, and continued to think of nothing but Madame Calas and Pape, with the boy, Antoine, thrown in for good measure.

It was unusual for him to feel at this stage that he was still a long way from a solution. But then, in this case, the problems were not amenable to police methods.

Murders in general can be classified under a few broad headings, three or four at most.

The apprehension of a professional murderer is only a matter of routine. When a Corsican gangster strikes down a gangster from Marseilles in a bar in the Rue de Douai, the police have recourse to standard procedures, almost as though tackling a problem in mathematics.

When a couple of misguided youths commit robbery with violence, injuring or killing an old woman in a tobacconist's shop, or a bank clerk, it may be necessary to pursue the assailants through the streets, and here too there is a standard procedure.

As to the *crime passionnel*, nothing could be more straightforward. With murder for financial gain, through inheritance, life insurance, or some more devious means, the police know themselves to be on solid ground as soon as they have discovered the motive.

Judge Coméliau, for the present, was inclined to the view that financial gain was the motive in the Calas case, perhaps because he was incapable of accepting the idea that anyone outside his own social sphere, especially people from a neighborhood like the Quai de Valmy, could have any but the crudest motives.

Given that Dieudonné Pape was the lover of Madame Calas, Dieudonné Pape and Madame Calas must have got rid of the husband, partly because he was an encumbrance, and partly to get hold of his money.

"They have been lovers for ten years or more," Maigret had objected. "Why should they have waited all that time?"

The magistrate had brushed this aside. Maybe Calas had recently come into possession of a substantial sum of money. Maybe the lovers had been waiting for a convenient opportunity. Maybe there had been a row between Madame Calas and her husband, and she felt she had put up with enough. Maybe . . .

"And suppose we find that, except for the bistro, which isn't worth much, Calas had nothing?"

"The bistro is something. Dieudonné may have got fed up with his job with Zenith Transport, and decided that he would prefer to end his days dozing in front of the fire in his carpet slippers in a cozy little café of his own."

Here, Maigret had to concede, was a possibility, even though remote.

"And what about Antoine Cristin?"

The fact was that the Judge was now saddled not with one suspect but two. Cristin too was Madame Calas's lover, and if anyone was likely to be short of money, it was he rather than Pape.

"The other two were just making use of him. You'll find that he was their accomplice, mark my words."

This, then, was the official view—or at least the view prevailing in one examining magistrate's office—of the Quai de Valmy affair. Meanwhile, until the real facts were brought to light, all three of them were being kept under lock and key.

Maigret was the more disgruntled in that he reproached himself for not having stood up to Coméliau. Owing to indolence perhaps, or cowardice, he had given in without a struggle.

At the outset of his career, he had been warned by his superiors always to be sure of his ground before putting a suspect through a rigorous cross-examination, and experience had confirmed the wisdom of this advice. A properly conducted cross-examination did not consist in drawing a bow at a venture, or hurling accusations at a suspect for hours on end, in the hope that he would break down and confess.

Even a half-wit has a kind of sixth sense, which enables him to recognize at once whether the police are making accusations at random or have solid grounds for suspicion.

Maigret always preferred to bide his time. On occasion, in cases of real difficulty, he had even been willing to take a risk rather than arrest a suspect prematurely.

And he had been proved right every time.

"Contrary to popular belief," he was fond of saying, "being arrested can be something of a relief to a suspected person, because, from then on, he does at least know where he stands. He no longer has to ask himself: 'Am I under suspicion? Am I being followed? Am I being watched? Is this a trap?' He has been charged. He can now speak in his own defense. And henceforth he will be under the protection of the law. As a prisoner, he has his rights, hallowed rights, and nothing will be done to him which is not strictly in accordance with the rules."

Aline Calas was a case in point. From the moment she

had crossed the magistrate's threshold, her lips had, as it were, been sealed. Coméliau had got no more out of her than if she had been the gravel in the hold of the Naud brothers' barge.

"I have nothing to say," was all she would utter, in her flat, expressionless voice.

And when he persisted in bombarding her with questions, she retorted:

"You have no right to question me, except in the presence of a lawyer."

"In that case, kindly tell me the name of your lawyer."

"I have no lawyer."

"Here is the membership list of the Paris Bar. You may take your choice."

"I don't know any of them."

"Choose a name at random."

"I have no money."

There was therefore no choice but for the Court to nominate counsel for her, and that was a slow and cumbersome process.

Late that afternoon, Coméliau had sent for Antoine who, having held out against hours of questioning by Lapointe, saw no reason to be more forthcoming with the magistrate.

"I did not kill Monsieur Calas. I didn't go to the Quai de Valmy on Sunday afternoon. I never handed in a suitcase at the checkroom of the Gare de l'Est. Either the clerk is lying or he's made a mistake."

All this time, his mother, red-eyed, clutching a crumpled handkerchief, sat waiting in the lobby at Police Headquarters. Lapointe had tried to reason with her, and, after him, Lucas. It was no good. She was determined to wait, she repeated over and over again, until she had seen Chief Superintendent Maigret.

She was a simple soul, who believed, like many of her kind, that it was no good talking to underlings. She must, at all costs, see the man at the top.

The Chief Superintendent could not have seen her then, even if he had wanted to. He was just leaving the bar in the Quai de Valmy, accompanied by Judel and Dieudonné Pape.

"Don't forget to lock up, and bring the key to Headquarters," he said to Moers.

The three men crossed by the footbridge to the Quai de Jemmapes, only a few yards from the Rue des Ecluses-Saint-Martin, behind the Hospital of Saint-Louis. It was a quiet neighborhood, more provincial than Parisian in character. Pape was not handcuffed. Maigret judged that he was not the man to make a run for it. His bearing was calm and dignified, not unlike that of Madame Calas herself. He looked sad rather than shocked, and seemed withdrawn, or was it resigned?

He said very little. He had probably never been a talkative man. He answered, when spoken to, as briefly as possible. Sometimes he did not answer at all, but just looked at the Chief Superintendent out of his lavender-blue eyes.

He lived in an old five-story building, which had an appearance of respectability and modest comfort.

As they passed the lodge, the concierge got up and peered at them through the glass. They did not stop, however, but went up to the second floor. Pape went to a door on the left, and opened it with his key.

There were three rooms in the apartment: bedroom, dining room, and kitchen. There was also a large store-cupboard converted into a bathroom. It surprised Maigret to see that there was a well-equipped bathroom. The furniture, though not new, was less old-fashioned than that of the house in the Quai de Valmy, and everything was spotlessly clean.

"Do you have a daily woman?" Maigret asked in surprise.

"No."

"You mean you do your own housework?"

Dieudonné Pape could not help smiling with gratification. He was proud of his home.

"Doesn't the concierge ever give you a hand?"

There was a meat-safe, fairly well stocked with provisions, on the kitchen window sill.

"Do you do your own cooking as well?"

"Always."

Above the sideboard in the dining room hung a large gilt-framed photograph of Madame Calas, so much like those commonly to be seen in the houses of respectable families of modest means that it lent an air of cozy domesticity to the room.

Recalling that not a single photograph had been found at the Calases', Maigret asked:

"How did you come by it?"

"I took it myself, and had the enlargement made somewhere in the Boulevard Saint-Martin."

His camera was in the sideboard drawer. On a small table in a corner of the bathroom, there were a number of glass dishes and bowls and several bottles of developing fluid.

"Do you do much photography?"

"Yes. Landscapes and buildings, mostly."

It was true. Going through the drawers, Maigret found a large number of views of Paris, and a few landscapes. There were a great many of the canal and the Seine. Judging from the striking effects of light and shade in most of the photographs, it must have cost Dieudonné Pape a great deal in time and patience to get the shots he wanted.

"What suit were you wearing when you went to your sister's?"

"The dark blue."

He had three suits, including the one he was wearing.

"We shall need those," Maigret said to Judel, "and the shoes."

Then, coming upon some soiled underclothes in a wicker basket, he added them to the rest.

He had noticed a canary hopping about in a cage, but it was not until they were leaving the apartment that it occurred to him that it would need looking after.

"Can you think of anyone who might be willing to take care of it?"

"The concierge would be only too pleased, I'm sure."

Maigret fetched the cage and took it to the lodge. The concierge came to the door before he had time to knock.

"You're surely not taking him away!" she exclaimed in a fury.

She meant her tenant, not the canary. She recognized Judel, who was a local man. Possibly she recognized Maigret, too. She had read the newspapers.

"How dare you treat him like a criminal! He's a good man. You couldn't hope to find a better."

She was a tiny little thing, of gipsy complexion and sluttish appearance. Her voice was shrill, and she was so enraged that it would not have surprised him if she had sprung at him and tried to scratch his eyes out.

"Would you be willing to look after the canary for a short time?"

She literally snatched the cage out of his hand.

"Just you wait and see what the tenants and all the other people round here will have to say about this! And for a start, Monsieur Dieudonné, we'll all be coming to see you in prison."

Elderly working-class women quite often hero-worship bachelors and widowers of Dieudonné Pape's type, whose well-ordered way of life they greatly admire. The concierge followed the three men onto the pavement, and stood there sobbing and waving to Pape.

Maigret turned to Judel:

"Give the clothes and the shoes to Moers. He'll know what to do. And I want the bistro kept under surveillance."

In giving instructions that a watch should be kept on the bistro, he had nothing particular in mind. It was just to cover himself if anything were to go wrong. Dieudonné Pape waited obediently on the edge of the pavement, and then fell into step with Maigret, as they walked alongside the canal in search of a taxi.

He was silent in the taxi, and Maigret decided not to question him further. He filled his pipe, and held it out to Pape.

"Do you smoke a pipe?"

"No."

"Cigarette?"

"I don't smoke."

Maigret did, after all, ask Pape a question, but it had, on the face of it, nothing to do with the death of Calas.

"Don't you drink either?"

"No."

Here was another anomaly. Maigret could not make it out. Madame Calas was an alcoholic. She had been drinking for years, presumably even longer than she had known Pape.

As a rule, a compulsive drinker cannot endure the companionship of a teetotaler.

The Chief Superintendent had encountered couples very like Madame Calas and Dieudonné Pape before. In every case, as far as he could remember, both the man and the woman drank.

He had been brooding abstractedly over this at dinner, unaware that his wife was watching him. And that was not all, by any means. Among other things, there was Antoine's mother, whom he had found waiting in the lobby at the Quai des Orfèvres. Handing Pape over to Lucas, he had taken her into his office.

He had not forgotten to instruct Lucas to let Coméliau know that Pape had been brought in:

"If he wants to see him, take him there. Otherwise, take him to the cells."

Pape, poker-faced, had gone with Lucas into an office, while Maigret led the woman away.

"I swear to you, Superintendent, that my son would never do a thing like that. He couldn't hurt a fly. He makes himself out to be a tough guy because it's the thing at his age. But I know him, you see. He's just a child."

"I'm sure you're right, Madame."

"In that case, why don't you let him go? I'll keep him indoors from now on, and there won't be any more women, I promise you. That woman is almost as old as I am! She ought to know better than to take up with a fellow young enough to be her son. It's shameful! I've known for some time that there was something going on. When I saw he was buying hair cream, brushing his teeth twice a day, and even using scent, I said to myself . . ."

"Is he your only child?"

"Yes. And I've always taken extra care of him, on account of his father having died of consumption. I did everything I could for him, Superintendent. If only I could see him! If only I could talk to him! Surely they won't try to stop me? They wouldn't keep a mother from her son, would they?"

There was nothing he could do but pass her on to Coméliau. He knew it was cowardly, but he really had no choice. Presumably she had been kept waiting all over again, up there in the corridor, on a bench. Maigret did not know whether or not the Judge had finally granted her an interview.

Moers had got back to the Quai des Orfèvres just before six, and handed Maigret the key of the house in the Quai de Valmy. It was a heavy, old-fashioned key. Maigret put it in his pocket with the key to Pape's apartment.

"Did Judel give you the clothes and the shoes?"

"Yes, I've got them in the lab. It's blood we're looking for, I suppose?"

"Mainly, yes. I may want you to look over his apartment tomorrow morning."

"I'll be working here late tonight, after I've had a bite to eat. It's urgent, I imagine?"

It always was urgent. The longer a case dragged on, the colder the scent, and the more time for the criminal to cover his tracks.

"Will you be in tonight?"

"I don't know. In any case, you'd better leave a note on my desk on your way out."

He got up from the table, filling his pipe, and looked uncertainly at his armchair. Seeing him so restless, Madame Maigret ventured:

"Why not give yourself a rest for one night? Put the case out of your mind. Read a book, or, if you'd rather, take me to the movies. You'll feel much fresher in the morning."

With a quizzical look, he said:

"Do you want to see a movie?"

"There's quite a good program at the Moderne."

She poured his coffee. He could not make up his mind. He felt like taking a coin out of his pocket and tossing for it.

Madame Maigret was careful not to pursue the subject, but sat with him while he slowly sipped his coffee. He paced up and down the dining room, taking long strides, only pausing from time to time to straighten the carpet.

"No!" he said at last, with finality.

"Will you be going out?"

"Yes."

He poured himself a small glass of sloe gin. When he had drunk it, he went to get his overcoat.

"Will you be home late?"

"I'm not sure. Probably not."

Perhaps because he had a feeling that he was about to take a momentous step, he did not take a taxi or ring the Quai des Orfèvres to order a police car. He walked to the Métro station and boarded a train for Château-Landon. He felt again the disturbing night-time atmosphere of the place, with ghostly figures lurking in the shadows, women loitering on the pavements, and the bluish-green lighting in the bars making them look like fish-tanks in an aquarium.

A man standing a few yards from the door of Chez Calas saw Maigret stop, came straight up to him, and shone a flashlight in his face.

"Oh! Sorry, sir. I didn't recognize you in the dark."

It was one of Judel's constables.

"Anything to report?"

"Nothing. Or rather there is one thing. I don't know if it's of any significance. About an hour ago, a taxi drove past. It slowed down about fifty yards from here and went by at a crawl, but it didn't stop."

"Could you see who was in it?"

"A woman. I could see her quite clearly under the gas lamp. She was young, wearing a gray coat and no hat. Farther down, the taxi gathered speed and turned left into the Rue Louis-Blanc."

Was it Madame Calas's daughter, Lucette, come to see whether her mother had been released? She must know, from the newspaper reports, that she had been taken to the Quai des Orfèvres, but no further details had been released.

"Do you think she saw you?"

"Very likely. Judel didn't tell me to stay out of sight. Most of the time, I've been walking up and down to keep warm."

Another possible explanation was that Lucette Calas had intended to go into the house, but changed her mind when she saw that it was being watched. If that were the case, what was she after?

He shrugged, took the key out of his pocket, and fitted it into the lock. He had some difficulty in finding the light switch, which he had not had occasion to use until now. A single light came on. The switch for the light at the far end of the room was behind the bar.

Moers and his assistants had put everything back in its proper place before leaving, so that there was no change in the little café, except that it felt colder, because the fire had been allowed to go out.

On his way to the kitchen, Maigret was startled to see something move. He had not heard a sound, and it took him seconds to realize that it was the cat, which he had left with the butcher earlier in the day.

The creature was rubbing its back against his legs now, and Maigret, bending down to stroke it, growled:

"How did you get in?"

It worried him. The back door, leading from the kitchen to the courtyard, was bolted, and the window was closed too. He went upstairs, turned on the light, and found that a window had been left open. There was a lean-to shed, with a corrugated iron roof, in the back yard of the house next door. The cat must have climbed onto it, and taken a flying leap over a gap of more than six feet.

Maigret went back down the stairs. Finding that there

was a drop of milk left in the earthenware jug, he poured it out for the cat.

"What now?" he said aloud, as though he were addressing the animal.

They certainly made an odd pair, alone in the empty house.

He had never realized how deserted, even desolate, a bar could look with no one behind the counter and not a customer in sight. Yet this was how the place must have looked every night after everyone had gone, and Monsieur and Madame Calas had put up the shutters and locked the door.

There would be just the two of them, man and wife, with nothing left to do but put out the lights and go upstairs to bed. Madame Calas, after all those nips of brandy, would be in her usual state of vacant torpor.

Did she have to conceal her drinking from her husband? Or did he take an indulgent view of his wife's addiction to the bottle, seeking his own pleasures elsewhere in the afternoons?

Maigret suddenly realized that there was one character in the drama about whom almost nothing was known, the dead man himself. From the outset, he had been to all of them merely a dismembered corpse. It was an odd fact that the Chief Superintendent had often noticed before, that people did not respond in the same way to parts of a body found scattered about as to a whole corpse. They did not feel pity in the same degree, or even revulsion. It was as though the dead person were somehow dehumanized, almost an object of ridicule.

He had never seen Calas's face, even in a photograph,

and the head had still not been found, and probably never would be.

The man was of peasant stock, short and squat in build. Every year he went to the vineyards near Poitiers to buy his wine. He wore good suits, and played billiards in the afternoon, somewhere near the Gare de l'Est.

Other than Madame Calas, was there a woman in his life, or more than one perhaps? Could he possibly have been unaware of what went on when he was away from home?

He had accidentally encountered Pape, and, unless he were crassly insensitive, he must have seen how things stood between Pape and his wife.

The impression they created was not so much of a pair of lovers as of an old married couple, united in a deep and restful contentment, born of mutual understanding, tolerance, and that special tenderness which, in the middle-aged, is often a sign that much has been forgiven and forgotten.

Had he known all this, and accepted it philosophically? Had he turned a blind eye or, alternatively, had there been scenes between him and his wife?

And what about the others who, like Antoine, were in the habit of slinking in to take advantage of Aline Calas's weakness? Had he known about them too, and if so, how had he taken it?

Maigret was back behind the bar, his hand hovering over the bottles on the shelf. In the end he took down a bottle of Calvados, reminding himself that he must leave the money for it. The cat had gone over to the stove, but instead of dozing as it usually did, was restless, bewildered to find no heat coming from it.

Maigret understood the relationship between Madame Calas and Pape. He also understood the role of Antoine and the casual callers.

What he did not understand at all was the relationship between Calas and his wife. How and why had those two ever come together, subsequently married, and lived with one another for so many years? And what about their daughter, in whom neither of them seemed to have taken the slightest interest, and who appeared to have nothing whatever in common with them?

There was nothing to enlighten him, not a single photograph or letter, none of those personal possessions which reveal so much about their owners.

He drained his glass, and grumpily poured himself another drink. Then, with the glass in his hand, he went and sat at the table where he had seen Madame Calas sitting, with that settled air which suggested that it was her usual place.

He tapped out his pipe against his shoe, refilled it and lit it. He stared at the bar counter, the glasses and bottles, and the feeling came over him that he was on the brink of a revelation. Maybe it would not answer all his questions, but it would answer some of them at least.

What kind of home was this, after all, with its kitchen where no food was served, since the Calases ate their meals at a table in a corner of the café, and its bedroom which was only used to sleep in?

Whichever way you looked at it, this was their real home, this bar, which was to them what the dining room or living room is to an ordinary family.

Was it not the case that on their arrival in Paris, or very

soon after, they had settled here in the Quai de Valmy, and remained ever since?

Maigret was smiling now. He was beginning to understand Madame Calas's relationship with her husband, and more than this, to see where Dieudonné Pape came into it.

It was very vague still, and he would not have been able to put it into words. All the same, there was no denying that he had quite shaken off his earlier mood of indecision. He finished his drink, went into the telephone booth, and dialed the number of the Central Police Station.

"Chief Superintendent Maigret speaking. Who is that? Oh! It's you, Joris. How is your new arrival getting on? Yes, I do mean the Calas woman. What's that? Oh! What are you doing about it?"

It was pitiful. Twice she had called for the guard, and each time she had begged him to get her something to drink. She was willing to pay anything, anything at all. Maigret had not foreseen the terrible suffering that this deprivation would cause her.

"No, of course not . . ."

It was not possible for him to suggest to Joris that he should give her a drink in breach of the regulations. Perhaps he himself could take her a bottle in the morning, or have her brought to his office and order something for her there?

"I'd like you to look through her papers for me. She must have been carrying an identity card. I know she comes from somewhere round about Gien, but I can't remember the name of the village."

He was kept waiting some time.

"What's that? Boissancourt-par-Saint-André. Boissan-

court with an a? Thanks, old man. Good night! Don't be
too hard on her."

He dialed Directory Inquiries, and gave his name.

"Would you be so kind, Mademoiselle, as to find the
directory for Boissancourt-par-Saint-André—between Montargis and Gien—and read out the names of the subscrib-
ers."

"Will you hold on?"

"Yes."

It did not take long. The supervisor was thrilled at the
prospect of collaborating with the celebrated Chief Superintendent Maigret.

"Shall I begin?"

"Yes."

"Aillevard, Route des Chênes, occupation not stated."

"Next."

"Ancelin, Victor, butcher. Do you want the number?"

"No."

"Honoré de Boissancourt, Château de Boissancourt."

"Next."

"Doctor Camuzet."

"I'd better have his number."

"Seventeen."

"Next."

"Calas, Robert. Cattle dealer."

"Number?"

"Twenty-one."

"Calas, Julien, grocer. Number: three."

"Any other Calas?"

"No. There's a Louchez, occupation not stated, a Pied-
boeuf, blacksmith, and a Simonin, corn dealer."

"Will you please get me the first Calas on the list. I may want the other later."

He heard the operator talking to the intermediate exchanges, then a voice saying:

"Saint-André Exchange."

Boissancourt-par-Saint-André 21 was slow to answer. At last, a woman's voice said:

"Who's speaking?"

"Chief Superintendent Maigret here, from Police Headquarters, Paris. Are you Madame Calas? Is your husband at home?"

He was in bed with influenza.

"Have you a relative by the name of Omer Calas?"

"Oh, him! What's happened to him? Is he in trouble?"

"Do you know him?"

"Well, I've never actually met him. I don't come from these parts. I'm from the Haute-Loire district, and he left Boissancourt before my marriage."

"Is he related to your husband?"

"They're first cousins. His brother is still living here. Julien. He owns the grocer's shop."

"Can you tell me anything more about him?"

"About Omer? No, I don't know any more. What's more I don't want to."

She must have hung up, because another voice was asking:

"Shall I get the other number, Superintendent?"

There was less delay this time. A man's voice answered. He was even more uncommunicative.

"I can hear you perfectly well. But what exactly do you want from me?"

"Are you the brother of Omer Calas?"

"I did have a brother called Omer."

"Is he dead?"

"I haven't the least idea. It's more than twenty years, nearer twenty-five, since I last heard anything of him."

"A man by the name of Omer Calas has been found murdered in Paris."

"So I heard just now on the radio."

"Then you must have heard his description—does it fit your brother?"

"It's impossible to say after all this time."

"Did you know he was living in Paris?"

"No."

"Did you know he was married?"

Silence.

"Do you know his wife?"

"Now, look here, there's nothing I can tell you. I was fifteen when my brother left home. I haven't seen him since. He's never written to me. I just don't want to know. I'll tell you who might be able to help you: Maître Canonge."

"Who is he?"

"The notary."

When, at last, he got through to Maître Canonge's number, a woman's voice, that of Madame Canonge, exclaimed:

"Well, of all the extraordinary coincidences!"

"I beg your pardon?"

"That you should call at this moment! How did you know? Just now, when we heard the news on the radio, my husband was of two minds whether to get in touch with you by telephone or go to Paris and see you. In the end, he decided to make the journey, and he caught the eight twenty-two train, which is due in at the Gare d'Austerlitz shortly after midnight. I'm not certain of the exact time."

"Where does he usually stay in Paris?"

"Until recently the train went on to the Gare d'Orsay. He always stayed at the Hôtel d'Orsay, and still does."

"What does your husband look like?"

"Good-looking, tall and well-built, with gray hair. He's wearing a brown suit and overcoat. He has his brief-case with him, and a pigskin suitcase. I still can't imagine what made you think of phoning him!"

Maigret put down the receiver with an involuntary smile. Things were going so well that he considered treating himself to another drink, but thought better of it. There would be plenty of time to have one at the station.

But first, he must ring Madame Maigret, and tell her that he would be late getting home.

Chapter 8

The Notary

Madame Canonge had spoken no more than the truth. Her husband really was a fine-looking man. He was about sixty, and in appearance more like a gentleman farmer than a country lawyer. Maigret, waiting at the end of the platform near the barrier, picked him out at once. He stood head and shoulders above the other passengers on the 12:22 train, and walked with a rapid stride, his pigskin suitcase in one hand and his brief-case in the other. His air of easy assurance suggested that he knew his way about and was probably a regular traveler on this particular train. Maigret noted all this when he was still quite a long way off.

Added to his height and impressive build, his clothes set him apart from the other passengers. He was almost too well dressed. To describe his coat as brown was to do less than justice to its color, which was a soft, subtle chestnut such as Maigret had never seen before, and the cut was masterly.

His fresh complexion was set off by silvery hair, and even in the unflattering light of the station entrance he looked

well groomed, smooth shaven, the kind of man whom one
would expect to complete his toilet with a discreet dab of
eau de Cologne.

When he was within fifty yards of the barrier, he caught
sight of Maigret among the other people meeting the train,
and frowned as though trying to recapture an elusive mem-
ory. He, too, must often have seen the Chief Superintendent's photograph in the newspapers. Even when he was
almost level with Maigret, he was still too uncertain to
smile or hold out his hand.

It was Maigret who stepped forward to meet him.

"Maître Canonge?"

"Yes. Aren't you Chief Superintendent Maigret?"

He put down his suitcase and shook Maigret's hand.

"It can't be just a coincidence that I should find you here,
surely?"

"No. I telephoned your house earlier this evening. Your
wife told me that you were on this train, and would be staying at the Hôtel d'Orsay. I thought it advisable, for security
reasons, to meet the train rather than ask for you at your
hotel."

The notary looked puzzled.

"Did you see my advertisement?"

"No."

"You don't say! The sooner we get out of here the better,
don't you think? I suggest we adjourn to my hotel."

They got into a taxi.

"The reason I'm here is to see you. I intended to call you
first thing tomorrow morning."

Maigret had been right. There was a faint fragrance of

eau de Cologne blended with the lingering aroma of a good cigar

"Have you arrested Madame Calas?"

"Judge Coméliau has signed the warrant."

"What an extraordinary business!"

It was a short journey along the quayside to the Hôtel d'Orsay. The night porter greeted Maître Canonge with the warmth due to a guest of long standing.

"The restaurant is shut, I suppose, Alfred?"

"Yes, sir."

The notary explained to Maigret, who knew the facts perfectly well:

"Before the war, when the Quai d'Orsay was the terminus for all trains on the Paris–Orléans line, the station restaurant was open all night. It was very convenient. A hotel bedroom isn't the most congenial place in the world. Wouldn't it be better if we talked over a drink somewhere?"

Most of the brasseries in the Boulevard Saint-Germain were closed. They had to walk quite a distance before they found one open.

"What will you have, Superintendent?"

"A beer, thanks."

"And a brandy for me, waiter, the best you have."

Having left their coats and hats in the cloakroom, they sat at the bar. Maigret lit his pipe, and Canonge pierced a cigar with a silver penknife.

"I don't suppose you know Saint-André at all?"

"No."

"It's miles from anywhere, and there are no tourist attractions. If I'm not mistaken, according to the afternoon news bulletin, the man who was carved up and dropped in the Saint-Martin Canal was none other than that swine Calas."

"Fingerprints of the dead man were found in the house in the Quai de Valmy."

"When I first read about the body in the canal, although the newspapers hadn't much to say about it then, I had a kind of intuition, and I toyed with the idea of phoning you even then."

"Did you know Calas?"

"I knew him in the old days. I knew her better, though— the woman who became his wife, I mean. Cheers! The trouble is, I hardly know where to begin, it's all so involved. Has Aline Calas never mentioned me?"

"No."

"Do you really think she's involved in the murder of her husband?"

"I don't know. The examining magistrate is convinced of it."

"What has she to say about it?"

"Nothing."

"Has she confessed?"

"No. She refuses to say anything."

"To tell you the truth, Chief Superintendent, she's the most extraordinary woman I've ever met in my life. And, make no mistake, we have our fair share of freaks in the country."

He was clearly accustomed to a respectful audience, and he liked the sound of his own voice. He held his cigar in his elegant fingers in such a way as to show off his gold signet ring to the best advantage.

"I'd better begin at the beginning. You'll never have heard of Honoré de Boissancourt, of course?"

The Superintendent shook his head.

"He is, or rather was until last month, the 'lord of the manor.' He was a rich man. Besides the Château de Boissancourt, he owned some fifteen farms comprising five thousand acres in all, plus another two and a half thousand acres of woodland and two small lakes. If you are at all familiar with country life, you can visualize it."

"I was born and brought up in the country."

And what was more, Maigret's father had been farm manager on just such an estate.

"Now I think you ought to know something of the antecedents of this fellow, Boissancourt. It all began with his grandfather. My father, who, like myself, practiced law in Saint-André, knew him well. He wasn't called Boissancourt, but Dupré, Christophe Dupré, son of a tenant farmer whose landlord was the former owner of the château. Christophe began by dealing in cattle, and he was sufficiently ruthless and crooked to amass a considerable fortune in a short time. You know his sort, I daresay."

To Maigret, it was as though he were reliving his own childhood, for his village had had its Christophe Dupré, and he too had amassed great wealth, and had a son who was now a senator.

"At one stage, Dupré speculated heavily in wheat, and the gamble paid off. With what he made on the deal, he bought one farm, then a second and a third, and by the end of his life the château and all the land attached to it, which had been the property of a childless widow, had passed into his hands. Christophe had one son and one daughter. The daughter he married off to a cavalry officer. The son, Alain, came into the property on his father's death, and used the name of Dupré de Boissancourt. Gradually the Dupré was dropped and, when he was elected to the County Council, he changed his name by deed poll."

This, too, evoked memories for Maigret.

"Well, so much for the antecedents. Honoré de Boissancourt, the grandson of Christophe Dupré, who was, as it were, the founder of the dynasty, died a month ago.

"He married Emilie d'Espissac, daughter of a fine old family who had fallen on hard times. There was one daughter of this marriage. The mother was killed in a riding accident, when the child was only a baby. I knew Emilie well. She was a charming woman, though no beauty. She sadly underrated herself, and allowed her parents to sacrifice her, without protest. It was said that Boissancourt gave the parents a million francs, by way of purchase price one must assume. As the family lawyer, I am in a position to know that the figure was exaggerated, but the fact remains that a substantial sum of money came into the possession of the old Comtesse d'Espissac as soon as the marriage contract was signed."

"What kind of man was Honoré?"

"I'm coming to that. I was his legal adviser. For years, I have been in the habit of dining at the château once a week, and I've shot over his land ever since I was a boy. In other words, I know him well. In the first place, he had a clubfoot, which may explain his moody and suspicious disposition. Then again, his family history was known to everyone, and most of the county families refused to have anything to do with him. None of this was exactly calculated to bring out the best in him.

"All his life he was obsessed with the notion that people despised him, and were only out to cheat and rob him. He was forever on the defensive.

"There is a turret room in the château, which he used as a kind of office. He spent days on end up there, going through the accounts, not only those of his tenants, but all the household bills as well, down to the last penny. He made all his corrections in red ink. He would poke his nose into the kitchen at mealtimes, to make sure that the servants weren't eating him out of house and home.

"I suppose I owe some loyalty to my client, but it's not as if I were betraying a professional secret. Anyone in Saint-André could tell you as much."

"Was he the father of Madame Calas?"

"Exactly."

"What about Omer Calas?"

"He was a servant at the château for four years. His father was a drunken laborer, a real bum.

"Which brings us to Aline de Boissancourt, as she was twenty-five years ago."

He signaled to the waiter as he went past the table, and said to Maigret:

"Join me in a brandy this time, won't you? Two *fines champagnes*, waiter."

Then, turning back to the Superintendent, he went on:

"Needless to say, you couldn't possibly have any inkling of her background, seeing her for the first time in the bistro in the Quai de Valmy."

This was not altogether the case. Nothing that the notary had told Maigret was any surprise to him.

"Old Doctor Petrelle used sometimes to talk to me about Aline. He's dead now, unfortunately, and Camuzet has taken over the practice. Camuzet never knew her, so he wouldn't be any help. And I myself am not qualified to describe her case in technical terms.

"Even as a very young child, she was different from other little girls. There was something disturbing about her. She never played with other children, or even went to school, because her father insisted on keeping her at home with a governess. Not one governess, actually, but at least a dozen, one after the other, because the child somehow contrived to make their lives a misery.

"Was it that she blamed her father for the fact that her life was so different from other children's? Or was there, as Petrelle believed, much more to it than that? I don't know. It's often said that girls worship their fathers, sometimes to an unnatural degree. I can't speak from my own experience. My wife and I have no children. But is it possible, I wonder, for that kind of adoration to turn into hatred?

"Be that as it may, she seemed prepared to go to any lengths to drive Boissancourt to distraction, and at the age of twelve she was caught setting fire to the château.

"She was always setting fire to things at that time, and she had to be kept under strict supervision.

"And then there was Omer. He was five or six years older than she was, tough and strong, a 'likely lad' as country folk say, and as insolent as you please as soon as the boss's back was turned."

"Did you know what was going on between them?" inquired Maigret, looking vaguely round the brasserie, which was now almost empty, with the waiters obviously longing for them to go.

"Not at the time. I heard about it later from Petrelle. According to him, when she first began taking an interest in Omer she was only thirteen or fourteen. It's not unusual in girls of that age, but as a rule it's just calf love, and nothing comes of it.

"Was it any different in her case? Or was it just that Calas, who wasn't the kind to allow his better feelings to stand in his way, was more unscrupulous in taking advantage of her than most men would be in a similar situation?

"Petrelle, at any rate, was convinced that their relationship was suspect right from the start. In his opinion, Aline had only one idea in her head, to defy and wound her father.

"It may be so. I'm not competent to judge. I'm only telling you all this, because it may help you to understand the rest of the story.

"One day, when she was not yet seventeen, she went to see the doctor in secret, and asked him to examine her. He confirmed that she was pregnant."

"How did she take it?" asked Maigret.

"As Petrelle described it, she gave him a long, hard look, clenched her teeth, and spat out the words:

" '*I'm glad!*'

"I should tell you that Calas, meanwhile, had married the butcher's daughter. She was pregnant too, of course, and their child was born a few weeks earlier.

"He carried on with his job at the château, not being fitted for any other work, and his wife went on living with her parents.

"It was a Sunday when the news burst upon the village that Aline de Boissancourt and Omer Calas had vanished.

"It was learned from the servants that, the night before, there had been a violent quarrel between the girl and her father. They could hear them in the breakfast room, going at it hammer and tongs for over two hours.

"Boissancourt, to my certain knowledge, never made any attempt to find his daughter. And, as far as I know, she never communicated with him.

"As for Calas's first wife, she suffered from fits of depression. She dragged on miserably for three years. Then, one day, they found her hanging from a tree in the orchard."

The waiters by now had stacked most of the chairs on the tables, and one of them was looking fixedly at Maigret and the notary, with a large silver pocket watch in his hand.

"I think we'd better be going," suggested Maigret.

Canonge insisted on paying the bill, and they went out into the cool, starlit night. They walked a little way in silence. Then the notary said:

"What about a nightcap, if we can find a place that's still open?"

Each wrapped in his own thoughts, they walked almost the whole length of the Boulevard Raspail, and eventually, in Montparnasse, found a little cabaret which appeared to be open, judging from the bluish light shining into the street, and the muffled sound of music.

"Shall we go in?"

They did not follow the waiter to a table, but sat at the

bar. The fat man next to them was more than a little drunk, and was being pestered by a couple of prostitutes.

"The same again?" asked Canonge, taking another cigar out of his pocket.

There were a few couples dancing. Two prostitutes came across from the far end of the room to sit beside them, but they melted away at a sign from Maigret.

"There are still Calases at Boissancourt and Saint-André," remarked the notary.

"I know. A cattle dealer and a grocer."

Canonge sniggered:

"Suppose the cattle dealer were to grow rich in his turn, and buy the château and the land for himself. What a laugh that would be! One of the Calases is Omer's brother, the other is his cousin. There is a sister as well. She married a policeman in Gien. A month ago, just as he was sitting down to his dinner, Boissancourt dropped dead of a cerebral hemorrhage. I went to see all three of them in the hope that one or the other might have news of Omer."

"Just a moment," interposed Maigret. "Didn't Boissancourt disinherit his daughter?"

"Everyone in the district was convinced that he had. There was a good deal of speculation as to who would inherit the property, because, in a village like ours, most people are more or less dependent on the château for their livelihood."

"You knew, I daresay."

"No. Boissancourt made several wills over the past few years, all different, but he never deposited any of them with me. He must have torn them up, one after another, because no will was found."

"Do you mean to say his daughter inherits everything?"

"Automatically."

"Did you put a notice in the papers?"

"Routinely, yes. There was no mention of the name Calas, because I couldn't assume that they were married. Not many people read that kind of advertisement. I didn't think anything would come of it."

His glass was empty, and he was trying to catch the barman's eye. There had evidently been a restaurant car on the train, and he must have had a couple of drinks before reaching Paris, because he was very flushed, and his eyes were unnaturally bright.

"The same again, Superintendent?"

Maigret, too, had perhaps had more to drink than he realized. He did not say no. He was feeling fine, physically and mentally. It seemed to him, in fact, that he had acquired a sixth sense, enabling him to penetrate the mysteries of human personality. Had he really needed the notary to fill in the details? Might he not, in the end, have worked the whole thing out for himself? He had not been far from the truth a few hours earlier. Why else should he have put that call through to Saint-André?

Even if he had not dotted the *i*'s and crossed the *t*'s, the impression he had formed of Madame Calas had been very close to the truth. All that he had been told confirmed this.

"She's taken to drink," he murmured, prompted by a sudden urge to have his say.

"I know. I've seen her."

"When? Last week?"

This was another thing that he had worked out for himself. But Canonge would not let him get a word in edgewise. In Saint-André, no doubt, he was used to holding forth without interruption.

"All in good time, Superintendent. I'm a lawyer, remember, and in legal circles matters are dealt with in their correct order."

He guffawed at this. A prostitute sitting at the bar leaned across the unoccupied stool between them, and said:

"Won't you buy me a drink?"

"If you like, my dear, but you mustn't interrupt. You might not think it, but we are discussing weighty matters."

Mightily pleased with himself, he turned to Maigret.

"Well, now, for three weeks there was no answer to my advertisement, other than a couple of letters from cranks. And, in the end, it wasn't the advertisement that led me to Aline. It was pure chance. I had sent one of my guns to a firm in Paris for repair, and last week I got it back. It came through a firm of long-distance truckers. I happened to be at home when it was delivered. In fact, I opened the door myself."

"And the truckers were Zenith Transport?"

"How did you know? You're quite right. I invited the driver in for a drink, as one does in the country. Calas's grocery store is just opposite my house in the Place de l'Eglise. We can see it from our front windows. The man was having his drink when he suddenly noticed the name over the shop:

" 'Would that be the same family as the people who have the bistro in the Quai de Valmy?' he said, half to himself.

" 'Is there a Calas in the Quai de Valmy?'

" 'It's a funny little place. I'd never set foot in it until last week, when I was taken there by one of the warehouse men.' "

Maigret was willing to take a bet that this warehouse man was none other than Dieudonné Pape.

"He didn't happen to say whether the warehouse man had red hair?"

"No. I asked him if he knew the Christian name of this Calas. He thought about it for a bit, and then said he vaguely remembered seeing it over the door. I asked, could it be Omer, and he said yes, that was it.

"At any rate, next day, I left by train for Paris."

"The night train?"

"No. The morning train."

"What time did you go to the Quai de Valmy?"

"In the afternoon, shortly after three. The bistro is rather dark, and when I first saw the woman, I didn't recognize her. I asked her if she was Madame Calas, and she said she was. Then I asked her Christian name. I got the impression that she was half drunk. She does drink, doesn't she?"

So did he drink, not as she did, but enough, all the same, to make his eyes water now.

Maigret had an uneasy feeling that they had just had their glasses refilled, but he was not too sure. The woman had moved to the stool next to the notary, and was lolling against him with her arm through his. For all the expression on her face, she might not have heard a word of what he had said.

" 'Your maiden name was Aline de Boissancourt, is that right?' I said.

"She didn't deny it. She just sat there by the stove, staring at me, I remember, with a great ginger cat on her lap.

"I went on:

" 'Your father is dead. Did you know?'

"She shook her head—no sign of surprise or emotion.

" 'As his lawyer, I am administering his estate. Your father left no will, which means that the château, the land, and all he possessed come to you.'

" 'How did you get my address?' she asked.

" 'From a truck driver who happened to have been in here for a drink.'

" 'Does anyone else know?'

" 'I don't think so.'

"She got up and went into the kitchen."

To take a swig from the brandy bottle, of course!

"When she got back, I could see that she had come to some decision.

" 'I don't want anything to do with the money,' she said, as though it was of no importance. 'I suppose I can refuse it if I want to?'

" 'Everyone has the right to renounce an inheritance. Nevertheless . . .'

" 'Nevertheless what?'

" 'I would advise you to think it over. Don't make up your mind here and now.'

" 'I've thought it over. I refuse it. I imagine I also have the right to insist that you keep your knowledge of my whereabouts to yourself.'

"All the while she was talking she kept peering nervously into the street, as though she were afraid someone would come in, her husband, perhaps. That's what I thought, at any rate.

"I protested, as I was bound to do. I told her I hadn't been able to trace anyone else with a claim to the Boissancourt estate.

" 'Perhaps it would be best for me to come back another time and talk things over again,' I suggested.

" 'No. Don't come back. Omer mustn't see you here. I won't have it.'

"She was terrified.

" 'It would be the end of everything!' she said.

" 'Don't you think you ought to consult your husband?'

" 'He's the very last person!'

"I tried to argue with her, but it was no use. As I was leaving, I gave her my card. I said that, if she changed her mind in the next few weeks, she could telephone or write, and let me know.

"A customer came in then. He looked to me very much at home in the place."

"Red-haired, with a pock-marked face?"

"Yes, I believe he was!"

"What happened?"

"Nothing. She slipped my card into her apron pocket, and saw me to the door."

"What day was it?"

"Last Thursday."

"Did you see her again?"

"No. But I saw her husband."

"In Paris?"

"In my study at home, in Saint-André."

"When?"

"On Saturday morning. He arrived in Saint-André on Friday afternoon or evening. He first called at the house on

Friday evening, about eight. I was out, playing bridge at the doctor's house. The maid told him to come back next day."

"Did you recognize him?"

"Yes, although he had put on weight. He must have spent the night at the village inn, where, of course, he learned that Boissancourt was dead. He must also have heard that his wife was heir to the property. He lost no time in throwing his weight about. He insisted that, as her husband, he was entitled to claim the inheritance in the name of his wife. As there was no marriage contract in this case, the joint-estate system applies."

"So that, in fact, neither could act without the consent of the other?"

"That's what I told him."

"Did you get the impression that he had discussed the matter with his wife?"

"No. He didn't even know that she had renounced the inheritance. He seemed to think she'd got hold of it behind his back. I won't go into the details of the interview, it would take too long. What must have happened is that he found my card. His wife probably left it lying around. Very likely she forgot I'd given it to her. And what possible business would a lawyer from Saint-André have in the Quai de Valmy unless it were to do with the de Boissancourt estate?

"It was only while he was talking to me that the truth gradually dawned on him. He was furious. I should be hearing from him, he said, and stormed out, slamming the door."

"And you never saw him again?"

"I never heard another word from him. All this happened on Saturday morning. He went by bus to Montargis, and caught the train to Paris from there."

"What train would that be, do you think?"

"Probably the one that gets in at the Gare d'Austerlitz just after three."

Which meant that he must have arrived at about four, or earlier if he took a taxi.

The notary went on:

"When I read about the dismembered body of a man recovered from the Saint-Martin Canal, right there next to the Quai de Valmy, it shook me, I can tell you. I couldn't help being struck by the coincidence. As I said just now, I was in two minds about calling you, but I didn't want to look like a fool.

"It was when I heard the name Calas mentioned in the news this afternoon that I made up my mind to come and see you."

"Can I have another?" asked the girl next to him, point-ing to her empty glass.

"By all means, my dear. Well, what do you think, Super-intendent?"

At the word "Superintendent," the prostitute started, and let go of the notary's arm.

"It doesn't surprise me," murmured Maigret, who was beginning to feel drowsy.

"Come now, don't tell me you've ever known anything like it! Things like that only happen in the country, and I must say that even I . . ."

Maigret was no longer listening. He was thinking of

Aline Calas, whom he was now able to see in the round. He could even imagine her as a little girl.

He was not surprised or shocked. He would have found it hard to explain what he felt about her, especially to a man like Judge Coméliau. On that score, he had no illusions; he would be listened to tomorrow with amazement and disbelief.

Coméliau would protest:

"They killed him just the same, she and that lover of hers."

Omer Calas was dead, and he certainly had not taken his own life. Someone, therefore, had struck him down, and subsequently dismembered his body.

Maigret could almost hear Coméliau's acid voice:

"What can you call that but cold-blooded? You can't imagine, surely, that it was a *crime passionnel*? No, Maigret, you've talked me around before, but this time . . ."

Canonge held up his brimming glass:

"Cheers!"

"Cheers!"

"You look very thoughtful."

"I was thinking about Aline Calas."

"Do you think she took up with Omer just to spite her father?"

Even to the notary, even under the influence of several glasses of brandy, he could not put his feelings into words. For a start, he would have to convince him that everything she had done, even as a kid in the Château de Boissancourt, had been a kind of protest.

Doctor Petrelle, no doubt, would have been able to express it better than he could. To begin with, the fire setting; then, her sexual relations with Calas, and finally, her flight with him in circumstances in which most other girls would have procured an abortion.

This too, perhaps, had been an act of defiance? Or revulsion?

Maigret had often tried to persuade others, men of wide experience among them, that, of all people, those most likely to come to grief, to seek self-abasement and degradation with morbid fervor, almost with relish, are the idealists.

To no avail. Coméliau would protest:

"If you said she was born wicked, you'd be nearer the truth."

At the bistro in the Quai de Valmy, she had taken to drink. This, too, was in character. And so was the fact that she had remained there without ever attempting to escape, allowing the atmosphere of the place to engulf her.

Maigret believed he understood Omer too. It was the dream of so many country boys to earn enough money in domestic service, or as a chauffeur, to become the proprietor of a bistro in Paris. For Omer the dream had come true.

It was a life of ease, lounging behind the bar, shuffling down to the cellar, going to Poitiers once or twice a year to buy wine, spending every afternoon playing billiards or *belote* in a brasserie near the Gare de l'Est.

There had not been time to investigate his private life. Maigret intended to go into that in a day or so, if only to satisfy his own curiosity. He was convinced that, when he was not indulging his passion for billiards, Omer had had a succession of shameless affairs with local servant girls and shop assistants.

Had he counted on inheriting the Boissancourt property? It seemed unlikely. He must have believed, like everyone else, that de Boissancourt had disinherited his daughter.

It had taken the notary's visiting card to arouse his hopes.

"I've had to do with all sorts in my time," Canonge was saying, "but what I simply can't understand—indeed, I confess it's quite beyond me, my dear fellow—is how, with a fortune landing in her lap out of the blue, she could bring herself to turn it down."

To Maigret, however, it seemed perfectly natural. As she was now, what possible use could she make of the money? Go and live with Omer in the Château de Boissancourt? Set up house with him in Paris or elsewhere—the Côte d'Azur for instance—in the style of rich landowners?

She had chosen to stay where she was, in the place where she felt safe, like an animal in its lair.

Day had followed day, all alike, punctuated by swigs of brandy behind the kitchen door, and Dieudonné Pape's company in the afternoons.

He too had become a habit, more than a habit, perhaps, because he knew. She need not feel ashamed with him. They could sit side by side in companionable silence, warming themselves by the stove.

"Do you believe she killed him?"

"I don't think so."

"It was her lover, then?"

"It looks like it."

The musicians were putting away their instruments.

Even this place had to close sometime. They found themselves outside in the street, walking in the direction of
Saint-Germain-des-Prés.

"How far do you have to go?"

"Boulevard Richard-Lenoir."

"I'll walk with you part of the way. What could have induced the lover to kill Omer? Was he hoping to persuade
her to change her mind about the estate?"

They were both unsteady on their feet, but quite up to
roaming the streets of Paris, which they had to themselves
but for an occasional passing taxi.

"I don't think so."

He would have to take a different tone tomorrow with
Coméliau. At the moment, he suddenly realized, he was
sounding quite maudlin.

"Why did he kill him?"

"What would you say was the first thing Omer would do
when he got back from Saint-André?"

"I don't know—lose his temper, I imagine, and order his
wife to accept the inheritance."

Maigret saw again the table in the bedroom, the bottle of
ink, the blotter, and the three sheets of blank paper.

"That would be in character, wouldn't it?"

"No doubt about it."

"Supposing Omer ordered her to write a letter to that
effect, and she still refused?"

"He'd have thrashed her. He was that sort—a real peasant."

"He did resort to violence on occasion."

"I think I can see what you're getting at."

"He doesn't bother to change when he gets home. This is

Saturday afternoon, around four. He marches Aline up to her room, orders her to write the letter, uses threatening language, and starts knocking her about."

"At which point the lover shows up?"

"It's the most likely explanation. Dieudonné Pape knows .is way about the house. He hears the row in the bedroom, and rushes upstairs to Aline's rescue."

"And does the husband in!" finished the notary, with a snigger.

"He kills him, either deliberately or accidentally, by hitting him on the head with something heavy."

"After which, he chops him up!"

Canonge, who was distinctly merry, roared with mirth.

"It's killing!" he exclaimed. "I can't help laughing at the thought of anyone carving up Omer. I mean to say, if you'd known Omer . . ."

Far from sobering him up, the fresh air, on top of all he had drunk, had gone to his head.

"Do you mind walking back with me part of the way?"

They faced about, walked a little way, and then turned back again.

"He's a strange man," murmured Maigret, with a sigh.

"Who? Omer?"

"No, Pape."

"Don't tell me he's called Pape, on top of everything else!"

"Not just Pape, Dieudonné Pape."

"Killing!"

"He's the mildest man I've ever met."

"No doubt that's why he chopped up poor old Omer!"

It was perfectly true. It took a man like him, self-sufficient, patient, meticulous, to remove all traces of the crime. Not even Moers and his men, for all their cameras and apparatus, had been able to find any proof that a murder had been committed in the house on the Quai de Valmy.

Had Aline Calas helped him scrub the place from top to bottom? Was it she who had got rid of the sheets and clothes, with their tell-tale stains?

Pape had slipped up in one particular: he had not foreseen that Maigret would be puzzled by the absence of dirty linen in the house, and would make inquiries of the laundry. But how could he have foreseen that?

How had those two imagined their future? Had they believed that weeks, possibly months, would elapse before any part of Calas's body was found in the canal, and that by then, it would be beyond identification? That was what would have happened if the Naud brothers' barge had not been weighed down by several extra tons of gravel, and scraped the bottom of the canal.

Where was the head? In the river? In a drain? Maigret would probably know the answer in a day or two. Sooner or later, he was convinced, he would know everything there was to know, but it was of merely academic interest to him. What mattered to him was the tragedy and the three protagonists who had enacted it, and he was certain he was right about them.

Aline and Pape, he felt sure, once all traces of the murder had been eradicated, had looked forward to a new life, not very different from the old.

For a while, things would have gone on as before, with Pape coming into the little café every afternoon for a couple of hours. Gradually, he would have spent more and more time there. In time, the neighbors and customers would have forgotten Omer Calas, and Pape would have moved in altogether.

Would Aline have continued to receive Antoine Cristin and the other men in the kitchen?

It was possible. On this subject, Maigret did not care to speculate. He felt out of his depth.

"It really is good night, this time!"

"Can I phone you tomorrow at your hotel? There are various formalities to be gone through."

"No need to ring me. I shall be in your office at nine."

Needless to say, the notary was not in Maigret's office at nine, and Maigret had forgotten that he had said he would be. The Superintendent was not feeling any too bright. This morning, in response to a touch on the shoulder from his wife, he had opened his eyes, with a feeling of guilt, to see his coffee already poured out for him on the bedside table.

She was smiling at him in an odd sort of way, with unusual maternal tenderness.

"How are you feeling?"

He could not remember when he had last waked up with such a dreadful headache, always a sign that he had had a lot to drink. It was most unusual for him to come home tipsy. The annoying thing was that he had not even been aware that he was drinking too much. It had crept up on him, with glass after glass after glass of brandy.

"Can you remember all the things you were telling me about Aline Calas in the night?"

He preferred to forget them, having an uneasy feeling that he had grown more and more maudlin.

"You talked almost like a man in love. If I were a jealous woman . . ."

He flushed, and was at some pains to reassure her.

"I was only joking. Are you going to say all those things to Coméliau?"

So he had unburdened himself about Coméliau as well, had he? Talking to Coméliau was, in fact, the next item on the agenda—in somewhat different terms, needless to say!

"Any news, Lapointe?"

"Nothing, sir."

"I want you to get an advertisement into the afternoon edition of the newspapers. Say that the police wish to interview the young man who was given the job of depositing a suitcase at the Gare de l'Est last Sunday."

"Wasn't that Antoine?"

"I'm sure it wasn't. Pape would realize that it had much better be done by a stranger."

"The clerk says . . ."

"He saw a young man of about Antoine's age, wearing a leather jacket. That could be said of any number of young men in the district."

"Have you any proof that Pape did it?"

"He'll confess."

"Are you going to interrogate them?"

"At this stage of the proceedings, I imagine, Coméliau will be wanting to do it himself."

It was all plain sailing now, a mere matter of putting questions at random, or "fishing," as they called it among themselves.

Anyway, Maigret was not at all sure that he wanted to be the one to drive Aline Calas and Dieudonné Pape to the wall. Both would hold out to the bitter end, until it was no longer possible to remain silent.

He spent nearly an hour upstairs in the judge's office. He rang Maître Canonge from there. The telephone bell must have waked the notary with a start.

"Who's there?" he asked, in such comical bewilderment that Maigret smiled.

"Chief Superintendent Maigret."

"What time is it?"

"Half past ten. Judge Coméliau, the Examining Magistrate in charge of the case, wishes to see you in his office as soon as possible."

"Tell him I'll be right over. Shall I bring the Boissancourt papers?"

"If you will."

"I hope I didn't keep you up too late?"

The notary must have got to bed even later. God knows where he landed up after I left him, thought Maigret, hearing a woman's sleepy voice asking: "What's the time?"

Maigret returned to his office.

"Is he going to interrogate them?" Lapointe asked.

"Yes."

"Starting with the woman?"

"I advised him to start with Pape."

"Is he more likely to crack?"

"Yes. Especially as he was the one who struck Calas down, or so I believe."

"Are you going out?"

"There's something I want to clear up at the Hôtel-Dieu."

It was a small point. Lucette Calas was in the operating theater. He had to wait until the operation was over.

"I take it you've read the papers, and know of your father's death and your mother's arrest?"

"Sooner or later, something of the kind was bound to happen."

"When you last went to see her, was it to ask for money?"

"No."

"What was it, then?"

"To tell her that, as soon as he gets his divorce, Professor Lavaud and I are going to be married. He might have asked to meet my parents, and I wanted them to be presentable."

"Don't you know that Boissancourt is dead?"

"Who's he?"

She was genuinely bewildered.

"Your grandfather."

Casually, as though the matter were of no importance, he said:

"Unless she's convicted of murder, your mother is heir to a château, eighteen farms, and goodness only knows how many millions."

"Are you quite sure?"

"Go and see Maître Canonge, the notary, at the Hôtel d'Orsay. He's administering the estate."

"Will he be there all day?"

"I imagine so."

She did not ask what was to become of her mother. As he walked away, he gave a little shrug.

Maigret had no lunch that day. He was not hungry, but

a couple of glasses of beer settled his stomach more or less. He shut himself up in his office the whole afternoon. In front of him on the desk lay the keys to the bistro in the Quai de Valmy and Pape's flat. He polished off a mass of boring administrative work, which he usually hated. To-day, he seemed to be taking a perverse delight in it.

Each time the telephone rang he snatched it off the hook with uncharacteristic eagerness, but it was after five o'clock before he heard the voice of Coméliau on the line.

"Maigret?"

"Yes."

There was a note of triumph in the magistrate's voice. "I have had them formally charged and arrested."

"All three of them?"

"No. I've released the boy Antoine."

"Have the other two confessed?"

"Yes."

"Everything?"

"Everything that *we* suspected. I decided that it would be a good idea to start with the man. I outlined my recon-struction of the crime. He had no choice but to confess."

"What about the woman?"

"Pape repeated his admissions in her presence. It was impossible for her to deny the truth of his statement."

"Did she have anything else to say?"

"No. She just asked me, as she was leaving, whether you had seen to her cat."

"What did you say?"

"That you had better things to do."

Maigret could never forgive Judge Coméliau for that.

weather and spunky repartee. Spunky repartee at that
the morning, Lance felt, was unnatural. He suspected
ere on speed.

elentlessly energetic young person guided him over a
f thick serpentine cables and had him crouch down just
camera range, waiting for a commercial break to go up
e set.

ur next guest," said the suspiciously spunky woman
he break, "is a man who single-handedly sailed from
York City to the Isle of Skye using only a dinghy and a
ade out of a bed sheet."

ce looked around the studio for the man she might be
bing and found that the relentlessly energetic young
n was motioning for *Lance* to go up to the ersatz
fast nook.

, I think there's been some mistake," said Lance in
sion.

od morning, Mr. Lerner," said the spunky young man.
tended his hand for a shaking and pulled Lance on
a.

od morning," said Lance, "but I think there's been a
e here."

want to hear all about Mr. Lerner's voyage across the
ic in that *dinghy*," said the spunky woman, "but first
ve to pause for one more commercial message."

red light on the camera went out.

ten," said Lance, "I think there's been a mistake

spunky man frowned.

at kind of a mistake?" he said.

out who I am," said Lance.

en't you the author of *Gallivanting?*" said the spunky
, now also frowning.

s," said Lance, "but the book is a novel about a young
ating and having romantic relationships with women,
s not about sailing across the Atlantic in a dinghy with a
et for a sail."

man and woman looked at each other, no longer
.

re must have been some mix-up," said the man, "but
ttle too late to do anything about it. We've got the stills
on the easels and everything."

use me?" said Lance.

re a live show, Mr. Lerner," said the woman. "Our

194

57

Upon boarding the plane to Pittsburgh, he was not at all
surprised to find that the temperature in the cabin was
approximately ninety-eight degrees Fahrenheit. Shortly after
takeoff it usually dropped to a degree or two above freezing.
He generally brought with him a long underwear T-shirt and
a sweater to ward off frostbite, and changed clothes in one of
the plane's tiny lavatories. Any time it took him more than
sixty seconds, some shmuck was banging on the door, asking
if he was all right in there—if you were in the john any longer
than the time necessary to urinate they figured you were
having a stroke or engaging in unnatural sex acts.

When the drink cart came down the aisle after takeoff,
Lance obtained two Bloody Mary mixes without vodka. As
soon as the stewardesses were three rows past him, Lance
reached into his shoulder bag and withdrew a flask of vodka
and surreptitiously poured a couple of fingers into each drink.
He resented paying two-fifty apiece for vodka miniatures that
cost the airline a couple of cents, but sneaking his own vodka
into their Mr. and Mrs. T or Snap-E-Tom made him feel like
an axe murderer.

By the time he reached Pittsburgh, he was slightly juiced.
His schedule of interviews indicated that his first one was
tonight, on a live radio program from midnight till two a.m. It
was called *Middleman at Midnight*.

When he got out of the terminal at the Pittsburgh airport
he was surprised to find it was about fifty degrees and raining.
When he'd left New York it had been at least ninety. He
flagged a cab, put his luggage inside, and gave the cabdriver
the address of the radio station.

The cab let him off at a quarter to twelve in what looked
like a deserted industrial park. As the rain slanted into his

191

face, Lance slowly circled a series of rakishly modern buildings, unable to find either a street number or an unlocked entry door. From a public phone across the street, he dialed the radio station. It was now midnight, and he was supposed to be on the air.

After forty-five rings a grouchy male voice answered.

"Hi," said Lance, shivering in the cold, trying to speak above the whine of the wind and the splatter of rain. "This is Lance Lerner. I'm a guest on your show, *Middleman at Midnight,* but I can't seem to find the entrance to your building."

"Who'd you say this was?" said the voice.

"Lance Lerner," said Lance. "Author of *Gallivanting?* I'm supposed to be on *Middleman at Midnight.*"

"I doubt it," said the voice.

"What do you mean you doubt it?" said Lance.

"I mean," said the voice, "that *Middleman at Midnight* was never *on* this station, plus which it went off the air about six or seven months ago. I sure don't know what you're doing here now."

"I sure don't either," said Lance with disgust and hung up the phone. By the time he managed to get another cab to go to his hotel he was soaked to the bone. And his first interview the following morning was at six-fifteen a.m.

It was a great beginning.

58

When the wakeup call came it was still dark out. He knew he'd had only four hours of sleep and that getting out of bed in his condition was going to be a major accomplishment. With four hours of sleep he had the capacity to fall asleep instantly at any stage in the getting-up process. Fortunately, he had a technique:

He reached for his battered Porsche
so hard the pain in his hand kept him aw
up and swing his legs over the side of th
legs were over the side of the bed he dro
did fifty pushups. By the time he had fini
was breathing hard enough to keep him
the bathroom.

Once he'd washed his face and brushed
up the phone again and called room servi
eggs over easy, a large grapefruit juice an
how long it would take to be delivered. A
Hispanic voice at the other end of the line

He went back into the bathroom and go
mentally reviewing all the steps in his daily
ready to face the world—exercising, showe
shaving, brushing, blow-drying, dressing,
those things to do every morning and
experienced in merely getting out of bed
complete waste of time to be up and around
before beginning the whole process all over
going to *get* up, you might as well *stay* up for
a crack.

Within sixty seconds of entering the sho
violent knocking on his hotel-room door. C
his head out of the shower and yelled, "Wh

"*Rune sorbis!*" said a heavy Hispanic acce

It never failed. When you asked room ser
would take for your food to arrive they al
minutes. If you waited thirty minutes before
shower, they came in thirty-one. If you waite
came in forty-seven. If you jumped in the sho
ly upon ordering, they came in a minute and
an uncanny ability to know when you were na
wet. Once he'd outwitted them—he had wait
and they still hadn't come, so he turned
without getting into it. Sixty seconds after
water, room service knocked on the door.
been palpably disappointed to find he was st

He arrived at the TV station at six-ten a.
young man and woman were sitting at an
nook beside a window through which could
lovely ersatz pastoral scene. They were a

visuals were set up on easels by the art department some time ago. It's too late to change them."

"So?" said Lance.

"So," said the man, "do you think you could just be a good sport and talk about what we're prepared to talk about?"

"About voyages across the Atlantic in a dinghy?" said Lance incredulously.

"Yes."

"But I don't *know* about voyages across the Atlantic in a dinghy," said Lance.

"Ten seconds!" called the floor director.

"Can you just talk about sailing in general then?" said the woman.

"I've never sailed in my *life*," said Lance. "I get *nauseated* on the water."

"Five seconds!" called the director.

"Won't you just please do this for us, fella?" said the man with a tightly set face. "It's not a helluva lot to ask."

"Three . . . two . . . *one* . . . " said the director.

"I'll see what I can do," mumbled Lance, but he knew it was going to be a farcical experience at best.

59

Following the show in which Lance had to spend sixteen minutes making up anecdotes about seagoing voyages he'd never taken, he was scheduled to appear on a TV talk show with a large studio audience. At certain intervals in this show, the host, for no discernible reason, spun a huge wheel with numbers on its face and then made local phone calls at random and asked inane questions of whoever answered.

Lance was scheduled to be on the show after a woman who had learned to be a gourmet cook despite the fact that she had no arms, and right after a female animal trainer and her two star pupils—a tiger that could sit on its hind legs and play a concertina, and a python that could light its trainer's cigarette —and right before an eighty-year-old woman wearing jogging shorts and a T-shirt on which was emblazoned the message JOGGING FOR JESUS. The elderly jogger had made her way from Seattle as far as Pittsburgh on a coast-to-coast journey to promote the religious sect of which she was a member, and Lance rather liked her at first.

Unfortunately, the tiger shit on the floor, the python vomited up a half-digested rabbit, and the cooking demonstration of the armless gourmet went awry when the woman in her nervousness knocked a Cuisinart bowl full of béarnaise sauce off the counter with her hooks. By the time they cleaned up the tiger turds and python vomit and got the armless gourmet through her segment, they were running late.

A talent coordinator informed Lance and the elderly jogger in the Green Room that although they'd been promised two segments each, they would now only be able to do one. Lance accepted the news with equanimity. The elderly jogger was furious.

"Goddamn it," she said, "you give the cripple, the tiger and the snake two segments, you can't give the Lord only *one!*"

The talent coordinator tried to reason with her, but the octogenarian runner just got madder and madder. Eventually the Lord lost His only remaining segment, and Lance had to take it on for himself.

The next show Lance did that day was a taped radio show and he was informed that there was no telling when it would air, if ever. It was hosted by a smooth, fast-talking deejay who never got either Lance's name or the title of his book.

The next interview was on a listener-sponsored FM radio station, and the ponytailed young man who interviewed him was also his own engineer. The ponytailed man was either very new at both jobs or very inept, because he kept cutting them off the air and apologizing for it, and when they *were* on the air there was constant screeching feedback from the microphone.

"Hey, man," said the ponytailed fellow by way of explanation, "I'm so stoned I'm lucky I can do *this* good." Lance had to struggle through an hour and a half of this before the ordeal was over.

Lance's fifth show of the day was also an FM radio show, and he was pleasantly surprised to find that his female interviewer was not only literate and articulate but had also done quite a bit of research on Lance and on his writing. Maybe too much research. She asked him questions about his previous books, the answers to which he had long since forgotten. Why did people expect you to remember your own books?

His sixth interviewer of the day turned out to be a pleasant enough blind chap who, the moment they went on the air, said: "What ever made you write such a sensationalistic, opportunistic, superficial and crassly commercial piece of trash as *Gallivanting?*"

Lance was momentarily dumbfounded. It seemed possible that the sightless interviewer was kidding, in the hostile way that people who have no sense of humor seemed to think was funny. Lance hoped that was what the man was doing. It wasn't. The man had simply decided to be vile. Since there was an hour allotted to the show, and since Lance hadn't the sense or the guts to walk off the show, the guy had a lot of time in which to be vile. Lance began to fight back and got in some good counter-punches, but when the show was over he was bathed in sweat.

"Did you really hate my book that much?" said Lance as they were leaving the studio.

"Hell, no," said the young man. "In fact, I kind of liked it."

"Then why did you attack it?" said Lance.

"Controversy makes for better broadcasting," said the fellow, flashing Lance a victory sign and a sightless wink.

Lance's seventh and eighth interviews of the day were with newspapers. Interviewer number seven was a salty woman of about fifty-five who typed with a cigarette dangling out of her mouth, *Front Page* style, raining ashes on her blouse. Interviewer number eight was a nervous young girl straight out of journalism school who took notes on a lined green pad and asked not a single question that couldn't have been answered by reading the biographical handouts which were sent to all Lance's interviewers in advance.

Between the end of his eighth interview and his evening plane to Cleveland he had about an hour and a half. As usual when he had any time left over in a tour city, he tried to visit as many bookstores as he could. Not to see whether his book was in stock—it usually wasn't—but to meet the people who actually sold the books on the floor. With the number of new titles that appeared every month in this country most books got lost in the shuffle. If the salespeople he introduced himself to liked him, then maybe they'd read his book. If they read his book, and if they liked it, maybe they'd recommend it to their customers.

After a fast look in the "Books, Retail" section of the classified directory, Lance scribbled down the addresses of six bookstores whose names he recognized. He flagged a cab and gave the driver extra money to wait while he ran into each store and introduced himself to as many salespeople as he could, buying copies of his book retail, if available, and autographing them for the salespeople who seemed the most sympatico.

The cabdriver seemed mystified by all these lightning stops in bookstores. After the fifth stop he suggested that if Lance didn't find the book he was looking for in the next store he ought to try the public library.

Lance made the plane to Cleveland by about nine minutes, but he was back in the familiar rhythms of fast-paced book promotion tours, he knew that he did it well, and he began to feel very good about himself.

The trip, he suspected, would go all right now, at least for a while. The disaster, whatever it was, was still out there somewhere, waiting for him, biding its time, but it hadn't caught up with him yet, and he had just started hitting his stride.

60

He arrived at his hotel in Cleveland and immediately ordered dinner from room service and requested a wakeup call for five-thirty a.m. He fell asleep watching TV and when the wakeup call came he was still dressed and the TV set was buzzing unpleasantly. Room service brought breakfast as he began to rub shampoo into his scalp in the shower. The nine interviews in Cleveland went no better or worse than they had in Pittsburgh, except that the weather in Cleveland was hot and humid and running around town was a bigger energy drain in the heat.

He taped a TV show along with a group of guests who, if they had anything in common other than something to plug, only the talent coordinators knew for sure. Sitting on the couches with Lance and attempting to hold a conversation were Pittsburgh Steeler quarterback Terry Bradshaw, Yiddish novelist Isaac Bashevis Singer, fast-food king Tom Carvel, Supreme Court Justice Whizzer White, dwarf Latin actor Hervé Villechaize, and the Dalai Lama. All had written books. None could find them in bookstores in the cities they'd been touring. Every time Lance started to speak, the Dalai Lama cut him off.

Cincinnati, which he got to shortly after sundown, was warmer even than Cleveland. He liked the fact that the Cincinnati airport was not in Ohio but in Kentucky—he felt it was thoroughly consistent with the other absurdities in his life.

When he got to his first TV interview of the day he found it canceled. The show felt itself in competition with his second interview of the day, the *Joe Shine Show,* and said that since Lance was already doing Shine they wanted no part of him. It was a phenomenon he had encountered in other cities so he was not surprised, although he'd heard that if the guest was famous enough the rule didn't apply. When he got to the *Joe Shine Show* the producer took him aside for a hurried conversation.

"Have you heard anything about this show?" asked the producer. Lance shook his head. "Joe tends to be a little rough on his guests," said the producer, "but it really sells books. Now, I don't want to make you nervous, but whatever you do, don't try to shake hands with Joe and don't mention cancer or wooden legs."

It wouldn't have occurred to Lance to mention cancer or wooden legs, but by the time the show began taping, he was concentrating so hard on not shaking hands and not mentioning cancer or wooden legs that he could barely speak at all.

Chicago, his home town, was the next stop after Cincinnati, and it was hotter and more humid than Cincinnati by half. It was also a better book town—possibly the best, surpassing even New York. He loved the lakefront and the architecture and the Ritz-Carlton Hotel—one of the few new hotels he'd stayed in that did not feature outside elevators and revolving penthouse restaurants, both of which made him queasy—and he even managed to squeeze in forty minutes to have lunch with his parents.

"Look how he eats," said his mother to his father, painfully watching Lance as he wolfed down a chicken salad sandwich from room service in his room. "If I had known you like chicken so much, I would have brought you a whole one."

"That's wonderful, Mom," Lance said, "but what would I do with a whole chicken on the road?"

"Maybe you'd give some to the other authors," said his mother. "Maybe you'd send a piece to Cathy. How's she doing, by the way?"

It was clear his mother was dying to know more about his separation. It was also clear that transitions were not her long suit.

"I saw Cathy for her birthday," said Lance casually.

His mother and father exchanged pregnant glances.

"And?" they said in unison.

"And it doesn't really look like we're going to be getting back together after all," he said. "At least for a while."

"Is it another fellow?" said his father, leaning in close so nobody in the hotel should hear.

Lance debated about how much to tell them. A little knowledge with them, he'd always found, was a dangerous thing.

"There may or may not be another fellow," said Lance, "but that's not the point. The point is that Cathy thinks she has to live alone for a while and grow some more."

"How much does she need to grow?" said his mother. "She's already five foot nine."

"I didn't mean that kind of growing, Mom," he said.

"I know, I know," said his mother sighing. "Your mother isn't as dumb as you think she is, don't worry."

After his last interview of the day in Chicago his Dad drove him around to bookstores, and he was able to squeeze in an even dozen before tearing off to O'Hare airport.

"Racing around like this is the worst possible thing for your digestion," said his mother as she kissed him goodbye at the terminal. She pressed a cold foil-wrapped package into his hand as he disengaged himself from her arms.

"What's this?" he said.

"Poison," she said. "I'm trying to feed you poison. It's just a piece of brisket for your dinner tonight, so you shouldn't have to order up a chicken salad sandwich in your room."

Although he had the thawing piece of brisket in his pocket, when they served dinner on the plane Lance decided to give airline cuisine a try. When asked his choice of entrées, the man in the seat next to him waved the stewardess away.

"Don't talk to me about airplane food," said the man to Lance, who had thus far not talked to him about anything.

"Why is that?" said Lance.

"Oh, I know," said the man, "they've upgraded the plastic dishes they used to have in Coach to real china. They've upgraded the plastic knives and forks to real stainless steel. They've even upgraded the entrée selection from one to three. But whether you order the steak, the chicken or the pasta, what you get is a lump of plastic glop suspended in amber mucilage."

"I know what you mean," said Lance.

"You do, do you?" said the man. "One time I'm sitting on an airplane, trying to eat my amber mucilage, and I notice that the guy in the seat next to mine, where you're sitting now, is vomiting quietly into his dish. The stewardess comes by, whisks it away from him and serves it to the fellow in the seat ahead of me as a hot snack."

Lance looked carefully at the man to see if he were joking, but the man continued talking.

"I once brought some airplane food home with me in a little bag and gave it to my pussycats," he said. "No *way*. They'll eat fish heads, chicken necks, spoiled meat, even their own vomit—but airplane food? *Huh*-uh. *Sorry*, Charlie. *Forget* it."

When Lance's meal arrived he sent it back. The stewardess seemed genuinely pissed.

When Lance got off the plane in Detroit he was not terribly surprised to find that Detroit was just as hot as Chicago. He took off his jacket and opened his shirt all the way to his bellybutton in the cab ride to his hotel.

As he was checking in, the clerk behind the desk noted his registration and then said:

"You have a little surprise waiting for you in your room, Mr. Lerner."

"I have?" said Lance. He didn't like surprises, especially since his fortieth birthday party. "What *kind* of a surprise?"

"I probably shouldn't tell you this," said the clerk, "but your wife checked in an hour ago. She's waiting for you in your room."

61

Lance was insanely happy. Cathy! Here in Detroit! Waiting for him in his hotel room to surprise him! But how did she know where to find him? Easy. Howard had his schedule. She had got it from Howard. She'd obviously told Howard about her birthday dinner, about Lance's discovery of the snapshots, about Lance asking her to come back to him. Howard had doubtlessly tried to dissuade her, but she'd been adamant. How could she give up Lance for a balding, paunchy man with an effeminate accent? She couldn't.

He left his bags with the bellman, and went racing around

the neighborhood, looking for a florist. He found one just about to close.

"Please!" he hollered through the locked glass door. "It's an emergency! My wife has come back to me and I have to buy her flowers!"

The diminutive old man who owned the shop sold him two dozen lavender roses and Lance raced back to the hotel. Too impatient to wait for the elevator to arrive, he sprinted up six flights of stairs and stopped outside the door of his room. He took a deep breath, unlocked the door and let himself into the room.

She had drawn the drapes and gotten into bed to await his arrival. He rushed to the bed, still holding the flowers, and reached out to her with his free hand.

"Darling!" he whispered. "What a wonderful surprise!"

"I thought you'd appreciate it," she said.

It was Claire.

Claire!

Claire, not Cathy!

He staggered backwards. The roses slipped from his hands, fell to the carpet.

"Lance, what's wrong?" said Claire.

He shook his head. The sense of loss, of crushing, over-powering disappointment, almost collapsed his lungs. He backed into a desk chair and sagged into it.

"My God, what is it?" she said, getting out of bed.

She was wearing a fantastic ivory silk nightgown and she looked sensational. But she wasn't Cathy.

"I'm sorry, Claire," he said. "I guess I was . . . expecting someone else."

She lowered her eyes.

"I thought you might," she said. "I realized that after I told the clerk at the desk. But he wouldn't have let me come up here any other way, and I did want to see you."

He nodded. He could see she was hurt. He didn't want to hurt her. He liked her. He really liked her. But she wasn't Cathy.

"Maybe I should go," she said.

"No, no," he said. "Please stay. I'll be all right in a minute. It's just that I'm kind of worn out from the tour. Just give me a minute, OK?"

She came over to him, started to touch him, then pulled back. She seemed insecure for the first time since he had met her. She really *is* vulnerable, he thought. How about that? He reached out for her, caught her hands and pulled her towards him. He pressed his face to her flat belly. It was soft. And warm. And it wasn't Cathy's.

"I'm glad you came," he lied. "It was a lovely surprise."

"And it would have been lovelier if I had been Cathy," she said gently.

He sighed.

"That's not untrue," he said at last.

They ordered dinner in the room. They talked about Cathy. Unexpectedly, Claire took Cathy's side against Lance. As they talked, Claire became more and more despondent. She said she no longer liked her life. She said her marriage was a joke.

"I thought you told me your marriage was *good*," said Lance. "I thought you told me your husband was an excellent provider, a strong protector, a considerate lover, and someone who hadn't bored you once in eighteen years."

"I did tell you that," she said.

"And it isn't true?" he said.

"And it isn't true," she said. "Austin neither provides nor protects, nor does he make love to me. And the reason that he doesn't bore me is that he's never around. If he *were* around, he *still* wouldn't be around. And that *is* boring."

"Why don't you leave him?" he said.

"I can't."

"Why not?"

"Because. I've gotten too used to the lifestyle. And I'm too old now to start over with somebody else."

"At forty?"

"Yes," she said. "Besides, I doubt that anybody who'd want me now wouldn't bore me even more than Austin."

"Do I bore you?" said Lance.

She shook her head.

"Why don't I?" he said.

"I don't know, Lance. At least with you there's somebody home. You actually listen when I speak, which is quite rare. And you even seem to care about my feelings, which is positively exotic. And you're something of an innocent, so it was fun for a while to play games with you and to try and shock you."

"It *was* fun, you say?"

She nodded.

"It was. It was enormous fun to force you to make love to me in your apartment, and in the limousine, and in my office. It was even *sort* of fun surprising you here in Detroit. Until you showed up, I mean. But now it's not fun anymore."

He kissed her cheek.

"I'm sorry," he said. "If the clerk had said anything at all except that my wife was waiting in my room . . ."

"I know. Well, that's the way it goes."

She slipped out of her nightgown and began to get dressed.

"Why are you getting dressed?" he said.

"There's still one plane I can catch back to New York tonight."

"Don't go, Claire," he said.

She stopped dressing and looked at him.

"Why not?"

"I want you to stay," he said. "I want to make love to you."

"I don't understand," she said.

"I like you," he said. "I like making love to you."

He walked over to her. He took her face in his hands and kissed her tenderly on the forehead, on her nose, on her chin, on her lips. He gently took off all the clothes she'd put on.

They went to bed. Their lovemaking was much fuller than the other times. He felt that she was much more present than the other times. He felt touched. He felt that she was getting emotionally involved.

Just as she was ready to climax, the telephone rang. He didn't move to answer it. He never answered ringing telephones when he was making love. The phone continued to ring. It broke their concentration completely, but they continued just to win out over the accursed ringing. It rang twenty times. It rang thirty times. It rang forty times.

"Answer it," she said.

He shook his head.

"Please answer it," she said.

"There's nobody I want to talk to now," he said.

The phone continued to ring. Finally *she* picked it up.

"Hello?" she said.

There was silence at the other end of the line. Then a woman's voice asked if she had the right room, if this was Mr. Lerner's room.

"Yes," said Claire, "this is Mr. Lerner's room."

The voice asked who Claire was.

"This is *Mrs.* Lerner," said Claire.

There was another silence at the other end. Then the

woman asked to speak to Lance. Claire handed Lance the phone.

"Lance Lerner speaking," he said into the phone.

"Lance? It's Cathy."

"Cathy!" said Lance.

"Oh my God," said Claire.

"Who was that woman who said she was Mrs. Lerner?" said Cathy. "*I'm* Mrs. Lerner."

"It . . . doesn't matter," said Lance.

"Was that Claire Firestone?" said Cathy.

Lance was astonished.

"Why would you ask me that?" he said.

"Because. Howard said Claire Firestone requested your current itinerary. Howard said he thought there might be something going on between you two. Is there, Lance? Is that who's with you?"

Lance thought Cathy might be crying.

"Cathy, what is it?" he said.

"Is that who's with you, Claire Firestone?" she said.

"What's the difference?" he said.

"Are you making love to her?"

"No," he said.

"Yes, you are," she said.

"Whatever you like," he said.

She was definitely crying. Well, the hell with her. She's fucking Howard. She deserves this, he thought. But the sound of her crying was more than he could bear.

"Cathy, what's wrong. Can I help you?"

"I need to talk to you," she said.

"Go ahead," he said. "I'm here."

"Not on the phone," she said. "When are you coming home?"

"Next Friday."

"Oh," she said.

"Do you want to see me next Friday?"

"I guess so," she said. "Call me when you get in. Call me from the airport."

"Can't you at least tell me what it's about?" he said.

"I'll tell you next Friday."

They said goodbye and he hung up the phone. Whatever it was wasn't that urgent if it could keep till next Friday. Could it be that she wanted to come back? Great. She decides to come back, she calls to tell me, and a woman answers the

206

phone and says *she's* Mrs. Lerner. Is that why Cathy was so upset? It seemed the likeliest possibility.

"I'm sorry," said Claire. "I should never have answered your phone. It was just driving me crazy."

"Don't worry about it," he said.

He put his arm around her, but she pulled away. She got dressed without speaking and went back to New York.

He wondered how he was going to be able to wait until next Friday.

62

It was going to be harder than she thought.

Not getting the information—getting the information was the easiest part. She had gotten Lance's phone number and address right out of the Manhattan directory. She was amazed that anybody as famous as Lance was listed in the Manhattan directory. But when she called him up, some kid answered the phone and said he was out of town, promoting his new book. She had used her head and told the kid that she wanted to interview Lance and needed to know when he'd be back. And the kid said Friday night late.

If the kid hadn't told her, she would have called his publisher and got the information. So all she had to do now was go to his apartment Friday night and tell him the good news—that she, Gladys Oliphant, was going to have his baby.

All well and good. All easy as pie.

So now it was Friday night, and she had put on her sexiest Antron nylon dress, and she had gotten her hair all sprayed and gussied up, and she was shaking so badly that she had to knock down about six beers and a couple shots of rye to give her courage. She was shaking less now, but she was not quite so steady on her feet.

She telephoned Lance's apartment again and the same kid

answered. She asked for Lance and was told that he wasn't expected for another hour or so. She went to his address and waited for him across the street. Telling him would be the hardest part. But then he'd know and he'd be so happy there wouldn't be anything to worry about.

63

Lance got off the plane at JFK. Although it was ten o'clock at night the air outside was like a steam room. What was August weather doing at the end of September?

He was completely exhausted. Ten cities in two weeks in all this heat, with an average of four hours' sleep each night, had taken its toll. At least the book was beginning to move. Howard had telephoned him in Los Angeles to say that all he needed to make it onto the bottom of the bestseller list was one network TV appearance. *Merv Griffin, Mike Douglas, Phil Donahue, Good Morning America,* the *Today Show* or the *Tonight Show.* Any one of them could do it. Every one of them had turned him down. Howard was going to try the *Tonight Show* again. It was a fifty-fifty shot, he said.

Lance went to a pay phone in the air terminal and called Cathy. She was relieved to hear he was back. At first she suggested he come to her apartment, but then she changed her mind. If he went directly home and she left in a little while, they could meet at their old apartment at about ten-thirty or so and save a good twenty minutes.

Lance called Dorothy and Janie at his apartment. They were overjoyed to hear from him and wanted to know all about the trip. He said he'd give them the details later—right now he needed a favor: Get lost for a couple of hours while he talked to Cathy at the apartment. They said they'd see him later.

Lance got in line for a cab, and when it was time to lift his bags into a taxi, he was so weak he almost fell over. The cabbie figured he was a wino.

Lance dragged himself up the stairs, opened the door and collapsed onto the floor of his apartment, sweating profusely and breathing hard.

After a few moments he was strong enough to stand up. He was just about to go into the bathroom to wash his face and brush his teeth when the doorbell rang. He considered a lightning fast trip to the bathroom, then said the hell with it. He buzzed her in.

He opened the door and looked down the steps and beheld, not his beautiful slim wife, but a monstrously fat woman, wet with perspiration and drunk as a skunk. It took him a moment before he realized it was Gladys Oliphant.

"Hi there, gorgeous," she said through the alcoholic vapors. "Remember me?"

"Gladys," he said without enthusiasm, "what a wonderful surprise."

"I jus' happened to be in the neighborhood," she said, "and I thought, 'why not drop by and see if old Lance is in.'"

"Well well," said Lance, "that's really nice. The thing is, though, Gladys, now is not a good time for a visit, because—"

"So that's jus' what I did—dropped by and saw if old you were in. And you were. And here I am."

Gladys had gained the topmost step and now, breathing hard, she pushed her way inside the apartment.

"Gladys, I wonder if I could ask you a tremendous favor."

"Anything," she said expansively, waving her hand and knocking over a floor lamp, "ask old Gladys anything at all. After all, we are more than friends, am I right? We have known each other carnally, as the Bible says, isn't that correct?"

"Yes, well, look, Gladys, the thing is that right now I'm expecting—"

"*You're* expecting! *I'm* expecting! That's what I came to talk to you about."

"Pardon me?" he said.

"I'm *expecting*. I'm preggers. And so are *you*. You're going to be a *father!*"

Lance was praying he hadn't heard what he was afraid he'd heard.

"Gladys, what are you *saying?*"

"Preggers. Pregnant. With child. In the family way. Gravid. Knocked up. Got a bun in the oven. And speaking of ovens, it feels like one in here. Mind if I get comfortable? Whooh!"

Gladys began taking off her clothes.

"Gladys, wait—hold on there! Please don't take off your clothes now! Please don't!"

"Why not?" she said, unbuttoning her dress. "Afraid I'll turn you on again? Afraid you won't be able to resist me?"

As fast as she unbuttoned buttons, Lance was rebuttoning them in a futile attempt to keep her clothed. Gladys pulled ahead of him and popped her enormous breasts out of their mammoth brassiere.

"Well, big boy, here they are," said Gladys, half nude and holding out her arms to him. "Why not take all of me?"

She began to sing "All of Me."

"Gladys, listen to me! Will you listen to me? I am expecting my wife here at any moment, I can't have—"

"Your *wife!*"

Gladys was outraged.

"Yes, my wife," said Lance. "She's going to be here at any moment to discuss a very crucial problem. She—"

"You never told me you had a wife!" she said. "If I knew you had a wife, would I have given myself to you? I would most certainly *not*, sir. A wife *indeed!*"

"Gladys, will you please *listen* to me!" he screamed.

That appeared to quiet her momentarily. He felt a flash of compassion for the large, seminude woman who might now be carrying his child, but there were more pressing matters at hand.

"Now listen, Gladys," he said, "I heard what you were telling me, that you're pregnant, and I'm very concerned about it. Very concerned. And I really want to discuss with you what we should do about it, I really do. But I can't do it now. Now my wife is coming. And she can't find you here without your clothes on."

"I should think *not!*" said Gladys.

"So if you would please *please* just get dressed and leave right now, I promise you on my word of honor that the moment she leaves I will call you and meet you anywhere at all to discuss this. All right? Will you do that for me?"

"I don't see why not," said Gladys, trying unsuccessfully to stuff her gigantic boobs back into her brassiere.

"Wonderful, wonderful," said Lance. "Just put your—"

The doorbell rang.

"Oh no," said Lance.

"Oh-oh," said Gladys.

"Too late," said Lance. "Oh my God!"

Lance looked wildly around for someplace to hide her. It was no mean assignment. The bedroom! He could hide her in the bedroom! The doorbell rang again.

"In here, Gladys!" he said, pushing her through the high double doors in his bedroom.

"Oh no you don't, smooth talker," said Gladys. "You're not getting *me* into your bed, no sir! That's how all this started in the *first* place!"

"Gladys, please. Just get dressed in here and wait for me. And don't make a sound, all right? Be as quiet as a mouse!"

He pulled the double doors closed behind him and went to answer the doorbell. In the bedroom Gladys had begun singing "All of Me" again. He dashed back into the bedroom, made shooshing noises and then had a brainstorm and turned on the TV.

The doorbell rang insistently. He pulled the double doors closed behind him and buzzed her in.

"Hi, Cathy!" he called down the steps. "I'm sorry it took so long—I was in the john!"

Cathy didn't say anything. By the time she got to the top of the steps he could see that she was crying. He took her in his arms and hugged her. In the bedroom, above the TV, he could still hear Gladys singing "All of Me."

"Cathy," he said, "what is it?"

"I don't know what to do," she said.

"About what?" he said.

"About Howard," she said.

"About Howard?" he said. "What *about* Howard?"

"I think he's getting tired of me," she said.

"He is?" said Lance. He didn't understand how he was supposed to feel about this extraordinary piece of news.

"He's stopped being spontaneous and romantic—just like you did—only with you it took two years, and with him about two weeks."

So here it was again, the same old complaint. You'd think she'd at least be diplomatic enough not to criticize him while asking for his help. Come to think of it, what kind of help was she asking for?

"How can I help you, Cathy?"

"You know him," she said. "And you know how a man's

mind works. What can I do to keep him from getting tired of me?"

Lance had to laugh in spite of himself. It was too ridiculous —being asked to counsel his own wife in renewing his rival's flagging ardor!

"Cathy, I love you dearly, you know that," he said. "But why in the world would I want to help keep you and Howard together?"

"Because," she said. "So far I don't love him. But if he continues to reject me, I'm afraid I'll fixate on him and I won't be able to see him objectively anymore, and then who *knows?*"

Gladys's singing in the bedroom had grown louder. Lance was frantic to silence her. Cathy had begun to cry again.

"Let me get you some Kleenex," said Lance, slipping into the bedroom and swiftly closing the door behind him. To his horror he saw that Gladys, instead of getting dressed, had removed every last article of clothing and was lying on the bed completely naked.

He turned up the volume on the TV and got down on his knees.

"Please, Gladys, please," he said. "Put on your clothes and be quiet. If you do I'll promise you anything in the world!"

"Even marry me?" said Gladys with delight.

"Uh, well, maybe not that," said Lance. "But anything else."

"Awww," said Gladys. "Why wouldn't you marry me?"

"Religious differences," said Lance. "But I will promise you anything else in the whole entire world."

"Lance?" called Cathy. "What are you doing?"

"Getting you some Kleenex," Lance called back. "Be right there!"

"Would you take me to dinner at Elaine's?" said Gladys.

"Absolutely," said Lance. "You get those clothes on and be quiet like a good girl, and I'll take you to Elaine's."

Gladys squealed and clapped her hands. Lance opened the double doors a crack and slid back out of the bedroom. Cathy looked at him curiously.

"Were you out?" she said.

"No, no," he said, "I was just in the bedroom."

"I meant out of Kleenex," said Cathy.

Lance realized with disgust that he'd come out of the bedroom empty-handed.

"Oh, out in *that* sense," said Lance. "Yes I am. I definitely am. But why don't you use my handkerchief . . ."

He searched his pockets for a handkerchief.

"That's OK," she said. "I don't need one."

"Yoohoo!" called Gladys from inside the bedroom.

Lance's heart stopped. Cathy turned in the direction of the bedroom doors.

"Yoohoo, Lance!" called Gladys again. "What night?"

"I don't *believe* it," said Cathy, suddenly furious. "You have a *woman* in our bedroom! You knew I was coming over, and you still have a *woman* in there!"

"Hold on a second," said Lance. "That's just Gladys."

"*Gladys?*" Cathy snorted. "Who the hell is *Gladys?*"

"Gladys is the woman that I have come in on Fridays. To clean. She's in there now, cleaning the bedroom. Watching TV and cleaning the bedroom."

Breathing fire, Cathy whirled and threw open the bedroom doors. Gladys, still naked, lay on the bed like a beached whale.

"I can explain this!" cried Lance, as Cathy went into hysterics and headed for the front door. "This is not what it seems, I swear to God, Cathy! Won't you let me explain?"

But Cathy was already halfway down the stairs and beyond recall.

There was at least one small consolation, thought Lance as Cathy slammed the door and ran out into the night—at least I *didn't* have to explain.

213

64

Julius Blatt was on top of the world. His hundred-dollar-a-plate dinner to free the Dalton Two was fast becoming one of the hottest charity events of the summer.

Already Blatt had formed a coalition of a number of unlikely groups, including the Authors Guild, the NAACP, the American Booksellers Association, the Black Panthers and the United Jewish Appeal. Plans for a telethon were being formed, and Sammy Davis, Jr., had agreed to co-host with Lillian Hellman.

An editor at Firestone Publishing by the name of Howard Leventhal had called Blatt personally and made an offer on the book that Ernest was reported to be writing on the Dalton Two: $250,000 hardcover advance against royalties, and a $100,000 guaranteed advertising and promotion budget.

Blatt told Leventhal he didn't know how good a deal that was and would have to ask his old friend, Lance Lerner. Leventhal said that he, personally, was Lance Lerner's editor, and that he could guarantee that the deal was much better than that which Lance himself had on his current book.

Blatt asked why Leventhal was offering a better deal on Ernest's book than on Lerner's, and Leventhal said that it was because Lerner was a known quantity on the market and Ernest wasn't. Blatt said he'd think about it.

Then a producer at Universal called Blatt, having read in Claudia Cohen's column that Ernest had signed a book contract on the Dalton Two, and offered $300,000 for the movie rights. Blatt said he'd gotten a better offer than that already from Warner Brothers, and that very afternoon Warners called and offered $575,000. Fox came in at $625,000 and Paramount at $800,000. Universal's final offer was $902,000, with Ernest writing the first-draft screenplay and Blatt executive-producing, and Blatt took it.

65

June Wedding.

If Hiram Wedding had loved his baby daughter any less he might not have burdened her with so self-conscious a name as June Wedding. If Hiram Wedding had loved his delicate and beautiful bride any less, she might not have died in childbirth scarcely eight months after they had married.

But Hiram hadn't loved either less, and so now here he was with a motherless baby and a dead wife and, little by little, he was starting to hit the bottle and to let his grip on reality loosen up and up, till finally there would be no grip left at all.

Hiram was a longshoreman on the Brooklyn docks. His body was so solidly packed with muscle that there were no soft places on it. Luckily for him his work on the docks depended on a firm grip on many things more important than reality. He would be able to earn enough to support Baby June for several years to come.

Baby June was not, alas, a pretty baby. Her name would prove to be a cruel joke. No one would ever wish to involve her in any kind of wedding, June or otherwise. She seemed to have inherited nothing from her beautiful dead mother but her sex. Instead June got her father's squat, powerful body and blunt-featured face. Hiram, in narcissistic and paternal blindness, thought that June was the queen of Sheepshead Bay.

As Baby June grew into young girlhood, even Hiram could see that she was turning out blunt and squat instead of finely honed and delicate. He tried to compensate, buying her only the frilliest of feminine clothing. It looked ridiculous on her squat, muscular body, but not to Hiram.

Since his wife's death, Hiram had been drinking more and more. Every night after leaving the shipyard he would go home and get loaded. Through the liquorish vapors his growing daughter occasionally looked to him like his poor dead wife. He held June in his drunken arms at night and sometimes he caressed her in places where fathers were not supposed to caress their daughters. Little June sensed that it was as wrong as it was physically pleasurable, and she grew to hate him for it.

When she was thirteen, June Wedding left her father's home. She left behind all her ludicrously inappropriate feminine clothing, and took with her only denim overalls and flannel shirts. In years to come she would buy satiny underwear like the things her father had forced on her while she was growing up and wear it secretly under her denim work clothes like a furtive male transvestite.

June Wedding held a number of jobs while she was growing up that most men wouldn't have been able to endure—loading and unloading trucks, servicing and repairing heavy machinery, driving tractor trailers as soon as she was old enough to get her license. She never finished school, but she was writing a bitter yet poetic first novel and she knew things that most men and women didn't. She was an able carpenter, plumber, electrician and mason. She could tear a transmission down and put it back together again. She could fly a plane and had nearly enough hours for a commercial pilot's license, although she doubted that any airline would hire her because she was a woman.

June's face was homely and she wore her hair chopped very short. She sought out the company of tough, masculine women. She hated men, but she didn't lust for women. She had, as far as she could tell, no desire for sex of any kind. When a female co-worker made a drunken pass at her, June almost tore her in half.

June stood for nothing. June stood *against* a number of things: She detested job discrimination based on sex. She detested male chauvinism of any kind. She detested male sexual aggression. Above all else, June Wedding detested rape. She read in the *New York Post* and the *Daily News* accounts of women being raped by men which could bring her to the boiling point. She had no fear of rape herself—she was stronger than most men—but she feared for the safety of her weaker friends. When a woman she worked with at a moving company called the Motherloaders was assaulted on the Lexington Avenue subway, she organized a small group she dubbed MATE—Men Are The Enemy.

The members of MATE began to do research on rape.

They photocopied newspaper stories on rape and discussed them endlessly. They took out of the public library and devoured every psychological study ever written on rape. They wrote an outline and a sample chapter for a book on rape and took it to several publishers, but they were turned down by thirty-two of them before they realized what was going on: the male pig editors had rejected their book for political reasons, and the female editors were Uncle Toms and Aunt Tessies and were scared to death to rock the boat and get in bad with their pig bosses. It was clear they would never be able to get it published. Not till after the revolution.

There were never more than four members of MATE— June and the three women at the Motherloaders whom she worked with most. They were all built short and squat and powerful like June. Like June, none of them had any sexual interest in either men or women.

Alix was the only member of MATE who had either long hair or breasts. They were not soft, feminine breasts, however. They were hard, muscular pectoralis majors, and they came from working out with weights. Alix did not need a bra.

Sandy had freckles, sandy-colored hair, heavy thighs, a nice smile, an ugly temper, and a broken nose. She had been a semi-pro boxer before joining the Motherloaders.

Wanda had a pretty face, a relatively trusting nature, and thighs as big around as Sandy's. She had the most feminine voice of the four of them and had a look of vulnerability that most men responded to. It was Wanda who'd been raped in the subway.

Two Hispanic men had caught Wanda in the sparsely populated Brooklyn Bridge station on the Lexington Avenue line. It was not late—about nine o'clock in the evening. The men seemed stoned. They began making sexual remarks to Wanda, and when she didn't respond, they took out folding knives. One held his blade against her neck, and the other pulled her pants down and raped her. There were at least a dozen and a half people in the subway station. None of them tried to help or to call for a transit policeman.

When both the men were finished raping Wanda, they threw her on the floor, called her a *puta*, and left. When the men had disappeared, some of the people in the subway station offered to help Wanda, but she refused and went into the ladies' room to wash off the filth.

Wanda didn't go to the police. She could not bear the prospect of a bunch of leering men asking her accusatory

217

questions. She went home and called her friends. Alix, Sandy and June immediately came over to her depressing furnished apartment in the East Village. They listened to the account of Wanda's degradation, they soothed her, they cursed and swore vengeance on her attackers.

For the next two weeks, they went with Wanda to the Brooklyn Bridge subway station and hung around there between the hours of eight-thirty and ten-thirty p.m., hoping to see the two Hispanic men again. They saw many Hispanic men. None of them looked to Wanda like her attackers.

On the nineteenth night, just as they were about to give up for another evening, the four women spotted a group of noisy Hispanic men at the end of the subway platform. They moved closer. There were three of them. One Wanda had never seen before, but the other two looked familiar to her.

Wanda wanted to leave. June told her to stay out of sight. Then she and Alix and Sandy strolled over to the three men and began making suggestive comments. The men responded. Joking loudly in Spanish, they drifted over to the three women and began to evaluate their sexual attributes. At a signal from June, each woman grabbed one of the men. Before the startled men knew what was happening, each found himself in a powerful hammerlock, with a straight razor pressed against his jugular vein.

June called out to Wanda to come and identify her attackers. But when Wanda drew close to them she was certain she had never seen these men before. June, Alix and Sandy were disappointed. They had been on their quest for nineteen consecutive nights now and they were eager for a taste of blood.

June said that although they may not have been the men who raped their friend, they were ugly male chauvinist pigs. They pulled the men into a nearby ladies' room and made them lie down on the floor. At June's direction, Wanda took out the scissors with which they had planned to castrate her attackers and merely cut off all the men's clothing.

When the three men were naked, the four women took turns disparaging the men's bodies, especially their genitals. Alix pulled down her jeans and sat on each of their faces. Sandy pulled down her jeans and peed on them. Then June took a can of aerosol paint and wrote slogans on the men's bodies. "RAPE IS A POLITICAL CRIME" and "MAKE WAR, NOT LOVE" are what she wrote.

66

Helen and the group were absolutely livid. What was Lance going to do about Gladys's pregnancy? Was he going to try to talk her into having an abortion? What if she refused? What if she wanted to have the baby? Was Lance willing to take responsibility for the child?

How could Lance possibly allow the situation between himself and Cathy and Howard to exist without confronting Howard about it? Didn't Lance see that all his apparent victimizations by women were actually things that he himself set up out of his repressed hostility to women and his subconscious desire to control them? Didn't Lance know that when you tried to repress your feelings in order to avoid losing control, they ended up controlling you, and that angry feelings accumulate until they explode?

Helen and the group urged Lance to have a serious talk with Gladys, and to come clean with Howard and let him know how he felt about what Howard had done. Various members of the group took turns being Gladys and Howard in a succession of psychodramas. Finally Lance agreed to confront both Gladys and Howard—more to halt the psychodramas than for any other reason. Lance telephoned Howard and made a lunch date with him for the following day. One o'clock in the Four Seasons Grill.

Howard was twenty minutes late. Lance was not surprised. With the load of ambivalence that Howard must be carting around these days, Lance was surprised that he showed up at all.

Howard did not look at all well. His thinning hair was thinning more than usual, his paunch was increasing, and his effeminate way of speaking had developed a soupçon of a stutter.

Howard observed that Lance looked unusually haggard, even for an author who'd been out touring. Howard said the book was still holding its own in sales, but that the *Tonight Show* had once again said no. Howard continued to talk, long after he had run out of things to talk about, and Lance realized he was simply trying to fill dead air because, were there to be a silence of any duration, something dreadful might pop out.

"Howard," said Lance after a while, "shut up."

Howard looked at Lance with alarm. All right, Lerner, thought Lance to himself, you've got your audience, now what are you going to do with it?

"Howard," said Lance, the anger beginning to well up inside of him, "I *know*."

Howard looked as if Lance had just pulled a gun on him.

"Y-you know w-*what?*" he said.

"Everything," said Lance. "I know everything that you've been doing with Cathy. I know you've been playing tennis with her. I know you've been romantic and spontaneous with her. I know you've been *un*romantic and *un*spontaneous with her. I know you've been fucking her brains out. I know everything. And I am vastly tempted to punch your fucking heart out, right here in the middle of the Four Seasons Grill."

Lance didn't quite know what Howard would do with the news. He certainly didn't expect Howard to do what he finally did. Howard burst into tears.

"Oh, my *God*," Howard blubbered, wetness spilling out of his eyes and nostrils. "Oh my dear sweet G-God in H-*Heaven!*"

Lance watched Howard bawl and decided it wasn't fair. When you finally got somebody dead to rights on something as serious as cuckolding and you were entitled to do anything at all to the guy and no court would be likely to convict you, what does the guy do but burst out crying. Could you attack a man who was crying? You could not.

"I f-feel so *horrible*," said Howard. "I f-feel like *scum!*"

"You *are* scum, Howard," said Lance.

"I f-feel like a g-gigantic bag of h-*horse manure!*" said Howard.

"You *are* a gigantic bag of horse manure, Howard," said Lance.

"I am s-so *ashamed* of myself I could d-*die!*" said Howard.

"That," said Lance, "would be a blessing."

"W-would it help at all to t-tell you I wasn't t-totally to b-*blame?*" said Howard.

"Are you going to tell me that my wife *seduced* you?" said Lance. "That would not be a fruitful direction to pursue."

"I d-don't mean to tell you *that*," said Howard, "b-but she certainly m-met me more than *halfway.*"

"I told you that isn't a fruitful direction to pursue, Howard," said Lance, "and cut out that stuttering. If you can't speak without stuttering, *sing.*"

Howard started to say something, began to stutter, started to apologize for stuttering, stuttered on the apology, and stopped talking altogether. Lance's anger at Howard dribbled away. In its stead stood disgust and pity. Picking on Howard was like beating up a paraplegic.

"All right, Howard," said Lance, "this isn't very satisfying. Let's not talk about it anymore."

"I'm so *s-sorry,* Lance," said Howard.

"I expect you are," said Lance.

"Does that mean you f-*forgive* me?" said Howard.

"It means that I think you're too pathetic to chastise," said Lance.

"Thank you," said Howard. "You're a much better p-person than I am."

"You can say *that* again," said Lance.

67

At 4:55 p.m. on a warm day in late September, four Hispanic-American youths—Tony Garcia, Vince Lopez, Juan Rivera and Pablo Moreno—walked into the big Brentano's bookstore at Fifth Avenue and 48th Street and announced that they were conducting a holdup.

Three cashiers brought them fistfuls of currency which they dumped into a flight bag emblazoned with the insignia of Lot

Polish Airlines. The most remarkable aspect of the crime was that, in lieu of fleeing, Garcia, Lopez, Rivera and Moreno hung around and chatted with the cashiers until the police arrived some forty minutes later.

When arresting officers Friedman and O'Rourke took them to the 17th Precinct to book them, the four demanded the right to call a public defender named Julius Blatt as legal counsel. In the ensuing telephone conversation between Garcia and Blatt, the following agreements were reached: (1) The group's slogan would be "Free the Brentano's Four"; (2) Blatt would represent them for 15% of all hard- and softcover royalties, 25% of all gross income from motion picture and television rights, and 50% of all gross profits from games, toys, and T-shirts.

68

Lance felt sick about Cathy's walking in on Gladys naked in his bed. He tried to reach Cathy many times by phone, but she hung up on him every time she heard his voice.

He wrote her a six-page letter, typed single-space, but after mailing it he feared that the Postal Service was too perverse to deliver it unsabotaged, and so he hand-delivered the carbon to her building and walked upstairs and slid it under her actual door.

He tried to reach Gladys several times by phone, but failed—it was either busy or there was no answer.

He went to his therapy group and told them about the latest developments in his life. Instead of the sympathy and encouragement he was expecting, the group gave him disapproval and disgust.

"What hidden payoff do you get from feeling weak and pushed around?" said Helen.

"What are you talking about?" said Lance.

"If you act shy and nebbishy, you think people will love

you more," she said. "If you act helpless, you think they'll take care of you."

"You let everybody control you," said Arnold. "You must love being victimized."

"You're crazy," said Lance. "Who have I let control me?"

"Everybody," said Arnold. "You let Dorothy and Janie move in on you. You let Gladys rape you and become pregnant by you. You let Cathy have an affair with your editor. You let Claire force you to have sex with her whenever she likes, wherever she likes, and under the most stressful and demeaning circumstances. You—"

"Now just hang on there a minute, Arnold," said Lance, beginning to get angry. "In the first place, I didn't *have* to let either Dorothy *or* Janie move in with me. I *wanted* them to move in with me. And—"

"*Sure* he wanted them to move in with him," said Jackie. "Because he wanted to *shtoop* them."

"That's not true," said Lance. "I haven't laid a glove on them and I'm not going to either."

"Bullshit," said Jackie.

"Bullshit yourself," said Lance. "You're just jealous."

"Jealous?" said Jackie. "Listen, bubie, if I wanted to have two teenybopper chink dykes sleeping on my living-room floor, I'd have them sooner than you could say 'Ho-ho-ho, Ho Chi Minh.'"

"Let's get back to what Arnold was saying, if you don't mind," said Helen. "About needing to be controlled by women."

"Yeah," said Lance, "let's get back to that. Now as far as Claire is concerned, I had sex with her under . . . exotic circumstances, but it was by choice. Nobody was *forcing* me to do anything at all. *I* was the one who decided if I wanted to do it. Not her. *Me.* I'm a completely free man—that's why she considers me such a challenge."

"A completely free man, eh?" said Roger. "Were you a completely free man when she said if you didn't have sex with her she'd tell her husband you made a pass at her?"

"Well," said Lance, "in a way, sure."

"Bullshit," said Jackie.

"Look," said Lance, "maybe the thing with Claire is a bad example. Publishing is a strange business, and sometimes you have to do some peculiar things to get your book before the public. Let's take another example. Like Cathy. I certainly didn't want Cathy to have an affair with my editor."

"You certainly did set it up, though," said Laura.

"What do you mean I set it up?" said Lance.

"You made a bare-assed pass at her best friend in front of all those people, causing her to leave you," said Arnold. "And then you informed your editor that she'd left you."

"If that's not setting it up," said Helen, "I don't know what is."

"All right," said Lance, "maybe Cathy's not the best example either. But you certainly can't say I wanted Gladys to rape me and then get pregnant because of it."

"Don't you take responsibility for your own ejaculations?" said Laura, blushing furiously.

Lance was shocked. He'd never heard Laura use a word like "ejaculations" before. Besides, he'd thought she liked him.

"Ejaculation," said Lance in a wounded tone, "is an involuntary physiological response."

"Bullshit!" said Jackie. "You mean to say you have no control over whether you come?"

"Well, sure I do," said Lance, "but—"

"How much effort did you exert to prevent yourself from coming?" said Helen.

"Well, none, really," said Lance, "but—"

"Did you try to discourage her in *any* way from having sex with you?" said Roger.

"I . . . I don't remember," said Lance.

"And you still maintain you had nothing to do with getting her pregnant?" said Arnold.

"Look," said Lance, "I was handcuffed to the *bed*. What could I have done to discourage her?"

"You could have said you didn't want to have sex with her," said Laura.

"How did you get handcuffed to the bed in the *first* place?" said Arnold. "Was the policewoman holding a gun to your head?"

"Hey," said Lance, "what's the point of all this? Are you trying to get me to say that everything that's happened to me is my fault?"

"We're trying to get you to see what part you played in each one of these situations and to take responsibility for them," said Helen. "If you can't take responsibility for what happens to you—if you can't see how the things you do contribute to what happens in your life—then you'll never be able to take charge of your life. You'll always be a victim."

So, he thought, even Helen, his own *therapist* was against him. What did *she* want? If he were at all paranoid, he'd have imagined she got them all together before he arrived and planned this. He had half a mind to not let them help him at all. Why was he paying thirty dollars a group session and fifty for private ones to be attacked like this? He could avoid all this grief and simply quit therapy. And if he really missed having people attack him, he could just go and walk the streets of New York and get it all for free.

"You know," said Helen, "I think Lance wouldn't be so eager to be controlled by women if he weren't so ambivalent about them."

"Ambivalent?" said Lance. "That's a laugh. I'm not ambivalent about women—I *love* women."

"I think you also have a lot of hostility toward them," said Laura.

"Hostility? Fuck you, Laura!" said Lance.

"You mean to tell me that when you thought Cathy was screwing Les you didn't feel hostile toward her?" said Roger.

"Well, sure," said Lance, "but that was only natural. *Anybody* would have felt hostile under those circumstances."

"But not everybody would have decided to remedy the situation by trying to fuck her best friend," said Helen. "That, to me, shows real hostility. That, to me, is like trying to assassinate somebody."

Lance thought it over.

"No," he said. "I didn't want to assassinate her. I just wanted to balance the scales, that's all."

"And what about the night you made love to her on her birthday, and then found out she was having an affair with Howard?" said Helen. "Did you want to assassinate her *then?*"

"No," he said. "Mostly I wanted to assassinate *Howard.*"

"If you can't feel the hostility," said Helen, "then you'll never be able to feel the love."

"I feel," said Lance, "all I want to feel."

"That I believe," said Helen.

225

69

The following afternoon Claire dropped by his apartment without warning to say hello. He was glad to see her and said so. Then Dorothy and Janie passed them on the staircase, headed for Lance's bathtub. Both girls were in their underwear, and when Claire caught sight of them her jaw dropped.

"That's, uh, Dorothy and Janie," said Lance. "They're staying here for a while till they find someplace else to live."

"I see," said Claire somewhat frostily.

"They're friends of mine," said Lance.

"I can imagine," she said.

"Look," said Lance, "there's nothing going on between us, if *that's* what you're thinking."

"I'll bet," said Claire.

He leaned in close to Claire and whispered.

"They're lovers," he said. "They have all they want in each *other*—they don't need me."

"Right," said Claire.

"You know," said Lance, "if I didn't know you better, I'd say you're jealous."

"Maybe I am," said Claire.

"Well, that's very flattering," said Lance, "but you shouldn't be."

Claire paced back and forth for several moments, thinking hard.

"All right," she said. "I *am* jealous. It's not a familiar feeling for me, so I guess I didn't recognize it at first. But that's definitely what it is. Do you know why someone gets jealous?"

"Why?"

"Because they start valuing someone too much and they begin to be afraid of losing them. They kid themselves that losing that person would be intolerable."

226

"I suppose you're right," said Lance.

"Oh, I'm right," said Claire, "don't worry. Anyway, I just realized I have started feeling that way about *you.*"

"You have?" said Lance. "That's nice."

"Not necessarily," said Claire. "Because I can't let myself get into those kinds of situations. So to protect myself here is what I propose to you: You give up your other women, and I will see to it that you never lack for sex, love, luxuries, or influence in the publishing world."

"What are you saying?" said Lance.

"I'm saying what I want—I don't want you to have any other women but me."

Lance smiled.

"Claire, get serious, will you? What am I supposed to tell people. that I'm going steady with Austin Firestone's wife?"

"We are not amused," she said.

"Well, I think you're being silly," he said.

"I'm not being silly, I'm being serious. If you agree to give up other women, I will give you everything you ever needed. You'll be one of the most successful writers in the world."

"And if I don't?" he said. "What will you do then, ruin my career?"

"Perhaps," she said.

Rage began to well up inside of him. How dare she try to buy him like that? How dare she try to control him? How dare she threaten him? Well, the group and Helen were wrong—he was damned if he was going to be controlled.

"OK, Claire," he said. "Go and do your worst."

"That's your answer?" she said.

"That's my answer," he said. "I'm a free man. Nobody buys me, nobody controls me, and nobody threatens me. And I'm not afraid of anything you could ever do to me either."

She wheeled and charged through the door. She stopped on the stairway and looked back up at him.

"You may be under the deluded impression that your wife and Howard Leventhal are almost finished with their seamy little liaison, and that you can get her back again," she said. "If so, you're an even bigger fool than I think you are."

"What's that supposed to mean?" said Lance. "What are you talking about?"

But she had got to him and she knew it. She was down the stairs and out onto the street and into her limousine before he could stop her.

70

Claire's parting shot had really rocked him. He didn't think she was bluffing. He thought she knew of a recent development. He had to know what it was.

He telephoned Cathy repeatedly through the day and night, but she didn't even pick up the phone. He took a cab to her building, rang her doorbell, but there wasn't any answer. He stood out in the middle of the street and tried to figure out where her windows were to see if they were lit. It was impossible to tell.

Well, he thought, if I can't find out through Cathy, then I'll find out through Howard. He telephoned Howard's office.

"Mr. Leventhal is out," said his secretary. "I'll tell him you called when he returns."

"When do you think he'll return?" said Lance.

"I'm not exactly sure," she said. "Two weeks, at the very least."

"Two weeks!" said Lance.

"Yes," said the secretary. "Mr. Leventhal has finally decided to take a long-overdue vacation. But perhaps one of his assistants can help you while Mr. Leventhal is gone."

"I had no idea he was going away on vacation," said Lance. "I just saw him and he didn't mention it."

"Yes," she said, "the opportunity to get away came up quite suddenly. He grabbed it. To his credit, I might add."

"Listen," said Lance, "it is terribly urgent that I reach him. Do you know for sure that he's already left?"

"I believe he has," she said. "But if it has to do with publicity on your book, Mr. Lerner, I'm sure that Mr. Fieldston or Charlene or Judy could take care of it for you."

"It doesn't have to do with my book," said Lance. "It's a personal matter."

"I see. Well, I'm afraid you'll have to wait till his return, then."

"There's nowhere I can reach him?" said Lance.

"On a yacht? Oh my, heavens, no."

"A yacht, you say? What kind of yacht?"

"He's on the *Claire de Lune,* Mr. Firestone's yacht."

"The *Claire de . . . ?*"

A light bulb exploded inside Lance's head.

It took all of seven minutes to grab a cab and get to the Firestones' apartment building on Park Avenue. The doorman assured Lance that the Firestones had already left on holiday, but there was no mistaking the long gray limousine parked outside—he knew it intimately.

He finally lied his way past the doorman, and the elevator man took him up. The valet who answered the door said that, yes, madam was still here, but that she did not wish to receive visitors as she was just about to go off on holiday. To the extreme surprise of the valet, Lance pushed past him and ran down the hall, checking rooms until he finally found Claire.

She was just finishing packing. If she was surprised to see him she didn't let it show.

"Hello, Lance," she said pleasantly. "How nice to see you. I'm sorry I don't have time to stop and chat. If you ask Charles, however, he'll bring you a kir royale or whatever else you may wish."

"What I *wish*," said Lance, "is to know what's going on here?"

"A vacation," she said. "Austin and I suddenly felt we had to get away from it all."

"Austin and you and Howard Leventhal," said Lance.

"That's right," said Claire, "and Howard Leventhal."

"And Cathy Lerner?" said Lance.

Claire shrugged.

"I know Howard said he was bringing a playmate," she said, "I'm not sure which one."

"You arranged the whole thing," said Lance, "didn't you? You arranged the whole thing just to get me."

Claire smiled.

"'Vengeance is mine,' saith the Lord."

She snapped her suitcase closed.

"Claire, don't do this," said Lance. "I beg you, don't do this."

Just then Firestone strode by the room and stuck his head in. At first he didn't recognize Lance and seemed puzzled at his presence. Then he remembered who he was and a dark look crossed his face.

"What the hell are *you* doing here, Lerner?" he said.

"Uh, well, I was just, uh, chatting here with Claire . . . with, uh, Mrs. Firestone, and uh . . ."

Firestone turned to Claire.

"What is Lerner doing here?" he said.

"I don't know," she said. "He seems to think he has some kind of crush on me. He seems to think he wants to sleep with me. It's all quite baffling."

Firestone turned back to Lance.

"Lerner," he said in a terrifyingly quiet voice, "I wish you to leave here *instantly.*"

"Can I just say one thing before I go?" said Lance.

"*Instantly,* Lerner," said Firestone.

"Oh, fuck off, Firestone," said Lance.

Firestone walked calmly to the bureau, opened the top drawer, pulled out a blue-black .38 caliber revolver and pointed it at Lance's chest.

"Fuck you, Firestone," said Lance, but he said it very, very softly, and he was moving backwards so quickly that it was possible Firestone never heard him speak.

71

Lance waited in a taxi across the street from the Firestones' apartment building. The Firestones' valet and doorman came out and put luggage into the trunk. The Firestones came out and were helped into the limousine. The limousine took off.

"OK," said Lance, "follow that limousine."

The cabbie turned and gave Lance a pained expression.

"What are ya," he said, "a cop?"

"No," said Lance, "an author."

The cabbie nodded, as if he'd been in an equal number of car chases with both cops and authors, and put the cab in gear. The limousine headed north as far as 79th Street, then across town to the West Side. Lance still had no idea what he was going to do, but the idea of Cathy alone on a yacht for two weeks with Howard and the Firestones was more than he could bear.

The limousine pulled up in front of the 79th Street Boat Basin. The chauffeur got the Firestones' luggage out of the trunk and put it into a small motor launch. The Firestones climbed into the launch and it cast off. Lance paid the cabbie and ran down to the dock, looking for somebody who would take him out to the Firestones' yacht. He figured Cathy and Howard were probably already aboard.

Lance finally located a gnarled old gent in a yellow slicker and a battered captain's hat who agreed to row Lance out to the yacht in his boat for twenty-five dollars. Lance thought this was a little steep, but there didn't seem to be any alternative. He agreed. The gnarled gent wanted his fee in advance. Lance paid him, then understood why—the boat was a rickety old dinghy half full of water.

Sitting in water up to his shins, Lance watched the yacht anxiously for signs of Cathy as the elderly sailor rowed toward it. There were a couple of people out on deck, but the sun was in Lance's eyes and he couldn't make out who they were.

When they pulled up alongside the yacht, Lance saw that the figures on deck were Firestone and Claire.

"Permission to come aboard," said Lance, wondering if that were the correct phraseology.

"Permission denied," said Firestone.

Lance looked at the ladder on the side of the yacht, bobbing tantalizingly close. If he jumped, he could catch it easily. Well, fairly easily. He focused in on the motion of the ladder and rose to a half crouch.

"Permission *denied*," said Firestone, seeing Lance's intention.

Lance sprang and caught onto a rung of the ladder.

The gnarled sailor looked alarmed.

"Coming aboard," said Lance, starting to climb the ladder.

Firestone took his pistol out of his pocket.

"The hell you are," he said.

A shot rang out and smacked into the water a yard from the

bottom rung of the ladder. The gnarled old sailor grabbed his oars and started rowing back towards shore at a speed that Lance wouldn't have thought possible.

"Hey, wait for me!" yelled Lance to the disappearing dinghy, hanging on to the ladder for dear life.

The old salt never so much as paused. When the second shot rang out, Lance let go of the ladder and dropped into the water. It was not cold at this time of the year, but Lance's swimming progress was somewhat slowed by his shirt, trousers and boots. He managed to catch up with the dinghy and haul himself over the side, only to splash down in the standing water at the bottom of the boat.

"What the hell's going on?" demanded the old coot.

"The guy on that yacht is a smuggler," said Lance. "I'm a Treasury man."

"Holy shit," said the man, "you coulda got us *killed* out there. How come you didn't call in the Coast Guard or something?"

"I thought I could take him alone," said Lance. "We T-men don't like to call in other agencies to do our dirty work."

Lance was not yet defeated. If the yacht could be boarded, he felt, Cathy could be taken off it. She'd be so impressed with the spontaneity and the romanticism of the gesture—qualities she had always complained he lacked—she would probably go along with him. Especially if he told her he was whisking her off to Paris on the Concorde or something equally romantic.

The problem was how to get past his triggerhappy publisher. He didn't think Firestone would actually have the guts to shoot him on purpose, but there were always accidents. If he were James Bond he could dress in a tuxedo, put a scuba-diving suit on over it, and swim out to the yacht during a late-night soirée. But he was not James Bond, he didn't think he could find any scuba suit to fit over his tux, and he doubted that the Firestones were planning any late-night soirées before they left.

As he stood on the dock, dumping water out of his boots and wringing it out of his shirt, he saw Firestone's crew cast off and begin moving out to sea. At the rate they were moving he guessed he had at most an hour to hatch a scheme to catch up with them in some faster form of transportation before they were irretrievably lost at sea. Too bad, he thought, that he didn't have access to something like a police launch.

Come to think of it, though, maybe he did.

72

"The thing you fail to appreciate," said Stevie when he finally located her at the 9th Precinct, "is that the NYPD has better things to do with its launches than to retrieve runaway wives from yachts."

"I do appreciate that," said Lance. "I also appreciate the fact that under certain unusual circumstances, some members of the NYPD have occasionally managed to utilize various NYPD vehicles in a distinctly unofficial capacity."

"What," said Stevie, "are the unusual circumstances in this particular case?"

"That the member of the NYPD who furnishes said vehicle gets taken to such a dinner the likes of which she has never before seen," said Lance.

"And where would such a dinner be served?" said Stevie.

"Wherever the member of the NYPD who furnished the vehicle most wanted it to be served," said Lance.

"Like, for example, the Seventh Regiment Armory on Park Avenue on the night of the hundred-dollar-a-plate dinner for the Dalton Two?" said Stevie.

Lance sighed.

"Sure," he said, "like that."

"In that case," said Stevie, "we are now talking turkey."

Stevie was not able, on such short notice, to get anyone to give her access to a police launch. But when Lance suggested a police helicopter, Stevie's face brightened.

"I have this writing student at John Jay College," said Stevie. "He flew choppers in 'Nam. Now he flies them for the city."

"You think he'd be up for it?" said Lance.

"He'd be impressed to meet an author as hot as you," said Stevie. "You never know."

"The thing I can never quite get," shouted Sparky Connors over the deafening noise of the chopper, "is the structure for a nonfiction piece!"

Lance peered down at the Hudson River below him, trying to spot the Firestone yacht, and trying to make out his own shape in the shadow of the giant dragonfly drifting downstream.

"That's easy!" shouted Lance. "It's 'Tell-'Em-What-You're-Going-To-Tell-'Em,' then-'*Tell*-'Em,' then-'Tell-'Em-What-You've-Told-'Em!' "

"That's it?" shouted Sparky.

"That's *not* it!" yelled Stevie.

"It is so!" screamed Lance.

"Is not!" screamed Stevie. "The most important part is the lead!"

"What's the lead?" shouted Sparky.

"That's what they call the Five W's!" yelled Lance. "Who, What, Where, When and Why! That's part of the Tell-'Em-What-You're-Going-To-Tell-'Em."

"Oh!" shouted Sparky.

It had been close to an hour since the Firestones had cast off. Sparky had swooped low over the river every time they saw a boat that Lance thought might be the one. None of them was. Now they were out over the Atlantic, and still there was no sign of the Firestone yacht. Lance feared Firestone had pulled a fast one—doubled back and gone the other way perhaps. And then suddenly he saw it.

"There it is!" he shouted.

Stevie and Sparky looked in the direction he was pointing. Sparky brought the chopper down to hover directly overhead. There was no doubt about it—it was definitely the *Claire de Lune*. Two people were standing out on deck, gazing upwards at the helicopter. Now three. Now four. Now five. Stevie took a microphone from the instrument panel and flipped on the chopper's public address system.

"Attention!" she said, her voice booming, "This is the police! We are preparing to board your vessel!"

Sparky dropped the ladder and hovered lower, so that its bottom rung just grazed the deck of the yacht. Stevie looked at Lance.

"You want me to go down and get your wife, champ?" she shouted at Lance.

Lance looked down at the deck, which was pitching and tossing in the choppy water. Fortunately, fear of heights was not among his many neurotic afflictions.

"No!" yelled Lance, "I guess the gesture means nothing unless I do it myself!"

"You realize we can't permit you to do this, don't you?" yelled Stevie.

"I realize that!" yelled Lance.

"If you fall and break your neck or drown," shouted Sparky, "we'll say we never knew you!"

"I understand!" shouted Lance. "Well, here goes nothing!"

Lance crouched over the top rung of the ladder, still standing on the helicopter's cabin floor. Then he carefully turned around and put first one foot and then the other on the ladder, hanging on to the side of the chopper with all the strength in his hands. Sparky tried to keep the chopper hovering nearly motionless as Lance carefully descended the ladder. A brisk ocean breeze and the propwash from the helicopter's rotor sent the ladder swaying back and forth. Lance felt more exhilarated than frightened.

When he had almost reached the end of the ladder he turned around to face the people on the deck of the yacht. Firestone was closest to him, looking exceedingly piqued. If he had the pistol with him he wasn't showing it. Claire, Cathy and Howard stood a few steps back. They seemed utterly entranced.

"So, Firestone, we meet again," said Lance.

"W-what are you doing here, Lance?" said Howard.

"I have come for Cathy," said Lance. "I am taking her back to the mainland, and then we are going on the Concorde together to Paris for a romantic second honeymoon."

Nobody could come up with an appropriate response to this statement, and so nobody said anything.

"Well, Cathy?" said Lance. "Are you coming with me?"

Everybody turned to look at Cathy. This was surely what she wanted, he thought, and yet it was apparent from the expression on her face that a number of forces were tugging her in a number of conflicting directions. There was certainly rage at Lance. There was loyalty to Howard. There was intense desire to go to Paris. There was pity for Howard if she left him here. There was loyalty to her hosts. There was,

235

conceivably, at some barely fathomable level, perhaps even *love* for Lance.

Howard, somehow sensing all of this, realizing how horrid it would be for him if his mistress consented to board a police helicopter and fly off to Paris with her estranged husband, took the only possible shot at winning—he capitulated.

"Cathy," said Howard, "I think you ought to go with Lance. You'll have a m-much better time and I'll manage fine without you, s-somehow."

Everyone on deck realized the brilliance of the move. Lance himself sensed that his own mother had never fired a more effective salvo of guilt.

"I think," said Cathy, "that my place is here with Howard."

Lance had underestimated his rival. Later he would go to pieces. Now he was desperate to save some kind of face.

"OK, Cathy," he said, "that's a noble and self-sacrificing decision."

The chopper hovered above. The deck of the yacht heaved up and down. The people on deck were in a state of suspended animation. It was still Lance's move. He smiled thinly and turned to Claire.

"How about you, Claire?" he said. "Care to fly with me to Paris?"

It was not a bad counter-move, but it was doomed to failure. There was no way that Claire could accept the offer under the circumstances.

"I think," said Claire, "that my place is here with Austin."

The time had come to leave. And still Lance lingered. He didn't know how to get out gracefully. He didn't realize that getting out gracefully was no longer an option. He looked at Howard.

"I think," said Howard, "that my p-place is here with Cathy. But th-thank you anyway."

Lance nodded, spun around, grabbed the ladder and began hauling himself up into the chopper. He was totally deflated, totally humiliated, totally demeaned.

He was definitely through with Cathy now—now and forever. He hoped he was going to be able to remember that.

73

Ever since his return from the ten-city tour Lance had been physically and emotionally depleted, and actively fighting off some gigantic physical collapse. Immediately following the fiasco with the thwarted helicopter rescue, he stopped fighting.

He went home and got into bed and had no further inclination to get up. His temples throbbed, his eyeballs ached, his throat burned, his nostrils flowed, his joints corroded and his temperature crawled up the thermometer.

He was a firm believer in the power of will to overcome disease or give in to it. He was fascinated by the placebo effect—the phenomenon which occurs when someone is told he is being given a certain medicine which is, in reality, only a sugar pill. The person's body reacts just as if it had actually been given the medicine it was told. What happens is that the body, not finding the chemicals in the bloodstream it expected to, goes ahead and manufactures them itself. If the body could do this, Lance believed, then it could either fight disease or succumb, depending on its particular emotional needs. There was little doubt in his mind that he now had an emotional need to fall ill, to get someone to take care of him.

Dorothy and Janie attended him, forced fluids down his throat, kept him warm, plied him with a ceaseless procession of medications. They checked daily with his internist by phone. They put hot compresses on his neck and cold ones on his eyes and forehead. They swabbed his flesh with alcohol. They spoon-fed him homemade chicken soup, albeit won-ton. Given how much attention we get for being sick, he thought, it's a minor miracle we are ever well.

Lance phased in and out of consciousness. He was frequently delirious and dreamed the half-mad dreams of the damned and the insane. He lost all track of time. And then, inevitably, the fever broke, the storm subsided. The attackers of his body spent themselves and withdrew.

He floated on a light, calm, peaceful plane. He was dizzy, weak, and had no desire to move. He opened his eyes and tried to see. His vision was blurred, but he could make out airy white shapes floating about him. Was this heaven or merely a hospital? He focused in on the airy white shapes and realized what they were: Dorothy and Janie. They were wearing white nylon nurses' uniforms! At first he was perplexed, and then he remembered telling Dorothy of a fantasy involving nurses. He smiled weakly up at them. He slept.

He awoke to a curious sensation. Slippery fingers kneaded his flesh. He opened his eyes. Dorothy and Janie, still in their nurses' uniforms, sat on either side of him, massaging moisturizing lotion into his skin. The bedclothes were drawn back. He was quite naked.

This had happened before, he was sure of it. On previous occasions he had barely been present to enjoy it. Today he was decidedly in attendance. As they gently and firmly manipulated his body, he began to get aroused. To his extreme embarrassment, his penis stiffened. What a cheap response to their therapeutic ministrations, he thought, but they didn't appear to be insulted. Quite the contrary. They took it as evidence of his recovery. They were overjoyed. They hugged him. They kissed him. They told him how worried they had been. Eventually, they slipped out of their uniforms and lay with him under the covers.

He sensed what was happening. He knew it was illegal. He supposed it was immoral. And he rationalized that he was too weak to resist. Naked flesh lay against naked flesh. Soft fingers probed nipples, hair and ticklish places. And soon they were making love. To him and to each other. He didn't have to move, they did it all. His feeling of exultation was so intense he knew he was having a spiritual experience. If God appeared at the climax and struck him dead it would have all been worth it.

But God did not appear, and he remained alive. The three of them slept intertwined. He dreamed ecstatic dreams. They awoke during the night and made love once more. It was less playful this time, and deeper emotions were plumbed. When they once more lay exhausted, they told him they were grateful. *They* were grateful! *They!* Why? To find out they were still turned on by men, they said.

They fell asleep in each other's arms again, but this time his dreams were heavy with foreboding. He was in a strange long room with a rounded ceiling. It was either a battlefield hospital in a Quonset hut or in the inside of an airplane. Whatever it was, he seemed to be in Holland. Through a window he could see a windmill. Something small lay still beside him. He reached out to touch it and found cold wetness. He opened his eyes and was aghast—lying beside him on the hospital bed was a bloody, slimy mess. He forced himself to inspect it and discovered it to be two premature human fetuses joined at the back. Siamese twins. Dead.

As he stared at the grisly sight, unable to shift his gaze, he heard footfalls in the corridor outside his room, and then a long shadow fell across the floor. He raised his eyes from the dead fetuses and beheld a mammoth gorilla staring down at him, reaching out for him. Terrified, he began to growl.

He awoke to the sound of his name being repeated over and over again. Dorothy was holding him in her arms. Janie was imploring him to wake up. They asked if he were all right. They said he'd awakened them by growling. He apologized for scaring them. He tried to make a joke of it, but he knew it was nothing to joke about. He sensed it had something to do with the disaster he frequently feared was going to befall him, but now there seemed to be a difference. Not only was it coming toward him, he was meeting it halfway.

74

"What do you suppose those dead fetuses symbolized to you?" said Helen, who'd been inexplicably delighted by the dream.

"I don't know," said Lance. "What do you think?"

"What they symbolize to *me* might not be what they symbolize to *you*," said Helen. "I'd rather hear *your* associations on this."

"All right," said Lance. "Well, maybe the dead fetuses represented Dorothy and Janie somehow. Maybe the windmill and the fact that it was in Holland was a subconscious pun on the word 'dike.'"

"Sounds good to *me*," said Helen. "Tell me more."

"That's about all I can think of," said Lance.

"Then make it up," said Helen.

Lance shrugged.

"All right," he said. "The fetuses were dead because . . . well, maybe because of me. Maybe I killed them."

"Go on," said Helen.

"Do you think I killed them?" he said.

"It's not what *I* think, its—"

"OK, OK," he said. "*I* think I killed them."

"Why do you think that?" said Helen.

"Because I had sex with them?"

"Are you asking me or telling me?"

"All right, because I had sex with them. They were . . . I don't know . . . they were too young to have sex, and so it killed them."

"What do you make of that gorilla?" said Helen.

"I don't know. Maybe he was going to kill me for what I did to the fetuses."

"Whom does the gorilla represent to you?"

"I don't know," he said.

"Make it up."

"All right. The gorilla represents . . . Daddy. Is that what you're thinking?"

"What *I'm* thinking doesn't matter. Is that what *you're* thinking?"

"Yeah. I guess so."

"So Daddy is going to kill you for having sex with Dorothy and Janie," she said.

"Yeah. Listen. Helen. Do you think I'm a monster for having sex with two teenaged girls?"

"No. Why do *you?*"

"I don't know. They're less than half my age. When they were born I was already twenty-three."

"And when you're seventy they'll be forty-seven. So what? Why do you think you're a monster? They certainly weren't innocent virgins—they're both very sensual, sexually sophisticated young women. And you didn't initiate the sex, *they* did."

"Wait a minute. Isn't that a direct contradiction to what

you and the group were saying to me last time? About Gladys? About being raped?"

"Why is it a contradiction?" said Helen. "All we said was that you had to take some responsibility for having had sex with Gladys and for impregnating her. And so does *Gladys*. And you have to take some responsibility for fucking Dorothy and Janie. And so do Dorothy and Janie. Responsibility isn't *blame*. Responsibility is *responsibility*."

"Mmmmmmm."

"The minute you take responsibility for what happens to you," Helen was saying, "you're in control of your life. The minute you stop, you're not."

"What if I should be flying in an airplane," said Lance, "and six wild geese fly into the engines and cause the plane to fall out of the sky? Would I have to take responsibility for that too?"

"You might not have to take responsibility for the six wild geese," said Helen. "You certainly would have to take responsibility for being on that plane, however."

75

The hundred-dollar-a-plate dinner for the Dalton Two was a huge success. The demand for tickets was so great that the event had to be moved from a good-sized dining hall on an upper story of the Seventh Regiment Armory to the much larger space on the Armory floor.

The affair was black tie. The day before the event, Blatt was able to get Ernest and Goose out on bail and into rented tuxedos that he paid for out of his own pocket. Ernest told Blatt he had written a short speech which he wanted to give at the banquet. Blatt read the speech and advised Ernest not to speak.

A dais had been set up at one end of the Armory floor. On it was the head table. Ernest and Goose sat together in the middle, flanked by Blatt on one side and the mayor on the other.

Lance had recovered sufficiently from his illness to make good on his promise to escort Stevie to the dinner. At their table were a literary agent named Arthur Black, who confided to Lance that he had bought his tickets from a scalper for $250, and Ralph Raitt, the homosexual movie critic from the *Daily News,* who had plaster casts on his right leg and his right arm. Raitt said he'd fallen down a flight of stairs that very day and broken his forearm and his shinbone, but he wouldn't have missed this dinner if they had had to wheel him in on a gurney.

Among the celebrities Stevie spotted at various tables on the floor were Barbara Walters, Flip Wilson, Mike Douglas, Jerry Lewis, Alan King, Jacqueline Onassis, Joe Papp, Henny Youngman, Andy Warhol, Sidney Poitier, Sidney Lumet, and Nipsy Russell. Camera crews from Channels 2, 4, 5, 7, 9 and 11 shot footage of Melvin Belli's opening remarks, of Blatt's brief introduction of Goose and Ernest, of Goose and Ernest refusing to be interviewed, and of John Denver singing a song called "Free the Dalton Two," which he had composed especially for the occasion. Stevie was in heaven.

At one point Blatt spotted Lance and tried to get him to move up to the head table. Stevie was all for it, but Lance begged off. Even attending the dinner at all, he felt, was lending the cause more of his support than he'd felt comfortable in lending.

76

Against his better judgment, Lance moved Dorothy and Janie into his bedroom, teddy bears and all. The conflicting feelings he had about such an arrangement were causing him to awake growling every two or three nights, but sleeping with them was so unbearably sweet that he was willing to risk the consequences.

Making love with two women brought up unfamiliar and tricky feelings. The problem occurred not when the three of them were loving each other simultaneously—complex and acrobatic combinations weren't terribly hard to figure out. No, the trouble came when two of the three were active and the third was not. Grade-school children had a saying: three kids can't play together. The first time Dorothy and Janie fell into love play with each other without including him he didn't know what to do. It was exciting to watch, but it felt so lonely. He began to wonder stupid things: Do they like each other better than they like me? Can they satisfy each other better than I can because they know what feels good better than a man does?

Fortunately for him, he was secure enough to snap himself out of it. But then it came up in another combination. Although he had always had a stronger affection for Dorothy, he found himself one night concentrating on Janie. The two of them got deeper and deeper into each other until they had totally forgotten about Dorothy. At the height of their passion they reached out for Dorothy to include her and they didn't find her. They stopped and looked around. Dorothy was gone. They got up instantly and began to search for her.

They found her upstairs, lying face down on her old sleeping bag, sobbing.

"Dorothy, what's wrong?" said Lance.

Dorothy shook her head.

"What is it, baby?" said Janie, taking her in her arms.

"I just started feeling left out," said Dorothy.

They both hugged her, feeling awful.

"The other day we were all making love," said Lance, "and you and Janie seemed to forget I was there. *I* felt left out for a while too."

"I felt like the two of you had forgotten about me," said Dorothy. "I felt like I was losing both of you. To each other."

"That's crazy," said Janie, covering Dorothy's face with kisses.

"I know it's crazy," said Dorothy. "That's just how it felt. It was like I was suddenly the little girl and the two of you were my parents—like you'd both been telling me in private I was your favorite, and then I saw you together making love, and I realized I wasn't."

They all went back down to bed together. Having a romantic relationship with two other people, Lance thought, was geometrically more difficult than with one. They were going to have to try to maintain an exquisite sort of balance. He felt they had displayed adequate sensitivity this time— realizing Dorothy was gone and rushing to find her and reassure her. But he didn't know how long such a delicate thing could last.

In the morning Lance suggested that Dorothy and Janie hire a moving company and move all of their things out of their parents' apartments into his. Both girls were delighted. Dorothy said she knew the perfect company to do the job—a group of women who called themselves the Motherloaders. Lance said it was the Seven Santini Brothers or nothing. Dorothy and Janie wondered at the vehemence of his response.

77

The experience with the non-rapists in the subway station had proven oddly satisfying for June, Alix, Sandy and Wanda.

No longer confining themselves to the hunting and castrating of Wanda's rapist alone, the group now addressed itself to rapists in general and began roaming Central Park late at night, looking for them. Disguised as elderly ladies—for elderly ladies were, oddly enough, sexually attacked as frequently as younger ones—they patrolled with pinking shears. Once more they met with initial failure. They saw no rapists. They saw drunken vagrants. They saw large bands of teen-aged muggers. They saw numerous old ladies, little knowing or caring that these were decoy policemen. They were once more growing restless. June toyed with the possibility of taking on a band of teenaged muggers just to relieve the monotony. They fretted that rape might be going out of style. And then, one night, success.

Shortly after midnight, they heard a woman's screams coming from deep inside a viaduct. They raced down an embankment, their hunters' blood pulsing warmly in their throats, and plunged into the viaduct. On the pavement lay a young Hispanic woman, her skirt torn half off her body, a young Hispanic man with his jeans at his knees about to thrust himself between her legs.

With shrieks of glee, June, Alix, Sandy and Wanda threw themselves at the rapist. The young Hispanic woman, hearing the shrieks of her deliverers and glimpsing their bared pinking shears, feared that worse things than rape were about to befall her and screamed the louder. Sandy and Alix pinned the amazed rapist to the ground, as June took his testicles in hand and deftly snipped them off.

The ensuing blood was more than June had counted on. Perversely, the rapist survived. His intended victim, stupefied by his spilled blood, almost did not. Paramedics, summoned by a worried MATE, swiftly transported both rapist and would-be victim to Bellevue. The young Hispanic woman was released two days after the man. June, Sandy, Alix and Wanda went to see the woman in her dreary East Harlem apartment to try to comfort her. When they told her who they were, she came at them with a machete.

The account of the castrating received scant attention in the media until MATE sent an open letter to the *New York Times,* claiming credit for the crime. In the letter the members of MATE deplored the act of rape, reviled rapists, took a healthy swipe at male chauvinists everywhere, and identified themselves as the commandos of the women's movement. So many outraged letters from feminists poured in to the paper that the *Times* featured an entire page of them. The National Organization of Women publicly dissociated itself from MATE and claimed no knowledge of its activities. The Rape Crisis Center in Cleveland said that with friends like MATE they needed no enemies.

June, Alix, Sandy and Wanda were quite hurt at the response of their sisters in the women's movement. They stopped dressing up as old ladies and roaming Central Park. They decided to focus their energies on less militant pursuits for a while.

They decided to radicalize nurses, stewardesses, waitresses, Vegas showgirls and topless dancers. They sent a test mailing of hundreds of mimeographed letters to nurses at several city hospitals, including Bellevue, St. Vincent's, Mount Sinai, New York Hospital and Doctors Hospital. They said that for too long nurses had passively stood by and let male chauvinist doctors rape them in spirit if not in body. They said that the time had come for this to stop, that old sex roles had to be reversed, that nurses had to begin getting as much respect and as much pay as doctors, and that if the nurses weren't willing to be part of the solution then they were part of the problem. The members of MATE asked to meet with representatives of nurses' groups to assist in radicalizing them. The representatives of the nurses' groups told the members of MATE to screw themselves.

June, Alix, Sandy and Wanda were quite offended at the responses of their sisters in the nursing profession. They issued a public statement that nurses were all Uncle Toms and Aunt Tessies and deserved what they got. They turned their attention to stewardesses.

They sent a test mailing of hundreds of mimeographed letters to stewardesses at several airlines, including TWA, American, Eastern, Delta and Pan Am. They said that for too long female flight attendants had passively stood by and let male chauvinist pilots and co-pilots and navigators rape them in spirit if not in body. They said that the time had come for this to stop, that the old sex roles had to be reversed, that female flight attendants had to begin getting as much respect and as much pay as pilots and co-pilots and navigators, and that if the female flight attendants weren't part of the solution then they were part of the problem. The members of MATE asked to meet with representatives of the female flight attendants' groups to assist in radicalizing them. The representatives of the female flight attendants' groups told the members of MATE to take a flying fuck at a rolling doughnut.

June, Alix, Sandy and Wanda were quite offended at the responses of their sisters in the female flight attending profession. They issued a public statement that female flight attendants were all Uncle Toms and Aunt Tessies and deserved what they got.

But instead of turning their attention to waitresses, Vegas showgirls and topless dancers, they decided to make a stand in the commercial airline business and dramatize their political views. They decided to create a media event which would get even more attention than the castrating of the rapist. They decided to hijack a jetliner and fly it to someplace that would be politically and promotionally appropriate. After considerable research and debate, they selected as their destination a remote island in the Pacific called Mannihanni, an island which Margaret Mead had once referred to as a society where women ruled and where men were second-class citizens.

78

Lance had never been sure during his seven-year marriage to Cathy whether or not he wished to have a child with her. He was absolutely certain now that he did not wish to have a child with Gladys Oliphant. He did not know how serious she was about going through with the pregnancy. Who knew for sure if she was really pregnant?

He finally reached Gladys by phone and suggested that they get together for a talk. She was delighted and suggested that they talk at Elaine's. She was anxious to get to know some of her fellow writers, she said, and she was eager to see one of the many celebrity fistfights she had read went on there.

Lance assured her that reports of celebrity fistfights were vastly exaggerated, but said that Elaine's was not the sort of quiet spot he'd had in mind for their discussion. Although this was not untrue, what was truer yet was that Lance was not overeager to show up at a place as visible as Elaine's with a two-hundred-forty-pound date in tow. It was the sort of thing that could get around town and give him a bad reputation.

Gladys said it was Elaine's or nothing. Lance decided he couldn't afford not to discuss Gladys's pregnancy and relented. He arranged to meet her that evening at Elaine's at six-thirty. He figured they could probably drink and eat and have their discussion and be out of there before ten when the regulars started showing up. Gladys asked whether six-thirty wasn't a wee bit early, and Lance assured her that six-thirty was the choicest time at Elaine's.

Gladys was a half hour late. Lance sat down at a table and ordered a bottle of Verdicchio. When she waddled in, Lance was talking to one of the waiters. He hailed her to his table and helped her into a chair. She was wearing a flowered rayon dress and had obviously gone to a lot of trouble with her hair

248

and makeup. Lance felt mean, small and relieved to have tricked her into coming so early.

Gladys looked around at the near-empty restaurant.

"Where *is* everybody?" she said.

"It's a slow night," said Lance. "You never know what are going to be the slow nights and what are going to be the ones when it's packed to the rafters with celebrities."

"Oh," said Gladys, her face falling about three chins. "I wish I had known beforehand. I was expecting to see a lot of famous writers."

"Well," said Lance, "that's the funny thing about this place. An evening may start out slow, like it is now, and then, suddenly, in come thirty or forty people and all at once things are happening. That's what may happen tonight."

"I doubt it," said Gladys, dubiously looking over the half dozen diners spread out across the room. "Who are those people? Are they anybody?"

Lance looked over the six people in the restaurant. Four of them were complete strangers and two of them he'd seen before but didn't know who they were. He didn't have the heart to give her so depressing a report. He leaned in close and said out of the corner of his mouth:

"Don't look at him now, but the little guy at the table in the back is a very interesting character."

Without moving her head, Gladys slid her eyes in the direction he had indicated.

"What's his name?" she whispered.

"He goes by many names," said Lance. "You wouldn't have heard of any of them. He's a double agent for the DIA."

"The what?" she whispered.

"The Defense Intelligence Agency. He works for them and he also works for the KGB, but each of them thinks he's loyal to *them.*"

"Who is he loyal to?" she whispered.

Lance shrugged.

"He himself isn't sure any longer," he said. "He's decided to write his memoirs and quit. When his book appears, he's going to have his looks altered by a plastic surgeon."

"Wow," she said. "Who else is here?"

"The rather plain-looking woman with the dishwater-blond hair two tables over?" said Lance.

Gladys slid her eyeballs in the opposite direction.

"Yeah?" she said.

"Her name is Letitia Loring," said Lance. "Big society

dame. A second cousin to the Hearsts. She's an editor at Viking. She's been living with her brother for eight years."

"I don't understand," said Gladys.

Lance raised his eyebrows.

"What do you mean?" she said. "Are you saying they're . . . ?"

Lance nodded.

"They're having an . . . *affair?*" she said.

"*I* didn't say it, *you* did," said Lance.

Gladys turned around and stared at the woman.

"Sssssstt," said Lance, "don't do that. They don't think anybody knows."

"Is that her brother she's with?" said Gladys.

Lance nodded.

"They don't look very similar," she said.

"One favors the mother, one the father," said Lance. "They're brother and sister, though, don't you worry."

"Wow," said Gladys.

"Let's talk about pregnancy now," said Lance, feeling he had placated her somewhat.

Gladys looked down at the tablecloth.

"Not yet," she said.

"You want to have something to drink first?" he said.

She nodded. He poured her a glass of Verdicchio and nodded to the waiter. The waiter came over and ran down the litany of specials. Gladys wanted to order one of everything, but Lance suggested she start with the stuffed mushrooms, the *paglia e fieno*, an arugula salad and a veal chop, then see how she felt. He himself ordered only a spinach salad.

When the food came she went through it all in the time it took Lance to eat his salad.

"This is nice," she said, "but it wasn't really what I thought it would be like."

"It'll pick up," he said. "I can feel it in my bones."

He finished his last glass of wine and ordered another bottle. He was feeling guiltier and guiltier as the time passed. What would the big deal have been to come later when the regulars were here? Was he so insecure he couldn't bear to be seen with an enormous fat woman? Was he truly afraid people would think he and she were an item? Why couldn't he see past his own petty insecurities and do something generous once in a while?

"I thought I'd see Woody Allen at least," said Gladys sadly. "I thought I'd see Jackie Onassis and Norman Mailer. I thought I'd see at least one fight and Elaine would have to throw people out on the street and Ron Galella would photograph them."

"It's not like that here," said Lance. "You've heard gross exaggerations of what goes on."

The door opened and four short balding men came in. Lance recognized two of them as agents at William Morris. They were seated next to the alleged incestuous socialites.

"You see those four guys who just came in?" Lance whispered.

Gladys turned to look.

"Yeah?" she said.

"They're agents at William Morris," he said.

She seemed let down.

"Is that all?" she said.

"What do you mean 'is that all?'" he said. "These four guys happen to practically run half of Hollywood between them."

"Yeah?" she said. "Name some of their clients."

"Well," said Lance, trying to think of names she might be impressed by, "they represent Ryan O'Neal and . . . Barbra Streisand and . . ."

"Ryan O'Neal is a client of ICM," she said.

"Look," he said, "I don't know who their clients are. I just know they're big. If you don't believe me, you don't have to."

"I'm sorry," she said and put her hand over his on the table. "That wasn't polite."

Oh God, he thought, don't be nice to me.

He drank another glass of wine and once more tried to get her to talk of her pregnancy, but still she hesitated. Perhaps if she saw one legitimate celebrity she might give in and speak about the fetus she was carrying and about why she had indicated to him that she intended to have the baby.

The idea of fathering a baby was, had always been, more than he could deal with emotionally. He was attracted and he was repelled. Attracted by the notion of co-creating a little human being and watching it develop the ability to communicate and show affection and absorb learning and go on to be a little Lance in one form or another—someone to whom he could give the benefit of his forty years of greater and lesser mistakes, someone who would perhaps carry on his name and spirit after he died. Someone who . . . well, but then there were the fears.

The fear of having conceived a monster, a grotesquely

251

disfigured baby who was either physically or mentally crippled, crippled enough to ruin the rest of his life while he
brought it up and tried to pretend to be leading a normal life
with it, and not crippled enough to languish and die merciful-
ly in the hospital. The fear of having conceived a normal child
and having it eat up so much of his working and leisure time
that it totally transformed his life into an appendage of the
child's and not his own. The fear of having conceived a child
as thankless and insensitive to its parents as he often imagined he was to his own. The fear of—

"A penny for your thoughts," she said.

He realized suddenly that Gladys's hand was once more
covering his and that she was gazing directly, if a bit
drunkenly, into his eyes. Who besides Gladys, he thought,
still used an expression like "A penny for your thoughts"? He
must not have spoken for quite a while.

"I'm sorry," he said. "I was just thinking about your being
pregnant. Can't we discuss it now?"

"Soon," she said. "But first I want to see what there is to
see here."

He looked around. More people had drifted in. It was now
nearly nine o'clock. Lance had drunk enough not to care
particularly who saw him and Gladys together. The table of
William Morris agents had obviously had a lot to drink. They
were getting loud and boisterous. Elaine appeared, and
walked over to their table and told them to keep it down.
They were too scared of her to answer back while she was at
the table, but when she turned her back and walked away one
of them gave her the finger. She spun around, like a grade-
school teacher who had convinced her students she had eyes
in the back of her head, and glared at them. Not one of them
could meet her gaze.

Lance told Gladys that, although he was not a regular at
Elaine's, he loved the idea that there was one restaurant in
New York where writers were given special treatment. He
told Gladys how Elaine had kept powerful people like Henry
Ford III waiting at the bar for over an hour while seating
her writers. He told how Elaine allegedly shifted some of
the food and bar charges off the checks of her down-and-
out writers and onto the checks of wealthy socialites who
wouldn't know the difference.

Gladys loved the stories as much as Lance had when they
had been new to him. He encouraged her to tell him about
herself. She told him about her writing, about her hopes of

252

being the next Barbara Cartland. About her tenants in the building, about Stevie Petrocelli. About Gladys's dismal history with men, about her rape by the Indians, about what it had meant to her to have made love to somebody as famous as Lance Lerner.

Extravagant praise and large amounts of wine combined to produce a warm, runny center. He found himself feeling very mellow toward old Gladys. He ordered another bottle of Verdicchio.

Shortly after ten, three agents from ICM came into the restaurant and were given a table adjacent to the agents from William Morris. The William Morris people had got considerably louder and were now hurling innuendoes at the ICM table. Lance glared in their direction. This appeared to incense the shortest of the William Morris agents.

"Why don't you keep your eyes on your cow?" he called to Lance.

"Why don't I *what?*" said Lance, instantly furious at the insult to Gladys and simultaneously horrified that people thought she was as obese as he had feared.

"*You* heard me!" retorted the fearfully short agent. "Why don't you get a pail and a stool and *milk* her?"

Lance sprang out of his seat and grabbed the tiny man by the front of his shirt and pulled him out of his chair. All the William Morris and ICM agents stood up and pressed forward.

"Are you going to take that back," said Lance, "or am I going to have to pound you into the ground and make you even shorter?"

In reply the diminutive drunk threw a haymaker at Lance's head. Lance ducked and the punch hit the closest ICM agent in the glasses. Instantly, the ICM man punched back, and before one knew it, eight men were trading punches.

Elaine waded into the midst of the fracas and began bum's-rushing agents out of the restaurant with awesome speed. Gladys stared, slack-jawed and delighted—this was what she had *known* Elaine's was like. This was what she had come to see. Gladys was not even dismayed when, over Lance's protestations of innocence, Elaine bum's-rushed *him* out of the restaurant and Gladys had to follow him out onto the street. And Gladys was the only person who was not surprised when Ron Galella *did* appear, and snapped photographs of Elaine wielding a barstool like a lion tamer and at least one shot of Gladys with her arms around her defender.

When the evening's entertainment was at last concluded, Lance took Gladys back to her apartment. He wanted to clean up, and they had still not discussed her pregnancy, and so he accepted her invitation for a nightcap and went inside.

Once they were both settled on her couch with glasses of Kahlua, Lance again approached the topic. Unexpectedly, Gladys began weeping uncontrollably.

"Gladys," he said, "what is it?"

She continued weeping, shaking now with sobs, till he worried about her well-being.

"I l-lost it," she said at last, between sobs.

"You what?" he said. He thought he'd heard her say she lost it, but that didn't make sense.

"M-miscarriage," she blurted, "I had a m-miscarriage . . . I thought if I t-told you, you wouldn't . . . go out with me."

So she wasn't pregnant! It was a relief, to be sure, but not, somehow, the precise emotional release he would have thought it to be. He tried to comfort her, and, to his utter astonishment, he began to be rocked by waves of grief for his now dead unborn child. To his even greater astonishment, he soon found himself sobbing as earnestly as Gladys.

They clung together in attempts at mutual consolation. He experienced a rush of overpoweringly sweet feeling for this gigantic woman who had briefly borne his child. He began to kiss her and hug her and, to his further amazement, he soon found himself drunkenly undressing her and making love to her. This time he wisely chose to be on top.

79

Lance arrived home from his date with Gladys at close to five a.m. He let himself into the apartment, conscientiously trying to be as quiet as he could so as not to wake Dorothy or Janie.

He undressed outside the bedroom door, then slipped

inside and made it to the bed before the light was snapped on.

There sat Dorothy and Janie, wearing their pajamas and staring at him with frigid fury.

"Where *were* you?" said Dorothy.

"We were worried *sick* about you," said Janie.

"You were?" said Lance.

It had truthfully never occurred to him that Dorothy or Janie would miss him if he stayed away all night.

"I called all the hospitals," said Dorothy.

"I called the morgue," said Janie. "We thought you had been killed by a mugger or hit by a *cab* or something."

"God, I'm sorry," said Lance. "I was out with Gladys."

"Till five a.m.?" said Dorothy.

"Hey, c'mon," said Lance, trying to jolly them a little, "you guys sound like I'm the teenager and you're my parents."

Neither one of them smiled. They were right, of course. It was typical of him that he forgot that other people had feelings too. He was not tremendously proud of himself.

"You're right," he said quietly. "I was very inconsiderate and unfeeling. I should have called you or something to let you know."

"You certainly should have," said Janie.

"I'm truly sorry. And I'll try not to have it happen again, OK?"

Eventually, somewhat grudgingly, they accepted his apology. By the time the sun came up they were even cuddling together again under the covers.

80

Hijacking a jetliner was going to be more fun than anything any of them had ever done before, they could see that. Every night after they got done working at Motherloaders they would go over to June's apartment and plot and discuss what they had learned.

The atlases said that Mannihanni was roughly the size of Staten Island. Its principal town was Port Pangaud on its northeastern tip. The total population numbered scarcely more than 15,000 women—Mannihanni didn't count its men. Mannihanni had been a French possession till 1945, when native guerrillas efficiently overthrew the small cadre of French officials who ruled it. The coup was as bloody as it was swift. The slaughtered French officials were decapitated, dismembered and put on display in the main square in Port Pangaud. All the guerrillas had been women. Shortly after the coup, France—which had no interest whatsoever in sending troops to deal with crazed guerrillas on a worthless island—officially granted independence to Mannihanni.

The revolution had been led by a tall, handsome, fiery young black woman named Josephine Taillevent. Shortly after the coup, Taillevent went to the United States and studied at UCLA, apparently earning her Ph.D. in philosophy before she returned to Mannihanni. Following her return, Dr. Taillevent—nicknamed "Mamma Doc" by her proud subjects—declared herself President-for-Life and had ruled since that time.

According to the atlases, the island's women ran the principal industries—sugar cane, rum, bananas, coconuts, coca, copra, jute, hemp and woven textiles—while the men stayed home, raised the children, and did the housework. In 1962, a huge repository of natural gas, some thirty million cubic feet of it, was discovered under the Presidential Palace in Port Pangaud. At this point, the United States, Russia, China and Japan began courting the Mannihannis, but Mamma Doc refused to recognize their diplomatic delegations because all their ambassadors were males. Males, in the opinion of Mamma Doc and her cabinet, were inferior to females and therefore unacceptable as diplomatic emissaries.

In 1969, a group of disgruntled Mannihanni househusbands stormed the Presidential Palace and tried to oust Mamma Doc. Several of the male insurgents were killed and publicly decapitated. The others escaped to Honolulu, where they were living as exiles. Since 1969, Mamma Doc had surrounded herself with a fanatically loyal group of armed female guards patterned loosely on Papa Doc Duvalier's Haitian *Tonton Macoutes*.

June, Alix, Sandy and Wanda scrutinized the location of Mannihanni on their maps. It lay south and slightly east of Honolulu. It was approximately as far west of Los Angeles as Los Angeles was from New York.

June said that hijacking the plane in Los Angeles made a helluva lot more sense than hijacking it in New York, but Alix said why should they have to pay for four tickets from New York to LA when they could just as easily hijack the damned plane out of JFK and save themselves some bread.

June said that if they hijacked it out of New York then they would have to stop somewhere around LA to refuel, which left them very vulnerable to any number of cute tricks on the part of the police, like recapturing the plane while they were refueling.

Wanda said that once they got to Mannihanni they might suggest to Mamma Doc that the four air fares they paid from New York to LA could be reimbursed to them.

They all agreed they would give notice to Motherloaders at the end of the week and then move to Los Angeles to begin planning the hijack.

81

His group ate up the latest developments in Lance's love life like miniature Reese's Peanut Butter Cups. They generally approved of his determined, if failed, attempt to take Cathy back with him on the helicopter. They heartily approved of his ending the affair with Claire in the decisive way he'd done it. They supposed they approved of his going to bed with Gladys again, since it had been his choice and since he was taking responsibility for it and not copping out by saying he had only done it because he was drunk—although that was actually the truth.

When it came to telling them about Dorothy and Janie, though, things got sticky. They all groaned and made faces when he told them how the girls had seduced him when he was weak from his illness, and although he maintained he took responsibility for it, they said he was just saying that so the group wouldn't jump on him. They were especially tough on him for staying out all night with Gladys and making Dorothy and Janie worry.

He was sorry he'd told them anything at all. It was clear they took anybody's side but his. He suspected they were jealous of his affair with the teenagers and couldn't admit it.

"I don't think you are in touch with your feelings," said Helen, "particularly your feelings about women. If you can't get in touch with the anger you feel towards them, then how are you ever going to get in touch with the love?"

"But I *am* in touch with the love," said Lance. "I'm in touch with the anger too—where it's appropriate, that is. I mean I'm sort of angry at Claire, and I'm sort of angry at Cathy, and I'm sort of—"

"'*Sort* of' isn't angry," said Laura. "'*Sort* of' isn't more than mildly annoyed. Why don't you tell us how you *really* feel?"

"How I really feel?" said Lance, beginning to get deeply annoyed. "I'll tell you how I really feel. I really feel like you are driving me *crazy*, that's how I feel."

"Who's driving you crazy?" said Laura.

"You, for one," said Lance.

"Who *else?"* said Helen.

"You too, goddammit!" said Lance, heating up fast.

"And who else?" said Jackie.

"You, you stupid cocksucker!" said Lance.

Arnold clapped his hands for joy.

"Shut up, asshole!" yelled Lance at Arnold.

"Why me?" said Jackie.

"Because not only are you an asshole," said Lance, "but you're Jewish as well, and you make non-Jews think all Jews are as big an asshole as *you* are!"

"I'm not Jewish," said Jackie. "I'm Episcopalian."

"Fuck you," said Lance.

"He's telling the truth, Lance," said Roger. "Jackie *is* Episcopalian."

"Then how come you use so many Yiddish words, asshole?" said Lance, sure they were putting him on.

"I'm a comedian," said Jackie. "You're a chef, you learn French. You're a comedian, you learn Yiddish."

"We're getting off the track here," said Helen. "I don't want to lose the wonderful feelings of anger that Lance was beginning to get to."

Lance turned to Helen.

"Is Jackie Jewish or Episcopalian?" he demanded.

"Episcopalian," she said. "But I don't want to—"

"How long has he been Episcopalian?" Lance interrupted.

"All his life," said Helen. "But I want to return to the feelings of anger you were beginning to get in touch with before—"

Lance wheeled on Jackie.

"Whatever church you worship in, Jackie," he snapped, "you're still an asshole!"

"Thanks, shmuck," said Jackie.

"Let's hear more anger," called Laura.

"Shut the fuck up with that!" said Lance. "Don't tell me how the fuck to feel!"

"Way to go!" cheered Roger.

"I said shut *up!"* shouted Lance. "Shut up, shut up, *shut up!* You are all driving me fucking bananas! I am sick and tired of you!"

"Who besides us?" said Helen.

"*Everybody!* Cathy, Claire, Gladys, Dorothy, Janie—*everybody!* What the fuck do they want from me, for Christ's sake?" he shouted. *"What the fuck do women want?"*

The group was momentarily paralyzed by his outburst. Lance's face was flushed, his breathing ragged.

"Forget what *women* want—what do *you* want?" said Helen.

"I want women to *leave me the fuck alone!*" Lance screamed at the top of his lungs.

"Why?" Helen demanded.

"Because I hate their fucking guts!"

Everybody in the group broke into spontaneous applause. Lance looked at them as though they were inmates in an insane asylum.

"What the fuck is going on here?" he said, breathing hard. "I tell you I hate you and you *applaud?*"

"Sure," said Laura. "Because now we know where we stand with you, you fuck!"

"Huh?" said Lance.

"You finally trusted us enough to show us your true feelings," said Helen.

Lance frowned and shook his head, totally baffled.

"Before you never showed us the feelings you claimed to have," said Helen. "Now you did. My guess is that you were *afraid* to show us your anger before. You were afraid it would kill us, or maybe that we would kill *you* for being so angry. But you see—you didn't kill *us,* and we didn't kill *you.* We don't even hate you for it."

Lance let out a long, exasperated sigh.

"Are you still so angry?" said Helen gently.

Lance shook his head.

"I guess not," he said.

"Why not?" said Helen.

"I guess it just boiled over and went away," he said.

Helen smiled.

"And what do you feel in place of your anger?" she prodded.

Lance shrugged.

"I guess relief," he said.

"I would suggest," said Helen, "that rather than continue asking what women want, you find out where that rage you have against them comes from and discover a way to release it."

"All right," said Lance, "I'll do that. I'll change. I'll become a whole new person."

"Don't tell me you're going to change," said Helen. "Tell me what you're getting out of what you're doing now, tell me what the payoff is in what you're doing now, or else you don't have a *prayer* of changing."

82

Lance thought over what he had said in the group about hating women. At the time he had really felt he did. Now he didn't. Collectively, he liked them a whole lot better now. Individually, he disliked them more, though. The more he'd seen of women in his life, the less he understood what it was they wanted, or, for that matter, what *he* wanted from *them*. He loved women, but they were, without a doubt, one of the biggest pains in the ass that God in His infinite wisdom had ever created.

In the years before he met Cathy and began living with her, dating women was a relatively uncomplicated matter. You took a woman out to dinner, to a movie or a play or a concert, and there was never any question but that you paid all her expenses. The tacit understanding was that, in exchange for doing this you eventually earned the right to try to coax her into some sexual or presexual activity. It was always understood that women had to be coaxed because sexual activities were somewhat distasteful to them.

It took Lance nearly twenty years to find out that it had all been pretense: women liked sex just as much as men did—possibly even *more* than men. And yet they still expected to have men pay for their dinners, their shows, and so on—and, for some reason, he had gone along with it. Just before he met Cathy, Lance had had a fairly intense relationship with a young woman who designed textiles and made quite a bit more money than Lance did, yet there was never any question that he'd pick up the checks. (In truth, he probably would have felt resentful if she had, but that was another story.)

One of the things that Lance was most annoyed about was that women were always demanding to be his equal in every way, and yet they still expected him to take care of them and be their protector. That, thought Lance, was trying to eat your cake and have it too.

Like men, women had a double standard of their own. They wanted to be able to let down their hair with a man and cry on his shoulder and be vulnerable. But if a man cried on *their* shoulder, or cried on it more than, say, once every twelve years—yicccchhhh! Who could stand a man who was a sniveling crybaby!

Shortly before Lance met Cathy there was a period in which he found himself telephoning women for dinner dates for the same evening, never more than two hours in advance. They all seemed genuinely sorry they'd made other plans that night, and all of them asked for rain checks. Lance never suggested alternative dates and became more and more furious at his seeming inability to get dates for dinner. It now occurred to him: the purpose of these calls was not to get dates for dinner, the purpose was to get more reasons to be mad at women.

Because of his anger at women Lance had invested an awful lot of energy since puberty in keeping them at arm's length, starting with his mother and continuing right on through his marriage to Cathy. He hadn't been aware of doing it at a conscious level most of the time, but he had done it nonetheless. Exactly why he felt the need to do it was hard to say.

There was certainly something in what Helen had said about the fear of intimacy. The way from the onset of adolescence he had begun to squirm whenever his mother tried to hug him and not unlike the way he sometimes began to squirm when Cathy tried to hug him. There was something about being that close that sometimes simply gave him the willies.

Perhaps it *was* what Helen said it was—the incest taboo. Perhaps, he thought, we are so conditioned never to lust after Mom or Sis or anybody else we live with that, once we get married and get into a familiar homey rut with a wife, there is some ancient sensing device which detects that we are getting too chummy with a member of the family and begins to send out warnings. Perhaps that's why sex with somebody outside the home is so much more exciting as a prospect—at least until it gets familiar and chummy and homey and that person begins looking like a member of the family too.

It was likely, Lance thought, that he had, at some level of consciousness, been avoiding intimacy with Cathy and other women all his adult life. Certainly that had been one function of his workaholic writing habits. If you were continually wrapped up in your work and were staying up till all hours to do it, there was a lot less opportunity to succumb to temptation and get involved in sexual activities that had been forbidden since childhood.

But perhaps the incest taboo was not the only reason to squirm away from closeness. There was a further fear. The fear that, if you were to let a woman get close to you, really really close to you, you might get hurt. She might tire of you and leave. "You think, if somebody left you once and you survived," Helen had said to him, "that the way you survive is to get somebody to leave you."

In the love affair all little boys have with their mothers, their mothers are continually leaving them for their fathers, and usually the little boys survive. Perhaps from the time that he was a little boy and his mother continually left him for his father and he survived, he had at some level indeed figured out that the way he got to survive was to get somebody to leave him. Perhaps that was, at bottom, why he managed to get Cathy to leave him—so he could survive.

There was another thing that Helen had said to him which, at the time, he'd not been able to appreciate: "All little boys are angry at their mothers for preferring their fathers," she said. "So staying angry at all women is a way of making all women your mother." It probably also followed that making all women your mother was a dandy way to avoid growing up. He had always recognized within himself a deep-seated fear of growing up. Growing up meant taking care of yourself. Growing up meant bringing yourself closer to dying.

"I have this great fear of this *normal* thing," said John Lennon early in 1975. "I don't want to grow up, but I'm sick of *not* growing up." Lennon had been separated from Yoko Ono for about a year at this point, bouncing from bed to bed, desperately avoiding anything that resembled normalcy, and doing his best not to grow up. At the end of the year Lennon returned to Yoko Ono, announcing, "The separation didn't work out," and immersed himself in grown-up and relatively normal things.

Perhaps Lance, too, didn't want to grow up but, like John Lennon, he was sick of *not* growing up. Perhaps Lance's separation hadn't worked out any better than had John Lennon's.

Getting his rage out in the group had somehow enabled Lance to get a lot clearer about his feelings for Cathy. He knew, in fact, exactly what he wanted to do about her now.

He asked his lawyer to begin divorce proceedings. His lawyer asked him if that was what he really wanted to do. Lance said it was what he really wanted to do, and to cut the shit. Lance's lawyer gave him the name of a fellow who specialized in divorce cases. Lance went to see the fellow that very afternoon. Lance said he wanted a divorce as quickly as possible. The divorce fellow said that he appreciated Lance's feelings, but that in New York State you had to have a cooling-off period, a year of legal separation, before you could obtain a divorce.

"Couldn't one simply go to Haiti or the Dominican Republic?" said Lance.

"One certainly could go to Haiti or the Dominican Republic," said the divorce fellow.

"And would the divorce be legal and everything?" said Lance.

"It would be legal in Haiti or the Dominican Republic," said the divorce fellow, smiling.

It seemed there was a difference between a cheap quickie divorce that might wear off and an expensive, excruciatingly long divorce that would last forever. Lance had always admired longevity in the things he bought. He told the divorce fellow to write him up an order for one of the latter.

83

Within one hour of Lance's arrival back at his apartment the doorbell rang. He buzzed, thinking it was Dorothy or Janie. He was eager to tell them of his decision.

It was not Dorothy or Janie. It was Cathy.

"Holy shit," said Lance when he saw her.

She did not look well.

"Hi, Lance," she said. "Can I come in?"

What the hell was Cathy doing here—today of all days?

"Sure," he said. "C'mon in."

She came in and looked around.

"Any unclad females about?" she asked.

Lance shook his head.

"I just got back," she said. "From the cruise."

"I see," he said. "And how did it go?"

There was a short pause.

"Not bad," she said. "Everybody enjoyed themselves."

"Good," said Lance. "I'm so pleased."

There was a longer pause.

"Shall I tell you how the cruise went *really?*" she said at last.

"I thought you already did," said Lance.

Cathy shook her head.

"It was a disaster," she said. "A nightmare. The absolute pits."

"What happened?" said Lance, secretly delighted.

"What didn't?" said Cathy. "Engine trouble. Stomach trouble. Terrible storms at sea. Horrendous *mal de mer*. We tossed more cookies out there than Famous Amos. By the third day nobody was speaking. When we landed in the Bahamas, Austin went ashore and flew to London. Claire went ashore and ran off with a beach boy. I stayed in my cabin and puked my guts out and had the runs for days on end."

"And Howard?" said Lance.

"Howard went ashore to buy native knickknacks and was mugged. He lost over three hundred dollars in cash, all his credit cards, his watch and his belt and shoes."

Lance burst out laughing.

"I'm sorry," he said, "but I don't harbor a lot of affection for old Howard."

"I don't blame you," said Cathy. "Howard probably had the worst time of all. He got into a terrible tiff with Austin on the second day. Austin called him a—what was it he called him now?—'a supercilious prig,' I think, and Howard resigned."

"Howard quit his job at the publishing house?" said Lance.

Cathy nodded.

"He said he was sick of the business anyway," she said. "He has this novel he has always wanted to write, so that's what he's going to do instead."

"How about that!" said Lance, relishing the prospect of Howard's having to put up with the same shit from *his* editor that Lance had had to put up with from Howard.

"He's not a bad guy really," said Cathy, "no matter what you think of him. Although what Austin said about him is certainly true."

"'Supercilious prig,' you mean?" said Lance, surprised.

Cathy nodded.

"I broke up with Howard on about the third day," she said. "I'm glad I did it then."

"How do you mean?" said Lance.

"I never could have done that to him after the mugging," she said.

"That's typical," he said.

"What's probably also typical," she said, "was my not being able to go with you on the helicopter."

"How do you mean?" he said.

"It was a wonderful gesture," she said, "—romantic, spontaneous, all the things I always said I wanted from you."

"So why didn't you come with me?" said Lance. "Because you didn't have the heart to leave Howard?"

She shook her head.

"Not really," she said. "I mean, that was part of it, sure. But the main reason was that I was too angry with you. I was too angry to give you the satisfaction of letting you come out of it a hero, even if it meant losing you and losing a trip to Paris and whatever else. I just couldn't bear to see you win."

Lance shook his head.

"Whew!" he said.

"I know," she said. "That was hard for me to admit. But I've been doing a lot of thinking. And what I mostly think is that, by not going with you on that helicopter, I probably became as big an asshole as you were at that surprise party I threw for you."

"Jesus," he said.

"We're almost even," she said.

"Almost?" said Lance.

"Well, having that fat whale naked on your bed when I came over last time still puts you *slightly* ahead of me," she said.

"Cathy?"

"Yeah?"

"Did you come over here to ask if you could come back to me?" he said gently.

"No," she said. "Why would you think that?"

"I don't know," he said. "Why *did* you come over here then?"

"To talk to you. To tell you what's been happening in my life. To maybe see if you wanted to occasionally go to dinner together."

"Before you ask me that and before I answer it, I have to tell you two things."

"What? That you're having an affair with a whale?"

"Not with her, no."

"With whom, then?"

"With two bisexual teenaged Chinese girls," he said.

"No, seriously," she said.

"I *am* serious," he said.

"You're really having an affair with two bisexual teenaged girls?" she said. "I refuse to believe that."

"It's true," he said.

"And what's the other thing?" she said.

"The other thing," he said, "is that I went to see a divorce lawyer today. I filed for a legal separation."

She stared at him for several seconds. He thought he saw flashes in her eyes of anger, hurt, and several other things before the invisible shield came down.

"I can't say I blame you," she said.

"It doesn't mean that we have to get a divorce," he said. "It just means that now *I* need a while to think."

"All right," she said. "I know that I still do myself."

She got up and walked to the door.

"I'll keep in touch," he said.

"Don't take any wooden fortune cookies," she said.

84

Lance felt rotten and elated about his meeting with Cathy. He honestly didn't know anymore if he wanted to continue the marriage. He had at first thought definitely yes, then definitely no, and now he had no idea at all. She had seemed so damned nice and so damned sensible and so damned vulnerable when she came to see him. He didn't know what he wanted to do about her.

He didn't know what he wanted to do about his novel either. His ten-city tour, although it had definitely hyped sales, had not put it onto the bestseller list. And now the sales were beginning to slide again. All he had left in the way of promotion was a book-and-author luncheon with a women's club in Westchester.

He called Mike Fieldston in advertising and promotion. Fieldston said the book was doing OK, but unless it got another shot in the arm it was just going to taper off and die. There wasn't any budget for another ad or another promotional tour, he said. Lance briefly regretted having severed his relationship with Claire—perhaps by engaging in a few more dangerous and demeaning sexual acts with her he could wangle another ad or a few more cities.

"Your only hope," said Fieldston, "is if one of the national TV talk shows, like *Donahue* or the *Tonight Show,* changes its mind and decides to put you on."

"What are the chances of that happening?" said Lance.

"It'll never happen," said Fieldston.

"So what you're saying," said Lance, "is that we're giving up?"

"Hey," said Fieldston, "you sold almost twenty thousand copies—that's not so terrible."

"I didn't even make back my advance yet," said Lance.

"So big deal," said Fieldston. "You're still a relatively young guy. Maybe you'll hit it really big on your next one."

"You mean that unless I get a big publicity break like *Donahue* or the *Tonight Show* I've had it?" said Lance. "Is that what you're saying?"

"That's it," said Fieldston. "A shot on Donahue or Carson would do it. Or maybe you could arrange to get stabbed to death in Macy's window."

85

Lance was dining with approximately one hundred fifty women in the ballroom of a Holiday Inn in Westchester. He was seated at the head table, next to a little lectern with a microphone on it from which, after the luncheon, he would address the assembled women on a number of self-serving subjects pertaining to his book. A little table had been set up at the back of the ballroom. On it were stacked about eighty or ninety copies of *Gallivanting*, which would be offered for sale after Lance's talk, personally autographed by the author. It was likely that Lance would sell at least six of them.

Lance munched on gray roast beef, drank white wine and alternately made small talk with the women at his table and pondered the women in his life. The women in his life—what had they seen in him? What had they wanted from him? Cathy had, at first, wanted a husband to look up to, to protect her, to fulfill her. Then she wanted a life of her own. Claire wanted a plaything to have kinky sex with and to control better than she had been able to control her own husband, perhaps. Stevie had wanted someone to introduce her to more celebrities whose names she would be able to drop. Dorothy and Janie had wanted a successful writer to emulate, and a father figure to feel ambivalent about sexually. Gladys wanted . . . God alone knew what Gladys wanted.

What, he wondered, do the women at this luncheon want from me? Surely not a chance to purchase a personally autographed copy of my book. Surely not gray roast beef and white wine. Surely not an hour-long speech about *Gallivanting*—so what *did* they want?

"What do you want?" said Lance to the woman on his immediate right, who was looking at him as though she were about to say something.

"A little more wine," she replied and extended her empty glass.

"I mean," said Lance, filling her glass, "aside from that."

"You mean in general?" she said.

"Yes. In general. In particular. In life. What do women want?"

"An end to televised sports," she said.

Lance chuckled good-naturedly and turned to the woman on his immediate left.

"What do women want?" he said.

"Sovereignty," she said.

Lance nodded, and turned to one of the women opposite him.

"What do women want?" he said.

"Acknowledgment," she said, "and unconditional love."

"What do women want?" he said to the woman on her left.

"Money," she said.

"What do women want?" he said to the woman on *her* left.

"Romance, excitement, and security," she said.

Lance nodded, impressed.

"And what do *men* want?" he said to her.

She thought a moment.

"Glamour, sex, and mother," she said.

"Aren't romance, excitement and security the same as glamour, sex and mother?" he said.

She shook her head.

"When I say mother," she said, "I mean a *disapproving* mother. My husband has made that very clear to me, and so that is the role I have decided to play with him."

"I see," said Lance, trying to envision the woman's marriage, and turning to the slightly spinsterly lady on her left. "What do women want?"

The spinsterly lady smiled sweetly at him.

"A good fuck," she said.

86

The second-to-last job that June, Alix, Sandy and Wanda did for the Motherloaders was to move all of the furniture out of an apartment on East 48th Street. It was actually kind of a funny scene. This chick was leaving her husband an empty apartment while she took all the furniture. Lerman or Lerner, the guy's name was, and he looked so amazed he must not have known she was going to do it. Served him right, the bastard.

The chick was friendly enough to them, but a little too good looking. June liberated a small jewelry box from her top bureau drawer when they were loading the truck. She figured the chick was rich enough that she probably wouldn't even know it was gone.

When June got home, though, and looked inside, she was disappointed. Inside the little purple velvet box was not a ring or a watch or a necklace—just these two gold balls, like steel ball bearings, only gold. June didn't see what they could be good for, but she thought maybe the gold was worth something at a pawnshop. In very delicate script somebody had engraved an inscription on them. It said: "For dearest Cathy, for when I can't be there. Love from Lance."

The guy at the hockshop seemed to know what they were all right, but when he tried to tell her he got kind of flustered. He said they were called boudoir balls or Ben Wa balls, and they were from the Orient. He said what you were supposed to do with them was to put them up inside your snatch and keep them there while you walked around and did the normal things you did during the day. June at first thought he was trying to come on to her and she almost decked him, but he didn't change his story even when she grabbed him by the shirtfront and shook him a little, so she figured he was probably telling the truth. After she let him go he squinted at

271

the balls through his little monocle and said that they were gold plated and not worth much, so June decided to hang on to them.

At home, just out of curiosity, she put the Ben Wa balls up inside her snatch like the guy had said you should. They didn't do all that much for her, to tell the truth, but they did sort of slide around in a pleasurable way, so June figured she'd keep them around and use them from time to time, when she needed an up.

June, Alix, Sandy and Wanda moved to Los Angeles. They found an apartment in El Segundo, not too far from the airport, and began planning the hijack in earnest.

Sandy located four pistols for them with no trouble at all—three .45 caliber Colt automatics and a .38 Smith & Wesson. At first they had thought they'd spend a lot of time transforming stilettos and swords and rifle barrels into metal crutches in order to get them past the metal detectors in airport security, but then Wanda remembered reading in *New York* magazine that you could get these lead foil bags for photographic film and put anything you like in them, even guns, and they wouldn't show up on the X-rays of the metal detectors, so that is when they switched to guns.

June found flights from Los Angeles to Honolulu that she liked on Braniff, TWA, Global and Pan Am. Wanda said she liked Braniff because of the great colors the planes were painted. June had read that the FAA had recently ordered Braniff to pay $1,500,000 for improper maintenance and other illegal procedures. Alix said she heard that Pan Am wasn't all that safe either. They finally settled on a Global flight to Honolulu departing Los Angeles on October 21st at 8:00 p.m., because it had a better movie than the equivalent flight on TWA.

87

The voice on the phone was not unfamiliar.

"Don't hang up, Mr. Lerner," it said, "I got a proposition I think you might go for."

"Who is this and why would I hang up on you?" said Lance.

"It's Julius Blatt, Mr. Lerner. The attorney for the Dalton Two? I'm sorry—the attorney for Ernest Roosevelt and Irving Washington."

"Yes, of course, Mr. Blatt," said Lance. "What can I do for you?"

"I know that you are not entirely pleased by our use of the slogan 'Free the Dalton Two' which you gave us, but not so displeased as to not attend the fund-raising dinner we had for them."

"Touché, Mr. Blatt," said Lance.

"What I am calling about," said Blatt, "is a matter of mutual benefit to both parties . . ."

"Go on, Mr. Blatt . . ."

"I understand that your current novel is doing good, but not so good that you would be averse to taking advantage of a good publicity break if you saw one staring you in the face."

"What is your proposition, Mr. Blatt?"

"Knowing your unhappiness with our use of the slogan which you gave us, do you think you would still appear with Goose and Ernest on a program and speak of the manner in which you conceived the campaign and the terrible injustice that you feel has befallen them?"

"What is the show you wish me to do this on, Mr. Blatt?" said Lance.

"The *Tonight Show*," said Blatt.

"Are you serious about this, Mr. Blatt?" said Lance.

"May my mother be hit by a tractor-trailer," said Blatt.

"And when would this show take place?" said Lance.

"They'll only take us as a package," said Blatt. "You, me, Goose and Ernest. They want us tomorrow. We'd have to fly out in the morning. I'll spring for the air fare."

It was, of course, exactly the promotional boost his novel needed, but to appear on national TV with the Dalton Two would be endorsing a cause that was entirely fraudulent. True, he had helped them before, but it had been inadvertent. This time it would be advertent, premeditated, and a total sellout. There were certain things a man had to avoid at all costs if he wanted to keep his self-esteem. Perhaps this wasn't one of them.

"Mr. Blatt," said Lance, "you have got yourself a panelist."

88

Lance gave Dorothy and Janie instructions about things to be done while he was gone, and then he took a cab to the airport. For some reason it did not occur to him on this particular trip to have a premonition of disaster.

Blatt and his two clients were not at the gate, and when he inquired whether they were listed as passengers on the flight he was given an envelope with his name on it.

"Mr. Lerner," said the letter inside, "I and the boys have decided to take an earlier flight so as to allow them to see something of Tinsel Town before the show. Hope this is AOK with you. See you in the Green Room." It was signed simply "Blatt."

Lance smiled a bemused smile. It was certainly AOK with him. He was not anxious to spend any more time than he had to with either The Dalton Two or their counselor.

The flight to Los Angeles was uneventful. Lance picked up his luggage and arranged to rent a Hertz car. He had plenty of time so he drove to the Beverly Hills Hotel, checked in, had

And when would this show take place?" said Lance.

They'll only take us as a package," said Blatt. "You, me, se and Ernest. They want us tomorrow. We'd have to fly in the morning. I'll spring for the air fare."

was, of course, exactly the promotional boost his novel ded, but to appear on national TV with the Dalton Two ld be endorsing a cause that was entirely fraudulent. e, he had helped them before, but it had been inadver-t. This time it would be advertent, premeditated, and a l sellout. There were certain things a man had to avoid at costs if he wanted to keep his self-esteem. Perhaps this n't one of them.

Mr. Blatt," said Lance, "you have got yourself a panel-"

88

nce gave Dorothy and Janie instructions about things to be ne while he was gone, and then he took a cab to the port. For some reason it did not occur to him on this rticular trip to have a premonition of disaster.

Blatt and his two clients were not at the gate, and when he quired whether they were listed as passengers on the flight was given an envelope with his name on it.

"Mr. Lerner," said the letter inside, "I and the boys have cided to take an earlier flight so as to allow them to see mething of Tinsel Town before the show. Hope this is AOK th you. See you in the Green Room." It was signed simply latt."

Lance smiled a bemused smile. It was certainly AOK with n. He was not anxious to spend any more time than he had with either The Dalton Two or their counselor.

The flight to Los Angeles was uneventful. Lance picked up luggage and arranged to rent a Hertz car. He had plenty of e so he drove to the Beverly Hills Hotel, checked in, had

86

The second-to-last job that June, Alix, Sandy and Wanda did for the Motherloaders was to move all of the furniture out of an apartment on East 48th Street. It was actually kind of a funny scene. This chick was leaving her husband an empty apartment while she took all the furniture. Lerman or Lerner, the guy's name was, and he looked so amazed he must not have known she was going to do it. Served him right, the bastard.

The chick was friendly enough to them, but a little too good looking. June liberated a small jewelry box from her top bureau drawer when they were loading the truck. She figured the chick was rich enough that she probably wouldn't even know it was gone.

When June got home, though, and looked inside, she was disappointed. Inside the little purple velvet box was not a ring or a watch or a necklace—just these two gold balls, like steel ball bearings, only gold. June didn't see what they could be good for, but she thought maybe the gold was worth something at a pawnshop. In very delicate script somebody had engraved an inscription on them. It said: "For dearest Cathy, for when I can't be there. Love from Lance."

The guy at the hockshop seemed to know what they were all right, but when he tried to tell her he got kind of flustered. He said they were called boudoir balls or Ben Wa balls, and they were from the Orient. He said what you were supposed to do with them was to put them up inside your snatch and keep them there while you walked around and did the normal things you did during the day. June at first thought he was trying to come on to her and she almost decked him, but he didn't change his story even when she grabbed him by the shirtfront and shook him a little, so she figured he was probably telling the truth. After she let him go he squinted at the balls through his little monocle and said that they were gold plated and not worth much, so June decided to hang on to them.

At home, just out of curiosity, she put the Ben Wa balls up inside her snatch like the guy had said you should. They didn't do all that much for her, to tell the truth, but they did sort of slide around in a pleasurable way, so June figured she'd keep them around and use them from time to time, when she needed an up.

June, Alix, Sandy and Wanda moved to Los Angeles. They found an apartment in El Segundo, not too far from the airport, and began planning the hijack in earnest.

Sandy located four pistols for them with no trouble at all—three .45 caliber Colt automatics and a .38 Smith & Wesson. At first they had thought they'd spend a lot of time transforming stilettos and swords and rifle barrels into metal crutches in order to get them past the metal detectors in airport security, but then Wanda remembered reading in *New York* magazine that you could get these lead foil bags for photographic film and put anything you like in them, even guns, and they wouldn't show up on the X-rays of the metal detectors, so that is when they switched to guns.

June found flights from Los Angeles to Honolulu that she liked on Braniff, TWA, Global and Pan Am. Wanda said she liked Braniff because of the great colors the planes were painted. June had read that the FAA had recently ordered Braniff to pay $1,500,000 for improper maintenance and other illegal procedures. Alix said she heard that Pan Am wasn't all that safe either. They finally settled on a Global flight to Honolulu departing Los Angeles on October 21st at 8:00 p.m., because it had a better movie than the equivalent flight on TWA.

87

The voice on the phone was not unfamiliar.

"Don't hang up, Mr. Lerner," it said, "I got a think you might go for."

"Who is this and why would I hang up o Lance.

"It's Julius Blatt, Mr. Lerner. The attorney f Two? I'm sorry—the attorney for Ernest R Irving Washington."

"Yes, of course, Mr. Blatt," said Lance. "Wha you?"

"I know that you are not entirely pleased by o slogan 'Free the Dalton Two' which you gave u displeased as to not attend the fund-raising dinne them."

"Touché, Mr. Blatt," said Lance.

"What I am calling about," said Blatt, "is mutual benefit to both parties . . ."

"Go on, Mr. Blatt . . ."

"I understand that your current novel is doir not so good that you would be averse to taking a good publicity break if you saw one staring you

"What is your proposition, Mr. Blatt?"

"Knowing your unhappiness with our use o which you gave us, do you think you would still Goose and Ernest on a program and speak of th which you conceived the campaign and the terr that you feel has befallen them?"

"What is the show you wish me to do this on, said Lance.

"The *Tonight Show*," said Blatt.

"Are you serious about this, Mr. Blatt?" said

"May my mother be hit by a tractor-trailer,"

himself paged at the pool and in the Polo Lounge so people would know he was there. Then he went out and hit several bookstores in the Beverly Hills area before finally heading over to Burbank to tape the show.

"Mr. Lerner," said Blatt, "may I present my clients, Ernest Roosevelt and Goose Washington."

"Mah man!" said Ernest.

"Mah man!" said Goose.

"Likewise," said Lance.

"Mr. Lerner, Goose and Ah, we very grateful for all that you done," said Ernest.

"It was nothing," said Lance truthfully.

"No," said Ernest, "we very grateful. Anything you want —Ah don't care *what*—you ask us."

"Well, thank you," said Lance. "That's very kind."

Lance was trying to be polite. It wasn't *their* fault they thought he'd expended a lot of effort on their behalf.

"So," said Blatt, "how were you planning to characterize the boys when you speak of them on the show?"

"Well," said Lance carefully, "I thought I would say that they were stunning examples of the lengths that talented ghetto youths will go to in order to find a showcase for their work."

"Sounds AOK to me," said Blatt, nodding his head approvingly. "How does it sound to *you*, boys?"

"Dy-no-*mite*, bro'!" said Ernest.

"Dy-no-*mite*, bro'!" said Goose.

"Well," said Lance during a longish pause that threatened to become awkward if not broken, "congratulations on your book deal, Ernest."

"Thanks," said Ernest.

"From what I hear," said Lance, "they gave you very good terms."

Ernest shrugged.

"Mr. Blatt say he can't get them to go no mo' than a fifty-fifty split on the paperback rights," said Ernest, raising his eyebrows.

"Well," said Lance, "Firestone hasn't done better than that for anyone else so far, either."

"Then it time," said Ernest.

"Well, you're right about that," said Lance. "As long as hardcover houses continue keeping fifty percent of their books' paperback advances, they're more in the business of selling rights than selling books—which probably explains why they don't do a better job at the retail level."

"You right," said Ernest. "That a fact."

Lance felt peculiar talking fairly sophisticated publishing jargon to a young black kid who couldn't even speak grammatically, but in a funny way he sensed that Ernest understood everything that he was saying.

"Hey, Mr. Lerner," said Blatt, "I want to ask you something."

"Please," said Lance, "call me Lance. All of you."

"OK then, Lance," said Blatt. "What would you say to a little proposition?"

"What sort of proposition?" said Lance uneasily. From Blatt's tone he could tell it would not be untainted.

"What do you say we talk after the show about maybe helping out a little on the writing of Ernest's book?"

"What sort of help did you have in mind?" said Lance.

Blatt held his palms parallel about a foot apart, then shrugged.

"What about ghost-writing it for him?" said Blatt.

Lance smiled and shook his head.

"No thanks," he said. "I've got more than enough of my own writing to do."

"Think it over," said Blatt. "Don't give me an answer till later."

"All right," said Lance.

"The money is good," said Blatt. "Better than you're getting on your present book."

"I'm aware of that," said Lance dryly.

"Don't give me an answer now," said Blatt.

"OK," said Lance, "I won't."

Lance turned and saw that Goose was grinning at him idiotically. Lance grinned back. Goose goosed him.

89

"My next guests," said Johnny Carson in the awed tones he might have used to introduce Albert Einstein or Sir Winston Churchill, "are two rather unusual and gifted men. Ernest Hemingway Roosevelt and Irving Goose Washington are two young black authors from Harlem who robbed a *bookstore* to call attention to their writing—writing which they felt would otherwise go unnoticed. They were convicted of grand larceny—is that right, Ed? Were they actually *convicted*, or . . . ?"

"*Indicted*," said Ed McMahon.

"I'm sorry," said Carson. "They were *indicted* for grand larceny, and through the efforts of Public Defender Julius Blatt and author Lance Lerner, they have become something of a cause célèbre in the literary and artistic community as The Dalton Two. Would you welcome, please, The Dalton Two and their defenders."

Ernest, Goose, Blatt and Lance came out, shook hands with Johnny and Ed, and then sat down. Carson seemed unsure of what tack to take with them and was apparently waiting to take his cue from them.

"Well," said Carson, "I must say you two gentlemen chose a somewhat . . . *unorthodox* method of calling attention to your work . . ."

The studio audience chuckled politely.

"If you robbed a bookstore to call attention to your writing," said Carson, "I suppose we ought to be grateful you aren't *munitions* manufacturers . . ."

A slight titter from the audience.

"Or distributors of . . . cesspools . . ."

A throatier laugh from the audience.

"Goose," said McMahon, sensing the segment was going to

bomb and taking a gamble on saving it, "why do they call you Goose?"

Goose turned to McMahon, grinning idiotically, and goosed him. The audience, taken totally by surprise, exploded into relieved laughter—these men weren't intimidating militant Negroes, they were vulgar down-home guys, just like the rest of us. Carson, unexpectedly delighted, touched the knot of his tie and did seven consecutive takes for the camera, milking at least three orgasms of laughter out of the audience. It was going to be a fun segment after all.

Ernest got to say a few words about writing, Blatt got to say a few words about the courage of young people today who came from disadvantaged ethnic communities, Lance got to say how important it was for the literary community to keep getting fresh infusions of life from the Third World and somehow managed to mention the title of his book three times. But the overwhelming favorite was Goose. He didn't say a total of three words the whole segment, but whenever the camera went to him, the audience fell down laughing.

They were the last segment or Carson would have held them over. As it was, he asked them to come back. They all said that they would.

When the show was through taping, Blatt asked Lance if he could take him to dinner. Lance pleaded previous plans with a sales rep from his publishing house. Blatt said he would see Lance the following evening on the plane back to New York. He and the boys were taking the 9:00 p.m. flight on TWA— the so-called red-eye—to enable the boys to spend the whole day taking in the sights of Tinsel Town, taking the studio tour at Universal and also taking a preliminary meeting there about the screenplay of Ernest's book.

Lance said that he had already made plans to go back on the 4:00 p.m. flight on American since he had a breakfast meeting in New York the following day. Blatt seemed disappointed but said he'd catch Lance in the city.

All in all, thought Lance as he left the studio, it had gone OK, but he doubted that the segment had sold many copies of his book. Well, he rationalized, at least it had done a lot for The Dalton Two. And since he was now publicly associated with the name, perhaps it would help him obscurely in whatever subsequent publicity they got on their own.

If he hurried, he could still visit one more bookstore before dinner.

90

His dread of flying was, for some reason, stronger than usual. He got to the Los Angeles airport with plenty of time to spare, turned in his rented car to Hertz, exaggerated only slightly on his form the amount of gas remaining in the tank as shown on the gas gauge, rode the Hertz courtesy bus to the American Airlines terminal and checked in at 3:25 for his 4:00 p.m. flight to New York. He inquired once more to make sure the plane wasn't a DC-10. It was not.

Within seconds of handing over his suitcase and watching it depart on its jolly little funhouse ride on the moving rubber belt and disappear, he was informed that the 4:00 flight was being delayed. How long or why, nobody seemed to know. Airline employees always tried to make it seem that the delays were caused by things like late deliveries of hollandaise sauce for the asparagus tips, but he knew better. He visualized drunken mechanics jamming dozens of pieces of delicate machinery into a jet engine that had fallen off onto the runway, then rubber-cementing it back onto the wing.

A smiling airline employee informed him at 4:00 that the plane was now scheduled to depart at 5:24 p.m. He was angry and demanded that his luggage be returned to him so he could take another flight. It was, the employee informed him, too late for that. Why didn't he simply go into the bar and relax? If he chose an earlier flight he would only have to wait at the other end for the plane with his luggage.

He decided to wait in the bar and keep his luggage company on the plane at 5:24. He resented the pretense on the part of the airline that they had enough assurance to pinpoint the time of departure that closely. He felt it would be more honest for them to say "sixish" instead of 5:24.

As he entered the bar he was dimly aware that he might be

receiving an extrasensory warning from his brain and from the collective unconscious that the flight with the baggage would crash on takeoff and that the sole purpose of the delay was to enable him to take another plane. He turned around and headed back to the gate, determined to let his luggage crash and take an earlier plane. But when he was within steps of the gate he got another extrasensory warning to ignore the previous message: it was not the flight with the *luggage* that would crash but the one he would *transfer* to, the one that departed earlier. If he did transfer onto the doomed plane at the last moment, his friends would speak of the tragic irony of his decision for years. He went back into the bar.

At 5:00 he paid for the three White Russians he had consumed, then walked to the gate. The lounge was empty. An airline employee he hadn't seen before was irritated when Lance inquired about his 5:24 flight. It was not a *5:24* flight, she said, it was a *4:00* flight, and it had departed, following a slight delay, at 4:45.

Lance was outraged. How could that have happened? He'd been told his flight was delayed till 5:24. He'd been told to wait in the bar.

The woman was not remorseful nor much impressed with his fury. It was true, she said, that the initial delay had been estimated at 5:24, but the trouble they'd had was then corrected and the new departure time had been duly announced on the p.a. system, and all of the other passengers had got on the plane and left without him. *Nobody,* she said, would have suggested that he wait in the bar, since it was common knowledge that the p.a. system could not be *heard* in the bar. If he hurried, she said, he could still probably get on the Global flight for New York which was scheduled to depart at 5:15 p.m. It was now 5:05.

Boiling with impotent rage, Lance raced away from the American departure lounge and headed down the hallway toward Global. At Global he was required to go through security once more, and although he had had no trouble at American, the metal detector at Global beeped when he went through it. The uniformed female security guard gave him a crappy little plastic box for his coins and keys and motioned for him to go through again, but when he did so it beeped again.

"I just went through security at American," he said. "It didn't beep there, even with my coins and keys."

"You've got too much metal," said the tight-lipped security woman. "Take some more off and try it again."

"But I have to catch a *plane*," he said, glancing at his watch. "It's after 5:10—my plane leaves at 5:15!"

The security guard did not appear to be alarmed.

"You should have thought of that earlier," she said, and motioned for him to go through again.

He took off his watch and put it in the plastic box and went through the metal detector again, and again it beeped.

"Take off your belt," said the security woman.

"If I take off my belt my pants will fall down," said Lance.

The security woman did not seem to be amused.

"Take off your belt," she repeated.

"And what comes next, the fillings in my teeth?" said Lance.

He took off his belt and put it in the crappy plastic box. His pants did not fall down, but the beeper beeped again when he went through it.

"Follow me," said the security woman.

"What for?" said Lance.

"We're going to have to search you."

"But I'll miss my *plane*."

The security woman unsnapped her holster. Lance sighed and followed her into a room marked "Security." It had a plain wooden table and a hard-backed chair and a metal locker. She closed the door behind them.

"Strip," she said.

"You're going to search me?" said Lance. "Not a *man?"*

"That's correct," she said. She took out a hard case of cigarettes, removed one, tapped the end on the box and lit it.

"I thought *men* searched men and women searched *women*," said Lance. "I mean I thought that's how it worked."

"Are you going to strip or aren't you?" said the security woman, removing her gun from its holster with elaborate casualness.

"Yes," said Lance. "Yes, I am."

He took off his jacket and tie and shirt and draped them over the back of the chair. She went through all the pockets and examined their contents. She was a plain-looking, even a homely, woman. She had doubtless been ignored or worse by most of the men in her life and she had probably deeply resented it. Here was an ideal opportunity to wreak vengeance on a proxy for the sex that had not appreciated her. He took off his boots and socks and handed them to her. She looked inside them, turned them over, found nothing.

"I'm sorry you feel you have to do this," said Lance. "You must not be a very happy person."

Her nostrils flared. She gave him a piercing look.

"Pants," she said between clenched teeth.

He unzipped his trousers and handed them to her. She went through his pockets with a vengeance. He resigned himself to having missed the second plane.

"I'm sure there are *plenty* of men who would love to go out with you," said Lance, realizing he was not pursuing a fruitful line of conversation, but unable to stop. "You seem like a nice person, and you aren't bad looking. I mean, you do have nice . . . *skin* and everything," he added, hastily scanning her for complimentable features.

"Drawers," she said.

"Pardon me?" said Lance.

"Take down your drawers."

Oh boy, he thought, I get to make up for at least six guys on this one. He pushed down his jockey shorts and handed them to her. She was staring quite frankly at his genitals.

"OK," he said, "you've searched me and you didn't find an M-16 or a hand grenade. Are you satisfied, now that I've needlessly missed my plane? Can I go now?"

"Up on the table," she said.

"What?"

"Up on the table on your knees and elbows."

"What the hell *for?*"

"I have to search your rectum."

"You're kidding me. What do you think you're going to find up there, a bazooka?"

The security woman leveled her pistol at him.

"Up on the table. Knees and elbows."

Angry and humiliated, Lance got up on the table on his knees and elbows, with his ass facing her. He was conscious of how ludicrous he looked and of how the security woman must be relishing his discomfort.

"Spread your cheeks," she said.

"Don't think this isn't going to be reported," he said. "I happen to know a few people in the Port Authority and in the Mayor's Office. You're going to regret your actions, I can promise you that."

"Spread 'em," she said and laid the cold butt of the revolver on his flank.

"You're going to be sorry you did this," he said. "You can't imagine *how* sorry."

The door opened and someone came in.

"Who the hell is that?" said a female voice, obviously referring Lance.

"Some asshole who knows people in the Mayor's Office," said the security woman.

"We're getting stacked up out there," said the visitor, "you better come and help."

"OK," said the security woman.

"Does that mean I can go?" said Lance.

The door opened. Lance turned around. The security woman and the visitor, also a security woman, were leaving. Several people outside the door, startled by the sight of a naked man on his knees and elbows on a table, were peering in at him. Lance hastily covered himself.

"You can go," said the visiting security woman. The one who had made him strip was already outside, having departed without so much as a cursory apology.

By the time Lance got dressed again it was 5:30. He was certain the Global flight had already departed, but having gone to so much trouble to gain entrance to the Global terminal he was loath to leave. He walked to the gate at a leisurely pace, and was rewarded for his peculiar brand of optimism—the 5:15 flight had boarded but had not yet left the gate. He gave his ticket to the flight attendant at the desk and scampered aboard.

91

They stood in the security area of the Global terminal and synchronized their watches. It was precisely 7:00 p.m., October 21st.

They wore khaki jumpsuits and carried small overnight bags. A lead-foil pouch containing a pistol was in each woman's overnight bag. The heavier bags they'd checked when they arrived at curbside on the Budget Rent-a-Car courtesy bus.

They had gone through every step of the plan over and over again, so there was no need to be nervous, but still they were nervous. Alix and Sandy were trying to pretend that they were calm, but June noticed that their hands were trembling. June thought Wanda looked so scared she might pee in her pants.

June herself betrayed nothing on the outside, but inside she was a wreck. She'd been up half the night with an upset stomach and a good case of the jitters. Before leaving the apartment that final time for the airport, June had gone into the bathroom with her overnight bag and closed the door and locked it securely behind her. She was going to do a few private things to give herself courage which she didn't happen to feel like sharing with the others and risk getting laughed at.

June took out a beautiful purple garter belt, a pair of purple stockings with seams up the back, a purple bra and a pair of beautiful purple panties. She had imagined it was her father and not she who had bought them for her, and that if she wore them in secret under her unfeminine jumpsuit during the hijack, in some way her father's immense physical strength would magically protect her.

She pulled off her jumpsuit and her white cotton underpants. She languidly drew on the sensuous lingerie, imagining that her father was watching her. Finally she put the jumpsuit back on, shoved the white underpants in her bag, unlocked the door and went out to join her co-conspirators.

Now, at a nod from June, the others got in line at the metal detector—first Sandy, then Alix, then Wanda, with June bringing up the rear. All four women had stopped breathing as they watched their overnight bags with the guns disappear on the moving black belt. Had *New York* magazine been right? Would the lead-foil pouches truly obscure the silhouettes of the pistols? Or would the guns be seen, whistles blown, alarms sounded, airport security police rush forward to clamp them into handcuffs and take them away to jail?

There was a silence. And then a gruff male voice behind them spoke:

"OK, girls—move it!"

June's heart stopped beating. Wanda's hands went halfway up in surrender. They all turned around to find, not the chief of security police, but a disgruntled passenger urging them to move on through the archway.

They breathed a collective sigh of relief. Sandy went through the archway. Nothing beeped. Alix went through next. No warning sounded. Wanda went through after Alix, and June stepped up to go through next. June could see their four overnight bags, neatly stacked at the end of the belt, waiting for them. It was going to work!

June stepped through the archway and the beeper beeped. A security woman walked up to her.

"Try it again," she said, handing June a blue polyurethane container.

With shaking hands, June reached into a zippered pocket, deposited keys and coins in the plastic box, went through the archway again. Again it beeped.

June looked at Sandy, Wanda and Alix. They stared back at her, afraid to move. June took off her watch and dropped it into the plastic box, then nodded to Sandy and looked in the direction of the four overnight bags. Sandy nodded, and swiftly took all four bags off the belt. June went through the arch again. Again it beeped.

"Follow me," said the security woman.

"What for?" said June, her pulse thundering in her ears.

"I'm going to have to search you."

"But we have a plane to catch. We're going to Hawaii on the 8:00 plane."

"Everybody's going *somewhere,* sister," said the security woman. "Do you have any carry-on luggage?"

"No," said June. "I checked everything at the curb."

"Good," said the security woman, guiding her gently toward a door marked SECURITY. "Less work for mother."

June followed the security woman into the room. There was a plain wooden table and a hard-backed chair and a metal locker. The security woman closed the door.

"OK, honey, strip," she said.

"Are you sure you have to do this?" said June, thinking of her purple lingerie and blushing deeply. "I'm not carrying any guns or explosives. I'm a working woman, same as yourself, going to Hawaii on vacation."

"If you strip fast enough," said the security woman not unpleasantly, "you might even make it onto that 8:00 plane with your friends."

June sighed. She unzipped her jumpsuit and peeled it down. The security woman's eyebrows went up. She whistled a wolf whistle.

"Is there some law against a woman wearing feminine underthings?" said June, her face hot with shame.

"Not at all, not at all," said the security woman. "I just didn't figure you as the type to wear stuff like that."

"Why not?" said June, but she didn't want to hear the answer.

"Let's see it, honey," said the security woman, holding out her hands.

Without looking her in the eye, June unhooked her bra and garter belt, slid down her stockings and panties, took them off and handed them to the security woman in a pile. The woman looked frankly at June's stocky body, then went through the lingerie.

"OK?" said June. "Are you satisfied now?"

The security woman took out a pocket-sized metal detector and passed it quickly over June's naked skin. When it reached her pubic area it emitted a high-pitched whine.

Oh, Jesus, thought June, the fucking Ben Wa balls!

"Up on the table, sister," said the security woman.

"Please don't do this," said June softly. "I think I know what's causing the metal detector to react, and I promise you it's not anything like a weapon or a bomb."

"Up on the *table,*" said the security woman. She put down her portable metal detector and unsnapped her holster.

"Have you ever heard of something called Ben Wa balls?" said June, cursing her stupidity for needlessly jeopardizing the entire hijack operation with such moronic self-indulgence.

"Up on the table. Knees and elbows."

The security woman leveled her pistol at June.

Furious and ashamed, June got up on the table.

"Spread 'em," said the security woman.

June did as she was told. The security woman let out another whistle.

"What the hell is that gold thing in your twat?" said the security woman.

"Ben Wa balls," said June, "I just asked you if you knew what they were."

"I think I'd better get the bomb squad in here on the double," said the security woman, unsnapping her walkie-talkie from her belt.

"No, wait," said June, *"please* wait. It's not a bomb, I swear to you. It's Ben Wa balls. Boudoir balls. It's an Oriental thing. A sex thing, all right?"

"How does it work?"

"You just put these two balls inside yourself and they sort of slide around in there. It feels very . . . sexy."

"I don't know. I think maybe the bomb squad should handle this. I don't know too much about this type of thing."

"Please don't call the bomb squad. I don't want a bunch of leering, sexist pigs sticking their fingers up my pussy—do you blame me?"

The security woman sighed.

"I guess not."

"Good," said June. "We women have to stick together, that's the only chance we've got against them—if we stick together."

"Well, you're sure right about *that,*" said the security woman.

"Damn right I am," said June. "We've got to stick together and fight back, even if the way we fight back sometimes looks kind of extreme."

"What do you mean extreme?" said the security woman.

"Well, like that group, MATE—Men Are The Enemy. Have you heard of them?"

"The ones that cut that rapist's balls off," said the security woman.

June nodded.

"What would you say if I told you I'm the leader of that group?" said June, aware that she was taking a chance.

The security woman looked at her oddly.

"You're the one that cut off his balls?"

June nodded, watching the security woman's face for a sign.

"Goddamn," said the security woman, breaking into a huge smile and reaching out to shake June's hand. "If it was me, I'd 've sliced off his goddamn pecker too!"

By the time June got done telling the security woman about MATE's activities—wisely deleting any mention of the impending hijack—and showing her the Ben Wa balls, it was too late to make the 8:00 flight to Hawaii. The security woman was very apologetic and went and found a schedule of flights to Hawaii while June was getting back into her clothes.

There were no other flights to Hawaii on Global that day, but the security woman found one on Braniff that left at 10:00 p.m. June was just about to voice her objections to Braniff when something else caught her eye: there was a 9:00 p.m. flight on TWA to New York which would serve her purposes quite nicely—once you hijacked an airplane, you could make it go in any direction you wanted to.

She told the security woman the Braniff flight would do, then went out and picked up her three very worried friends. They got to the TWA gate just as the 9:00 p.m. flight to New York began boarding.

92

Captain Eddie "Hap" Harrigan was getting madder than hell. His Global DC-10 had been scheduled for departure from LAX at 5:15, and now here it was 6:45 and they were no closer to departure than they had been an hour ago.

First the goddamned aft cargo door wouldn't lock, next the flight recorder was on the fritz, and after that somebody had kicked over an entire cart of First Class meals and Sky Chefs were taking their own sweet time about replacing them.

Hap pulled out his silver flask of Calvert Manhattans and took a healthy swig, and got a disapproving eyebrow-raise from his first officer, Bubba Bogan.

"Hey, good buddy," said Bubba, "go easy on that stuff, will ya? We don't need any more near misses on this flight."

"Hey, good buddy," said Hap, "up your giggy with a lighted ciggy."

Hap resented Bubba's implication that the near miss with the TWA L1011 on the way into LAX had had anything to do with his drinking. Any flight that you *didn't* have a near miss, as Bubba well knew, was a dull flight, plus which if he was going to have to fly an aircraft as shitty as a DC-10, he was damned if he was going to do it sober.

The DC-10, in Hap's opinion and in the opinion of a great many pilots, was an original piece of garbage, but he was not anxious to downgrade. Stepping down from the DC-10 to a smaller aircraft required a pay cut of $1,000 to $2,000 a month. He was not *that* interested in safety.

Besides, even if the aircraft were safe, there were other things to worry about. Like this airport, for instance. The International Federation of Airline Pilots Associations had awarded LAX its Black Star rating, a rating reserved for only the most dangerous airports. How the FAA allowed operations as suicidal as those that were permitted here was beyond him—planes took off and landed at LAX in opposite directions on parallel runways. Bubba himself had called it a 200-mile-per-hour game of Chicken.

No, the only way to not let it all get to you was never to fly sober, and let the chips fall where they may. If your number was up, then your number was up, and fuck the passengers.

A stew from the Coach section poked her head into the cockpit and asked what everybody wanted for dinner. Her name was Cindy or Trudy or something, and she was always fooling around with drugs. How could you respect anybody who took drugs? He was fairly sure she was the one who had complained about the size of his wang. Miserable little slut. Small wonder she thought he had a tiny wang—if she was the stew he was thinking she was, she had a crack the size of Bryce Canyon.

93

Lance was livid. For the past hour and a half he had been sitting patiently in his seat, waiting for the Global flight to take off for New York. His baggage, he figured, was now hurtling eastward somewhere over Arizona. It would arrive several hours before him and go trundling around on the baggage carousel, unclaimed, until somebody lifted it off and quickly stripped it of valuables.

Worse yet, he realized he had inadvertently stumbled onto a DC-10, after scrupulously avoiding the jinxed wide-bodies on all but one of his last dozen flights. He wondered if it was worth the bother of getting off and taking his chances on being able to still find a 707, a 747 or an L1011 this late in the day. With his luck, the DC-10 would land safely and the plane he transferred to would collide with a Cessna and land in several counties of Kansas simultaneously.

He looked around for somebody who might be able to give

him a progress report and realized he hadn't seen any flight attendants about in quite a while. He got out of his seat and moseyed over to the galley.

The curtains to the galley were drawn and he could hear hysterical female giggling coming from the other side. He didn't know if it was proper to simply pull back the curtain or if he should ask for permission first.

"Uh, excuse me," he called out, but the giggling continued with no acknowledgment of his having spoken. He didn't see why he had to seek permission to enter anyway. After all, what could they be doing behind that curtain, showering?

"Excuse me," he called again. His hand went up automatically as if to knock, but he realized the idiocy of trying to knock on a curtain and finally just pulled it open.

Two stewardesses looked up guiltily. They were both blond and young and fairly good looking in dissimilar ways. Each of them was holding a short plastic drinking straw in the vicinity of her nose. On the stainless-steel counter in front of them was an open plastic container full of white powder.

"Can I help you?" said the one nearest the curtain.

"Yeah," said Lance, eyeing the white powder, "I just wanted to know—are we almost there?"

Both stewardesses exploded with laughter. It had not been a witticism worthy of that kind of response, he knew. He figured they were stoned.

"C'mon in," said the one nearest the curtain.

He stepped into the galley and she drew the curtain closed again.

"Want some nose candy?" said the other stewardess.

"OK," he said.

The one nearest him handed him the container of white powder and the straw. He covered one nostril and breathed in deeply with the other.

"Hey," said the one farthest from him, "what's your name, *Hoover?*"

"No, Lerner," said Lance and snorted from the opposite side.

"I'm Trudy," said the far stew, "and this is Judy."

"Trudy and Judy," said Lance. "Say, you aren't twins by any chance, are you?"

Both stews looked stunned.

"That's really far out you should say that," said Trudy, "you know?"

"Oh?" said Lance.

"Yeah," said Judy. "We're both Geminis, and there's no way you could have known that."

"You're both Geminis?" said Lance. "Far out." He hated discussions like this, but was willing to see where it might take him nonetheless.

"Really," said Trudy. "I mean I'm on the cusp, but still."

"What are *you?*" said Judy.

"Jewish," said Lance.

"I mean what sign?" said Judy.

Lance was surprised, and *not* surprised, that people still spoke this way.

"I'm a Gemini too," said Lance, savoring the inevitable reaction.

Trudy and Judy looked at each other dumbfounded.

"I don't *believe* it," said Trudy.

"Three *Geminis,*" said Judy. "Talk about *synchronicity!*"

"What do you have rising?" said Trudy.

"What I have rising," said Lance, "is my gorge. Why have we been sitting on the ground in this plane for the past hour and a half?"

"Hey," said Judy, "don't lay that on *us,* OK? I mean, it's not *our* fault."

"I'm not saying it is," said Lance. "I just don't understand why we're sitting here and not moving, that's all."

"Oh," said Judy. "Well, if you really want to know, I'll tell you. First the aft cargo door wouldn't lock. Then some asshole kicked over the First Class meals, and we've been waiting for replacements."

"Plus which the flight recorder wasn't working either," said Trudy. "Flight recorders come in real handy when you crash."

"When you crash," said Lance, "or *if?"*

"When," said Trudy. "It's only a matter of time."

Judy nodded.

"Flying is Russian roulette," said Judy.

Lance looked at them carefully.

"Are you serious about that," he said, "or are you joking?"

Trudy and Judy inhaled another line of cocaine each.

"It's nothing to joke about," said Judy.

"You mean flying is really as dangerous as I've always feared it was?" said Lance, not sure how eager he was to get into this discussion.

"Oh, lots worse," said Trudy.

"You mean," said Lance, "the equipment itself isn't up to snuff, or the people who operate it aren't?"

Trudy and Judy looked at each other and sighed.

"You don't really want to know this, do you?" said Judy.

"In a terrible way," said Lance, "I do. I mean I feel I ought to. Not everything, maybe, just a couple things to kind of give me the picture."

"OK," said Trudy, "where do you want to start?"

"Equipment," said Lance.

"Equipment," said Trudy. "OK, well, the equipment you're on now is a DC-10, which is a lemon if I've ever seen one. Two stews we know died on the DC-10 that went down last week in Newark."

"I'm sorry to hear that," said Lance. "I knew DC-10s were dangerous, but I don't know why."

"First of all, the pylon that attaches the engines to the wing sometimes cracks and breaks off," said Judy. "Second, the aft cargo door doesn't stay locked very well and has a habit of blowing off, which causes the cabin floor to collapse, which happens to be where the control cables are located. Third—"

"If the DC-10s are so dangerous," said Lance, "how come you fly them?"

"Shit, I don't know," said Trudy. "Both Judy and me are planning to give them up. But then, we're planning to give up smoking too, and we haven't done that either."

"The thing of it is, is that it almost doesn't matter that the other planes are safer," said Judy. "Because the peckerheads that service DC-10s are just as out-to-lunch as the dorks that service the 747s and the L1011s."

"What do you mean out-to-lunch?" said Lance. "Aren't the mechanics who work on airliners certified by the FAA?"

"I've got a hot bulletin for you, sweetheart," said Judy. "Ninety per cent of the mechanics who service airliners aren't even A&Ps."

"A&Ps?"

"That's the FAA's term for qualified mechanics—it stands for 'airframe and power plant.'"

"Then there's the air traffic controllers," said Trudy, "who are about as big a bunch of booze-hounds as you'd never want to meet. And their equipment is so outdated it's a crime. Their computers that keep track of aircraft taking off and landing are always going out, and the controllers are left staring at a blank scope."

"I guess you were right," said Lance. "I guess I really didn't want to know about this stuff."

"Tell him about the fuel problem," said Judy.

"Right," said Trudy. "A DC-10 uses about $1,850 worth of kerosene every hour, so every flight—not just DC-10s—is allotted the smallest possible amount of fuel on board, especially since it *takes* fuel to *carry* fuel. Which is OK, unless you develop problems, or have to spend a while stacked up in a holding pattern, or you get diverted to another airport or something. Then you have a very good chance of flaming out and going down without fuel."

"Can't you just watch your fuel gauge and have a good alternative plan in mind or something?" said Lance.

"Sure," said Judy. "That's assuming your fuel gauge is *accurate*, of course. Fuel gauges on airliners can be off by several thousand pounds, though. And every once in a while, a plane runs out of fuel and crashes."

"I really don't want to hear anymore," said Lance, beginning to feel a little dizzy.

"You want to hear some shit about the pilot?" said Judy.

"What pilot?" said Lance. He was definitely getting dizzy, either from the coke or from the information the two stewardesses were taking such perverse delight in feeding him.

"The asshole who's about to take us into the wild blue yonder," said Trudy, "Hap-fucking-Harrigan. You want to know what keeps him going? Outside of jumping stews? Calvert pre-mixed Manhattans in a little silver flask."

"You're kidding me," said Lance. "Doesn't the FAA have some regulation about that?"

Trudy nodded.

"Federal law says that at least eight hours must elapse between consumption of any alcoholic beverage and the commencement of any flight. Go tell that to Hap Harrigan."

Lance backed unsteadily toward the curtain.

"OK," he said, "you've convinced me."

"What do you mean?" said Trudy.

"Where are you going?" said Judy.

"Off the airplane," said Lance, pulling the curtain open.

"Aww, we scared him," said Judy.

"C'mon back here," said Trudy, pulling him back into the galley and closing the curtain.

"No thanks," said Lance. "It's been lovely, but I really have to run."

"Don't go yet," said Trudy, suddenly seductive, snaking her arms around his neck.

"Why not?" said Lance.

"Because," said Trudy, giggling, and nuzzling her cheek against his, "we like you. And we want to fly with you."

"Yeah," said Judy, kissing him wetly on the lips, "if we have to go up there with old drunken Hap, we don't want to do it alone."

"You won't be alone," said Lance, beginning to get aroused. "There are about two hundred and seventy people on this junk heap to keep you company."

"We don't want *them* to keep us company," said Judy, "we want *you.*"

Judy began unbuttoning her uniform.

"Have you ever made love at thirty-five thousand feet with two stewardesses?" whispered Trudy in his ear.

"Not even with one," said Lance, instantly getting an image of the three of them writhing around together on the floor of the galley as the aft cargo door blew out, the cabin floor collapsed, the pylons fell off the wings, the slats withdrew and the aircraft began to come apart.

"What's your first name?" said Judy, reaching for his belt buckle.

"Lance," said Lance, "but I'm afraid I really do have to go now."

He lurched back toward the curtain, but both Judy and Trudy hung onto him, swaying a bit unsteadily on their feet.

"If *we* go," giggled Judy, unbuckling his belt, "we're taking you with us, Lance."

Trudy unzipped his fly and stuck her hand inside his pants.

Suddenly they heard the p.a. system switch on, and a somewhat boozy male voice addressed them:

"Ladies and gennumun," said the voice, "this is your captain, uh, Captain Harrigan speaking . . . The, uh, difficulties that we were waiting to be, uh, corrected have finally . . . been corrected. So, uh, we apologize for the delay and, uh, we'll be getting underway in just a moment here. And, uh, once we're aloft, the stewardesses will be bringing us all . . . uh, bring all of *you,* that is, a complimentary cocktail with my, uh, compliments . . ."

"Oh my God," said Lance, "we're *leaving.*"

"*Together,*" said Trudy, locating Lance's shvantz and pulling it slowly out of his fly.

"Flight attendants, uh, prepare for . . . departure," said the voice on the p.a. system.

Judy and Trudy were giggling like crazy. Trudy had sunk to her knees in front of Lance and taken his entire organ into her mouth. As it began to expand in the hot wet cavity, all of Lance's determination to save his life by leaving the aircraft drained out of his body.

Judy picked up the p.a. system telephone off the wall and spoke into it.

"Good evening, ladies and gentlemen," said Judy, repressing a giggle. "My name is Judy Hotchkiss. I'm the First Flight Attendant on your flight today. On behalf of Captain Harrigan and the entire crew, we'd like to welcome you to Global's flight number 323 to New York . . ."

Lance leaned back weakly against the stainless-steel counter as Trudy continued to work on him.

"Please check now to make sure that your seat belt is securely fastened for takeoff . . . despite the fact that it is virtually useless and, in a forced landing, it will rupture your spleen and fracture your pelvic saddle . . ."

Trudy almost gagged with laughter, dislodging Lance from her throat. Judy temporarily forgot what came next, then plunged onward.

"Be sure that your seat back and tray table are stowed in the upright and locked position and that all carry-on items are placed under the seat in front of you . . . Although your seats are securely mounted to the floor and stressed to nine g's, nine g's is less than the minimum requirement for automobiles, so if we have a forced landing they'll probably tear loose and severely injure you . . ."

Trudy was in convulsions over that one. She reached up, grabbed Lance's hand and placed it on Judy's bosom. Lance obediently started fondling Judy's breasts as skillfully as possible under the circumstances, aware that he was participating in a fairly ludicrous tableau.

"There are eight exit doors on our DC-10," Judy continued, "although the chances of even half of them opening in the event of a forced landing are . . . kind of remote. This aircraft is equipped with floatable lower seatback cushions for your assistance in the event of a water landing. The Coast Guard considers these seat cushions unsuitable for nonswimmers and children. If you are fortunate enough to have a life vest under your seat you will find it . . . extremely difficult to locate, extract, unpack, put on and inflate."

A stewardess stuck her head in the galley.

"Jude?" she said, then saw what was happening on the floor and quickly withdrew.

"In tests we've conducted with these life vests," Judy continued, as Lance diligently kneaded her breasts, "even trained members of the crew were unable to use them properly. If this aircraft does land in water, it will float anywhere from eleven seconds to four days, assuming it doesn't break up on impact . . ."

"Ladies and gentlemen," said the p.a. system, "this is Captain Harrigan . . ."

"Since we are cargo-loaded," Judy continued gamely, "it will probably float with the nose down . . ."

"Ladies and gentlemen," said the p.a. system, "the flight attendant who is addressing you, Miss Hotchkiss, is—"

"A Coast Guard helicopter can pick up twenty people from the water," Judy continued, raising her voice over that of the captain's, "one per minute. That's in ideal conditions, of course. But the size of the group on this plane will make a recovery from the water impossible, so most of us will probably freeze to death before it arrives . . ."

"Ladies and gentlemen," said the p.a. system, "I'd like you to ignore what Miss Hotchkiss has just told you. She appears to be, uh, somewhat under the influence of, uh . . ."

"Miss *Hotchkiss*," said Judy, interrupting him, "is under the influence of about six lines of Peruvian marching powder, which is *considerably* less debilitating than the twelve to fourteen Calvert Manhattans that the man who is *driving* this aircraft has just poured down his throat!"

Three stews ducked into the galley and tried to wrestle the phone out of Judy's hands.

"*Listen* to me, you little slut!" said the voice on the p.a. system. "You better shut that trap of yours or I'll—"

"*The man who is piloting your aircraft,*" screamed Judy, as the stews finally snatched the phone from her hands, "*has a penis the size of a cocktail frank!*"

The aircraft was returned to the gate. Judy, Trudy and Captain Harrigan were taken away to be interviewed by several people at the airline in very reasonable tones and then fired.

Lance reserved a seat on the very next flight to New York, which happened to be the 9:00 p.m. one on TWA—the notorious "red-eye." He had to hurry a bit, but he made it onto the aircraft just as the doors were about ready to close. Lance looked forward to a nice boring flight. If he had not at that point spotted Ernest, Goose and Blatt and gone to greet them, he might have noticed the four short, stocky women in the khaki jumpsuits at the back of the plane who were removing pistols from their carry-on luggage and preparing to address their fellow passengers.

94

The 9:00 p.m. TWA flight for New York took off right on time. The passengers were all chatting loudly. June nodded to Alix, Sandy and Wanda. They all unfastened their seat belts and stood up. Alix, Sandy and Wanda began moving rapidly up the aisle. June prepared to inform her fellow passengers about the life-changing alterations she was about to make in their futures.

Two stewardesses spotted the standing passengers and shook their heads in exasperation. They got up out of their seats and were just about to say that the captain had not turned off the "Fasten Seat Belts" sign, when June grabbed a public address phone off the wall and began to speak in a loud, no-nonsense voice.

"Your attention please," said June. *"I would like you to listen quite carefully to what I am about to say . . ."*

Heads turned toward June at the back of the plane. A few passengers figured she was a harmless loony and began to titter. June held her massive revolver aloft for everyone to see. The stewardesses halted and the tittering ceased immediately. Alix, Sandy and Wanda continued up the aisle past the stewardesses. They held their pistols in front of them. Several passengers gave gasps of fear and a general panicked buzzing began.

June fired a shot into the cushion of the seat she was standing next to. The sound of the explosion in the close quarters of the airliner was a tremendous shock and effectively froze the buzzing.

"*Good,*" said June. "*My next shot will go into flesh, not polyurethane. Since I finally have your attention, I would like to say a few words about what is happening. In case you haven't guessed, this is a hijack.*"

A few passengers began to speak, but June pointed her pistol in their direction and they shut up. Alix, Sandy and Wanda passed through to the cabin ahead.

"*As you know,*" June continued, "*Hijacking an airliner is a federal crime, with severe penalties for the hijackers should they be apprehended. For this reason we are quite prepared to kill anybody who attempts to interfere with us. If you wish to stay alive, I suggest that you follow precisely the instructions that we give you. Are there any questions so far?*"

A woman four rows ahead of June timidly raised her hand. She was about fifty-five and had tight gray curls all over her head.

"*Yes?*" said June.

The woman said something in a wee, shaky voice that was hard to hear.

"*Again, please?*" said June.

"Are we going to Cuba?" said the woman somewhat hopefully.

"*The question was, 'Are we going to Cuba?'*" said June. "*No, we are not going to Cuba. Next question.*"

A man raised his hand.

"*Yes, pig?*" said June.

The man looked as if he was about to object to the use of the word "pig" in addressing him, then he appeared to reconsider.

"Uh, can you tell us whether this hijack is motivated by political or by essentially financial motives?" said the man.

"*Political,*" said June. "*This hijack is a political act and a media event. When we arrive at our new destination, most of the female passengers will be permitted the choice of either staying with us or leaving of their own free will.*"

"Uh, what about the men?" said the man who had asked the question.

"*Did I say you could ask another question, pig?*" shouted June, leveling her gun at him.

"N-no," he said.

"*No what, pig?*" she shouted.

"No ma'am," said the man.

A woman of about sixty with white hair in a bun and granny glasses raised her hand.

"What *are* you going to do with the men?" she said.

"Any passengers of either sex whom we do not deem releasable for political reasons when we reach our destination," said June, *"will be obliged to remain with us as political prisoners. Until further notice, all male pigs on this plane are political prisoners."*

A young woman in a print dress with little poodles on it raised her hand.

"Can you tell us our destination, please?" she said.

"Our destination," said June, *"is not something you need to know yet. You will be informed of our destination at the appropriate time."*

An elderly man raised his hand. He was wearing a light tan straw hat with a jolly feather.

"Can't you at least give us a hint?" he said.

"No, pig, no hints," said June. *"This is a hijack, not a game of Twenty Questions."*

Some of the passengers were interested to see that even elderly men were classified as pigs. It seemed democratic, if rude.

A young woman wearing designer overalls raised her hand.

"Can you tell me where you got your jumpsuits?" she asked.

95

Lance stared at the stocky young woman in the khaki jumpsuit with a mixture of fear and relief. So this was it—what he'd been dreading for so long.

If it had been a normal hijack, he might have been able to look upon it as merely a dangerous adventure, one which he would probably be able to use in one form or another in some novel he would write in the future. But these hijackers had said they were members of MATE, the crazed women's group he told Cathy about and she'd thought he was making up. He knew he and all the rest of the men on board the plane were in serious trouble. He recalled an incident he had read about in which these same women had caught a rapist in Central Park and snipped his testicles off with pinking shears, and he shuddered.

The really strange thing about the woman who had addressed them, though, Lance thought as he stared at her, was that she seemed so familiar. In fact, all four of them had seemed familiar to him, and he couldn't say why. No photograph of them had ever appeared in the papers or on TV. He would have to think about it.

Ernest, Goose and Blatt seemed mesmerized by the proceedings. He wondered what they were thinking. He wondered what would happen to them and to him, and which of them—if any—would survive. He remembered asking Helen whether, if he were on a plane that crashed, he would have to take responsibility for the plane's crashing. He recalled her saying that if he didn't have to take responsibility for the plane's crashing, he at least had to take responsibility for being on the plane that crashed. He wondered if being on a plane that was hijacked was the same thing. He supposed it was. He tried to think what combination of elements had put him on this particular plane at this particular time, seemingly by chance. *Was* it chance that had put him here?

Well, for one thing, he was here on this plane because the plane he was on before this had stood on the runway for an hour and a half while the pilot was getting drunk and the stewardesses were getting stoned. Was that *his* fault? It was not. To be absolutely fair, however, the stewardesses were not getting stoned alone, they were getting stoned with his tacit approval and with one of them being further encouraged by his allowing her to nibble on his dork.

All right. Was it his fault he had gotten on that flight because the flight before it had left early without him? It was not.

When he thought about it, he would never have traveled to Los Angeles to be on the *Tonight Show* in the first place had he not written a novel which he was currently trying to promote. And he never would have been invited to appear on the *Tonight Show* if he had not come up with that stupid slogan, "Free the Dalton Two," which he'd intended as a satiric remark. So much for satiric remarks.

301

Of course, if you took it a bit further, if he had not come up with that stupid slogan, Ernest, Goose and Blatt wouldn't be on this plane now either. So, in a sense, he had to take responsibility for at least four people being on this plane.

He wondered how he felt about that. It made him a little uneasy to have that much responsibility. It also made him feel kind of, well, *protective* toward Ernest, Goose and Blatt. It was not a wholly unpleasant feeling. Perhaps, if he had had so much to do with all of them getting into such a mess in the first place, he might be able to have something to do with their getting out of it as well. Strange thought.

96

Wanda had remained at the rear of the forward Coach cabin. Alix and Sandy moved into First Class. The flight attendants and passengers they encountered had all heard June's address on the p.a. system and gave the women a wide berth, especially when they spotted their guns.

Alix remained in First Class. Sandy opened the door to the cockpit and stepped inside. The captain, the co-pilot and the flight engineer turned toward her and said nothing.

"I assume you heard on the p.a. system what is going on," she said curtly. None of the three men acknowledged her question. She turned to the flight engineer.

"Show me a map of the Pacific," she said.

The flight engineer looked at the captain, then turned to his maps, riffled through them and spread one out on the table in front of him. Sandy peered down at it briefly.

"South of Hawaii and a little east is an island called Mannihanni," she said. "That is where you are heading. I suggest you inform Air Traffic Control and begin making your turnaround immediately."

The three men continued to look at her.

"Do you have the use of your ears?" said Sandy.

"Can I say something?" said the captain in a relaxed-sounding drawl.

"What?" said Sandy.

"Why don't y'all come off this bullshit, sweetheart, and tell your galfriends to put away the guns. We'll crack open a case of champagne, we'll have a little party up here in the cockpit, and when we get to JFK we'll go back to the motel and we'll take y'all to a place that's one helluva lot better than Hawaii or Mannahanna or anything else."

Sandy regarded the captain soberly for several seconds. Encouraged by her silence, he and the co-pilot and the flight engineer broke into ingratiating, toothy grins. At length Sandy walked calmly over to the captain and stuck the barrel of her gun in his amazed mouth.

"If you don't turn this plane around immediately," she said quietly, "I am going to blow your tongue and teeth out the back of your head. If you have understood what I have just said to you, please nod your head."

Carefully, so as not to alarm the butt of the pistol or its owner, the captain nodded his head.

97

"I really needed this," said Blatt. "I really needed to get hijacked by a bunch of crazy broads with guns."

"If we do everything they tell us to," said Lance, "they may let us go once we get wherever we're going."

"Ah think we could take 'em, bro'," said Ernest. "What *you* think, Goose?"

Goose nodded.

"Ah think we *could*, bro'," he said.

"Yeah? Well, forget about it," said Lance. "Maybe you don't think they have the guts to use those guns of theirs. I'd say, judging from how they sliced that rapist's balls off, they have the guts."

"Say what?" said Ernest.

"You didn't hear about how they cut off a guy's balls who was raping some women in the park?" said Lance.

Ernest and Goose shook their heads.

"Well, they did," said Lance. "So before you get any swell ideas of trying to take them, you just think about that."

Ernest and Goose nodded their heads.

Lance decided he would think about that too.

98

By the time June took over for Sandy in the cockpit, they were nearly there. The flight had gone very smoothly. The passengers and crew seemed suitably impressed with the hijackers' seriousness and so far had complied with whatever requests had been made of them.

June had checked the flight engineer's maps and charts and was not surprised that there was virtually no data on either Port Pangaud in particular or Mannihanni in general. As far as they could tell there was some sort of airfield at Port Pangaud left over from World War II, but what state of repair it was in or whether the runways were long enough or smooth enough to land a jumbo jet was debatable.

The flight engineer tried several times to contact the tower at Port Pangaud without much success. After trying for close to fifteen minutes, he did get some kind of response, but it was very hard to hear over the static, and it was in a language no one in the cockpit understood.

There was a heavy cloud cover over the area where Mannihanni lay according to the maps. At 20,000 feet the full moon lit the cloud cover like an Arctic snowbank. Since no other aircraft responded to their radio calls, they decided it was safe to drop below the cloud cover and make a visual check.

At 8,000 feet they entered the cloud cover and could see

nothing at all. At 3,500 feet they finally got below it. There lay Mannihanni—a huge dark shape sprawled in the water like a dead animal. If there was life here it was hibernating. There were no lights.

The fuel gauges were showing very little fuel remaining. They had been burning 12,000 pounds of kerosene every hour for well over five hours and they had to find a place to land before they flamed out. If they couldn't find the airfield they might have to take their chances ditching at sea. The captain took it down to 1,000 feet. Four pairs of eyes in the cockpit raked the island for landing sites. The flight attendants had begun briefing the passengers for an emergency evacuation.

"Ladies and gentlemen," said the voice on the p.a. system, "this is First Flight Attendant Sharon Folsom speaking. At this time, all airline employees, police officers, firefighters and military personnel please identify yourselves to the flight attendants by ringing your call button. Please make sure that all eyeglasses, pens, jewelry and other sharp objects which might injure you during an emergency landing are placed in a safe area such as purse, side coat pocket, or the seat pocket in front of you. Please remove your shoes. High-heeled shoes must be removed and placed in the seat pocket in front of you. All loose items at your seat must now be safely stowed."

June saw it at the same moment as the captain: a glowing patch of ground lay just ahead—the airfield! It didn't seem very large, and the lights illuminating it were fairly weak, but at least it was better than putting her down in the ocean.

"Please make sure your seat belt is low and tight across your hips," Sharon continued. "Note the number and location of your assigned and alternate exits. If you have not already done so, please bring your seat back to the full upright position and make sure your tray table is safely stowed and locked . . ."

The captain sighed.

"OK," he said, "we're going to give it that old college try."

"I think we're going to lose an engine, old buddy," said the flight engineer.

"What's that?" said the co-pilot.

"Number three engine," said the flight engineer. "We're going to lose it."

"Why?" said the captain.

"Fuel," said the co-pilot, eyeing the gauges. "Open the cross-feeds."

"Whoops," said the flight engineer, "there she goes,

Number three just flamed out, good buddy. We'd better get down there while we still can."

It was relatively cool in the air-conditioned cockpit, but June's clothing was soaked from nervous perspiration.

"OK," said the captain, squinting down at the ground. "There seems to be what looks like a field or something down there on the far side of the strip in case we're short."

"Let's do it, pal," said the co-pilot, "before we lose the number one engine."

"Roger," said the captain. "Better tell the people."

The flight engineer picked up his microphone.

"Assume the brace position," he said over the p.a. system.

"Assume the brace position," echoed Sharon on the p.a. system. "With your seat belt still low and tight, lean forward and grab your ankles. If you are not able to grab your ankles, lean forward, cross your arms, place the palms of your hands against the seat back in front of you and press your forehead on your crossed arms."

"We're losing number one, old buddy," said the flight engineer.

"*Brace,*" said Sharon on the p.a. "Keep your head down until the plane stops. *Repeat.* Stay *down* in your brace position until the aircraft comes to a complete stop. As soon as the aircraft stops, leave it *immediately.* Do not take *anything* with you during the evacuation. *Repeat.* Do not take *anything* with you during the evacuation!"

"Here goes nothing," said the captain, beginning his approach.

99

In the rear Coach cabin passengers were praying, crying, and trying to remember all the instructions they had been given.

Lance had passed through depression, anxiety and sheer terror, and had come out in a place that was oddly calm and slow and detached. It was, Lance knew, a classic form of panic, but he preferred it to the other forms he was acquainted with.

No sooner had the passengers assumed the brace position than the plane bounced onto the runway with a tremendous jolt. Lance was hurled painfully into his seat belt, squeezing the breath out of his abdomen, then thrown violently backwards and then forwards again. People were screaming loudly enough to drown out the high-pitched whine of the engines. The aircraft continued to buck violently like a maddened bronco, and then suddenly it was over. They were stopped.

"Release your seat belts and get *out!*" shouted Sharon over the p.a. system.

Passengers were still screaming, many of them unaware that they had actually landed. Some of them appeared to be injured. Many were already out of their seats and pressing forward towards the emergency exits.

"Release your seat belts and get *out!*" shouted another flight attendant on the p.a. system.

Some of the emergency doors were jammed and wouldn't open. Lance was out of his seat, trying to assist passengers who were dazed or paralyzed with fear as he headed toward the one exit he now saw they had managed to open.

"Release your seat belts and get *out!*" shouted another flight attendant on the p.a. system, and then the p.a. crackled and went dead.

Ernest, Goose, Blatt, and most of the people in Lance's immediate vicinity now appeared to be moving toward the one open exit in their cabin. FAA regulations required that all aircraft be able to be fully evacuated within ninety seconds, Lance had been told. It was hard to see how such a thing could be accomplished if all emergency exits weren't usable. He wondered how long it would be before the gas tanks exploded and the interior of the cabin became a flaming inferno.

"Jump! Jump! Jump!" shouted a flight attendant and people jumped out of the exit.

"Run! Run! Run!" shouted another flight attendant, and Lance involuntarily thought of grade-school primers starring Dick and Jane and Spot.

Dear God, prayed Lance to himself as he pushed nearer to the exit, if You're listening, and if You exist, and if You care about such things, I promise if I get out of this plane alive that I will never ever have sexual relations with fat ladies or with female executives in their offices or limousines or with kinky policewomen or with teenaged girls of any ethnic derivation, and I will return to my own lawfully wedded wife and cohabit with her in harmony or do whatever in the world would please You the most.

And then Lance was at the opening of the emergency exit.

100

The crew had accomplished a minor miracle. They had managed to land a jumbo jet with two engines gone on a runway that was as full of cracks and potholes as a New York City street. The fact that the runway was scarcely half the length necessary to accomplish such a landing, and that the aircraft then traveled across three fields and stopped just short of a long, low building covered with rusting corrugated tin, which contained several drums of kerosene, made the feat even more laudatory.

Twenty-two passengers were injured in the forced landing,

none of them seriously. While the passengers were still evacuating the aircraft, several four-wheel-drive vehicles jounced across the field toward it. The vehicles jolted to a stop and a number of people jumped out of them.

The people were all wearing what looked like army combat clothing: paratroopers' jumpsuits, jumpboots, berets, and—although it was quite dark out—sunglasses. They were almost all carrying automatic rifles and submachine guns. They were all black women.

The soldiers, if that's what they were, quickly herded the passengers together and began loading them onto what appeared to be old World War II military trucks. They yelled at the passengers in a language they had never heard before and prodded them with the butts of their automatic weapons until they began getting into the trucks.

June let herself be shoved into a truck. She was in a state of shock. What kind of monsters *were* these Mannihanni women, and why couldn't they recognize their sisters from America? These women were horrible. These women were—yes!—as bad as men!

"Excuse me, Miss," said Blatt to one of the soldiers, "but where are you taking us? *Donde est vous* taking us?"

The soldier looked blankly at Blatt.

"They not understan' you, bro'," said Ernest.

"I know," said Blatt. He sighed a deep sigh. "I don't know, Ernest. I don't think it looks too good for us, pal."

"Ah knows what you mean, bro'," said Ernest.

"I got to be honest with ya, Ernest," said Blatt. "I'm sorry I ever started the whole business with Free the Dalton Two. I hope you don't mind my saying that, pal."

"No, not at all, bro'," said Ernest.

101

It had taken almost two hours, but the half-dozen army trucks finally delivered them to a large building that appeared to be the reception area and waiting room of a partially constructed air terminal.

The modernistic architectural style was, Lance recognized, one that had been popular in the States about twenty-five years ago. The construction apparently had started and stopped roughly fifteen years ago. In the far half of the terminal there were plywood forms still in place, patiently waiting to be filled with poured concrete that whoever was in charge had long since decided not to pour. Framework for large plate-glass windows that would never hold glass was quietly rustling away in the warm, moist, heavy tropical air.

About a hundred and forty people—passengers and crew members—had been dumped into the terminal by the female soldiers, who now stood at parade rest, their automatic weapons slung over their shoulders, their eyes undetectable behind dark aviator-style sunglasses. Lance tried to think who these soldiers reminded him of, and then he had it—the old *Tonton Macoutes* of Haiti's Papa Doc Duvalier. Shortly before they landed, the leader of the hijackers had gotten on the p.a. system and told them they were going to an island called Mannihanni—an island, the hijacker had said with evident pride, where women ruled. Lance wondered what the hijackers thought about Mannihanni now.

The passengers and crew had been loosely segregated by sex and now huddled together on the cement floor in little groups, trying to console and reassure one another. In Lance's group were Ernest, Goose, and Blatt. They were in a state of shock, which was hardly surprising given the fact that they had been hijacked, threatened with shooting, flown five and a half hours to a strange island in the Pacific and crash-landed.

"I guess we should all be thankful we survived the landing," said Lance.

"That right, bro'," said Ernest.

"That right, bro'," said Goose.

"I hope," said Blatt, "that we're still thankful tomorrow, or whenever it is we find out what they plan to do to us."

102

They had been lying on Lance's king-size bed, watching *Casablanca* on the *Late Show*, when the newsbreak interrupted the movie.

"Authorities at the Los Angeles International Airport have just reported that a nine p.m. TWA flight to New York has been hijacked," said a black newsman with a frowning smile. "The hijackers are a militant group of women calling themselves MATE. It is not known at this time where the hijacked plane has been rerouted. Names of the passengers and crew members have not yet been released, pending notification of their families."

Dorothy and Janie looked at each other and raised their eyebrows. They did not see how this piece of news was relevant to their lives. Lance was flying to New York tonight, but he had taken a much earlier flight. They were irritated that the newsbreak had caused them to miss several critical moments of the film.

Cathy had not been watching TV that night. She'd taken a long leisurely bubblebath, then picked up a copy of Lance's first published book, which she had found, remaindered, in a bookstore that afternoon, and climbed into bed to reread it.

Cathy did not know if she wanted to get back together with

311

Lance, but she resented the realization that, for the first time in their separation, he no longer appeared bent on their reconciliation at all costs. She had enjoyed his pursuit of her while it lasted. She had a profound need to be pursued, to offer resistance, and to succumb. The worst part about being married was that, once you succumbed, nobody pursued you again, unless you had affairs or at least did some serious flirting and teasing.

She was surprised to see how well Lance's first book was holding up in the rereading. It had been the first thing that had attracted her to him. She had read that book and then contrived to meet its author—writing him an extravagantly literary and witty fan letter which had taken her a week to compose. He had responded almost immediately, of course, and she made him court her on the phone before she agreed to see him face to face. Not because she had any doubt that she wanted to, but because she suspected—correctly, it turned out—that he would not be interested in her if she were too available, especially after her extravagant letter.

She finally consented to see him for a drink, and refused to be picked up at her apartment because she was ashamed of the tiny fourth-floor rooms she shared with Margaret and Cheryl. They agreed to meet in the bar at Trader Vic's in the basement of the Plaza Hotel. She arrived twenty minutes late so as not to risk waiting for him alone, and he was forty minutes late, so it hadn't helped.

They ordered frivolous fruity drinks, heavy with rum, and little Polynesian tidbits on skewers. They got high. They teased and enjoyed each other. She let him take her home with him, and she let him hug and kiss her, but she did not let him put his hands inside her clothing. Eventually she said she had to go home. He tried to get her to stay over, but she refused. She was as determined as he was. He offered to escort her home. She allowed him to put her in a cab.

He called her the next day and asked her to dinner. She had already made tentative plans with another man. He talked her into breaking them. She agreed, feeling wicked. They went to a little steak house on First Avenue called Billy's. It had antique lamps and old polished wood wainscoting. They ate and drank and began to fall in love. They went back to his house to hug and kiss. She allowed herself to be talked into sleeping over, with the proviso that he promise not to try to make love to her.

He promised. He swore an oath on his mother's head. He

said if he broke his word that God should strike him dead. Fortunately, he broke his word. Fortunately, God neglected to strike him dead. They made wondrous love all night, and slept briefly and started all over again. She never went back to her own apartment. She thought he was the most wonderful man in the world. She was certain that all she needed in this world was to make him happy and to be his wife. She was wrong.

Being his wife and making him happy had not paid off as advertised. She felt eclipsed by his shadow when she stood behind him in the public spotlight. She felt she was competing with his writing for his attention, and coming in second. Her job at the *Times Book Review* was not fulfilling either. There she felt eclipsed by the famous authors whose books she sent out for reviews and by the famous reviewers who reviewed them.

Outwardly, she and Lance continued to be the perfect couple. Even to each other they maintained the image of contentment. Inwardly, each felt responsible for the unrest they shared. But rather than doubt their love for each other, they began to doubt the other's love for them. They gave each other secret tests of love. Each ran the test until the other failed. The tests were designed for failure. They tried to make each other wrong. They nursed hurts and grudges. They sulked. They began to grow apart.

She began to flirt with others. Men clustered around her, wondering whether they had a chance with her. They had more of a chance than they knew. None pressed his luck and she remained faithful to her husband by default. The closest she came to adultery was agreeing to go to an afternoon movie with a married man who was a mutual friend of theirs and then necking with him in the theater like a high-school girl. It was an exciting but stupid act—anybody might have seen them. But maybe that had been the point—to be seen.

At a boozy dinner party in the Hamptons one summer she allowed herself to be led out onto the terrace by one of the male guests and kissed him hungrily with an open mouth. What neither she nor the young man on the terrace realized was that everyone at the dinner table could see precisely what she was doing. Lance had been surprisingly understanding about the incident. She felt it was because she had given him an excuse to cheat on her, redeemable at any time.

Lance's editor, Howard Leventhal, had pursued her harder than anyone. It was not that she was attracted to him. It was rather that she was attracted to his attraction to *her*. It seemed a welcome change from Lance's lack of attention to her. Many times she considered submitting to Howard—to get back at Lance, if for no better reason—but she held back. Not because of strength of character. Not necessarily because of strong moral beliefs. Probably more because the timing had never really been right.

She continued to resent Lance's lack of attention both in and out of bed, and his constant expectation to be waited on. And then Lance got caught bare-assed at his surprise birthday party. More than shock, she felt relief. She had often toyed with the fantasy of leaving him. Now she finally had a reason.

Howard had been a huge disappointment. She had wearied of his lovemaking before they were more than halfway through their first night together. If Lance had been inattentive and unspontaneous, Howard was simply inept. Lance may have been reluctant to fondle her as long as she wanted to be fondled, but Howard didn't quite know what it was you were supposed to fondle. And being with Howard *outside* of bed wasn't any better. Lance was preoccupied with his writing, but once you finally got his attention he was fascinating and fun. It was no problem getting Howard's attention, but once you had it you wondered what you wanted with it. Howard was a supreme bore. He had no sense of humor, no sense of adventure, no views of anything that could not be obtained from the *New York Times*, the *New York Review of Books*, or the *Wall Street Journal*. The one good thing about that God-awful cruise to the Caribbean on the Firestones' yacht was that she finally had an excuse to get rid of Howard.

She was sad that Lance had discovered the photographs of her and Howard together. Lance had probably been right about her subconsciously wanting him to find them. Even Dr. Freundlich thought so. She told Dr. Freundlich that she had been more aroused making love with Lance while they were separated than she had for the last six years of her marriage. It was clear that he could be spontaneous and imaginative in bed and engage in all the foreplay she could ever hope for if he only wanted to. And if sex with Lance could go on being as good as it was that night after her birthday dinner, then both of them would want to make love a lot more often than they had in the last few years.

After several sessions with Dr. Freundlich it was clear to her that she could influence how much attention Lance paid to her and how much he expected to be waited on. It was clear to her she could be as much her own person living with Lance as she had been living alone. She could listen to rock music, she could write her own novels, and she could be in the limelight as much as her own ambivalence about success would allow. In any case, whenever she felt eclipsed by Lance it was her own doing, not his.

She was chagrined to find that Lance had filed for a legal separation. She was tired of living alone. She was tired of having to make do without the luxuries his income afforded, and she no longer felt unentitled to them. She missed sharing with Lance the reports of each other's daily doings, their common outlooks on things and people, their private jokes. Cathy and Lance were, fortunately or not, a couple. And she missed him. If she really worked at it, she thought she could get him back again.

She closed the book which had drawn her to Lance originally and turned off her reading light in her tiny white bedroom and composed herself for sleep. The following morning an employee of TWA would telephone to inform her that her husband was a political prisoner on a tropical island on the other side of the globe.

103

Lance slept fitfully for a couple of hours, trying vainly to find a comfortable position on the cement floor of the air terminal. He was hot and sweaty and filthy and his muscles ached. He had taken off his boots and rolled up his shirt and stuck it under his head for a pillow, but it wasn't much help.

A couple of hours after dawn a truck pulled up outside the terminal, and several guards dumped piles of carry-on luggage from the plane into the middle of the floor. As the guards watched from behind their dark glasses and darker automatic weapons, the passengers were permitted to poke through the piles for their possessions. Lance was fortunate to find his shoulder bag, which contained toilet articles, several bottles of vitamins and other pills that Lance was sure would come in handy.

Another truck arrived with breakfast, but many of the passengers were sufficiently put off by the unfamiliar smells and tastes of the food not to consume very much of it. There was a mushy, yellowish, fruity thing which Lance thought might be a kind of melon. There were flat brownish things that looked like giant pea pods. There was something spiky that smelled disgusting and looked like a kind of sea creature. Lance nibbled on the melony thing and on one of the pods, but neither seemed to be anything you would want to put inside your actual body.

All attempts to communicate with their captors fell on deaf ears. The female soldiers either grunted or pretended not to hear. Since they were armed, nobody pressed them hard for a response.

By the time the sun came up, the temperature inside the airline terminal had risen from the eighty-five degrees it had been during the night to the upper nineties. All of the men had removed their shirts and shoes. The older ones rolled up their trouser legs. Some of the younger ones stripped down to their undershorts. Lance was interested to see that a number of the women on the other side of the terminal had done the same thing. The sight of so many women clad in underwear was the only interesting thing about his situation. He did not feel it was adequate compensation for his predicament.

Shortly after nibbling the breakfast fruits, it occurred to Lance to visit the bathroom. He got up and began making his way around the terminal, looking for the facilities. Two guards came over and asked him something he didn't understand.

"Bathroom?" he said. "Toilet? Men's room?"

They stared blankly. His intestines communicated an urgent message to him.

"*Toi*-let," he said, shaping one in the air with his hands. They continued to stare at him.

"*Rest* room," he said. "Commode? Crapper? Pissoir? *Toi*-let."

He pantomimed sitting down, pulling down his pants and straining. One of the women laughed uproariously, and turned to the other.

"Koh-ler," she said, by way of explanation.

"Koh-ler," he said, nodding enthusiastically, "very good! Yes! You call it *Koh*-ler? We call it *toi*-let."

"Koh-ler," said the other guard, chuckling, and made the sound of a Bronx cheer with her mouth.

"Where *is* the *Koh*-ler?" said Lance.

One of the guards inclined her head in the direction away from the entrance and indicated that Lance should follow her. He loped after her, as cramps began to clutch at his innards.

She stopped before a door. He was terribly grateful.

"Koh-ler," she said.

104

The day after the hijack, October 22nd, was a relatively slow news day, and so most of the print and broadcast media featured the story.

The *New York Times* focused on the political background of Mannihanni and President Taillevent. It speculated upon what Mannihanni would do with the hijackers and spoke of the United States' virtual lack of diplomatic ties to the matriarchal island. It quoted various feminist leaders denouncing the members of MATE for their irresponsibility in hijacking the jetliner and once more dissociating the women's movement from all such extremist tactics.

The New York *Daily News* published a list of the passengers and crew and featured interviews with the air traffic controller who had been the last person to speak with anyone aboard the hijacked plane. The captain of the jetliner had told him they were going to "some cockamamy island in the South Pacific," and hoped he had enough fuel to get there and a decent place to make a landing.

The *New York Post* featured exclusive and heartrending interviews with the members of the passengers' families. Because there had been no official word about the status of the landing, nobody knew if their loved ones had survived or died in a crash.

NBC pointed out that four of the passengers had been guests on the *Tonight Show* the night before the hijack, and featured an exclusive short interview with Johnny Carson, who expressed admiration for all four men, particularly Ernest and Goose, and concern for their safety.

CBS featured an interview with an FAA official who said that there was talk of putting FBI men on all international flights from now on, and when it was pointed out to him that the hijacked plane had not been an international flight he seemed annoyed.

ABC scooped everyone with an exclusive bulletin on the landing. An undisclosed source in the federal government received a report from Honolulu that the hijacked plane had landed safely at the Port Pangaud Airport in Mannihanni, that all passengers and crew members had survived, and that the four hijackers had been shot while resisting arrest. The report did not say what provisions had been made for the transportation of the survivors back to the United States.

The following day, as national attention began to shift to other stories, there was a new report from Mannihanni: An official emissary of President Taillevent issued a statement that one hijacker and twenty-two passengers and crew members had died of injuries sustained in the emergency landing at Port Pangaud. The rest were being detained at the Port Pangaud air terminal, said the statement, pending the outcome of an investigation. President Taillevent's aides were said to be trying to determine whether any of the Americans on the plane were involved in an attempt to assess the size and vulnerability of the extensive Mannihanni natural gas deposits.

A minor official in the State Department expressed bemused irritation at the notion that the United States would be at all interested in the possibility of any potential petroleum deposits on an island as small as Mannihanni. When informed of the supposed three million cubic feet of natural gas reported to have been discovered underneath the Presidential Palace in Port Pangaud, the official said that was nonsense and angrily concluded the interview.

Network switchboards were besieged with calls from frantic members of passengers' and crew members' families, trying to find out whether their loved ones had survived the crash. It was not until the third day following the hijack that a list of casualties could be obtained from the undisclosed source in Honolulu. The list numbered only twelve, not twenty-two. It was published in several papers, and the *New York Post* devoted the entire front page to the list, framed in black. In a later edition, a front-page editorial in the *Post* called for immediate military action to force Mannihanni to surrender the American hostages. This was the first time the word "hostages" had been used to describe the survivors.

The under secretary of state was interviewed on *Meet the Press* and tried to soft-pedal the situation in Mannihanni. He pointed out that neither President Taillevent nor any of her emissaries had said that any of the passengers or crew were either "hostages" or "prisoners," just that they were being temporarily detained. He called upon the news media to try to resist escalation of a potentially delicate diplomatic situation in an attempt to stimulate newspaper sales and television viewership.

Lance's novel, *Gallivanting,* finally made it onto the *New York Times* bestseller list. There was a run on bookstores, on map stores and on public libraries for information on Mannihanni. There was a run on anthropologists to appear on radio and TV talk shows and discuss the matriarchal society on Mannihanni. Mannihanni gags began to appear in the monologues of stand-up comedians in little clubs across the country. Johnny Carson had the restraint to resist making jokes about Mannihanni or Mamma Doc for the first week of captivity.

To Cathy Lerner the hijack was not remotely amusing. From the moment TWA notified her that Lance was aboard the hijacked plane she went into a mild state of shock. She refused to believe at first that Lance had actually been on the plane at all. She telephoned the apartment and spoke with Dorothy and Janie, who were also terribly distraught. When they heard news of the hijack it never occurred to them to worry about Lance, since he had telephoned them the night before and said he was taking a 4:00 p.m. flight back to New York. When he hadn't arrived that night they began to worry. When TWA phoned the following morning, they realized Lance must have somehow decided to take a later plane and been unlucky enough to pick the one that was hijacked.

Until the list of casualties was printed and Lance's name was not found among them, Cathy had convinced herself that Lance was dead and that this was God's punishment for her affair with Howard Leventhal. After the list was published,

Cathy felt reprieved—God was giving her a second chance. She didn't know how long Lance and the other passengers and crew members were likely to be held captive. She knew that she, Cathy Lerner, was not going to allow what happened to the hostages in Iran to happen to her husband. She did not know what it would take to get him back. She knew only that getting him back had suddenly become the thing in the world that she wanted most.

Cathy kept the television on constantly, frantically switching back and forth between the channels for the latest bulletins on the situation in Mannihanni. When the news wasn't on, she telephoned the network switchboards and, when the switchboards could no longer handle the volume of calls about the hostages, she telephoned every hour the special number that ABC had set up with recorded updates on the situation.

Cathy also called the offices of her senator, congressman, and the Manhattan borough president. Nobody she spoke to in local government was able to tell her even as much as she had learned from the news on television and from the special ABC recorded bulletins. She was intensely patriotic but had come to hate the government. She thought it was scandalous that the U.S. Treasury was allowed to print up money without additional gold backup, thereby devaluing everybody's money and making inflation worse. She thought the U.S. Treasury should be arrested as counterfeiters. Still, the government ought to be able to do *something* to get the hostages released—step in and do it by force, if necessary. Surely the United States armed forces weren't afraid of whatever military defense could be mounted on the tiny tropical island of black women. And yet . . .

And yet, maybe they were. Before Vietnam Cathy had always taken for granted the fact that the United States was so powerful that nobody could stand up to her militarily. After Vietnam, and after Iran, she no longer knew. It was just possible that a bunch of black women on an island in the South Pacific was enough to scare the military leaders of a nation that had apparently lost its nerve. When she was a little girl in grammar school, the toughest boy in her class inexplicably had been beaten in a schoolyard fight by a somewhat smaller student. From that day on the tough kid shied away from fights, and even the littlest kid in class delighted in taking swipes at the former tough guy, knowing he had lost his nerve and would never fight back.

Well, the joint chiefs of staff might have lost their nerve, but not Cathy Lerner. And if the military was chicken to take on the Mannihannis, then there was always the private sector. TWA was a gigantic corporation, larger than many nations. Surely *they* would be quite anxious to resolve the situation in Mannihanni, if only to effect the return of their jetliner, which must be worth millions upon millions of dollars.

As an editor she'd been trained to get information. There were a number of time-consuming stratagems she could employ, and then there were certain people, like Claire Firestone, who were useful red-tape cutters. She went to see Claire Firestone.

Claire was surprisingly pleasant to her, considering how horrible the cruise had been and how nobody who had been aboard appeared to want to have anything to do with anyone else who'd been. Claire said that she wasn't sure what they could do themselves, but seemed willing to at least find out what efforts were being made by the government and by the private sector to have the hostages returned.

Claire took Cathy to meet with a vice-president at the airline named Boynton. Boynton was a large florid-faced man of about fifty, who seemed simultaneously glad and nervous to see Claire. Cathy assumed Claire had had an affair with the fellow.

"Terrible situation in Mannihanni," said Boynton, "simply terrible. I hope they get those poor people out of there faster than they did the hostages in Teheran."

"What's being done, Arthur?" said Claire.

"Precious little, I'm afraid," said Boynton, sneaking a covert peek at Claire's legs, which were crossed at the knee and visible to at least mid-thigh.

"Does the airline plan to do anything if the government doesn't act quickly enough?" said Cathy.

"The airline?" said Boynton, regarding Cathy warily.

"I don't think the airline is really as eager as you might think it would be to get its airplane back, Cathy," Claire said.

"Why not?" said Cathy.

"The aircraft on this airline are insured," Claire explained. "The insurance more than covers every crash—which is, for example, why the airlines are not as interested in air safety as you or I."

"Now, Claire," said Boynton, taking out his handkerchief again, "that is not fair and you know it."

"The hell it isn't," said Claire. "What incentive do you

321

have to improve your safety record if it doesn't cost you anything when you lose a plane?"

"What about the insurance company?" said Cathy. "Maybe *they'd* be interested in mounting some kind of effort to get the airplane back."

Claire shook her head.

"The insurance company doesn't care either," she said. "They're tickled pink to collect their premiums, invest them, raise their rates, then pay out a relatively small settlement with inflated dollars whenever a plane is lost."

"Now, Claire," said Boynton, forcing an unimpressive chuckle, "this young lady may not know you as well as I, and she may actually think you're *serious.*"

"You're goddamned *right* I'm serious," said Claire. "These insurance companies are so rich, Cathy, they don't even *wince* picking up a 747 or a DC-10. Forty or fifty million dollars over three or four years is chopped *liver* to these guys."

"Claire, please," said Boynton.

"Most airlines," said Claire, "could double or triple the number of planes they lose without any problem at all."

"I hope you don't believe all this, Mrs. Lerner," said Boynton with a strained smile.

"*Believe it,* Cathy," said Claire. "A few years ago National Airlines crashed one of its 727s into Escambia Bay in Florida. National made an after-tax profit from the crash of $1,500,000 because of excess insurance coverage on the aircraft. That amounted to eighteen cents a share on their stock. Ten days after the crash, National issued a press release which said that this profit came from 'the recent involuntary conversion of a 727 aircraft.'"

"Is this really true, Claire?" said Cathy.

"Ask *him,*" said Claire. "He knows the case very well."

Cathy turned to Boynton, who was rapidly patting his forehead and cheeks with his still-folded handkerchief.

"Did that really happen, Mr. Boynton?" said Cathy.

"I don't know," said Boynton. "I'm not familiar with the case."

"He worked at National when it happened," said Claire.

Cathy regarded Boynton for a moment, then nodded and stood up.

"Well, Claire," she said, "I don't think we're going to get a lot of really gutsy support from old Boynton here."

105

Although the meeting at TWA had made Cathy angry and despondent, Claire seemed relatively unaffected. It had been, said Claire, exactly the response she'd expected.

They walked north on Fifth Avenue, discussing the meeting and scanning department-store windows. Cathy asked if Claire knew anyone in government who might be able to help, and Claire didn't respond. At first Cathy thought Claire hadn't heard the question, but then she could see that Claire was thinking. From the way that Claire looked while she was thinking, Cathy felt it was not so much a matter of running a list of former lovers through Claire's mental computer to see if any of them were in government so much as running a list of former lovers in *government* to see which might be effective and willing to help.

"All right," said Claire, validating Cathy's suspicions, "there are two. One is a congressman, the other is CIA."

Cathy was impressed. What would it be like to go to bed with a congressman, to have an affair with someone in the CIA? All she could summon were images from old James Bond movies. What would it be like to permit yourself to hop into bed with any man you wanted to? What price, if any, was being exacted upon Claire for such promiscuity? Was it the obviously wretched state of Claire's marriage to Austin? If so, there was no justice—until she'd left Lance, Cathy hadn't hopped into bed with *anyone,* and *her* marriage was just as wretched as Claire's.

"May I ask you something very personal?" said Cathy.

"What?" said Claire.

"Are these men—Boynton, and the congressman and the CIA man—all people you've . . . been intimate with?"

Claire did not respond.

"Why do you ask that?" said Claire after several moments.

"I don't know," said Cathy. "I'm sorry. I know it's none of my business. Please forgive me."

"I'm not offended by your question," said Claire, "just interested why you would ask it."

"I don't know," said Cathy, blushing furiously. "It just seemed to me that you're more . . . at ease with your sexuality than I am, and I wondered how . . ."

"You wondered how . . . ?"

". . . it felt," said Cathy.

"I see," said Claire.

"I'm really sorry I asked," said Cathy. "I really had no right to be so presumptuous."

"I *told* you I wasn't offended," said Claire, "so stop apologizing. The answer is yes—Boynton and the congressman and the CIA man are all people I've been intimate with. And how it feels to be at ease with one's sexuality I couldn't tell you."

Cathy regarded Claire quizzically.

"You're saying you're *not* at ease sexually?" said Cathy.

"To do something frequently is not necessarily evidence that you're at *ease* with it," said Claire.

"I guess you're right," said Cathy. "It could just as easily be evidence of the *opposite*. Tell me, do you at least . . . enjoy sex? I'm sorry, you don't have to answer that if you don't want to."

"I don't mind answering it," said Claire, "but if you're going to continue asking me presumptuous and intimate questions, at least stop pretending that they just slipped out and you don't really want to know the answers."

Cathy smiled a slow smile.

"OK," she said. "I'll stop pretending."

"Good," said Claire.

They crossed the street and Claire stopped to look at something in one of the Mark Cross windows.

"Do I at least enjoy sex . . ." said Claire, seemingly more intent on evaluating the leather object in the window than rating her level of sexual enjoyment. "Well, that's a complex question. I enjoy many *aspects* of sex, but the most pleasurable ones are not necessarily those centered in my erogenous zones."

"What do you mean?" said Cathy, realizing she knew.

Claire again allowed several moments to elapse before replying, then turned to face Cathy.

"The reason that I'm taking so long to reply to your

324

question," said Claire, "is not that I'm trying to figure out the answers. It's that I'm trying to figure out how candid I want to be with you."

"If you're wondering whether you can *trust* me," said Cathy, "all I can tell you is that I have no reason to betray you."

"Well, maybe you do and maybe you don't," said Claire. "But don't worry, I don't trust anybody anyway."

"Well," said Cathy, snorting with laughter, "I guess that settles *that.*"

"Not necessarily," said Claire. "Just because I don't *trust* you doesn't mean I can't be *candid* with you. I could tell you things that don't cost me very much. Or I could tell you things that wouldn't do me much harm if I were candid about them. Or I could tell you things which would do *you* more damage than *me* if you revealed them."

Cathy chuckled with unexpected amusement. There was something about this woman's outrageousness that tickled her.

"Are you this guarded with your friends?" said Cathy.

"I don't have any friends," said Claire. "I have acquaintances, I have people I use, I have people who use me. I don't have friends."

"I feel sorry for you," said Cathy.

Claire nodded.

"I feel sorry for myself," she said. "Maybe that's why I'm talking like this. I don't know. Maybe it's because it's time I tried to *have* a friendship."

"With me?" said Cathy.

"Maybe," said Claire. "I had an opportunity to observe you quite a lot on that horrible cruise. And I liked what I saw."

"What did you see?" said Cathy. "Besides a miserable lady tossing her cookies, I mean?"

"I saw a woman who was fairly decent and straightforward as women go," said Claire. "I don't know many women who are either decent or straightforward. Most of them would just as soon stab you in the back as look at you."

Cathy nodded.

"I'm not sure that I'm not one of those myself," said Claire. "I just thought I'd warn you."

"All right," said Cathy. "I'll take my chances. I'm a big girl."

They passed a black beggar with a seeing-eye dog. He had a

sign strapped to his chest which said THANK GOD YOU CAN SEE. Cathy took a handful of change out of her purse and dropped it into the blind man's cup. He nodded at her as she passed.

"People like that make me feel so guilty," said Cathy.

"Why?" said Claire. "Just because you're so much more fortunate than they are?"

"No, because I always find myself wishing something dreadful would happen to them so I wouldn't have to look at them."

Claire laughed. They continued north on Fifth Avenue. They passed vendors selling hot chestnuts, mixed nuts, pretzels, hot dogs, orange juice, pencil drawings of animals, umbrellas, handbags, costume jewelry. They passed musicians playing trombones, violins, flutes, guitars, steel drums, with their hats and instrument cases open before them on the pavement and sprinkled with small change.

"I remember when Fifth Avenue used to be an elegant boulevard," said Cathy. "Now it's a combination minstrel show and flea market."

Claire chortled.

"Are you usually this crotchety," said Claire, "or are you just trying to get in my good graces?"

"I'm not changing how I feel," said Cathy, "just how much I express."

Claire nodded.

"Look, Cathy, I don't know if we can be friends, but I do want to clear the air about something."

"All right."

"How do you feel about the fact that you called your husband at a hotel in Detroit and I answered the phone?"

Cathy stopped to drop a few more coins in the cup of a blind man in ragged clothing who was sitting on the street, stroking a large black and white rabbit. She wasn't sure what part the animal played in the man's life, unless it was a seeing-eye rabbit.

"I don't love it," said Cathy, "but I figure I deserved it. I mean Lance and I were already separated at the time, and I *was* having an affair with his editor. I don't see how I could really be too convincing in the role of the wronged wife."

"Yes," said Claire, "but how do you feel about *being* with me, knowing I've slept with your husband?"

"That depends," said Cathy.

"On what?"

"On whether or not you're planning to sleep with him in

the future," said Cathy. "Assuming there *is* a future," she added quickly.

"You want him back, don't you?" said Claire. Cathy nodded. "I mean you want to live with him again, don't you?"

Cathy nodded again.

"You haven't answered my question," she said.

"I know," said Claire. "Well, I'm *not* planning to sleep with him in the future. Although, to be brutally frank about it, I suspect that is more his decision than it is mine."

"Do you . . . love him?" said Cathy.

"I don't think I love *anybody*," said Claire. "I do find Lance terribly attractive and fun to talk to and to be with and to . . . manipulate. I was able to manipulate him for a while, and then he realized he didn't have to allow it. When I saw he wasn't letting me manipulate him anymore, I got really angry. But I also started respecting him a lot more than before."

"How were you manipulating Lance?" said Cathy.

"It's not important," said Claire. "I tend to manipulate everybody, especially men. It's always amazing how easy men are to manipulate."

"Because they're weak or stupid or what?" said Cathy.

"Because they want to be manipulated," said Claire.

"Yeah, you're right," said Cathy. "Having a woman manipulate them reminds them of their mommies. And if they're being manipulated they don't have to take responsibility for their actions."

"You sound like you've been talking to a shrink or two."

"I've been going to a shrink ever since my separation. It's one of the smartest things I've ever done," said Cathy.

Claire made a face.

"What do you need with a shrink?" she said. "You're not crazy."

"That's where you're wrong," said Cathy. "We're *all* crazy. But people who go to shrinks tend to screw up their lives a little less than people who don't."

"My life isn't screwed up," said Claire. "My life is great."

"You're full of shit," said Cathy smiling. "Your life is so great you don't trust anybody, you don't have any friends, you feel you have to manipulate men into having sex with you, and when I asked if you at least *enjoy* the sex, the most you could say was that you enjoy certain *aspects* of it."

Claire sighed.

"OK," she said, *"touché.* You know, what I most enjoy

327

about sex is the excitement of seduction. Of being the seducer."

"Why do you think that is?" said Cathy.

"It's about the only way I can feel in control," said Claire.

They passed by Tiffany's and both women paused to look at the contents of the windows.

"Control comes in a whole lot of different forms," said Cathy. "Sometimes it's hard to know who's controlling whom."

"I know," said Claire.

"Why do you think you have to feel in control all the time?" said Cathy. "Is that the only way you think you can survive?"

"Could be," said Claire.

"To control everybody you come in contact with all the time?" said Cathy.

"Every single second," said Claire.

"Are you controlling me now?" said Cathy.

"I guess I must be," said Claire, "by definition."

"It doesn't seem like you are," said Cathy. "It seems like you're being really candid and vulnerable."

"That could just show how insidious and sneaky I am at controlling you," said Claire.

"Yeah," said Cathy. "Or it could show you're so vulnerable that you try to convince people you're manipulating them even when you're being completely honest."

"It could show that," said Claire.

"You're a strong woman," said Cathy. "You don't have to manipulate people in order to survive."

"Perhaps," said Claire.

"I'm not as strong as you are," said Cathy. "And when I finally assert myself and do something I should have done for myself a long time before, I feel so guilty I can hardly enjoy it."

They passed a man in dark glasses, sitting on the pavement, holding a cup. Cathy reached into her purse and dropped the last of her coins in his cup.

"Hey," he said, "what are you doing?"

"What?" said Cathy, confused.

The man stood up and poured the coins out of his cup and handed them back to her.

"I'm not a beggar," said the man.

"I'm so sorry," said Cathy, "I saw the dark glasses and the cup, and I—"

"I'm a guy on a coffee break on a sunny day," said the man. "Gimme a break, for God's sake, will ya?"

Claire burst into laughter. Cathy babbled apologies. The man walked away, muttering.

106

Lance was aware of his fellow passengers to only a limited degree. Blatt had withdrawn into a deep despondency and spoke very little. Ernest and Goose chattered to each other and tried to flirt with the guards. As inept as Goose must have been with the women in the States, the Mannihannis appeared to be amused by him. Goose entertained the guards with headstands, cartwheels, and grotesque faces. Two or three guards would stand together, watching him and giggling. They appeared to be more than a little intrigued by a clumsily designed tattoo Goose had on his right bicep. In homage to Muhammad Ali, or perhaps to Goose himself, it said "THE GREATEST."

Ernest and Goose were of the opinion that the only way out of their predicament was through a romantic liaison with the guards, and to this end they were ceaseless in their attempts to endear themselves. On the fourth day of captivity, Goose finally succeeded.

He had been doing mock obeisance to them, touching his head to the floor, kissing the toes of their combat boots, and then, on an impulse, he began kissing his way right up the leg of the guard who was closest to him. When his kissing neared her crotch, she became alarmed. She seized his head in both her hands and began to scream at him in her native tongue.

The passengers who had been watching Goose's clowning held their breaths to see what she'd do next. Several guards clustered around her and began a heated argument. At length the guard who held Goose's head between her hands asked him a question. Goose grinned idiotically at her and didn't answer. Once again the guard asked him her question. It was impossible to guess what she was asking, but nonetheless Goose decided to agree. He nodded his head and smiled. The guard turned toward her colleagues and conferred briefly with them.

Lance tried to make out what they were saying, but could understand nothing. The language at times sounded almost French, but there were no recognizable French words. It also sounded a little Spanish and a little Indian and a little African. The one sound Lance heard repeated was a name: Monte.

Monte? Monte *what?* Monte *who?* Monte Cristo? Monte Carlo? Monty Python? Monty Clift? Monte Hall? Monte Rock? The guard turned back to Goose and asked him another question containing the name Monte. Once more Goose grinned idiotically and nodded his head. This appeared to please the guard, for she stroked his face. She then motioned for Goose to follow, and led him out of the terminal. Just before he went through the front door, he turned back and waved to Ernest, Blatt and Lance, and then he disappeared.

Ernest turned to Blatt and Lance and gave them an I-told-you-so look.

"Well," said Ernest, "it look like mah man has made the grade."

"Maybe," said Lance.

"Maybe?" said Ernest. "What you mean, 'maybe,' Mr. Lerner?"

"I mean," said Lance, "I want to hear what he tells us about his experience before I draw any conclusions about whether or not he made the grade."

Lance took the edge of his thumbnail and carefully etched a graffito in the soft plaster of the wall. "Free Lance Lerner," it said.

He liked the look of that. He felt it worked on several levels. As an exhortation to his captors. As a professional title. As a memo to his restrictive super-ego. He thought he might one day have it set in type and hung above his desk. Assuming, of course, that he would one day be able to *return* to his desk.

The only other such sign on the wall of his study in New York was one which he had appropriated from a *New Yorker* cartoon shortly after he became a full-time freelancer. The cartoon was of a kid in a very progressive kindergarten asking his teacher, "Do we *have* to do what we want to do?" He had had the caption set in Old English type and framed. He sat staring at it for hours on end when the sense of too much freedom in his new professional capacity threatened to overwhelm him. DO WE HAVE TO DO WHAT WE WANT TO DO? For a long time it had had the power for Lance of a Zen koan.

On the way back from the men's room to the floor space he shared with Ernest, Goose and Blatt, Lance passed the four hijackers. The leader looked up at him, frowned, and snapped her fingers.

"Shit!" she said.

"What is it?" said Lance.

"I just realized where I know you from."

"Where?" said Lance.

"Did you live in an apartment in the East Forties in Manhattan?" she said. "Forty-eighth Street?"

"Yes . . . ?"

"And your old lady walked out on you and took all the furniture?"

"Yes . . . ?"

"Shit!" she said. "We're the ones who moved her!"

"You're a *Motherloader?*" said Lance.

"Yeah."

"I'll be goddamned!" said Lance. "I *thought* you looked familiar!"

"Yeah," she said. "Small fucking world, huh?"

"You're not kidding," said Lance.

They smiled and shook their heads in bafflement, a sudden bond of kinship formed between them.

"Yeah," she said, "Alix, Sandy and Wanda were the other three on the job that day—we were a team. Small fucking world."

"Jesus," said Lance. "And you're the same group that castrated that guy in the park? The rapist?"

"Yeah."

"How about that," said Lance. "Listen, I hope you don't mind my asking, but how did you go from moving my wife's furniture to castrating rapists to hijacking airplanes?"

June shrugged.

"How does anybody do anything?" she said. "You do

331

something that doesn't particularly interest you for a while, and then one day something better comes along."

When Goose did not reappear that night, Ernest took it as a very good sign—Goose was spending the night in bed with at least one of the guards, and possibly even more than one. And however rustic the guards' accommodations might be, they had to be luxurious compared to the floor of the terminal.

When Goose did not reappear the following day, Ernest said it must mean that he had managed to please the guards enough to make them want to keep him with them. Ernest himself now began to play up to the guards, but he was too self-conscious to clown around the way that Goose had, and so he was not successful. The guards did not smile when he tried to speak to them, and soon he stopped trying.

There seemed to be fewer people lying about on the terminal floor than when they first arrived. It was impossible to say if this was actually so, but that was Lance's impression. He wondered what had happened to the others, if indeed anything had happened to them at all. He wondered if they had charmed their way into other guards' beds, or had merely died of dysentery. He felt it was time for him to try to improve his situation.

On his next trip to the men's room, he indicated to the guard that he wished to communicate a request.

"*I*," he said, pointing to himself, "wish to *speak* to someone."

The guard looked blank.

"*I*," he repeated, pointing to himself, "*speak*." He pantomimed exaggerated processes of speaking, yelling, declaiming, shaping billowing clouds of verbiage from his mouth. "I . . . *speak*," he repeated.

"I . . . *speek*," parroted the guard.

"Good," said Lance, nodding enthusiastically. He knew she hadn't understood, but at least she appeared to be willing to listen to him.

"*I*," he said, "*go* speak." He pantomimed exaggerated walking and then speaking.

The guard looked confused. Well, thought Lance, confusion is a slightly higher state than blankness. Next comes noncomprehension, and from then on it's all uphill.

"I," he said, "go speak to *boss. Your* boss. Do you have a *boss?*"

"Boss," said the guard, clearly having no idea what the term connoted.

"Boss," he said, trying to think of a way to act out the concept. He mimed an angry employer shaking his fist, yelling, pointing, pounding his desk. He mimed a scared employee smiling nervously upwards, cringing behind his upraised arms, warding off blows. By the time Lance thought of saluting, the charade had been going on for ten minutes. The guard's face immediately registered comprehension.

"Boss," she replied excitedly, and returned the salute.

"Wonderful," said Lance, *"very* good. I don't know why I didn't think of that sooner. Here I am, trying to convey the concept of boss by enacting a melodrama in an office, when a simple salute would have . . ."

"Boss!" said the guard again, whipping off another smart salute.

"I," said Lance, "go *speak* . . . to *boss."* He mimed going, speaking, and saluting. The guard was beginning to put it together.

"I," she said, pointing to Lance. *"Speak,"* she said, miming his speaking motions. *"Boss,"* she concluded, whipping off another crisp salute.

"Yes!" said Lance delightedly. *"Yes!* Very *good!"*

The guard appeared to think this over, then arrived at a decision. She grabbed him by the upper arm and began to pull.

"Speak boss," she said. Lance could have kissed her.

107

The guard led Lance to an American jeep. It was painted black and had a somewhat familiar-looking insignia on its doors and hood. Lance didn't at first know where he had seen it before, and then he remembered—it was a gigantic blow-up of the symbols the guards wore around their necks.

He assumed the symbol to be either religious or political or both.

The guard motioned for Lance to climb into the jeep. He did. She climbed in the other side.

"What's that?" he asked, pointing to the symbol around her neck.

She looked at him uncomprehendingly.

"*That,*" he said, and pointed directly at the symbol.

She pulled in her chin and peered down at it with crossed eyes. She looked back up at him and pointed to the symbol, obviously surprised that he didn't know what it was.

"*Monte,*" she said.

"*Monte?*" he said. There it was again, the name he'd heard in their conversation about Goose. Whoever this Monte fellow was, he was pretty popular to be on the jeeps and around the necks of the soldiers. The guard said something with the name Monte in it, but realized he wouldn't understand. She smiled and shook her head, then started the engine and took off across the bumpy terrain.

Once they left the airfield, the terrain grew greener and hillier. To Lance's right was, he guessed, the Pacific. It seemed utterly calm, and the glare bouncing off it was too painful to look at. To Lance's left were low hills choked with palm trees and vines.

The road they were traveling on was a two-lane dirt road, but it appeared to be the major thoroughfare along the ocean. They passed a number of native women on the road, driving oxen and cows and pigs. The only motorized vehicles they passed were army trucks with the same symbol of Monte on their sides.

After about thirty minutes of driving, they entered a populous area. Dozens of corrugated-tin huts, adobe huts, and huts made of what looked like blocks of dung. A primitive gas station with one rusting pump. A handful of tiny stores with corrugated-tin roofs and open stalls. A couple of open-air bars, with large bottles of cheap rum standing on a table, and groups of native women sitting on stools, drinking and conversing. Lance had traveled in Mexico, Guatemala, and many islands in the Caribbean, but he could not recall seeing housing and living conditions as poor as these.

They stopped at a military checkpoint, manned by two female guards with the same uniforms as those who guarded the terminal, except that these wore white patent-leather Sam Browne belts and holsters. The guards at the checkpoint had slung submachine guns and the pistols in their patent-leather holsters were automatics. The driver of Lance's jeep spoke with them briefly. The guards peered in at Lance, then let him pass.

Once past the checkpoint, the road got flatter and better tended. The bushes on both sides of the road were dotted with red and purple flowers. Lance didn't know their names. Up ahead was some kind of castle. They went through another checkpoint, and then Lance could see the castle clearly. It was enormous. It was made of huge stones, and it appeared to be several stories high. It had high conical turrets, with flags sporting the symbol of Monte, and it was surrounded by a moat.

The jeep stopped at a third and final checkpoint, and then clattered across the wide drawbridge. They entered a beautiful courtyard. Parked at the far end of the courtyard were two army trucks and three Mercedes-Benzes. One of the Mercedes-Benzes was a white stretch limousine. Four little flags with the Monte symbol flew from the corners of the limousine.

He pointed to the limousine.

"Boss?" he said.

The guard nodded and rolled her eyes.

"Mamma Doc," she said.

Mamma Doc—then the scuttlebutt on the terminal floor had been accurate. Mamma Doc Taillevent—President-for-Life—was the power here. Was this the Boss he was being taken to see?

The guard parked the jeep and motioned for Lance to get out. He stepped carefully to the ground, wobbling slightly, and steadied himself by leaning against the side of the jeep. The guard got out and motioned for him to follow. Several female soldiers stopped to stare at Lance as they made their way to the castle entrance. Lance realized that he hadn't seen a single native man on Mannihanni since his arrival. He wondered where they were.

They entered the main doors, went through yet another checkpoint, and then turned down a passageway lined with rock. It was much darker inside and about thirty degrees cooler. Lance followed the guard into a large office. Behind a desk sat a receptionist, also in uniform, typing with two fingers on an old upright typewriter.

The guard said something to the receptionist. They both looked at Lance, and then they spoke some more. The guard motioned for Lance to sit down on a worn wooden bench, then waved goodbye to him and left. Lance was sorry to see her go. Although they hadn't communicated more than three or four words, he felt that she was his first friend on Mannihanni. He wondered whom it was she'd brought him to see. He sensed that it would not be Mamma Doc.

After he had waited for perhaps an hour, two more guards appeared, and walked up to him without smiling. They motioned for him to get up. He followed them into a large dark room with a desk and three chairs. One of the chairs was made out of steel. It had been painted over several times, and was fairly dirty. Next to the steel chair was a large rectangular metal box with numerous dials and switches. Lance figured it was a shortwave radio.

The guards motioned for Lance to sit down in the steel chair. As soon as he did so, they swiftly bound his wrists to the arms of the chair with leather thongs.

"Hey," said Lance, "what's going on here?"

One of the guards bent down and tried to tie Lance's ankles to the chair, but he moved his legs out of her reach. The second guard brought the muzzle of her submachine gun up to Lance's jaw and he let his ankles drop back down again. The first guard bound his ankles to the chair legs with leather thongs.

Lance was beginning to get really nervous. What had he gotten himself into by asking to see the boss? Who was this boss who was going to see him, and why was it necessary to have one's wrists and ankles tied to a chair when one saw this boss? Lance began to get very nostalgic about his old home on the cement floor of the stinking terminal and wished that he was back there.

The first guard stood up, ripped open Lance's shirt, and unbuckled his belt.

"Uh, listen," said Lance, "I changed my mind, I *thought* I wanted to see the boss, but it turns out I didn't want to after all. It turns out I completely forgot an appointment I had made in the terminal to see—"

The second guard unzipped Lance's fly and yanked at Lance's trousers. He felt a sudden spasm in his bowels.

"Please," said Lance, forcing a pained smile, "I really do have to leave now."

The second guard yanked again, and pulled Lance's trousers down below his knees. In a perfect world, he thought, he would have had clean underwear. In a perfect world he would probably also not be tied to a steel chair in a castle on a strange island in the Pacific, having his trousers yanked below his knees. He had spent the ten years before his marriage trying to yank down the pants of women, and ever since his separation it seemed that every woman he met was trying to retaliate in kind.

When the guard yanked down his undershorts as well, Lance got even more nervous than he was already, but not nearly as nervous as he got as soon as he saw what they were up to. What they were up to was attaching wires to terminals on the shortwave radio and bringing them over to where Lance was sitting.

Please, God, he prayed, let them be hooking me up to the shortwave radio to hear a stereo concert from Prague while I'm waiting to talk to the boss and not what I think they're doing.

The guards attached wires to Lance's wrists and ankles by means of perforated rubber straps with metal terminals on them. One thing now was certain—they were not hooking him up to a shortwave radio to hear a stereo concert from Prague. Please, God, he prayed, let them be hooking me up to an electrocardiograph machine as part of an exhaustive physical examination.

The guards attached more electrodes—to his chest, his right ear, his right nostril, and his penis. It was looking less and less like an electrocardiograph hookup every second. Finally the guards finished their hookups and withdrew.

Lance had seen *Midnight Express,* he had read countless stomach-churning charitable solicitations from Amnesty International, and he could no longer pretend that what was going to happen to him was anything other than what he dreaded most: he was going to be tortured.

Even when Lance was a small boy growing up during the Second World War and heard stories of how soldiers were tortured by the Japs and the Germans, he never understood how anybody could endure it. He himself had never fostered any illusions about whether he could endure torture. He would admit to the Mannihannis whatever they wanted him to admit to—it didn't matter what.

"Just tell me what you want me to admit to," he said aloud, although the room was empty. "I'll swear I've done it."

108

Lance had been sitting, strapped to the steel chair and wired to the machine, for about ten minutes when he heard somebody enter the room behind him and close the door. The somebody walked slowly and heavily to the desk.

The somebody was a very tall, very husky black woman in a black uniform, a black Fidel Castro hat and dark glasses. She was smoking an enormous cigar. She looked carefully at Lance, as if trying to figure out what he was doing there, and then sat down heavily in the chair behind the desk.

Lance waited, with pounding heart, for something to happen, but the woman continued to stare at him and smoke the cigar and say nothing.

Lance cleared his throat.

"Uh, I'd like to go to the toilet, if I may," said Lance, aware that the person behind the desk probably could understand him no better than the guards at the terminal.

There was no reaction from the large person behind the desk.

"*Koh*-ler," said Lance carefully. "I . . . wish . . . *Koh*-ler."

The person behind the desk erupted in laughter. Lance was startled. The person behind the desk seemed to find Lance's request the height of wit.

"Hew don't have to say *Koh*-ler," said the person. "Hi understand 'twalette.'"

"Good," said Lance, genuinely heartened, having enormous faith in his ability to communicate verbally, provided one spoke his language.

"Hi em General Maxime," said the person behind the desk.

"Ah," said Lance, impressed at the rank. "How do you do, General Maxime. I am Lance Lerner. I'd shake hands, but

338

I'm afraid they've tied my wrists to this chair for some reason."

The General did not apparently find this humorous. She did not reply.

"I wonder, General, if I might go to the toilet just now? I have a severely upset stomach, and I really have to visit the toilet."

"Hew may not veeseet the twalette," said the General. "Hew are a prisoner."

"A prisoner," said Lance. "Yes. I know that. But why, General? Why am I a prisoner? What have I done wrong?"

The General smoked silently for a while before replying.

"Hew deed not come here because hew were hijacked," said the General.

"I didn't?" said Lance. "Then why did I come?"

"Hew weesh to spy on our natural gaz supply," said the General. "Hew theenk les Etats Unis can capture thees natural gaz from Mannihanni, but hew are wrong."

She leaned over to what looked like an intercom on her desk and pushed a lever. Instantly, searing pain sped through Lance's body and he realized the torture had begun. He bit down hard on his lower lip to keep from screaming, and the pain eventually stopped.

He was amazed. He hadn't screamed. He hadn't made a sound at all.

"I am not a spy," he said, and tensed.

The General hit the switch again. Once more searing pain shot through his body, once more Lance bit down on his lower lip, once more it stopped, and once more he had not cried out.

"I am not a spy," he said again. "I'm an author."

Suddenly he felt courageous. He had withstood two electric shocks and he hadn't crumbled as he was always certain he would. Maybe he wasn't the coward he had always feared he was.

"Hew are what?" said the General.

"I'm an author," said Lance. "I write books."

"Books?" said the General. "Wheech books?"

"Novels," said Lance. *"Knuckle Sandwich, Fresh When Available, Modern Lit, Cut to the Chase, You Can't Get There from Here*—those are all the titles of novels I've written. *Gallivanting* is the latest one."

"Gallivanting?" said the General.

"Yes," said Lance. "Why, have you heard of it?"

The General grew suddenly livid and smashed down on the lever on the box on her desk. Once more the fiery pain attacked his body. Lance bit through his lower lip and blood ran warmly down his chin, but once again, miraculously, he had survived and not made a sound.

"Hew deed *not* write *Gallivanting!*" said the General. "Hi know thees to be a *fact!*"

"How would you . . . know such a thing?" said Lance.

He was beginning to lose consciousness now, but he didn't care. If he was going to die, at least he could die content that he hadn't been a coward after all.

"How Hi would *know* such a theeng?" thundered the General. "How Hi would know such a theeng ees that I hev seen who wrote *Gallivanting* on the *Tonight Show!* And *hew* are not *heem!*"

"I am . . . Lance Lerner . . ." he said, now barely able to speak. "I am . . . the person you saw on . . . the *Tonight Show* . . ."

The General lurched out of her chair and came over to where Lance was sitting. She aimed her desk light at Lance's face, and held up his chin.

"Hew do not look like heem," said the General less certainly.

"I don't . . . look like him because . . . when you saw me on the . . . *Tonight Show* . . . I had shaved and . . . showered and . . . was dressed . . . differently . . ." Lance mumbled.

The General lifted Lance's chin a bit higher.

"Now that hew mention eet," said the General, "Hi theenk there *ees* a slight resemblance."

"Good . . ." mumbled Lance, genuinely pleased that he was able to look at all like himself, even now.

"So," said the General, "hew are the author of *Gallivanting.* Tell me sometheeng."

He was sinking in black fur. It was a lovely feeling. But somebody had asked him a question. It would be possible to answer it before he left. It would be impolite not to.

"What . . . can I . . . tell you . . . ?" whispered Lance.

"What ees Jawnny Carson really like?" said the General.

109

Lance awoke between cool sheets in a clean bed.

He was back in New York, he knew it. The whole nightmare in Mannihanni had been just that—a nightmare, and now he was awake and back in the land of the living.

He opened his eyes.

"Hew slept?" said a familiar voice.

He was not back in New York. The nightmare was still on. The person who had spoken was seated opposite his bed in a big wicker rocking chair, smoking a cigar.

At least he was alive.

He was still weak, his wrists and ankles and nostril and ear and chest and penis hurt where the electric shocks had been administered, but at least he was still alive. Not only was he alive, but somebody had given him a bath, a shave, possibly even washed his hair, and dressed him in what felt like cotton pajamas. Who had done this and why?

"Hi owe you an apologize," said the General. "Hi have checked your story and hew are who hew say. Hew are famous auteur. Hew are not a spy."

"No kidding," said Lance weakly. He wondered why they were mutually exclusive—why you couldn't be a famous auteur *and* a spy—but wisely he did not raise this philosophical point.

"None of us is a spy," said Lance, "and I suggest that we all be released and allowed to return to our homes in America."

The General continued puffing her cigar.

"Ees not my job to decide thees," she said between puffs. "Ees job of our President-for-Life, Madame Taillevent."

"Well then," said Lance, "I would appreciate having an opportunity to speak to her about this."

"Madame Taillevent ees very busy woman," said the

341

General. "But porhops she weel find time for the friend of Jawnny Carson."

Two more days passed before Lance was able to arrange an audience with Mamma Doc. On the evening of the third day, a guard appeared in his room carrying an old black wool tuxedo on a hanger, reeking of mothballs. She handed it to him as if he was supposed to know what to do with it.

"What's this for?" he said.

The guard merely extended the tuxedo to him.

"Thank you," he said, taking it from her, "but what is this *for?*"

"Mamma Doc," said the guard.

Lance brightened.

There was a white wing-collar shirt and a white bow tie. The jacket sleeves and trousers were four inches too short, and the body of the jacket was far too roomy, but there didn't appear to be time to visit a tailor. Lance wasn't able to tie much of a bow in his tie, and no shoes had arrived with the rest of the clothing. He was forced to follow the guard down the hall barefoot. Considering all that had happened to him thus far, it did not seem to be a noteworthy detail.

After a long walk down many stone corridors, Lance was ushered into a baronial dining room. At the end of a table that was easily twenty feet long and set with white linen, china, and gold flatware, sat Mamma Doc. She was much as Lance had imagined—tall, husky, black and female. Her hair, unexpectedly, was white, and she was dressed in a white silk variation of the General's modified army uniform, but without the hat or the cigar.

The guard saluted her and motioned to Lance. Lance bowed. The guard withdrew. Nobody had yet said a word. Lance prayed she spoke English.

"Hello," said Lance, enunciating clearly. "My name is Lance Lerner."

"We are Madame Taillevent," said Mamma Doc. "Please to be seated."

Mamma Doc motioned Lance to a chair at the other end of the table. He sat down. He realized that he was to dine with Mamma Doc—certainly a great honor, and one that would doubtlessly not have been conferred upon him were it not for his intimate friendship with Johnny Carson.

"Well," said Lance, "this is an unexpected pleasure, Madame Taillevent. I mean I had no idea that we would be dining together."

Mamma Doc gave him the briefest of smiles and inclined her head.

"Eet ees not often that we are able to dine weeth a fameuse auteur."

A guard appeared with a bottle of champagne and filled the gigantic crystal goblet in front of Lance's plate. Mamma Doc, he noted, had a filled glass already.

"Well," said Lance, raising his glass to Mamma Doc, "I, uh . . ." He suddenly found himself unable to think of a toast suitable to a female president who used the royal "we." In fact, the only toast that came to mind was one that he'd seen Bogart use in the movies. "Here's looking at *you*, kid," he said to her at last.

Mamma Doc appeared to find the toast acceptable. Either she was a Bogart fan or else she assumed it was a traditional American toast to royalty.

"Heer's looking at *hew*, keed," she intoned solemnly.

They drank. It was surprisingly good champagne.

The champagne was a little *too* good—before he knew it he had drained the glass. The moment he put it down a guard appeared from nowhere and swiftly filled it up again.

"So, Meestair Lerner," she said, "how hew theenk of Mannihanni so far?"

Lance smiled uncomfortably, then opted for politeness.

"I, uh, like it fairly well," he said. "What I've seen so far, I mean."

"Yais?" she said. "Hew like fairly well the grinding poverty of the peasants?"

"Uh, heh heh, well, now that you mention it, I *don't*," he said, somewhat unnerved. "I was just being polite, as a matter of fact."

"Not to be polite, Meestair Lerner," she said. "We een Mannihanni are not polite. Politeness ees a luxury we cannot to afford."

"Well then," said Lance, "to be brutally candid, Madame President, I was *shocked* at the living conditions of the peasants that I saw on the way to your palace. Especially in contrast to the way you yourself live—your champagne, your crystal glasses, your gold flatware, your Mercedes limousine."

"How we leev een the Palace," she said, "ees not so much

for our own plaisir as for the peasants. The peasants demand that their leader leev een splendor—eet geev them dignity."

"Dignity?" said Lance. "What kind of dignity can they have if you live in splendor and they live in rusting corrugated shacks?"

"Hew do not understand our ways, Meestair Lerner," she said. "Eef we were a reech country like les Etats Unis, then all our peoples could to have the champagne, the crystal glasses, the gold flatware, the limousine. Seence we are not, they weesh for *us* to have eet at least."

"I find that hard to believe," said Lance. "I'm sorry, but you did ask me to be frank."

"We do weesh hew to be frank, Meestair Lerner," she said. "We weel tell hew, then, that we deed at first, followeeng the revolution, leev een the corrugated-teen shacks as the peasants. But the peasants tell us, '*No*, Madame la Présidente, *no*, Mamma Doc—eef hew leev as we do, then the leaders of the beeg countries like les Etats Unis weel not respect us."

"Then why don't you do something to improve the quality of their lives?" said Lance.

"We do," she said. "Every Sunday we go ride een the limousine and veeseet weeth the peoples. We tell them of the advances we making een the government. We throw to them the gold coins."

Lance sighed.

"Look," he said, "what you do with your own people is your business, I guess. What you do with mine upsets me a lot more. Why are you holding us prisoner?"

"We do not hold hew preesoner, Meestair Lerner," said Mamma Doc.

"No?" said Lance. "You mean we're free to leave?"

"Yais, of course," said Mamma Doc. "Only we must to determine first why hew come here."

"Look," said Lance, "the General says you think we're spies, that we're interested in your natural gas deposits. We never even *heard* of any natural gas deposits before we arrived here. We never even heard of *Mannihanni* before we arrived here."

"You no like the General?"

"That would be a gross understatement."

"You no like her because she ees woman or because she ees Negro?"

"I no like her because she tortured me when I was first brought to the castle."

344

Mamma Doc appeared truly shocked.

"No! The General do thees to *hew?*" said Mamma Doc. "Eet ees not possible!"

"I thought she did it at your behest," said Lance.

"No!" said Mamma Doc vehemently. "Not our behest! The General tortures only at behest of the *General.* The General ees vicious, weecked, *evil* person!"

"Then why do you allow her to continue in such a position of power?" said Lance.

"Why?" said Mamma Doc. "We *tell* hew why. Mamma Doc ees good—the peoples all loving Mamma Doc, yais? But the General ees evil—the peoples all hating the General. So eef sometheeng unfortunate have to be done that the peoples weel hate, we have the General do eet, and the peoples not hating Mamma Doc."

Lance nodded. He supposed Mamma Doc was right. Two guards brought several platters of food to the table. One of the dishes appeared to be some kind of meat. Another appeared to be fish, and a third was neither meat nor fish, though probably not fowl either. Smaller platters contained varieties of mashed fruit and what looked like seaweed.

"Ees not like your food een les Etats Unis," said Mamma Doc. "Ees not like your McDonald's homboorgers."

"It's certainly not," said Lance.

Mamma Doc seemed vastly amused.

"Een les Etats Unis," she said, "we have experience the same deefeeculty weeth the food as you do in Mannihanni."

"You were in the United States?" said Lance.

Mamma Doc nodded.

"Shortly followeeng the revolution against the accursed French," she said. "We deed not have the education. A world leader must to have the education. So I go to les Etats Unis for the education."

"Where did you study?" said Lance.

"UCLA," said Mamma Doc. "We study Heestory, Pheelosophy, Engleesh, French . . ."

"I would have thought you already *knew* French," said Lance.

"We *deed,*" said Mamma Doc. "We take French because we theenk maybe we can *ace* eet."

Lance chuckled. There was something fairly ingratiating about this woman, he thought. Ingratiating and oddly familiar.

"How did you pay for the tuition?" said Lance.

"The people of Mannihanni geev me scholarsheep," said Mamma Doc.

"And what degree did you attain there?" said Lance. "A Ph.D.?"

"No no," said Mamma Doc. "We go only one semester. Then we feel we serve better the people of Mannihanni in Port Pangaud than een West Los Angeles."

"If you only went to school one semester," said Lance, "then why do they call you *Dr.* Taillevent and Mamma *Doc?*"

"Ah," she said, "that ees because we receive the Doctor of Deeveeneety degree from the Universalist Chorch. By mail."

"I see," said Lance.

"No," said Mamma Doc, "we deed not weesh to stay more than one semester een les Etats Unis. Your country ees, forgeev me, not to my taste."

"Why not?" said Lance.

"For many reason," said Mamma Doc. "The McDonald's homboorgers, the poleeteecal seetuation, the pollution of the atmospheres, the commercialism of everytheeng. But most of all, ees too unpleasant for me to be een society wheech ees not separateest."

"Which is *not* separatist?" said Lance, incredulous. "You mean you'd like blacks and whites to be *segregated?*"

She shook her head impatiently.

"Not black and white," she said, "man and *woman.*"

Lance laughed.

"So that's why I haven't seen any men so far in Mannihanni," he said. "Where do they live?"

"The men of Mannihanni," said Mamma Doc, "they are not a problem weeth us. They know their place."

"And what is that?" said Lance.

"The usual," said Mamma Doc. "The work of the house. The procreation. The care of the small babies. The work wheech does not tax the mind—that ees what they like the best."

As they continued to chat, Lance noticed with utter astonishment that a hairy black spider the size of a soup bowl had suddenly dropped onto the tablecloth from above and was now ambling in a leisurely fashion toward the food. He watched it, frozen with fascination, not daring to breathe for fear that it would be attracted to him.

If Mamma Doc saw the spider she was giving no indication. When it was two feet from her plate, Mamma Doc soundlessly raised her fist above her head and brought it swiftly down

346

on the spider. Lance heard a sickening splat. The spider's legs twitched and curled into a ball.

Lance turned away, certain he was going to vomit. When he glanced back at Mamma Doc he noted that she had covered the spider's remains with a large cloth napkin and had already resumed eating her dinner. These people are barbarians, he reasoned, why should I be surprised?

"Meestair Lerner," chided Mamma Doc. "Hew do not eat your deener."

"I'm, uh, not too hungry tonight, thanks," said Lance.

"Do hew grieve for the spider?" she said.

"No," he said, "I scarcely knew him."

Mamma Doc laughed.

"Hew have a droll manner to express yourself," she said.

"Death brings out my antic side," he said.

"Do hew appear often on the *Tonight Show?*" she said.

"Not that often," he said. "Once every few years."

"What ees he like?"

"Johnny Carson?"

"Yais."

"He's a good guy. Smart, smooth, handles himself nicely. I don't really know him that well, if you want to know the truth."

"Last night he say your book ees on the bestseller leest."

"No kidding?" said Lance. "Did he happen to say what number it was?"

"Eight," said Mamma Doc.

"Far fucking out," said Lance. "Well, next time a young author asks me how to publicize his novel, I'll know what to advise: get hijacked."

"Hew are quite eentelligent for a man," she said.

"Thanks a lot," he said.

"Do hew have the fortune to be married?" she said.

"Sort of," said Lance.

"Please?"

"Well, yes, I'm married," said Lance, "but my wife and I no longer live together."

"Ah," said Mamma Doc. "And does thees condeetion deestress hew?"

"It did at one time," said Lance. "A great deal."

"Not at present?" said Mamma Doc.

"Not that much," said Lance.

"We een Mannihanni could to use a man of your eentelligence."

"Oh?" said Lance. "In what way?"

"The men of Mannihanni have leetle eentelligence," she said. "They adding nothing to the bloodlines when they breed. A man weeth your eentelligence would add much to the bloodlines."

"I see," said Lance.

"Porhops hew would to conseeder to stay een Mannihanni when the others leave," said Mamma Doc.

"And become a stud horse?" said Lance.

"That and other theengs," she said.

"What kind of other things?" said Lance.

The notion of staying in Mannihanni for any purpose at all, even as a court stud, was not enthralling.

"We have the weesh," she said, "to write a book."

"Stop the presses!" said Lance. "Tear out the front page!"

"Please?"

"I'm sorry," said Lance. "I was being impolite. I know a great many people who are writing books."

"Ah," she said. "But thees book *we* weesh to write weel be our autobiography. Porhops hew would weesh to help us."

"Hey, listen," said Lance, "I really appreciate the offer—I'm really knocked out by the offer and all—I mean I'm really honored that you would even ask me. But I'm afraid that it just isn't the kind of thing I like to do."

Mamma Doc nodded slowly.

"Een les Etats Unis hew have the expression 'every man have hees price,' no?"

"Yes," said Lance. "But I'm afraid that there isn't anything you could offer me that would change my mind."

Mamma Doc took a last bite of food, chewed it slowly, swallowed.

"What eef we say to hew, 'Mestair Lerner, eef hew stay een Mannihanni to help us to write our book, then we letting everybody else go home'?"

"I thought you said that you were going to let all of my people go anyway," said Lance. "I thought that's what you said a few minutes ago."

"What we say," said Mamma Doc, "ees that we weel eenvestigate eef all the peoples on the airoplane come heer because they are forced, or eef they weesh to spy. *Then* we letting them go."

"And now you're saying that you'll release them only if I stay and help you write your autobiography?" said Lance.

Mamma Doc nodded.

348

"Hew are not required to geev us answer tonight," said Mamma Doc. "Hew may cogitate about thees for a while."

"All right," said Lance.

The guards began clearing dishes.

"Hew weesh a brondy, Meestair Lerner?" said Mamma Doc.

"Oh, no thanks," said Lance.

"Hew weesh to come to our bed now and make sex?" said Mamma Doc.

"Uh, not tonight, thanks," said Lance, trying to suppress his shock at her question.

"Hew theenk we are too old for hew?" she said.

"Old?" said Lance. "Oh *no*, Madame Taillevent. Not too old at *all*. I *love* older women."

"How old hew theenk we are?" said Mamma Doc.

"How old?" said Lance, stalling for time. He had absolutely no idea how to play this. He figured she was around seventy-five.

"How old?" said Mamma Doc.

"Oh. Well, uh, I'd say, about . . . forty-nine?"

Mamma Doc let out a shriek of laughter which startled him.

"Hew theenk we are *forty-nine?*" she cried, helpless with mirth.

"You aren't?" said Lance.

"We are seexty-seex," said Mamma Doc.

"Sixty-*six*," said Lance, playing up the surprise angle. "You're *kidding* me! I don't *believe* you? Sixty-*six!* That simply isn't *possible!*"

Mamma Doc beamed with satisfaction.

"How many years have *hew*, Meestair Lerner?" said Mamma Doc.

"Me?" said Lance. "I'm forty."

"Forty," said Mamma Doc. "Forty ees not too old for me. I have made sex weeth boys of only twelve."

"Is that so?" said Lance. "When you were how old?"

"Not how *old*," said Mamma Doc, "but what *time?*"

"Excuse me?" said Lance.

"We make sex weeth a twelve-year-old boy only thees morning."

"Ah," said Lance.

"Hew find thees unusual?" said Mamma Doc. "That we take a boy thees age for sex?"

"Well," said Lance, "I guess it *does* sort of surprise me. I mean I guess I'm always surprised to find out what a woman wants."

"What a woman wants?" said Mamma Doc. "A woman wants energy."

"Energy?"

"Energy from the act of making sex," said Mamma Doc. "We store it up. It geev us strength. That ees why we ordered to make sex by our god."

"Your *god* orders you to have sex?" said Lance.

Mamma Doc nodded.

"Monte," she said.

"Why does Monte order you to have sex?" said Lance.

"Eet make Monte hoppy eef we make sex," said Mamma Doc. "The act of making sex geev strength to us, then we geeving strength to Monte. Hew certain hew don't weesh to come weeth us now to bed and make sex?"

"Uh, well, not tonight, I'm afraid," said Lance.

"Hew weesh rain check?" said Mamma Doc.

"Yeah," said Lance. "I'll take a rain check."

A guard appeared to escort Lance back to his room. Mamma Doc extended her hand to Lance. He didn't know whether he was expected to shake it or kiss it. Playing it safe, he did both.

"Please to theenk about whether hew weesh to help us weeth our book," said Mamma Doc. "Please to take all of the time that hew require. Only give us your decision sometimes tomorrow."

It wasn't fair. Why should the fate of all the passengers hang on whether Lance was willing to sacrifice himself by remaining in Mannihanni? Most of them he'd never even met. Would they sacrifice themselves for *him*? On the other hand, how was he going to feel if their imprisonment lasted months or even years—knowing all the time that he could have saved them? How was he going to feel as the elderly and sickly passengers began to die, knowing that he could have spared their lives by giving up his freedom?

What if he *did* stay in Mannihanni? Would it be any better than death? What kind of life would he have here? He would certainly be given exceptional treatment—wonderful living quarters, champagne, perhaps his own limousine. He would evidently be given an endless supply of Mannihanni women to impregnate, and would watch as dozens—possibly even hundreds or thousands—of his children were born and grew to maturity. The notion of having that many children was momentarily intriguing, but then he remembered that in Mannihanni it was the men who raised the children and his fantasy dissolved.

If he stayed in Mannihanni, he would be forced to become Mamma Doc's lover. The huge, sixty-six-year-old black woman was not exactly his ideal mate. On the other hand, how many more years would she even *want* to have sex? Probably well into her late nineties, with his luck.

Needless to say, he would never again see anyone he loved back in America. Never see Cathy. Never see his folks. Never see Dorothy or Janie or Stevie or Claire or any of the others. How could he face that? The notion of a future in which he would never know anyone but Mannihannis plunged him into despondency.

Lying in his bed, Lance debated the decision that Mamma Doc had asked him to make by the following day. He fell asleep debating.

110

Maybe it was because they'd been frisked and the guards knew they no longer had weapons. Maybe it was because they were women and the guards therefore considered them either weaker than men or simply less hostile. Whatever the reason, on one of the nights when June, Alix, Sandy and Wanda were escorted to the women's room, their armed attendant made the mistake of propping her automatic rifle against the wall and relieving herself alongside her captives.

No sooner had the guard squatted over one of the holes in the floor than June knocked her cold with a karate chop. Alix bolted the door from the inside. Sandy boosted herself up to the window ledge, smashed out the glass, crawled through the empty frame and dropped to the ground outside. Wanda and Alix went next. Just as June was about to boost herself up onto the ledge, somebody outside tried the door, found it locked, and began to pound on it. June jumped for the ledge, missed her handhold and slid back into the room just as the door burst inward.

The guard who had kicked down the door fell forward with the momentum and temporarily lost her balance. Within the next second all these things occurred: the guard regained her balance, June saw that it was too late to jump for the ledge again because she would be shot in the back, the guard registered her unconscious compatriot on the floor and June as the probable attacker. June saw that she was too far away from the guard to use karate on her. Within the following two seconds these things occurred: June's right hand went inside her jumpsuit to her crotch. The guard's submachine gun was raised into position. June's thumb and first two fingers of her right hand entered her vagina and found the first of two Ben Wa balls. The guard clicked off the safety and began to squeeze the trigger. June's right hand came out of her pants, snapped back over her right shoulder, and hurled the gold-plated ball with all her might at the guard's forehead.

The submachine gun chattered, but the bullets thunked harmlessly into the wall, because the owner of the finger which had pulled the trigger was in the process of falling onto the floor unconscious. June leaped for the ledge, and this time she made it. She crawled through the window and dropped to the ground. The four women were already across the field and into a corrugated-tin shed before the searchlights went on and the yelling started.

111

Lance awoke, drenched in his own sweat. He got up, washed, put on his tuxedo, and buzzed for a guard. When his door was unlocked and the guard appeared, he said simply: "Mamma Doc." The guard evidently understood what he wanted, for she immediately nodded and disappeared.

Within twenty minutes the guard had reappeared and led him through the dark, damp stone corridors of the castle to see Mamma Doc.

Mamma Doc sat in a bed that must have been twice king-size, dressed in white satin pajamas, watching a game show on television. The guard brought Lance into the room, bowed to Mamma Doc, and withdrew.

"Good morning, Madame Taillevent," said Lance.

"Good morning, Meestair Lerner," she said. She inclined her head toward the television set. "You know thees program, *Fomeely Feud?*"

"Uh, sure," said Lance. "How are you able to get American TV shows on Mannihanni?"

"Eet arrive on the satellite," she said, then grimaced. "Thees show ees excellent exomple of the decadence of les Etats Unis."

"Why is that?" said Lance.

"What do they compete to know—answers to questions one find een the Encyclopedia Britannica or the Koran or the Judeo-Chreestian Bible? No. They compete to know answers to questions wheech most numbers of peoples geev when asked. The highest aspiration een les Etats Unis ees to *be* like everybody else and to *theenk* like everybody else."

"Well, that's certainly true of *some* people in the United States, but I don't think it's fair to say that *everybody* in the country feels that way," said Lance.

"Yais?" said Mamma Doc. "Porhops hew tell us now hew

not part of the attacking of our girls that happens yesterday een the night!"

"What attacking of girls happened last night?" said Lance.

"Hew standing there and saying hew not *know?*" shrieked Mamma Doc. "Weeth your name on one of the weapons of the *attacking?*"

"I have absolutely no idea of what you are *talking* about," said Lance. "I *swear* to you!"

"Tell me, Meestair Lerner," she said, "your Christian name is wheech?"

"Lance," said Lance.

"Lance," she repeated, withdrawing something small from the pocket of her gown and holding it out to him so he could get a close look at it.

It was a small gold ball. It was . . . Lance couldn't believe what it was she was showing him—one of the two Ben Wa balls he had given Cathy years ago in New York! And now, for some reason that God alone could grasp, here it was, on the other side of the world, in the hand of the dictator of an obscure South Sea island!

"I . . . have absolutely no idea what that is doing here," said Lance incredulously.

"So!" said Mamma Doc. "Hew confess that hew *know* thees object!"

"I confess that I know it," said Lance, "but I—"

"Hew confess that hew throw thees object een the head of one of our girls yesterday een the night een the lavatory of the women?" said Mamma Doc.

"Absolutely not!" said Lance. "How could I have been in the lavatory of the women last night? I was here in the palace, locked up in my room, asleep."

Mamma Doc pondered this a moment. It was undeniably true that Lance had been in the palace the night before and locked up in his room.

"Very well," she said, "we weeling to believe hew not responsible. But unteel we finding out who *ees* responsible, we keep your peoples here."

"That's really ironic," said Lance.

"Why ees ironic?"

"Because," said Lance carefully, "I came here this morning to make you a counter-offer on the writing of your autobiography in exchange for the release of my people."

Mamma Doc looked at him for several moments before replying.

"Your mind ees eenteresting to me, Meestair Lerner," she said. "Porhops we shall ask Monte what we are to do weeth your people."

Lance was tempted to suggest that if she refused to let his people go, Mamma Doc could expect locusts, floods, and the slaying of her firstborn, but he thought better of it and restrained himself.

"Perhaps we could ask Monte together," is what he said instead.

Mamma Doc's eyebrows raised themselves, seemingly independently of their owner's intent.

"Hew weesh to take part een ceremony to honor Monte?" she said.

"Yes," he said. "I would consider it a great honor."

"Ees great *great* honor," she said, "but we weesh to be certain thees ees what hew truly weesh to do."

Lance sensed this might well be the tipoff to back down, but he somehow felt that going through with it would win him many more points than he'd lost with the Ben Wa ball.

"Taking part in a ceremony to honor Monte is what I truly wish to do," said Lance.

"Een thees case," said Mamma Doc, "we cannot refuse hew such an honor."

"Thank you," said Lance.

"Porhops hew weesh now to have the further honor to breeng hyour meelk-white body to our bed to make sex weeth us?"

"Oh, not just now, thanks."

"Porhops hew weesh another rain check?"

"Yes, a rain check would be better."

"Eet amuse us to pretend we geeving you thees choice."

"I beg your pardon?"

"We know anytime we weesh hew to come to our bed and make sex weeth us, we have but to send for hew and hew weel do what we weesh."

"I will?"

"Yais. Because hew so attrocted to us and because hew weesh to keep hyour penis and hyour balls attached een the place wheech they now attached."

Lance was speechless. Mamma Doc smiled a smug smile and returned to her televised game show.

112

By the time Lance was returned to his room and locked in to eat his lunch, he was trembling with anger. Mamma Doc's insinuations that he belonged to her, that he was sexually on call whenever she wanted at peril of castration, filled him with rage and fear. More rage than fear. Did she honestly think she could force him to service her sexually whenever she wanted? On the other hand, did he honestly think she *couldn't*? What kind of a man would he be if he acquiesced to such an arrangement? On the other hand, what kind of a man would he be if she had his gonads amputated? It was a paradox—the only way to keep his balls intact was to pretend he didn't have any, the only way to show he had balls was to lose them.

What would his group say now—that he was letting himself be victimized again? That once more he was willing to let a woman control him sexually? That what Mamma Doc wanted was a grotesque parody of what he felt all women wanted? That the feelings engendered in him by Mamma Doc's pronouncements were merely an exaggeration of the feelings he sometimes had about the sexual demands made upon him by his own wife?

Maybe it wasn't so farfetched after all. Maybe the anger toward women he had apparently been feeling all his life stemmed from fear. Fear of women. Fear of sex with women. Fear of what sex with women led to—commitment and permanence. Commitment and permanence, in his mind, led to having children, to having grandchildren, to growing old, to dying, to death.

When Lance was about eight, his parents took him to a resort in the Indiana Sand Dunes called Duneside Inn. One night, shortly after they'd put him to bed, he began to think about such matters as how far out did outer space go, where did it end and, more important, what lay beyond the end? Then, perhaps logically, he began to think about death. For the first time in his life he realized that when he died that would be the end of him.

He got nauseated and claustrophobic and felt he couldn't breathe. It seemed he was falling slowly upward into a black infinity. He called out tearfully for his Dad to come and explain away his fears, to make it all right as he always had before. But for the first time in his life his Dad wasn't able to make it all right. He told little Lance that we lived on through our children, that we lived on through our work, but that we didn't really know what happened after death, if anything at all.

Lance found no solace in his father's words. He couldn't bear the thought that he would die someday, that he would cease to exist for the rest of time. Did others know they were going to die? If they did, then how could they just go about their lives as if nothing were wrong, as if they were going to live forever? He wanted to run up to people on the street and ask them if they knew they were all going to die and what they planned to do about it.

Eventually he calmed down. He pretended to himself that everything was all right, that everything was still the same, that nothing had changed, but he knew better. He never overcame his fear of death, he just repressed it to some subconscious level where he didn't have to deal with it. The same level at which he probably truly believed that having sex with women put you on a cosmic conveyor belt that led inevitably to death. If you could avoid sex with women, then maybe you could avoid getting on that conveyor belt and somehow manage to avoid death. If that was how he had it pegged subconsciously, then it was certainly useful to harbor anger at women. Harboring anger at women was an effective barrier against being intimate and sexual with them.

He sat down at the table and began picking at his lunch. There was a meatlike dish which looked like what he had been served at dinner with Mamma Doo—*carpus* she had called it, he seemed to recall. There was also a fishy thing again, and seaweed, and several things that looked like mashed fruit, and something that looked like squid or octopus with two big eyes staring up at him from the plate.

He took a large piece of seaweed and covered the creature with the two big eyes and took experimental bites out of the fish. Possibly it had not been refrigerated very well, because it tasted less than fresh. He took little bites of the mashed fruits but found them rather bitter. He cut off a piece of the meatlike *carpus* and began to chew it. It didn't taste quite as sickly sweet as it had at dinner with Mamma Doc. He swallowed the piece he was chewing and put another, somewhat larger piece in his mouth.

The larger piece was a mistake. It was just too chewy and tough. He took it out of his mouth and put it on the side of his plate. It looked like leather. He peered closely at it. It *was* leather. It even had lettering on it. He couldn't quite make out what it said because of the brown sauce on it. He wiped off the brown sauce and picked it up and held it close to his eyes. The letters were E . . . A . . . T. Eat? Was this some kind of a gag? Why would they serve him, along with his lunch, a small piece of leather encouraging him to eat?

He wiped at the small piece of leather and looked closely at the word EAT. There was something about the lettering that looked faintly familiar. Where had he seen it before? How *could* he have seen it before? The letters were a poor imitation of the lettering in the Superman logo. Where was the last place he had seen lettering like that?

An image flickered through his consciousness, no longer-lasting than a subliminal image in a television commercial. He knew better than to chase it. The best thing to do when you were trying to summon a forgotten word was to just let it go, relax, and let it come back of its own accord. He closed his eyes and relaxed. The image came flickering back briefly, and then was gone again, but this time he had had enough time to read it. What it said was THE GREATEST.

THE GREATEST—the Muhammad Ali tattoo he'd seen on Goose's skin! That was it, he was certain of it now. The EAT was taken right out of the middle of the tattoo! The Mannihannis had cooked Goose's goose and served it to him. He had just eaten human flesh!

Lance got up from the table so violently that he upset the tray. He had just chewed and swallowed part of a fellow named Goose Washington, a person he had known and spoken with and even appeared with on the *Tonight Show*.

He lay down on the bed. He had to make sense of this extraordinary piece of information immediately, because it related very directly and very immediately, he sensed, to his own well-being.

The last time he had seen Goose was in the airline terminal, flirting with the guards. One guard in particular had been the focus of Goose's attention. It had seemed that she was interested in Goose sexually. She had discussed Goose's behavior with her fellow guards. She had asked Goose something, and he, having no idea what it was, had nodded agreement. The question the guard had asked of her colleagues and of Goose had the name Monte in it, Lance was almost positive of that. And then the guards had taken Goose out of the terminal, presumably to fuck, and that was the last anybody had ever seen of Goose again. Till now, that is.

Had Goose unwittingly volunteered to participate in a religious ceremony honoring Monte—the same kind that Lance himself had recently committed himself to with Mamma Doc? And was the standard consequence of the Monte ceremony that the volunteer was killed, cooked and eaten? When Lance had still been in the terminal it had seemed to him that there were slightly fewer passengers than when they had first arrived. Were the Mannihannis simply cannibals who were keeping them like cattle to be slaughtered for food?

Perhaps Lance was wrong. Perhaps the piece of meat was not part of Goose's tattoo at all. Perhaps it really *was* a piece of leather with the word EAT on it which Mamma Doc had slipped into his lunch as a prank. He devoutly prayed that this was the case. He devoutly prayed that the Monte ceremony was simply a pagan religious ceremony and that nothing more occurred in it than that a group of people got together, did some drumming and dancing and chanting, and then Monte was pleased enough to grant them good health or great wealth or whatever it was they wanted, and that was that.

Surely that was the extent of the Monte ceremony. Surely there was nothing more sinister about it than that. And yet. And yet, the Mannihannis were a violent people. And they had at least in part modeled themselves on the Haitians, who were also black, descended from Africans, and former subjects of the French. They had even appropriated the uniforms of the Haitian *Tonton Macoutes,* and the nomenclature of the Haitian presidency—Mamma Doc Taillevent, President-for-Life. Didn't it therefore follow that the Mannihanni religion might be patterned after voodoo, with the same sort of bloody sacrifice to the gods as a requisite part of every ceremony? If the Haitians butchered pigeons, chickens, pigs and sheep in *their* ceremonies, wasn't it possible the Mannihannis butchered men in *theirs?* Many primitive tribes ate the brave animals they hunted to absorb their strength or courage—wasn't it possible the Mannihannis ate men they sacrificed in their ceremonies for the same reason? Wasn't it possible that when a Mannihanni woman said she wanted to have sex with you and eat you, that she wasn't merely using a figure of speech?

This is insane, thought Lance, I am going insane here. I am being swept up in paranoid fantasies and convincing myself that these people are cannibals and that I am about to be slaughtered and eaten, and the only evidence I have is a little piece of leather with the word EAT on it. There has to be a saner and more conventional explanation to all of this. There has to be. Perhaps if I just lie here and try to relax and not think about the food all over the floor and the creature with the two big eyes and the little piece of leather with the word EAT on it, the truth will come to me.

Lance lay across his bed, staring up at the Monte symbol on the wall, trying to decide what was paranoia and what was real. The answer lay in Monte. The Monte symbol was doubtlessly an abstraction of something, but what? It looked like a peace symbol that had sprouted legs, sticklike legs. Or arms. Or claws. Claws like a crab or a lobster. Claws like some kind of hideous insect. Like some hideous, carnivorous, grasping, preying . . . mantis. Praying mantis. That's what the damned thing looked like—a praying mantis! Mantis pronounced with a French accent was . . . MONTE! The praying mantis, whose chief claim to fame is that, when it has finished mating, the female bites the male's head off!

Lance buzzed for a guard, his chest pounding.

113

Mamma Doc looked up from the TV as the guard led Lance back into her bedroom.

"So," she said with a raucous laugh, "do hew return to tempt us weeth sexual favors, Meestair Lerner?"

"No," said Lance carefully, "I return to ask you a question: What happens in the Monte ceremony?"

"Please?"

"What happens in the Monte ceremony?"

"Releegious copulation."

"Religious copulation and . . . death?"

"Yais, of course, death. Copulation and death they are always close. Een hyour language sometime the sexual climax ees called 'the leetle death,' no?"

"Yes, but that isn't intended as a literal—"

"Thees ees what sex ees *about*—death. You have sex and then you have death. Death and tronsfiguration."

"In the Monte ceremony, *whose* death and *whose* transfiguration are we talking about?"

"The male who ees offer heemself to the High Priestess een releegious copulation. And the tronsfiguration of hees body eento sometheeng holy and perfect, wheech ees then come eento the body of the High Priestess where eet and the High Priestess and Monte Herself become one. Eet ees exqueeseet to die and sojourn weeth Monte."

"Yes, I'm sure it is. Tell me, how . . . I mean, by what means does the male who has offered himself to the High Priestess in religious copulation . . . achieve death?"

"Ees very sweeft," she said somewhat defensively. "Ees almost weethout pain."

"What is the means?" said Lance.

She seemed hesitant to answer.

"Is it by . . . beheading?" said Lance.

"Thees happen to be the very humane death," said Mamma Doc. "We don't expect somebody he come from les Etats Unis to appreciate the Monte ceremony."

"It's barbaric," said Lance.

"Hew calling our releegion barbaric?"

"Barbaric and totally immoral."

"Hew are releegious bigot, Meestair Lerner! We under the eempression een hyour country releegious bigotry has been outlawed!"

Mamma Doc seemed a little unsettled. She reached toward the bedside table, opened an ornately carved wooden box, extracted a cigar, bit off the head and lit it up. Beside the carved box was something that Lance hadn't noticed on his previous visit this morning—a wig stand. On it was a black wig. The General and Mamma Doc were one!

"You're cannibals, too," said Lance quietly, "aren't you?"

"Please?" said Mamma Doc.

"You're cannibals," said Lance. "You eat human flesh."

Mamma Doc raised her eyebrows.

"Yais, of *course* we eating human flesh. Ees very *tasty,* human flesh. Ees a great *delicacy,* human flesh. *Hew* have been eating human flesh as well, Meestair Lerner, seence the day hew arrive here."

Lance closed his eyes. There seemed little point in passing out now. Everything seemed so surreal. Surreal and more lethargic than real life, like a movie which has lapsed into slow motion. He felt a definite need to leave Mannihanni rather rapidly, before anyone processed him as a candidate for a transfiguration or a smorgasbord.

"This morning," said Lance, "I mentioned an alternative proposal to the one you offered me regarding your autobiography. I would now like to outline that proposal."

Mamma Doc gave him an interested look.

"I am not willing to ghostwrite your autobiography," said Lance. "I *am* willing to *write* your *biography.* If it's written in my voice rather than yours, the complimentary things in it will be more believable. But I will not write the book unless you agree to let me include some critical things about you as well. And I will not write the book unless all of the hostages are released by sundown tonight, and unless I am among them."

Mamma Doc erupted in maniacal laughter.

"Thees ees no proposal," said Mamma Doc, "thees ees *boolsheet!* Hew leaving Mannihanni tonight, we never seeing hew or the biography again! What hew theenk we are, Meestair Lerner, a bimbo?"

"I do not think you are a bimbo, Madame Taillevent," said Lance, letting his gaze stray to the box of cigars and the wig stand. "On the contrary, I know that only a bimbo would believe that any author in the world, no matter how successful, could make a deal on a book as important as this without spending considerable time meeting with editors in New York, querying them about their marketing and promotional capabilities, and ensuring that the book would be guaranteed an enormous amount of attention—attention that makes the difference between a book that sinks without a ripple, like thousands of books that come out every year, and a book that hits it so big that its author and its subject are asked to appear on the *Phil Donahue Show* and the *Mike Douglas Show* and the *Merv Griffin Show* and the *Tonight Show*."

He paused to let his words sink in, watching Mamma Doc's face intently for a reaction. She drew in a cheekful of smoke, held it briefly, then expelled it into the air. She thoughtfully shaped the ash in an empty bowl which had probably recently held delicacies, like parts of hapless fellow hostages.

"Tell us, Meestair Lerner," she said after a while, her eyes still on the ash of the cigar, "what make hew theenk Jawnny Carson weesh to put the President-for-Life of Mannihanni on hees show?"

"What makes me think that? First of all, you'd be a great talk-show guest. Second, Johnny does tend to put on whatever guests I ask him to whenever I'm on the show, although I must admit he usually doesn't bring them out of the Green Room till the very last segment."

Mamma Doc expelled another cloud of cigar smoke and appeared to be searching the swirl for guidance. After perhaps two minutes of silence she spoke again:

"Eef hew make heem guarantee us two segments, Meestair Lerner, hew have a deal."

114

Lance was unable to get the hostages released by sundown that day. But within forty-eight hours of making his verbal agreement with Mamma Doc, he was able to reach Kronk by radiophone at the beefalo ranch. Kronk offered the Taillevent biography to the six largest hardcover publishers in New York on a bidding basis, and a combined hardcover-softcover deal was struck for an advance of $775,000, the money to be divided equally between Lance and Mamma Doc. A cable outlining the terms of the deal arrived at the Presidential Palace just as the first of the three military C-130 cargo planes touched down on the ancient Port Pangaud landing strip.

Lance was the final person to board the last of the three cargo planes, and Mamma Doc herself accompanied him to the aircraft.

"Een the words of the accursed French, Meestair Lerner, *"au revoir,"* said Mamma Doc, clasping his hand.

"Au revoir, Madame Taillevent," said Lance, squeezing her hand in return and finding she was unwilling to relinquish his.

"Please, Meestair Lerner," she said. "Not to judge the releegious customs of theese country by hyour own. And please not to hate so much the General for what she does to hew when hew arrive. We shall puneesh her severely for thees atrocity."

"OK," said Lance, not quite sure how that was going to work.

As Lance turned toward the plane, Mamma Doc suddenly threw her arms around him and squeezed him so tightly he could scarcely breathe.

"Eef we not see hew again, hew break an old woman's heart," she whispered hoarsely into his ear, and planted a wet kiss on his lips.

* * *

The media were waiting for them in Honolulu with mini-cams and flowered leis. The freed hostages, when they learned that Lance had been the instrument of their deliverance, were adulatory. All three networks carried footage of Lance being hugged and kissed by scores of grateful men and women. The Royal Hawaiian Hotel insisted upon giving all the former hostages who didn't need to be confined to the military hospital at Pearl Harbor free room and board for three days on Waikiki Beach. Don Ho personally serenaded them with "Tiny Bubbles," and "Lovely Hula Hands." So many funny rum drinks with flowers in them were pressed upon Lance by grateful former hostages that he was stricken with a hangover worse than all the sickness he'd endured on Mannihanni.

After three days the media got bored and went back to hotter stories, and the former hostages began trickling home to the mainland. Lance telephoned Cathy and was surprised how clearly he could hear her voice. She must have been terribly self-conscious talking to him, though, because she went on at some length about matters that he'd ceased caring about during his incarceration in Mannihanni—about how bills he'd been unable to pay in his absence had caused his major-medical policy to lapse and his telephone and gas and electricity to be turned off, and so on. Lance supposed he would begin to care about such things again once he returned to a phoneless and gasless and electricityless apartment, but for now he was more concerned about what Cathy *wasn't* saying than what she was. She had avoided any talk of their relationship, except to say that her separation papers had come in the mail and that she had torn them up.

He supposed that meant she wanted to come back to him. He *wanted* her to come back to him, but he worried that the woman he'd loved for so many years had changed so much he wouldn't respond to her in the same way anymore.

He had so many wonderful moments with Cathy mounted in his mental album. Like the time he'd said "Ready when *you* are, CB," and she'd thought that CB stood for Cute Bunny. Like the time her robe fell open and she caught a glimpse of her sensational body in the mirror and gasped with surprised delight. Like the dinner party where she led him to discover she was wearing the garter belt and stockings he'd previously been unable to convince her to wear.

Lance fervently prayed that Cathy hadn't changed too much.

The flight in the cargo plane from Port Pangaud to Honolulu hadn't bothered Lance at all, but when his commercial jet took off from Honolulu, Lance began to get the shakes. At first he thought it was an enduring symptom of the hangover, but then he realized it was a recurrence of his old fear of flying. When the plane landed at Los Angeles to refuel, Lance got off, took a cab to the railroad station and bought a Pullman ticket to New York.

He'd expected the four-day train ride to be boring, but it wasn't. He reviewed more happy moments with Cathy in his mental album. He watched the often spectacular scenery roll by. He loved the sound of the wheels on the rails. He imagined he was Cary Grant in *North by Northwest*, then realized that what he'd endured in Mannihanni was no less harrowing than what Cary Grant had gone through on Mt. Rushmore. The train pulled into Grand Central Station slightly before four a.m. He walked outside and marveled at the city he'd accepted with little more than irritation for so many years. He took a cab to his apartment and gave the amazed driver a tip larger than the fare.

115

Cathy's life had taken a gratifying turn. She'd sold three chapters of her novel and an outline of the rest to Claire for fifty thousand and an unprecedented sixty-forty split on the softcover rights.

Dr. Freundlich was very impressed when Cathy told him the news in their weekly session, and even more impressed when she announced she was quitting her unfulfilling job at the *Book Review*. But when she told him her other news— that she was pregnant—he waited noncommittally till she indicated how she viewed this development herself.

How Cathy viewed her pregnancy was with great perplexity. Part of her confusion was that for the first time in her life she thought she didn't want an abortion, that she might be ready for motherhood, but she was not interested in raising the child by herself and she already knew the depth of Lance's own anxieties regarding children. The idea of raising a child with Lance appealed to her, but she doubted that he'd go for it, even under the best of circumstances. Under the best of circumstances she would have been clear whether the baby was fathered by Lance and not by Howard.

Well, the only thing to do was to try the idea out on Lance and see how he reacted. And at dinner at Lutece, with all that great expensive French food and after a couple bottles of French champagne, would be an ideal time to spring it on him.

116

Lance got to the restaurant promptly at eight. Cathy was already seated, having arrived early. An unopened bottle of Dom Perignon was in an ice bucket at her side. Each of them was so preoccupied with conflicting feelings of longing, dread, remorse, resentment, love, and terror at the meeting that at first they didn't even recognize each other. Then they did and embraced shyly and awkwardly.

Lance thought Cathy looked very beautiful and very elegant in her new blue blazer and tan slacks, but oddly strained and unfamiliar. My God, he thought, we were once so close we could complete each other's thoughts and never needed to speak in whole sentences. Now here we are, virtual strangers who don't recognize each other in a restaurant and who embrace like polite acquaintances. One of the great hazards of growth, he thought, is that you risk leaving someone you love behind. They had both grown enormously since their separation, but perhaps not on parallel paths. He'd been fairly sure before that they could still make it as a couple. Now he didn't know.

"Hello," he said, extending his hand. "My name is Lance."

"Glad to meet you," she said. "My name is Cathy. I've heard a lot about you."

"All of it good, I trust?"

"Not really," she said, but she was smiling.

They finished off the first bottle of champagne in just under ten minutes. The alcohol helped unfreeze some of their words. Lance told Cathy about the ordeal in Mannihanni. She seemed very sympathetic. Cathy told Lance about her novel. He was delighted for her. It was beginning to flow now. They were beginning to remember who each other was.

They were well into their second bottle of champagne when Cathy said she had more news. Lance looked at her expectantly, a smile on his face.

"I'm pregnant," she said.

The smile took on a slightly glazed patina.

"Well," said Lance, "I don't suppose that's as big a problem as it might appear to be."

"I'm not entirely sure whether it's yours or Howard's," she said.

The smile crumbled and fell to the table.

"I'll pay for the abortion," said Lance, "no matter *whose* kid it is."

"I don't think you understand," said Cathy, beginning to cry. "I'm thinking of *having* this child. And even if I wasn't, I certainly don't need *you* to pay for my abortion. I have more than enough money to do *that* now. But I don't want to *have* another abortion—I don't think I could face it. And I resent the callous and dismissive answer you gave me—'I'll pay for the abortion.' What a fast sexist response that was. I really thought you were past that kind of reaction by now."

The captain approached, smiling, bearing menus. He heard the tone of Cathy's voice and swiftly withdrew.

"Look," said Lance, "I won't deny that I or any other man is sexist or that we have treated women in a less than wonderful manner. I myself happen to have recently gotten in touch with my own bewilderment and anger at women, which I didn't even know I had. But just springing this on me now without warning, is, well . . ."

"Yes . . . ?"

"Well, *you* know my feelings about kids, Cathy, my fears of producing abnormal children and about the responsibility of

368

bringing somebody into the world that I'm going to have to . . . It's like opening up Pandora's box, for God's sake."

"So? Go ahead and open it. What do you think you'll find in there?"

Lance considered this. He had, as a matter of fact, been forced to deal with a lot of these kinds of thoughts when he was a prisoner in Mannihanni, and they hadn't done him in then. There was no reason why they should now. He drank off his glass of champagne, poured himself another, and opened up Pandora's box.

He took a long hard look inside, expecting horrible slimy things to slither out, the terror of the unimagined, the gaping black maw of the unconfronted, but to his extreme surprise the horrible things had left. They'd already been imagined, confronted and flushed in the expurgations of feeling resulting from Gladys's short-lived pregnancy and from the deep soul-searching that had been forced on him in Mannihanni by torture from the General, threats of castration from Mamma Doc, the prospect of his own death by beheading in the Monte ceremony, and from the ghastly realization that he'd been eating human flesh. No, there was nothing much left in Pandora's box but a few rather tired and pedestrian worries, the kind that most people have every day. And if having sex with women and conceiving kids and committing yourself to a relationship put you on a conveyor belt that ended in death, then it was also true that *not* doing all those things still put you on the same conveyor belt.

"You know what?" said Lance. "I'm not as scared as I thought I'd be."

Since the frightening negative thoughts were under control, he was now free to consider the positive ones—as he had when Gladys had admitted she'd miscarried. And the notion of a junior version of himself, of whatever sex, growing in the womb of his wife, was rather appealing to him—assuming it *was* a junior version of himself and not of Howard Leventhal.

"You're serious?" said Cathy, amazed. "You're really not scared?"

"No. Not if it's really *my* kid."

"I don't really think it's Howard's," she said. "I think it happened that night you took me to dinner on my birthday, because I wasn't using anything that night or the next morning either, and Howard always uses condoms—those silly multi-colored ones with the big—"

"I'm not interested in Howard's taste in prophylactic

fashion," said Lance cutting her short. "But if you believe the kid is really mine, I think I'd like to help you bring it up."

Cathy looked at him in astonishment.

"Are you seriously saying you want this child?" she said, her eyes once more filling with tears.

"Yes," said Lance, his own eyes beginning to moisten.

They stood up and embraced across the table. The captain, who had hoped the lowering of voices indicated it was safe to return with menus, once more withdrew.

"You know what?" said Cathy.

"What?"

"I love you."

It was going to be all right.

117

"You're pregnant, Mrs. Oliphant."

"*Miss* Oliphant," said Gladys.

The doctor raised his eyebrows.

"Oh, it's all right," she said, "it's a wanted child. My boyfriend and I have been trying to have this child for months. He'll be so glad to hear we finally managed to do it."

She had apparently conceived again the night Lance took her to Elaine's. To prevent the embarrassment of another false alarm, she wouldn't tell him this time till just before the baby was due.

"Your *boyfriend*," said the doctor uneasily, "must be a very unusual person."

"Oh, he sure is," said Gladys. "He's a famous author. You've probably heard of him. His name is Lance Lerner."

"The author of *Gallivanting?*" said the doctor.

"That's the one," said Gladys.

Epilogue

"Excuse me," said the tall young black man in the three-piece blue suit, the white shirt open at the neck, and the loosened rep tie. "Attention . . . May I have your attention, please? . . . Hello? Hi. I know it's a little crowded in here, but I'd like to beg your indulgence for a just a few moments here, if I might.

"As most of you know, we are celebrating tonight the fiftieth birthday of our good friend, Lance Lerner. I didn't get a chance to meet all of you yet, but, as most of you know, my name is Ernie Roosevelt, and Lance and I go back a long way. I hope your champagne glasses are full, because I would like to propose a toast. To Lance Lerner—my mentor, my friend, the godfather of my son, the man who is responsible for my marriage, my literary career, my new career in politics and, well, just about everything else in my life, including my life itself. May the second fifty, Lance, be as wonderful and as productive and as inspiring as the last. *L'chayim!*"

The more than two hundred guests jammed into Lance's living room raised their glasses in salute and drank.

Lance nodded and smiled back at them and felt his eyes fill up. Time was accelerating now at a rate he found alarming. When he was a little boy each day had seemed interminable, each weekend a holiday to be celebrated, the return of winter unimaginable. He remembered late afternoons in summer, with the distant cry of swallows and grackles, afternoons which seemed as though they would go right on until the middle of the night. He recalled long Sunday afternoons in winter with the light coming into his parents' apartment at an angle that now filled him with inexplicable sadness. As a child nothing passed fast enough to suit him. Time was something to be slogged through with difficulty and great resistance, like trying to run through waist-deep water. He had thought he

371

would never get out of grammar school. High school seemed exotic and grownup and highly unlikely.

But then it began to go a little faster. Grammar school *did* end, high school was more than likely, and then, wonder of wonders, he was even a college man. Time was speeding up. Like a rocket at Cape Canaveral, starting out so slowly you felt it was never going to even clear the launching pad, but then beginning to move a little faster, faster, faster yet, until it shot into the sky and disappeared.

His life had started speeding up in the same manner. Years which had previously contained as many as twenty-two months each when he was a kid contained scarcely more than eight by the time he was forty, while the years nowadays contained no more than five months each. There was barely enough time to dig your summer clothes out of the closet before it was time to put them away again. He watched his hair turn gray, the skin beneath his eyes and chin go slack and wrinkled, even saw his slim and always-firm buttocks begin to droop a bit. How many years did he have left? Thirty? Twenty-five? He had spent his thirties and forties trying to preserve the status quo, only to find that there had never *been* a status quo, that things had always been in flux and the illusion of stability in his life had been precisely that—an illusion. It had been a hard, exciting football game, and now he was in the third period and to his consternation found that the clock had been kept running even during time-outs, even at half-time.

Could it really have been ten years since he had been caught bare-assed at the surprise party Cathy had thrown for him, since he had tried so hard to get her back and stumbled into affairs with Stevie and Claire and Dorothy and Janie and Gladys and all the rest? Could it really have been ten years since his plane was hijacked and he'd nearly lost his life in Mannihanni? Ten years ago he had been consumed with the question of what it was that women wanted. He had ultimately concluded that women wanted what they'd *said* they wanted—romance, excitement, security, sovereignty, acknowledgment, unconditional love, money, a good fuck—everything, in short, that men wanted too.

God, it was overwhelming, all that had happened to him and to all whom he had known in the past ten years. *Gallivanting*, of course, had been at the top of the bestseller lists for over a year, and the movie they'd made of it had done surprisingly well before it began appearing on late-night TV.

The book he had written about his experience in Mannihanni, *I Remember Mamma Doc*, had replaced *Gallivanting* on the lists, and the movie of that had been not much of a hit, but then they'd made it into a TV sitcom and that was still in syndication.

His marriage to Cathy had resumed after his return to New York and for the most part was better than it had ever been before. He supposed part of it was that Cathy now had an identity beyond that of Mrs. Lance Lerner. Her writing had matured. Novels had not proven to be her ideal form of expression—trenchant literary criticism had. Cathy, writing under her maiden name, had become one of the most trenchant of literary critics in New York and had a column that was nationally syndicated.

Several months after Lance returned from Mannihanni, he and Cathy had a baby. A boy. They named him Michael. And despite all of Lance's fears, the baby was completely normal. And beautiful. And Lance loved him very much, and felt that the energy which had begun ever so slightly to drain out of him now had a place to be collected. Michael was eight years old. One of his closest companions was named Lanny. Lanny was the love child, as his mother described it, of America's favorite new romantic novelist, Gladys Oliphant, and a mysterious stranger. Although Lanny was quite a bit plumper than Michael, people marveled at how alike they looked. Almost like brothers, some said.

Lanny and Michael played a lot with Ernie and Dorothy's boy, Goose. Ernie had had to adapt his written experiences with the Dalton Two to include the incarceration in Mannihanni, but the book was an even bigger hit than *I Remember Mamma Doc*. Ernie's attempts after that to write a novel or anything else didn't work out, but Lance had insisted that Ernie go to college and get an education, and that *did* work out. Ernie had moved himself and Dorothy and little Goose to an apartment on the same block as Lance's and, at Lance's urging, finally campaigned for and won a seat in Manhattan's 18th Congressional District, the so-called Silk Stocking District.

Ernie and Dorothy were still somewhat friendly with Janie, although neither of them much cared for her lover Tamago, an overbearing Japanese woman who owned a sushi bar on East 48th Street. Janie and Tamago were considering adopting an orphan from the war in Peru.

The members of MATE were captured by Mamma Doc's

guards and given the choice of enlisting in the army or being beheaded. They chose the former.

It was largely through Lance's influence on Mamma Doc that Mannihanni had evolved into a modern nation—selling natural gas to the U.S., bringing heavy industry to Port Pangaud, discouraging cannibalism, and, just this year, finally giving its men the vote. Lance sometimes wondered whether that hadn't been Mamma's plan all along.

Claire divorced Austin shortly after their traumatic cruise with Howard and Cathy. Austin sold Firestone Publishing to Insurance International, Incorporated, which first kicked him upstairs and then kicked him out entirely, forbidding him to use his own name again in business. Austin had publicly stated that he was thrilled to be rid of the publishing business, never having understood it anyway. Austin professed not to care when I.I.I. hired Claire as chief operating officer of Firestone Publishing.

Lance, Ernie, and all the alumni of the Mannihanni saga who'd written books about their experience had been represented by Julius Blatt, who gave up being a public defender to become one of the hottest literary and show-business agents in the industry. After a year at William Morris he was hired by Creative Artists as a full partner, but had left only this year to become the head of Universal Studios. He was here tonight, wearing a silk shirt open to the navel and about a pound of gold chains around his neck.

Stevie had gotten into trouble with her superiors in the NYPD for appropriating the helicopter for Lance's abortive kidnap of Cathy and quit her job in a cold fury. Shortly afterwards, she opened a place in the Village which was a combination restaurant, bar and karate school. It was still fairly successful and you could always find a dozen or more celebrities present in the late hours, but it wasn't quite Elaine's. Stevie had supplied all of the booze and most of the food for Lance's party tonight, but Lance thought she was less happy as a restaurateur than she'd been as a cop.

After Lance dropped him as a protégé, Les found another older mentor, had an affair with the man's wife, but was never found out.

Margaret and Cathy never renewed their friendship. Margaret got married two more times, but neither union lasted more than six months. Margaret's friends told her it was the man's fault in both cases.

Lance heard that Howard, his editor on *Gallivanting*, had

become a novelist, and was tickled to learn that Howard's first effort sold fewer than a hundred copies because his editor allowed the book to go totally without advertising or promotion. Lance heard rumors that Howard had entered into a ménage-à-trois with a fifty-five-year-old woman and her husband, but hadn't believed it. Tonight Howard had shown up with a white-haired couple in their sixties who were always touching him, and Lance decided to believe the rumor.

Not far away from Lance stood his Mom and Dad, who were chatting enthusiastically with Helen. Lance's Mom had published three books of recipes and become a local celebrity in Chicago. Lance had stopped going to Helen for therapy when the baby was born, feeling he had finally graduated. And a year after that, Helen dropped the rest of her patients to become the host of an evening talk show on PBS. Helen, to her credit, had as guests on her show every member of Lance's group who'd published a novel, and often co-hosted with Jackie until he hit it big in Vegas and was no longer interested in educational TV.

Ernie drifted over to Lance and put his arm around him.

"Well," said Ernie, "how does it feel?"

"To be fifty?" said Lance. "Exactly the way it feels to be forty. At least physically. Hey, Ernie, am I imagining it or are you a little preoccupied tonight?"

Ernie looked at Lance and then sighed.

"It shows, does it?" he said.

"What is it, Ernie?"

Ernie sighed again, then steered Lance over to a less-populous corner of the room, and lowered his voice.

"I feel a trifle foolish even talking about this," said Ernie, "but I really need to verbalize it to someone."

Lance took a sip of his champagne.

"I want to preface what I'm going to say," said Ernie, "by saying that Dorothy and I have a good marriage, a really good marriage, Lance. And I don't at all begrudge her the fact that she was once, well, homoerotic. Dorothy tells me that that phase of her life is completely over, and I believe her. And yet . . ."

"And yet?" said Lance and took another sip of his champagne.

"And yet," said Ernie, "I have lately come to the inescapable conclusion that Dorothy is having an affair with our *au pair* girl and, frankly, I feel that that state of affairs has upset the balance of our relationship. You know, Sigmund Freud,

375

the father of psychoanalysis, put it so well when he asked, 'What do women want?'"

Ernie was now looking oddly at Lance, doubtlessly due to the fact that, while Ernie had been speaking his last sentence, Lance had choked and coughed out a spray of champagne.

"Are you all right?" said Ernie.

Lance caught his breath, wiped his mouth and nodded.

"Ernie old man," said Lance, putting his arm around his friend's shoulders, "I want you to listen very carefully to the story I am about to tell you. And I hope that you can profit from my own experience. . . ."